Trade Rumors

By: Jessica Terry

I0677785

This is a work of fiction. Similarities to real people, places, or events are entirely coincidental.

TRADE RUMORS

First edition. July 30, 2024.

ISBN: 979-8990176928

Written by Jessica Terry.

If you've ever sincerely supported me in any way, I appreciate you.

Chapter 1

• • • •

JOE DIDN'T EVEN WORRY about being seen as he strode right up to Raven's door, pounding loudly with his fist.

Raven swung the door open a moment or two later after evidently checking the peephole. The surprise on her face was obvious. "Joe?"

"Let me in," Joe demanded, brushing past her into the apartment and removing his jacket without invitation.

"Uhh...what's going on?" Raven asked curiously, closing the door.

"You know why I'm here." Joe was unbuckling his belt.

Realization washed over Raven's face. "Oh." She rubbed her hands over her thighs and hips, now nervous. "Look, I was drunk when I suggested that..."

"But you meant it." Joe lifted his shirt over his head.

Raven held a crying Joe in her arms after Van walked out. With Raven's help, Joe had commandeered a small restaurant for the evening so that he could set up an elaborate and romantic setting for Van, where he was going to propose like he had been planning to do for months. But she had shattered his world and his heart by dumping him and telling him she and her twins were moving in with another man; a man who had more money than he did. Raven was in shock, as well, as she had no idea that Van, her cousin and best friend, had been seeing her millionaire ex-boyfriend, Grant McCallister. She held Joe as he cried his eyes out, in too much shock to cry herself just yet. She offered him a drink, then took one herself;

after a while, they were both tipsy. Joe sat across from her, mindlessly fiddling with an unused place setting, and Raven impulsively leaned over and kissed him. Clearly shocked at first, Joe suddenly started returning her kisses, and they went at it desperately for several moments before Joe pulled back, seemingly coming to his senses.

"What are we doing?" he panted, his voice raspy. He rubbed the back of his neck. "I can't do this, Raven."

"Why not?" Raven asked desperately, leaning forward in her chair and placing her hands on his thighs. "We both just got kicked in the gut...let's help each other feel better."

Her hand eased to Joe's crotch and he gently pushed it away. "And when we were done we'd have to go right back to facing what happened. Us having sex is not gonna make us forget any of this," Joe informed her, waving a hand at their surroundings.

"For the time being, it will." Raven reached for Joe's crotch again.

Shooting out of the chair and stepping away from her, Joe shook his head. "I can't, Raven," he murmured. "My mind is all over the place right now and I'm still hoping I'm going to wake up from some really bad dream at any second. Look, I'm sorry...thank you for everything, even though it all turned out to be for nothing." He blinked back more tears and turned away from her. "I've gotta get outta here..."

"Joe..."

Joe shook his head again as he walked out as if he were still in a daze.

Raven propositioned Joe again when he stopped by her place a few days later to give her some money for everything she did to help plan Van's proposal, even though she had never asked him for a dime. Raven had been upset about the pro basketball player she'd been casually seeing, Donald Rogers, dumping her the night before, and impulsively suggested Joe take her to bed. She opened the robe she was wearing to reveal her nakedness underneath, both seducing and begging him with her eyes. Joe, aware that she'd been drinking again, had politely refused her (even though she could tell he liked what he saw), and quickly left.

Now, Raven bit her lip at the sight of Joe's muscular chest. She felt her body heating up and tried to ignore it. "Still, I had just gotten dumped and then I let myself get upset about what Van did again and...I wasn't thinking. Plus, Joe, that was a while ago. You and I both know this wouldn't be a good idea."

"I ain't worried about it being a while ago or a good idea. Take your clothes off."

"Joe."

"Now."

"You really think this is gonna fix anything?"

"I might not be quite as horny when I leave here. Tomorrow morning." Joe was now naked and daring Raven to resist him.

Raven felt her resistance weakening. Even though months has passed, she was still upset at her cousin and Joe's former longtime girlfriend Van Roseland for dogging both of them and getting with Grant McCallister, a millionaire that Raven had been previously seeing. But she didn't know if getting busy with Joe was the best way to deal with it, despite trying twice before to do just that. But the more she looked at Joe's dark, muscular body standing right in front of her, the more she felt herself not caring about sensibility.

"To hell with it," she muttered, yanking her own shirt off.

Before long, she was as naked as Joe and in his arms, kissing him wildly. Joe picked her up with ease and she wrapped her long legs around his waist, continuing their kiss as he carried her over to the wall. Hoisting her up to mouth-level as if she weighed two pounds, he dove forward to taste her wetness. The tip of his long tongue gave a few teasing first licks and he enjoyed how it made her shiver. He moaned as he stopped teasing and got down to business, feasting and savoring, spurred on by Raven's pants and loud moans. She was already begging for him to be inside of her.

"Joe, I can't take this..." she panted, writhing against the wall. "I want it *now*."

Joe continued to drive her crazy with his tongue, the same way he used to do to Van. He frowned, pushing that thought of out of his mind; she was the *last* person he wanted to think about.

When he eventually decided to spare Raven and let her slide down the wall, she immediately grabbed his jutting hardness as she dropped to her knees and slid almost all of it into her mouth, as eager to please him as he'd been to please her.

"Damn!" Joe exclaimed, pleasantly surprised. He braced a hand against the wall as Raven pleasured him like a bonafied pro. *Something told me this girl was a freak...does she even* **have** *a gag reflex??*

Raven grabbed Joe's taut backside, repeatedly and eagerly pulling him into her mouth. She was loving his moans and curses of pleasure, and a surge of pride hit her when his knees buckled. Part of her couldn't even believe this was really happening; this was *Joe*, of all people. During the almost six years he was with Van, she had never once looked at him in this way or thought she was attracted to him. But she couldn't deny how much she loved what they were doing. And if what had gone down so far was any indication of what was to come, she was going to have a *very* memorable afternoon. In her opinion, Joe had one of those kinds of dicks molds were made out of and sold in stores, in the *main* display.

My cousin is straight stupid to give all this up, she thought to herself as she continued to put in work.

Without any warning, Joe was on top of her on the carpeted floor, taking the quickest second possible to grab a condom from his pants pocket. He couldn't take any more and *had* to be inside of her. He bit his lip as he entered her then slowly increased his pace, his eyes fixed on her breasts bouncing with each thrust. He leaned down and flicked her dark nipples with his tongue, never breaking his stroke. Raven was in absolute heaven, arching her back and holding his head to her chest. Wrapping her legs around him, she repeatedly lifted her hips to meet his, matching him thrust for thrust almost as if she were being challenged to do so.

"Don't stop," she panted, digging her nails into his strong back.

"Trust me, I'm not."

"Harder, Joe...give it to me harder..."

"You sure you can take it?" Joe challenged, looking her right in the eyes.

"I can take whatever you got," Raven confidently replied. She clenched around him and smirked at his sharp intake of breath, his eyes closing momentarily. "Now give me what you came over here to give me."

And that's exactly what Joe did.

· · · ·

AFTERWARDS, RAVEN AND Joe laid side-by-side on their stomachs in the middle of Raven's living room, their chins resting on their folded arms. After almost two hours of aggressive sex, they were both spent yet still basking in post-coital euphoria.

"I cannot believe we just did that," Raven muttered, the smile still on her lips. She rested the side of her head on her arms, her brown eyes roaming Joe's face. Even now, she still thought his looks were just average, like she always had. But there was no denying the man was sexy and knew how to put it down; just thinking about what he did to her sent a shiver down her body.

"Yeah, me either," Joe agreed, turning his head to look at her, as well. He smirked. "But it was damn good, though."

"Damn good is an understatement." Raven continued to eye him. Her smile faded slightly. "You feel guilty?"

"For what?" Joe asked quickly, frowning.

"You know for what. For us having sex. I mean, I *am* Van's cousin and all..."

"And?"

"*And* she's your ex..."

"She's my *ex* because she dumped me, remember? I wasn't good enough for her 'cause my pockets weren't fat enough. She's with somebody else. So I don't have anything to feel guilty about."

"Technically, no you don't, but it's just the principal of the whole thing-"

"Fuck principal!" Joe exclaimed. "She's the bitch that threw damn near six years down the drain like it was nothing, cheating on me with a dude just because he could pay off all her and her dead former fiancé's bills. I worked my ass off trying to make a better life for us and she spit in my face, so I don't give a damn about any principal!"

Raven's eyebrows shot up in surprise; she had never heard Joe use such language, and especially about Van. Outside of his two daughters, Joe had loved Van more than anything, and he treated her like a queen the entire time they were together. To hear him talk about her like this now was shocking, even after what Van did.

"Okay, okay...I understand that," Raven conceded, not even trying to plead her cousin's case. Truth be told, she wasn't totally over what Van had done, either. She'd been dating Grant McCallister and then as soon as they parted ways, Van got with him. Granted, the *reason* Raven and Grant stopped dating was because Raven had foolishly listened to one of his jilted admirers and accused Grant of being gay, but that wasn't the point. Van broke the girl code.

"I hate her, Raven," Joe declared, his voice low. His intense dark eyes were focused straight ahead.

Raven eyed his profile. "Joe, come on; you don't mean that."

"The hell I don't."

"I can't say she's too high on my list of favorite people right now, either, but I wouldn't say I *hate* her."

"Well, that's you."

"You don't see yourself *ever* getting over what she did? You don't think you can forgive her?"

"Maybe eventually. Not any time soon, though."

Raven just continued to eye him, her expression thoughtful.

"I don't think you get it, Raven," he continued, his voice softening just slightly. "Ever since I met Van, she had me. Every *second* that I was her man, I was all about trying to please her and make things better for her and her twins the best way I could. And I loved those kids like my own, becoming their father, because I wanted to be. Did I always do the right thing or make the best decisions? No. Was I the best at managing what money I *did* have? Not at first but I got better. Did I let my baby mama get away with too much, in regards to child support? I absolutely did.

"But you know what nobody will *ever* be able to say about me? That I ever *once* disrespected, mistreated, cheated on, took advantage of, or abused Van in any way, shape, or form. I loved that woman more than I loved *myself*, Raven." Joe's voice rose slightly. "And to find out that after months of working overtime and going to school to better myself and be a better man for her, and planning a proposal she would never forget, saving every penny I could so I could buy her a nice ring and take her on a nice honeymoon, that I or anything I did wasn't good enough...and even worse, that she had progressed enough with this other cat that she and her kids would move into his house?? That meant she was seeing him while we were together, lying to my face for who knows how long while I was just focused on her. You don't just *get over* that."

Tears were in Raven's eyes but she tried to blink them back. She knew exactly how hard Joe worked to pull off the proposal and all the planning, because she was right there helping him do it. She saw how exhausted he was when they would meet up to go over things, but he never once complained; he always said Van was worth it. And the closer they got to the night of the proposal, the more excited he became. Raven had been just as excited about everything that was going on; she was so eager to help Joe because she knew how good a man he was, and how much he loved her cousin. And she and Van helping plan each other's weddings was something they had talked about since they were kids. But Raven was shocked right along with Joe when Van had revealed she would be moving out of the house she and Joe shared and moving in with Grant; like Joe, Raven hadn't had any idea anything was going on between them. She had never, ever seen a man as heartbroken as Joe was that night after Van walked out. For a while he was devastated and depressed; now, he was just angry.

"You're right, Joe; I can't even imagine that," Raven softly conceded. She inched a little closer and rubbed a hand along his strong back.

Joe shook his head. "I'm good," he insisted, starting to pull away.

"Stop," Raven admonished, gripping him. "You don't have to be all tough around me. I was there for the whole thing, remember? And I was blind-sighted, too. You cried on my shoulder." She leaned closer to him. "And I'm the one that tried to grab your dick an hour after you got dumped."

Despite himself, Joe laughed loudly at that, throwing his head back. Seeing him laugh made Raven smile. "I feel like that shouldn't be so funny but *damn*, Raven."

Raven giggled. "So you can relax with me, okay? No judgment."

Joe looked at her, the smile still on his lips. "I can get with that."

"Good." Raven's smile widened.

Joe's eyes roamed her face for a moment before he volleyed her earlier question back to her. "Do *you* feel guilty about what just went down?"

Raven's hand slid down to his firm backside. She bit her bottom lip, her eyes tightening. "Not in the slightest."

Joe's own eyes darkened with desire, recognizing that look. "I thought you were about the principal and all that."

"That was just the right thing to say. But I'll take this," her gaze roamed up and down his muscular body, "over some damn principal any day of the week."

"Is that right?" Joe pushed Raven onto her back and climbed on top of her, nestling himself between her long legs. He looked down at her face, realizing just how pretty she was. He noted that she wasn't adorned with her usual face full of makeup. She looked better without it, in his opinion.

He started slowly sucking her neck. "So you think you'll want to do this again?"

Raven's eyes slid closed in pleasure as she leaned her head back to give him better access, her hand sliding to the back of his bald head. "Hell yeah, I want do to it again. And again after that."

"I don't want a relationship," Joe quickly specified, lifting his head to look at her. "You good with that?"

"Please, after the past few months I've had, a relationship is the *last* thing I need right now," Raven assured him. She tightened her legs around his waist as her hips began a slow grind. "Now can you kindly get back to what you were doing?"

"Damn right I can."

Chapter 2

· · · ·

VAN KNEW SHE HAD NO right to complain.

Grant was working, as usual. Her twins, Canton and Cassie, were in their respective rooms, probably enjoying one of the many things Grant had bought for them. Van was able to come home from work and relax without having to worry about which bill that she couldn't afford to pay was going to pop up in her mailbox. She wanted for absolutely nothing. But she just wasn't as happy as she knew she should have been.

And she wasn't blind as to why, either. As much as she loved and appreciated her fiancé Grant, she still hadn't fully gotten over her ex, Joe. She thought she had, but getting him off her mind turned out to be a task she constantly failed at. The guilt over walking out on him when he was about to propose consumed her for months, at times so much that it actually physically hurt. The look on his face when she told him she was leaving him still haunted her.

Despite how it seemed, Van had loved Joe more than anything, outside of her kids. And there were more times than she would ever admit that she had questioned her decision, especially after he revealed to her everything he'd been working on to make things better for them. Money had been her main reason for leaving, and from what he told her, that was no longer going to be an issue; or at least, not as much of an issue. But she left him anyway. At the time, she felt justified in that. But the decision still ate at her.

The night Grant proposed, Joe had called her. Van was relieved because he'd been refusing her calls for months; she thought they were finally going to be able to talk things out and start paving the way towards at least being friends. But Joe had only one thing to say to her:

"I hate you. Lose my damn number."

That was it. He hung up on her and hadn't talked to her since.

Those words hurt Van, and she hadn't been able to shake that hurt. Even though she knew she broke his heart, she never thought the day would come where she would hear Joe say he *hated* her. He had always loved her, with everything in him. And she hated making him feel like that hadn't been good enough, but she knew that's exactly what she did.

Sighing, Van pushed herself off the chaise lounge in the alcove of her and Grant's master suite and headed down the hall to see what the twins were doing. Canton was at his computer studying, as usual; ever since Grant bought him that laptop, Canton spent a lot of his time staying up on the news, studying history and law, reading case studies and watching trials online. He was determined to go into law and then politics when he grew up and Van was incredibly proud of that, even though she often had to actually make him take his head out of the books and go play sometimes.

His twin sister Cassie, though, was all about making it to the bright lights of Hollywood. Van found her in her room, her iPhone in her hand and earbuds in her ears, dancing around her hot pink and gray-decorated bedroom. Van couldn't help but smile and shake her head. Cassie had long ago stated that she wanted to be a singing/dancing/acting/modeling superstar, and if she had her way, she would already be on the road to that. But Van wanted her to enjoy her childhood, so she didn't let her do all that much yet, agreeing to talk about letting her go on more auditions when she turned thirteen.

Not having the energy to cook, Van decided to order some takeout for dinner. As she rummaged through the menus she and Grant kept in the office desk, she got a text from him letting her know he was on his way home and couldn't wait to see her. Van smiled, then bit her lip guiltily. She hadn't told Grant about all of these thoughts and feelings she was having about Joe; as far as Grant knew, Van was over him, though he *was* aware that she still harbored some guilt over how she hurt Joe. But Van just couldn't bring herself to be honest with her fiancé about still feeling conflicted over how she left her ex-boyfriend for him, and how she spent way more time thinking about him than she should.

Grant also didn't know that this was the reason Van had been dragging her feet planning the wedding. Really, her heart just wasn't in it. Part of her wondered if she was doing the right thing.

Which was probably why she still hadn't told her parents about anything that happened. They thought she was still living happily with Joe; they had no idea she'd left him for another man that she was now engaged to. Every time she talked to her mother, she tried to keep the subject on anything but her love life. And when her mother *did* ask about Joe, Van stayed as vague as possible. She had always been close with her parents, but she was actually embarrassed to tell them the truth about everything; she didn't want them to think badly of her for leaving a perfectly good man just because he didn't have enough money in his bank account.

After Van placed the dinner order, she freshened up before going down to the kitchen to start preparing the table. She had just pulled some plates out of the cupboard when Canton walked in.

"Hey, baby," Van greeted him warmly.

"Oh...hey," Canton grunted, looking away. "I didn't know you were down here."

"Yeah, I'm just setting the table for dinner. I ordered Chinese."

"'Kay." Canton wasn't looking at her. "I just wanted to get an apple but I can come back later."

"No, go ahead. Get one," Van instructed as she headed into the dining room. Once there, she changed her mind and decided they could just eat at the kitchen table tonight. When she got back to the kitchen, Canton was gone.

Van sighed as she began to set the table. There was a time when Canton would have offered to help her. But now, he couldn't wait to get away from her, and it had been this way for a while now. Van knew why. Canton missed Joe and resented her for leaving him. She had tried to talk to him about it on several occasions but she didn't think he would ever really see where she was coming from. It had gotten so bad that Van had even gotten calls from Canton's teachers saying he wasn't as attentive or focused as he used to be, and had even been rude on occasion. That wasn't like Canton, and it worried Van. She hadn't expected him to stay this upset this long, but Canton had really grown to love Joe like a father and it hit him hard when he realized he wasn't going to be seeing him anymore. This made Van feel even worse because as much as she had agonized over her decision, one thing she didn't consider was how losing Joe would affect the twins. Cassie seemed fine, but Canton certainly wasn't.

• • • •

"HEY, RAVEN."

"Hey."

"I've been trying to reach you for a few days now. Where've you been?"

"Oh, I've just been kinda...busy," Raven responded, then giggled. It was then that Van realized Raven wasn't alone.

"I've left messages," Van persisted. "I thought you would've called me back by now."

"Yeah...sorry." Raven giggled again then whispered something under her breath. "What's up?"

Van sighed. She really hoped that her relationship with her cousin would have improved by now, but things were still strained. Raven and Van had always been as thick as thieves, ever since they were kids; but this was yet another relationship she had ruined by getting with Grant.

"Umm..." Van didn't even know what to say. She hated this, how withdrawn Raven was from her now. "Do you want to try and go see a movie sometime this weekend? Or do you have to be at the restaurant?"

"I'll have to let you know about that," Raven responded quickly. There was some rustling on her end and then a sharp intake of breath. "Ahhh...I'm gonna have to call you back," Raven informed in a shaky voice.

Van asked an obvious question. "Do you have company?"

"Hang up," she heard a man's voice say.

Van frowned. Even though the voice was low and muffled, she could have *sworn* it sounded like Joe. But she knew there was no way that could be.

"Van, I will call you back," Raven said breathlessly.

"When?" Van called out, sensing Raven was about to hang up. She knew she sounded desperate but she missed her cousin.

"Soon. *Oooh...*" Raven moaned. There was more rustling and whispers, then Raven cursed under her breath. "Yeah, I'll call you back soon. Bye." She hung up.

Van looked at the phone, as curious as ever. Raven was obviously getting busy so Van couldn't really blame her for not wanting to talk right then, but she couldn't help but wonder who Raven was with. She knew that basketball player Donald Rogers had dumped her a while back, but Raven hadn't mentioned seeing anyone else since. Maybe it was just a booty call not worth mentioning, though Raven always told her about those in the past, even if she ended up not keeping the guy around very long. But that was then and this was now, apparently.

But Van couldn't shake how much the male voice she heard sounded like Joe. She knew Raven had helped him plan her proposal but other than that, she never knew the two of them to hang out or even interact much when Van wasn't there.

And Joe wasn't even Raven's type; Raven never really understood why Van had been so into him, since Joe wasn't what most people would consider conventionally handsome. Van hadn't been able to get enough of him, though; it wasn't all about his looks. It was the kind of man he was. He was sweet, attentive, caring, romantic, hardworking, loyal; he was incredibly handy and could fix just about anything, which Van found incredibly sexy. She never had to ask him to help out around the house or with her kids; he did whatever he could proactively and willingly. He respected her, made her feel cherished and loved...and his bedroom skills were in a class by themselves. Even the thought of his excellent lovemaking sent a jolt to her center. At times, Van still missed that.

Yeah, her mind had to be playing tricks on her; her guilt was causing her to hear things. She had to be tripping. Whoever was making Raven moan right then *definitely* wasn't Joe.

Chapter 3

• • • •

GRANT KNEW SOMETHING was up with Van; he just didn't know what.

She hadn't been herself for a while, but of course whenever he asked her what was wrong or if anything was on her mind, she insisted she was fine. At times she actually seemed rather distant, and he didn't know whether to leave her alone and let her work through it herself or be more persistent in getting her to open up. He and Van might have been engaged, but in a lot of ways they were still getting to know each other; their relationship and engagement had come about so fast that at times Grant still couldn't believe he was actually about to be a husband and stepfather to twins. But he couldn't wait; Van had captivated him ever since he'd seen her pumping gas that random night at the gas station.

Which was why it bothered him that she didn't seem as interested or excited about planning their wedding as he was. He had left the actual planning to her because, as much as he might have wanted to, he simply didn't have time to plan a wedding *and* run his multimillion-dollar companies. But he definitely wanted to be in on the progress and was eager to give his opinion when she asked for it; he wanted her to have the wedding of her dreams so he told her she could get anything she wanted; spare no expense. But it had been six months since he proposed and they hadn't even set a date yet, let alone really decided on anything else concrete. They'd kicked a few ideas around;

that was it. Grant wanted to believe that this foot-dragging was because she was stressed with work or just wanted to take her time, and not because she was having any doubts.

"Do you think she is? Having doubts?" Grant's longtime friend Rick asked him when they talked about it one night after work, looking over at Grant as he wiped his mouth with a paper napkin. They were at the bar at their favorite hole-in-the-wall place, Coco's, diving into a mountain of chicken wings and drinking beer. Grant loved going there not only because of the delicious food and relaxing atmosphere, but because it was one of the few places where he usually wouldn't be bothered. No one cared that he was a millionaire and local celebrity and he needed that relief sometimes.

"I hope not but I couldn't tell you," Grant replied with a light shrug. "I know everything happened really fast and she's probably still trying to wrap her head around everything...she's barely been doing her new job a year, the twins are still getting acclimated to all these changes, I'm at work more than I'm at home, which I know she doesn't like..."

"I'm sure she knew that reality when she decided to be your woman, though, right?"

"Yeah, I guess...I admit we never really talked about it, though. We didn't really discuss how all of this was going to work or play out at all; we just kind of jumped in with both feet and hoped for the best. That might work with some things but not when you're planning a marriage and life together."

"Sounds like *you're* the one having doubts," Rick observed, eying his friend thoughtfully.

Grant shook his head. "There's not a doubt in my mind that Van is the woman I want to be with, man. But I *will* admit that at times, I wish I had gone about things differently."

"You mean how you pursued her when you knew she was with somebody else?"

"That, and other things," Grant mused. "We didn't really prepare the twins for all this; we just yanked them from one house to another and expected them to be fine with it. And Cassie, for the most part, seems to be. But Canton...I know he isn't happy about living in my house."

"You two don't get along?"

"It's not that. Joe, Van's ex, was like a father to him; really the only father he knew, since his biological father died when he was so young. And as sad as it is to admit, Van and I were so caught up in our own stuff and that we didn't even consider the impact all of this was going to have on them, losing Joe like that."

"That's rough, man," Rick shook his head. "And I must say, I thought it *was* a little fast when you told me you and Van were engaged; but I know you well enough to know that your impulsiveness only runs so far. If you asked her to be your wife, you didn't do it on a whim."

"Absolutely not. I take marriage seriously, man. And I pray to only do it once."

"I hear you; that's how it *should* be," Rick concurred, twisting his own gold wedding band around his finger.

His deep blue eyes turned back to his friend. "About Van, though...what are you gonna do?"

"I'm not sure what I *can* do, really," Grant admitted. "This is new territory for me so I'm kind of learning as I go. I went from living alone for years to having a fiancée and a set of prepubescent twins in my house. And don't get me wrong; I love it. But it's an adjustment for all of us, still. And I try to remember that when Van is dragging her feet with the wedding planning or seems like her mind is somewhere else."

Sipping his beer, Rick peered at his friend and contemplated if he should mention the possibility that was on his mind; that Van's apparent apathy might be due to her still being hung up on Joe or, even worse, wanting Joe back. But he didn't want to put that on Grant's mind and cause him to worry any more than he already was; he just hoped that it really was just a case of everyone still getting adjusted to all of the changes that had taken place in the past few months.

"Well, I'll just say this," he finally said, setting his beer on the bar. "Be patient with Van. I mean, there shouldn't be a real rush to get married, should there?"

"No, there's no *rush*, other than just wanting her to be my wife."

"Understandable. But just take your time, man...let things settle down, keep getting to know each other, build your relationship with the twins...just enjoy being together without any pressure. Don't push her. Try to understand where she might be coming from and why she might be a little gun-shy. You have the rest of your lives to be together; just enjoy the ride."

Grant pondered Rick's words, then nodded slowly. "Yeah, I see your point. You're right. I've been so laser-focused on getting Van, then getting Van to leave Joe and move in with me, then finding the right time to propose to Van, then trying to get Van to set a date...I haven't really just taken the time to *enjoy* Van. I love having her with me; she's honestly one of the best things to come into my life, ever. I just need to chill out, huh?"

"Yeah..." Rick hedged, weighing his next words as he ran a hand through his dark hair. "You do. But I feel the need to say this, also..."

Grant looked at him curiously. "Say what?"

"While you're *chilling out*, keep your eyes open," Rick advised gently. "I'm not trying to imply anything, but with how everything came about between you two...I'm just saying, trust your gut. Don't let your love for Van cloud your common sense and good judgement. I don't know Van very well at all and I'm not implying anything," he quickly clarified again when Grant's face morphed into a frown, "But I wouldn't be much of a friend if I didn't tell you this, man. All I'm saying is...just trust your gut. That's all."

• • • •

RICK'S WORDS WERE ON Grant's mind the entire ride to his house after leaving Coco's. As much as he initially started to take offense to his friend's warning, the more the thought about it, the more he couldn't deny Rick had a point. As much as he loved Van, he couldn't lose his head completely. He reminded himself to just keep his eyes open as he hoped that Van was being as sincere with him as he had been with her.

When he was about five minutes from home, Grant got a call from his mother, Bernice. Smiling, he pressed the button on the steering wheel to answer the call via Bluetooth. "Hey, Ma! Everything okay?"

"Yeah, baby, everything's fine. Why'd you ask that?"

"You hardly ever call me this late. I'm surprised you're not in the bed."

"Oh, I was up watching a movie on this thing you got me. You spent all that money on this big ol' TV; I might as well use it."

Grant laughed. He had to convince his mother to even accept the Netflix subscription; she still had a VCR and a shelf full of videotapes.

"Well, I hope you're enjoying it. I know I love mine."

"When do you have time to sit around watching movies?"

"Not that much, I admit. Van and I like to do that together, though, whenever we can."

"Speaking of Van, when am I going to get to meet my future daughter-in-law? All I've gotten to do is talk to her one or two times on the phone. She's a sweet lil' thing."

"Yeah, she is," Grant smiled as he usually did when he thought of his fiancée. "I don't know, though, Ma...I'm not sure when we'll be able to get up to South Carolina to visit. And you know you don't like coming down here."

"Atlanta got too many people in it for me," Bernice commented. "It's no rush but I would like to see her face before the wedding day. *In person*."

"I know, Ma," Grant shook his head, still smiling. He appreciated how his mother hadn't questioned his judgment when he called her to announce he was getting married and just chose to be happy for him. Before Van, he couldn't even remember the last time he told his mother about a woman he was seeing; nobody had lasted long enough or been special enough to mention. But the day after Van accepted his proposal, he called Bernice and told her all about Van.

"Y'all ain't set a date yet?" Bernice asked.

"Not yet."

"What's the hold-up?"

"No *hold-up*, really...we're just taking our time, that's all." Grant didn't want to mention that Van didn't seem to be as anxious to set a date as he was.

"Well, just be sure you let me know when it is so I can start making my dress."

"Ma, I told you, you don't have to make your own clothes anymore. All you have to do is tell me what you want or need and it's done."

"You already spoil me enough, baby. Plus, I like making my own clothes. Keeps my stress down."

"Stress? About what?"

"Oh, your sister's been calling me every other day about that boy she's messing with. One day she's all in love and the next she's fussing about something he did."

Grant chuckled. "I'm surprised she hasn't told me about any of this. I'll have to call her."

"I don't even try to figure out what's on that girl's mind or why she does stuff like she does it. As long as she's getting her lesson, that's all I'm really worried about."

"She better be."

"You driving?"

"Yes, ma'am."

"Well, let me let you go, then. You know I don't like you being on that phone when you're driving."

Grant chuckled again. As many times as he had explained to his mother that he didn't have to actually hold his phone in his hand while he drove, she would still end the conversation when she realized he was behind the wheel.

"Okay, Ma. I'll talk to you later, then. Do you need anything?"

"No, baby, I'm good. Thank you, though."

"Make sure you let me know if you do. I love you, Ma."

"I love you too, baby." Grant could hear the smile in her voice and it made him smile wider. "And I'm proud of you."

Grant was full-on grinning now. "Thank you, Ma."

A few minutes later, Grant arrived home and pulled his car into the double garage. He cut the engine and sat back in his seat, thinking about the conversation with his mother. It made him remember that he had yet to speak to Van's parents and he wondered if they had accepted the news of his and Van's engagement as well as his mother had. Van hadn't mentioned it either way, and now he was curious. He quickly got out of the car and went into the house to find his fiancée.

She was in their bedroom, folding laundry. Even though Grant utilized a cleaning service, Van insisted on doing her own laundry. She still wasn't entirely comfortable having everything done for her.

"Hey, sweetie," she greeted him when he entered the room. Her smile, as usual, made him melt inside.

"There she is." Grant walked over to her and grabbed her by the waist, pulling her to him. He leaned down and kissed her strawberry-shaped lips, inhaling her sweet scent as he held her tighter. She wrapped her arms around his neck, her warm hand resting on the back of his bald head, and they continued to kiss for several moments before finally tapering off.

"I missed you," Grant whispered, his forehead against hers.

"I missed you, too." The smile was still on Van's lips. "Did you eat? I can fix you something."

"Oh, no I'm good. I couldn't eat anything right now if I wanted to."

"You had a good day?"

"It was fine; busy, as usual," Grant shrugged. "Went and met up with Rick for a little while; we went to Coco's, which is why I'm so full. I talked to Ma in the car a little while ago."

"Oh yeah? How is she doing?"

"She's good. Finally using that Netflix subscription I got for her."

"I'm surprised; I didn't think she would ever use that," Van chuckled.

"Me either, really."

"Speaking of which, do you want to watch a movie tonight or are you too tired?"

"I think we can make that work." His hand roamed her back. "Where are the twins?"

"In their rooms, asleep. Surprisingly."

"Damn; I didn't even get to see them today. I'll try to get home earlier tomorrow. Listen, babe...there was something I wanted to ask you."

"Yes?"

"Have you told your parents about us getting married?"

He felt Van's body tense in his arms. "Why do you ask?" she evaded.

"Because it occurred to me I've never once spoken with them or anything. You've talked to my mother, and even my sister that one time. And you're always saying how close you and your parents are, especially you and your mother. I'm curious as to how they took the news."

"Oh..."

Several silent moments passed and Grant started getting a bad feeling. "Van."

"Hmm?"

He leaned back so he could look at her face. "You haven't told them, have you?"

Van averted her eyes. "Not...not really."

Frowning slightly, Grant stepped back. "What do you mean, not really? Either you have or you haven't, Van."

Biting her lip, Van looked up at him sheepishly under her bangs before turning her eyes away again. "Okay, I haven't exactly told them about...our engagement yet."

More upset than he expected to be (despite a part of him not being that surprised), he dropped his hands from her waist. "Any particular reason why?"

"It just...hasn't come up," Van answered weakly.

"It hasn't come up." Grant's eyes were unwavering as he peered at her, and Van looked at him timidly like a child about to be reprimanded. "Is it that it hasn't come up or that you just don't want to *bring* it up, for some reason?"

"Grant, please..."

"There's a reason you haven't told them by now, Van. We've been engaged six months."

"Please don't take this the wrong way, baby," Van pleaded, stepping closer and tentatively putting her hands on his waist. "Of course I'm going to tell them. Really. I'm just...it just hasn't been the right time."

"In six months, huh?" Grant stepped back again and turned away from her. He couldn't help the hurt that was spreading over him; he knew for a fact that Van talked to her mother, who lived out of state, at least once or twice a week. In all that time, she never mentioned anything about planning to marry Grant. That stung. And he didn't even want to think about what that might mean.

He turned to leave the room.

"Grant!" Van called out. He stopped but didn't turn around. "Where are you going?"

"To my office."

"But I'm almost finished folding these clothes; I thought we were going to watch a movie together."

"Watch it by yourself. I can't be around you right now."

Chapter 4

• • • •

JOE ROLLED OUT OF TANISHA'S bed, easing out
from under her arm. He glanced over at her, sprawled
across the bed and snoring, and shook his head as he stood
and stretched before heading towards the kitchen. He
opened the refrigerator and was glad she had some bottled
water for a change; probably just because he requested it.
Usually all she drunk was orange soda.

He grabbed a bottle and practically yanked off the cap
before taking a long swig. Leaning against the counter in
the small kitchen, he checked the time on the clock on the
stove, noting the upgraded appliances. He frowned when
he remembered who was responsible for that.

Tanisha was his ex and the mother of his two
daughters, Jillian and Tara. He broke up with her years ago
because she was a childish, negative woman (and because
he discovered that she had deceived him and gotten
pregnant on purpose) and he couldn't deal with that
anymore. And she'd been a thorn in his side ever since,
especially after he got with Van. Tanisha didn't like her
and never missed a chance to make that known, and when
she wasn't doing that, she was trying to make Joe pay for
not being with her by being the most annoying, petty,
aggravating pain she could be towards him. But everybody
knew she was mainly acting like that because she wanted
Joe back. After Van dumped Joe, he went back to Tanisha;
clearly on the rebound but Tanisha didn't care. She was just
glad he'd come back to her. They tried a relationship again

but Joe wasn't really into it, even though Tanisha's attitude had greatly improved now that he was no longer with Van. Tanisha wanted Joe to be her man again, but as long as he wasn't anybody *else's* man, she was satisfied.

Eventually, Tanisha dragged into the kitchen wearing nothing but a t-shirt and panties. She was rubbing her eyes and looking way more innocent than she was. Her long black hair was wild and all over the place.

"When'd you get up?" she asked, clearing her throat.

"Just a few minutes ago."

"Why didn't you wake me up when you got up?"

"For what?"

Tanisha just looked at him before she moved over to the refrigerator to get herself an orange soda. She leaned against the counter next to him as she popped the top on the can. "What's wrong with you?"

"Nothin'."

"You always got an attitude when you're here."

"Yeah, well. You know why that is."

"Joe-"

"Save it. I'm not in the mood."

Tanisha just shook her head as she took a long swallow from her soda can.

Grant McCallister had bought and renovated Tanisha's apartment building, and it burned Joe that he had to stay with Tanisha when Van had dumped him because he really didn't have anywhere else to go at the time. Van had told him he could keep the house they'd been living in, but it was in Van's name and he already felt like enough of a chump after how and why she dumped him; he wasn't going to take her pity offering on top of that. More importantly, there was no way he would have been able to stay there and sleep in the bed they shared for years. There were just too many memories and he knew it would drive him crazy. He went to Tanisha's and, of course, she never wanted him to leave. Joe tried to convince her to get another apartment somewhere else but she didn't want to move because of the reasonable rent, plus all of her friends lived nearby. She wouldn't be able to get an apartment as nice for the amount she was paying anywhere else. Usually Joe was able to put it out of his mind, the fact that Grant had anything to do with the apartment; but when he *did* think of it, it was an automatic mood-killer.

"When are the girls coming back?" Joe asked, referring to their daughters.

"They're staying at Mama's until later tonight." Tanisha set her can on the counter and stepped in front of Joe. She started raking her long nails up and down his chiseled abs. "Why?"

"I think I'm about to head out."

"Why?? We've got all day; you don't have to go nowhere." Tanisha looked up at him seductively as she slid her hand down to his crotch and squeezed. "Especially since you never let me get none of this when they here."

Joe started to respond when Tanisha dropped to her knees and pulled his dick out of his boxers, stroking him several times with her small hand before swirling her tongue around the tip. Joe groaned and closed his eyes when she finally slid her mouth over him, leaning his head back and gripping the edge of the counter. Tanisha never could get enough of him, and Joe couldn't deny that the sex with her was good. But he was a little surprised when he found himself comparing Tanisha's technique to Raven's. He tried to clear his mind of that and just enjoy what was being done to him in the moment.

A while later, after Tanisha finished with him and downed another can of soda, she followed him into the bedroom, where he started getting dressed.

"Still gon' leave, huh?"

"I've got some stuff to do," Joe grunted, not looking at her as he pulled on his jeans.

"You coming back later on?"

"Probably. Before the girls go to sleep." Joe didn't sleep there every night because he didn't want his daughters getting the wrong impression about him and Tanisha getting back together, though he had long since talked with them about their situation.

"Well, look, there's something I wanted to talk to you about."

Joe turned to her, his jeans unbuttoned. "What?"

"What do you think about us having another baby?"

Joe's eyebrows shot up, then he laughed and resumed buttoning his jeans. "I think you've lost your mind."

"What?"

"You have *lost* it if you think that's gonna happen."

"Why??"

"Because I don't trust your ass, that's why."

Tanisha frowned and put her hand on her hip. "Excuse me?"

"Don't act like you don't remember me finding out about you poking holes in the condoms around the time you ended up pregnant with Tara. I haven't forgotten about that."

Her expression faltering, Tanisha's hand fell. "That was years ago, Joe."

"So?"

"I wouldn't do that this time."

"You *couldn't* do that this time. I bring my own rubbers whenever I come over here."

"Okay, so what's the problem? Why can't we have another kid? Don't you want a son?"

Joe immediately thought of Canton, Van's son who he had long since grown to think of as his own. His sister, Cassie, too. He missed them something terrible, and it was just another reason to resent Van.

"I got enough kids," Joe grunted, yanking his t-shirt over his head.

"But I want to have another one."

"I said no, Tanisha, damn!"

"*Why*, though??"

"Tanisha, why don't you get real? You can barely afford the two kids you have now, not to mention that you hardly spend any *real* quality time with them. I'm just now getting on my feet, money-wise. And I am not in the frame of mind to be thinking about having another child, especially with a woman I don't even like all that much."

Tanisha recoiled as if Joe had slapped her across the face. Her expression was hurt. "That's a fucked up thing to say to me, Joe. Especially after I just got finished sucking your-"

"Didn't nobody tell you to do that."

"I didn't see you stopping me!"

"Why would I? That's *one* thing you're good at."

Tanisha's jaw dropped. "Why you gotta be so mean?"

Grunting, Joe just shook his head and stalked past her out of the bedroom.

"Where are you going?" Tanisha demanded, right on his heels.

"I told you I got stuff to do. I'm out."

"We were in the middle of a conversation!"

"If the conversation is about us having another baby, there is absolutely nothing to talk about. It ain't happening."

"Just like that? I don't get no say in it, huh?"

"Tanisha, if you just want to have another baby so bad, have one with somebody else. We both know I'm not the only one you're sleeping with."

"But they ain't you!"

"Oh well. Don't ask me about this no more."

"Joe."

He turned to look at her, his expression hard.

She looked at him, a hint of concern in her eyes. "You've changed ever since she left you," she informed him in a softened voice, stepping closer. "Even when I pissed you off, you never used to talk to me like you talk to me now. One of the reasons I always lo-, um...why I was always so into you was because you were tough but you were still nice. You were really one of the good guys. Now you're just...*bitter*."

Joe wanted to laugh but wasn't in the mood to do it. Tanisha was one to talk; she was bitter for years after he left her. The entire time he was with Van, Tanisha's attitude shot from bad-enough to insufferable and stayed there until Van left him.

And it also amused him how Tanisha could never tell anyone she loved them. The entire time he'd known her, he'd never heard her use the word; at least not in regards to her feelings about someone. Not even to their daughters. It used to bother him but now, he no longer cared about hearing it from her. Really, he thought it was sad.

"Yeah, well," Joe grunted as he unlocked the door and opened it. "Being a *good guy* obviously hasn't gotten me anywhere."

• • • •

VAN HAD FINALLY GOTTEN back in touch with Raven.

"What are you doing tonight? I miss hanging out with you; we need to get together," Van told her.

"We will," Raven replied, though Van suspected her response was more obligatory than sincere. "I might be having some company tonight, though, so I'll just have to let you know."

"Ooh, with the mystery man from the other night?" Van asked, hoping Raven would give up some details.

"There's no mystery man; just someone I'm getting down with whenever. A friends-with-benefits kind of thing."

"Who is he?"

"I don't want to say."

Van frowned. Raven was usually all too eager to dish; sometimes a little *too* eager. "Why not?"

"He just doesn't need to be mentioned yet, that's all. I'm keeping him to myself for a while."

"Oh..." Van wasn't quite sure if she should buy this explanation. "The sex must not be any good."

"Oh, that's not it at *all*. He's probably one of the best I've ever been with," Raven bragged, loving that Van had no idea she was talking about Joe. "That man does things to my body I can't even describe. Got me wanting to skip work and everything."

"Wow," Van marveled. "Can you at least tell me something about him? His initials? Where he lives? Where you met him? *Anything*??"

"We met through a mutual friend," Raven teased. She knew it was probably a mean thing to do but she loved keeping Van in the dark; she felt she deserved it after the way she snuck around with Grant all that time behind Raven and Joe's backs like she did. "He lives somewhere here in Atlanta."

"That's all I get, huh? What mutual friend did you meet him through?"

"Damn, Van, you writing a book or something? Why are you being so nosy?"

Shocked, Van actually looked at the phone as if making sure she was still talking to the right person. "I'm not trying to be nosy, Raven; I'm just trying to get you to talk to me. You never tell me anything anymore. We used to be able to talk about any and everything and now I have to beg you for every little detail."

Raven sighed. While she hadn't totally forgiven Van and wanted to see her squirm a little, she couldn't deny that at times she too missed the relationship they used to have.

"Things are different now, Van," she said after a moment. "I know you've apologized and all that, and I wish I could just forget about it like you want me to, but you're just gonna have to be patient. To be real...I don't look at you the same anymore."

That hurt. Tears pricked Van's eyes but she quickly blinked them back. "I see."

"I'm just being honest."

"I get it."

There was a moment of awkward silence before one of them spoke again. "How are my babies?" Raven eventually asked.

"They're doing okay," Van replied, still reeling from Raven's statement but glad that they were at least talking about *something*. Van's twins were just about the only subject Raven still spoke to Van freely about. "Cassie is already talking about what she wants for her birthday."

"They just turned eleven not all that long ago."

"Yeah, I know. And her little spoiled behind got treated like a queen, too; she and her friends got picked up in a limo and had a spa day with the works. You couldn't tell her anything after that. Canton and his friends just spent the day at the arcade."

"They're already having separate parties, huh?"

"I would've preferred they do something together, but they couldn't agree on anything. So Grant just suggested we..."

Van's voice trailed off, knowing Grant was still a rather touchy subject between them. She didn't want Raven any more upset with her than she already was.

"You might as well go ahead and say it; it's not like I don't know he's your man now," Raven said bitingly, the edge her voice clear.

"Umm...Grant suggested we just all have breakfast together as a...as a family and then let them do their own things," Van finished softly.

Raven remembered. She had been invited to that "family" breakfast but refused to go, opting to just call the twins to wish them happy birthday and then celebrate with them on her own.

"Good plan," Raven replied simply.

"Yeah..." Van absolutely hated this awkwardness. "It turned out well, except Cassie is probably going to expect bigger and better for next year."

And I'm sure you and Grant will give it to her, Raven thought to herself, but didn't want to be unnecessarily snide. "You know Cassie has always been over-the-top; that's nothing new."

"That's true. I have to check her about her attitude more than usual, though. And I'm especially worried about Canton."

"What's going on with Canton?"

"He's been acting up in school and has barely had anything to say to me in months. He's uncharacteristically short and rude, even with his teachers, and that's just not like him. I've never gotten so many calls about his behavior."

"Wow, really? I can't imagine Canton acting like that," Raven mused, genuinely concerned. She never wanted what was going on between herself and Van to affect her relationship with Canton and Cassie; she couldn't love them much more if they were her own children. "Why do you think he's acting like that?"

"I know exactly why he's acting like that. He misses Joe."

"I remember you mentioning that a while back but I didn't think it had gotten *this* bad, to the point of him acting up and all that."

"I'm surprised, myself. Canton never used to give me any trouble but now, he only talks to me when he has to. At least he's polite enough to Grant."

"Hmm."

"He and Joe were really close and I know he just misses that relationship," Van continued. "I tried to suggest he call Joe but apparently that's not good enough; he misses seeing him every day."

"Well, Van, Joe is pretty much all Canton knows, as far as a father figure. He was practically a baby when Calvin died," Raven commented, referring to the twins' biological father and Van's former fiancé who passed away from complications with diabetes that he didn't know he had until it was too late to do anything about. "Of course he's going to be upset about losing him. All the money in the world can't replace that kind of relationship."

Van figured this was supposed to be a dig, but it was also true. Cassie might have been in heaven living in what she considered the lap of luxury but Canton had always been the opposite of his sister; he had simple tastes. He never minded the old house they used to live in, and actually enjoyed learning from Joe how to fix anything that needed to be fixed there. Joe was always proactive in being as helpful to Van as he could and doing whatever he saw needed to be done without having to ask, and he had taught Canton to be the same way. Van just wanted her sweet little boy back.

"I can't argue with that," Van stated humbly. "But things can't keep going this way. Maybe I should call Joe and have him talk to Canton."

"Nope," Raven immediately replied. "Not a good idea."

Van frowned. "What do you mean? Why isn't it?"

"Because you and I both know that this is just an excuse to get Joe to talk to you."

Van's mouth fell open. "That is *not* it, Raven! I'm sincerely concerned about my son and I think Joe might be the only one that can talk some sense into him."

"I don't doubt your concern for Canton. But can you deny that you've been trying to contact Joe ever since he called you that night and told you he hated you, and he hasn't been trying to hear it?"

"Okay, yes...I *have* been trying to talk to Joe and he's been ignoring me," Van admitted. "But that doesn't mean I have ulterior motives now."

"Really?"

"Yes, really!"

"Well, I think you should just leave the man alone," Raven advised. "I mean, you've put him through enough."

Van was flabbergasted by her cousin's words. "Raven! This isn't *about* me; this is about Canton! And as upset as Joe might be at me, I can't imagine he'd turn his back on him if he knew he needed him!"

"So you want him to come in and fix the mess you made."

"Oh my god...seriously??"

"Van, I'm not trying to be mean, here. I'm just keeping it real with you. You all were happy; no, things weren't perfect, but real life isn't. The *one* thing Joe lacked, money, was something he was busting his ass to get, and you *still* left. You uprooted those twins from everything they knew and moved them in with a man they *hardly* knew. And now you really think Joe is going to want to come in and help you after that?"

Van started to protest, but she had to (grudgingly) admit that Raven had a point. It was an angle that Van honestly hadn't considered.

"Okay, I get it," Van finally acquiesced. "Even though I *am* mostly and sincerely concerned about Canton, I'm not gonna lie; I *would* like to finally really speak with Joe. And since we're keeping it real...I miss him."

Raven paused. "What do you mean, you miss him?"

"I just...miss seeing him, talking to him. We were friends first before anything and now we're nothing. I don't know if I'll ever get used to that, Raven."

"You sure this isn't just your guilt talking?"

"Of course I feel guilty! Who *likes* hearing that someone hates them? I certainly don't, and especially not from Joe. I've never heard him say he hated *anyone*, not even Tanisha. To know that *I* was the one to drive him to that..."

Raven sighed again. "Look, Van...I get where you're coming from. I do. But I still say you should figure out something else with Canton and leave Joe alone. Let that man heal. You can't have your cake and eat it, too."

"I'm not *trying* to-"

"You want Grant and his money and you want Joe to be okay with it. What is that?"

Van paused, frowning. "Since when did you get to be such an advocate for Joe? Once upon a time you would be on my side on this."

"It's not about being on anybody's side, Van. Right is just right."

Something was up. Raven had never gone to bat for Joe so hard, and Van couldn't help but wonder why. Had they become friends during the time Raven was helping him with the proposal? Van couldn't imagine they would stay in contact after that; why would they need to?

"I don't necessarily think that I'm *wrong*, though," Van replied after a moment. "I don't see how it's wrong to miss someone you loved."

"Yeah, well, I hate to sound cruel and insensitive, but you just need to get over it. He doesn't want anything else to do with you; he's made that clear. Get your fiancé to help you with Canton, or have him talk to a counselor or therapist or something. But just leave Joe alone."

Van was definitely suspicious.

Chapter 5

• • • •

GRANT HADN'T SAID MUCH of anything to Van in a few days, and Van was over the silent treatment. She cornered him in the bathroom one morning when they were getting ready for work.

"Can we please talk?" she requested, eying him as he stood in front of the mirror, shaving. "I cannot go another day like this, Grant."

Grant calmly swished his razor in the water in the sink before tapping it against the edge. His eyes remained ahead of him. "What is there to talk about?"

"Grant, please. I know you're upset at me for not telling my parents about our engagement. And I understand that. But nothing is going to get resolved unless we deal with it; going days without speaking isn't going to solve anything."

Grant calmly wiped his face with a towel and placed it by the sink before reaching for his aftershave, taking his time gently patting it onto his smooth skin. After several moments, he turned to look at her. "Have you still not told them?"

Instantly nervous, she hesitated slightly when she answered, "No, not yet."

Scoffing, Grant shook his head and started to turn away from her.

"Grant!" Van grabbed his arm, turning him back towards her. "Look, I understand you being upset, but-"

"I passed upset two days ago, Van. I'm *pissed*. Especially after what you just said," Grant interrupted bitingly, his hard eyes boring straight into hers.

Van swallowed nervously. "I'm so sorry. But please, let's just deal with it. Let's sit down and talk and get everything out in the open."

Grant eyed her for a moment before sighing and wordlessly turning and walking into their bedroom. Van followed him and climbed onto the huge bed, where he was already sitting and looking at her.

"Let me just say this first," Grant began, not wasting any time. "As incensed as I am about all this, I'm even more hurt. I'm trying not to think about what it means that you don't even want to tell your parents about us getting married."

"Please don't think the worst about that," Van quickly pleaded. "Grant, I would never have accepted your proposal if I didn't love you and want to be your wife. I still do. I've just had so much other stuff on my mind with work and the issues with Canton...even though it's been a while now, Grant, there are still times I can't believe all of this is real. I actually pinch myself when I wake up in your arms in this beautiful house, without all the stresses I used to have. But it has nothing to do with me being ashamed of you or anything of the sort."

"Does it have anything to do with Joe?"

"Wh-what?"

"You heard what I asked you, Van."

"Why would it have anything to do with Joe? Why would you ask me that?"

"Stop stalling and answer the question."

Van knew there wasn't much she could get over on Grant, at least not for very long. All of his business experience had taught him how to read people and their body language, and he could be almost scary when he was in no-nonsense mode. Van sensed he was in that mode now, and she knew she needed to just be honest and avoid getting deeper into the doghouse than she already was.

"All right. Honestly? It still doesn't sit well with me that he hates me so much," Van admitted. "I know you probably don't want to hear that and think I should be over it by now, or maybe that I just shouldn't care what he thinks of me, but I'm sorry...I can't help it. It kills me that I'm the one that drove him to such feelings, when he's always been such a kind and generous and loving man. This has nothing to do with my feelings for you; I want to be with *you*, Grant. But I still care about Joe. Maybe I shouldn't, but I do."

Grant just looked at her, and Van prepared herself for anything. Would he yell? Would he understand? Would he call off their engagement and put her and her twins out? She had no idea what was going through his mind and her nervousness rose with every passing second she waited for his reaction.

Finally, he spoke. "I can understand that, Van. Of course you would care about him. That's just the kind of person you are; you care about people. It's one of the reasons I fell so hard for you. But *now* the question is, do you want Joe back?"

"No," Van replied quickly. She shook her head, looking right into his eyes and grabbing his hand. "I told you; I want *you*, Grant. That hasn't changed."

He eyed her. "Are you sure?"

"Yes." Van didn't have the nerve to mention her recent doubts, but her response was true; she *did* still want Grant. She just didn't know if she wanted to marry him yet as much as she thought she did. And considering she'd agreed to be his wife, she spent too much time missing – even occasionally yearning for - her ex, regardless of the reason.

But if Grant caught that loophole in her response, he didn't speak on it.

Sighing, Grant reached over and cupped her face in his hand. "I don't want to lose you, Van. But I won't tolerate being kept in the dark about anything. Just be straight up with me; with our situation coming about the way it has, I can understand feelings and emotions being all over the place. I'd like to think that by now, you know I'm a patient and understanding man when I need to be."

Van smiled and rested her hand on top of his. "I *do* know that. It's one of the things I love so much about you."

He leaned over and kissed her gently on the lips, then pulled back, looking right into her eyes. "No more secrets, okay?"

Van hoped he didn't sense her guilt when she smiled tightly and nodded. "I promise," she managed to say, even though she knew that promise was already broken.

• • • •

"MS. ROSELAND? THIS is Mrs. Harris, Canton's science teacher."

Van tried to think positively but a sense of dread coursed through her. "Yes, Mrs. Harris, how are you today?"

"I'm good, thank you. Do you have few minutes to talk about Canton?"

"Of course; just give me one second." Van braced herself for this latest issue with her son as she got up to close her office door. Taking a deep breath, she picked her phone up as she retook her seat at her desk. "All right, I'm back. What's going on?"

"Well, Canton hasn't been turning in his homework assignments on a regular basis," Mrs. Harris informed her. "Out of six assignments, he might turn in three. His mind wanders in class and I can tell he's just not paying attention. On the last two tests, he didn't finish in time and his grades suffered because of it; one time, he actually fell asleep."

"What?" Van was shocked. She had a strict bedtime of 9:30 for the twins, so Canton should have been getting plenty of sleep. This was a new one. "That doesn't make any sense. I make sure he's in bed at a reasonable time every night."

"Well, he's certainly not the only student who does these things; kids at this age tend to have a hard time keeping their mind and attention on the task at hand. But what concerns me about Canton - and what differentiates him from most students who do this - is that when he *does* turn in his homework or complete any work in class, it's impeccable. When I can get him to answer a question, it's always correct. So it's not that he doesn't know the material; he just doesn't seem interested in doing it."

That was only a marginal relief to Van. She wasn't terribly surprised to hear that Canton's issue wasn't that he couldn't keep up or grasp the work; he had always been ahead of the game when it came to school. His heart just wasn't in it like it used to be.

Sighing, Van rested her head against the back of her leather chair. "I'm so sorry if he's been disruptive to your class, Mrs. Harris. I'll definitely address this with him when I get home."

"He's actually more disinterested than disruptive," Mrs. Harris clarified. "His apathy about even being here is evident. He could far and away be one of my best students if he wanted to be. I've tried to talk to him about it, but he wouldn't tell me anything. I don't mean to pry, Ms. Roseland, but I have to ask...is there anything going on at home that we need to know about?"

There was no way Van was going to get into everything that had brought about this behavior in Canton. She understood why the question was being asked, but there was only so much detail Van was going to give. Not only did she feel it wasn't any of Mrs. Harris' business, it also shed a not-so-favorable light on Van.

"There have been some changes at home that Canton unfortunately hasn't adapted well to," Van replied vaguely. "We've tried to be patient and understanding with him about it because it *has* been a big adjustment, but not doing his homework or finishing tests is unacceptable. I appreciate you bringing this to my attention and I will most definitely be talking to him about it tonight."

"Thank you, Ms. Roseland," Mrs. Harris replied. Van knew she probably wanted to get more details about these "changes" and "adjustments" that Canton had been going through at home, but thankfully she left it alone. "I appreciate you speaking with me. I just want Canton to reach his full potential. I've seen his transcripts; he's always had excellent grades. If he continues like he is now, though, he'll barely pass my class."

Van pinched the bridge of her nose, telling herself not to get upset. The last thing she wanted was for Canton to fall behind or just settle for passing grades when he was capable of so much more than that. "I'll do everything I can to prevent that. Please feel free to give me a call any time you feel there's something else I need to know about Canton's behavior or performance in class."

"I certainly will."

Van sighed as she disconnected the call and put her cell phone back on her desk. So add science class to the list of ones Canton was falling behind in. Van knew she had to figure something out; despite what Canton was feeling about her and their home situation, she knew he'd regret it eventually if he let his excellent grades go down the toilet. He always loved school and learning; he had long since declared that he was going to a top school and he was going to do it on a full scholarship so Van wouldn't have to worry about paying for it, and he stayed focused on getting the best grades he could so he could do just that. Van knew he was just in the sixth grade, but who knew how long this funk he was in would last if she didn't do something about it?

As soon as she got home that evening, Van headed straight for Canton's room. He was surprisingly not on his computer but lying on his bed, on his side, just mindlessly playing with the bedspread. His glasses were on the nightstand next to him.

"Hey, baby," Van greeted him, stepping into the room.

His eyes turned towards her briefly before looking back ahead of him. "Hi."

"Are you feeling okay? Why are you lying down?" Van went over to feel his forehead. He shifted away from her.

"I'm fine," Canton replied simply.

Telling herself to keep her cool, Van sat down at the foot of the bed and looked at him. "Canton. Canton, sit up and look at me."

With a heavy sigh, Canton slowly did as he was told. He looked at her, his disinterest in whatever she had to say already evident. He almost looked like a different boy without his glasses.

"I got a call from Mrs. Harris, your science teacher, today," Van informed him. "What is this about you not turning in your homework and not finishing your tests in class? That's not like you and you know we don't play that."

Canton just looked away, then halfheartedly shrugged a shoulder.

"I can't hear your shoulder shrugging."

"I do my work," Canton eventually said in a bored voice.

"You don't do *all* of your work. Your teacher said you could be ahead of the class if you did, but if you keep going like this, you'll barely pass. And I know that's not the only class you're slacking in. Canton, honey..." Van placed a hand on his leg and felt it immediately tense, "I know you're upset about Joe being gone. I know you miss him and I'm sorry about that. But that doesn't mean you can just stop doing what you need to do. You need to get it together with the schoolwork, ASAP."

Canton remained quiet.

Peering at him, Van persisted, "Is there anything else going on that I don't know about? Or is this just about Joe being gone? If it is, I understand; he's been like a father to you for most of your life. It's totally understandable that you're upset; I know things could have been handled differently, all of these changes that have happened in the past year or so. But I need you to work with me so we can try to make things better. I hate seeing you like this."

Canton still said nothing.

Determined not to give up, Van scooted a little closer to him on the bed. "Baby...have you called Joe? You know you can still talk to him; I know you'd prefer it if we were all still living together like we used to be, but, sweetie...things are just different now. Life doesn't always go the way we want it to and we have to learn how to adapt. Joe might be gone but you still have to keep moving; things can't stop just because you're disappointed."

Canton's brow furrowed, and he slowly turned his eyes to her. Van could almost see the wheels turning in his head.

"Why do you keep saying that?" he asked evenly.

Van frowned, confused. "Saying what?"

"That Joe is 'gone.'"

"Because...he *is*." Van didn't know where her son was going with this.

"Joe didn't die. He didn't move out of town. He didn't leave us. You *dumped* him."

Van gasped. She felt her heart start beating double time; she hadn't expected this. Canton was looking at her in that now-usual accusatory way and Van found herself momentarily stumped.

"Um...I, um..." she stammered. "Canton, look-"

"Didn't you?"

Finding her voice, Van tried to sound stern when she declared, "There are certain things I'm not going to discuss with you, Canton. That's grown folks business."

"It doesn't take a genius, Ma. You don't have to discuss it with me for me to figure out what went on. I pay attention. You and Joe were together for years. And you seemed happy, with how you two were always kissing and stuff. But you were mad sometimes about Joe not having any money. Joe started working all the time to try to get some. Then we started hanging out with Mr. McCallister, *without* Joe. Mr. McCallister happens to be rich. Next thing we know, you're telling us we're moving in with him, and we don't see Joe anymore. And after just a few months, now you're engaged, to *Mr. McCallister*. Joe just wasn't good enough for you 'cause he didn't have enough money."

He might as well have slapped her across the face, as much as that hurt. Van's whole body went as cold as ice. She knew her son was intelligent and perceptive, but she had no idea that he'd figured things out to that extent. And even worse, that he apparently thought of her as some kind of shallow, selfish gold digger.

Unable to control the tears stinging her eyes, Van wordlessly stood and hurried out of the room. Part of her expected Canton to call her back or follow her and apologize, if for nothing else than making her cry, but he didn't. He meant every word he said. He didn't *just* miss Joe. He was pissed at Van for kicking who he considered his father to the curb for being too poor. Van had been worried about losing Cassie's respect for leaving Joe for Grant, but apparently, she had lost Canton's.

Van shut the door behind her in the master bathroom and put her hand over her mouth, tears rolling down her face in steady streams. The look in her son's eyes and the words he said to her ran through her mind like breaking news, and she knew she wouldn't be forgetting them any time soon. The last thing she wanted was for either of her children to think badly of her, but once again, her well-intentioned decision to leave Joe for the betterment of her kids was coming back to bite her in the butt.

She moved over to the mirror and looked at her reflection. She ran some water over one of her face cloths and dabbed her eyes and cheeks with it, trying to catch her breath. She was glad Grant wasn't home; she didn't want him to take it personally that Canton preferred Joe over him. No, this was *her* problem; Canton was *her* son and she would have to figure out how to fix this mess she had unintentionally created.

After several moments of contemplation, she pulled her phone out of her pocket as she lowered the lid on the toilet and sat on top of it. Biting her lip nervously, she ran her fingertips over the screen several times before finally going ahead and dialing Joe's number. As expected, it went right to voicemail. Van chose her words carefully as she left a message:

"Joe, it's Van...look, I know you don't want to talk to me, but I'm calling you about Canton. I'm concerned about him and I think you might be the only one that can get him to see reason. He's falling behind in school, being short and rude with people, and you know that's not like him. Please...can you please give me a call so we can figure out how to help him get through this? He just misses you."

Van hung up, hoping that her Canton-focused message would be enough to get Joe to call her back this time.

Chapter 6

• • • •

JOE GOT VAN'S MESSAGE. He took his time listening to it, not bothering until the next day, but he was automatically concerned when he heard it was about Canton. There was part of him that wondered if Van was just saying what she said to get him to talk to her, but he had to make himself dismiss that notion. Despite what he thought of Van, he couldn't doubt the love she had for her kids. So if she said Canton was having issues, he believed it.

But he still didn't want to talk to Van.

Feeling the need to get another male point of view, he talked to his friend Duke, a co-worker he had started hanging out with occasionally, to get his perspective.

"Why don't you want to talk to his mom about it?" Duke asked him.

"I just don't have anything to say to her," Joe replied simply, not wanting to go into the details of him and Van's breakup.

"Y'all must have fallen out or something."

"That's one way to put it."

"But it's not about y'all, though, from what it sounds like; she's calling you about her son."

"I know; and I *do* want to help him. I miss little man; considered him my son. Still do, really."

"And how old is he?"

"Eleven," Joe answered, remembering the twins' recent birthday.

"Well, most likely you'll have to deal with his mama if you're gonna deal with him, if he's that young. Does he have his own cell phone? Most kids do nowadays."

"I don't know. Not that I know of."

"Well, man, you might have to just suck it up and talk to her. It doesn't have to be that long; keep the subject on Canton."

"Yeah, but I know her; she'll try to steer the conversation to us."

Duke peered at him. "Is she your ex?"

Resisting the automatic frown that wanted to form, Joe grunted, "Yeah."

"She cheat on you?"

Joe sometimes didn't really think of it like that; in his mind it was just that Van left him for another man. It was less hurtful and insulting that way. But cheating was what Van did, as he had noted himself on several occasions. The reminder only caused him to become more agitated. "Yeah."

"I'm not gonna ask for any details 'cause I can tell you don't really want to talk about it..."

"You're right."

"But if you can do anything to help Canton, you should. It sounds like he needs you and you don't want him to think that you don't care about him anymore just because you and his mom are no longer together."

Joe didn't want that because that wasn't the case at all. He missed the talks he used to have with Canton; telling him stories from his childhood and how he came up, advising him to avoid the mistakes he made, teaching him how to treat a woman and take care of his mother and sister, as well as fix things around the house. Canton was almost the total opposite of how Joe was at his age (and they really didn't have a whole lot in common now), but they had always shared a tight bond. He smiled when he remembered how Canton would follow him around the house when he was little; everywhere Joe went, Canton was right behind him. And when he got older, Canton would often ask for his advice on things, or come to him when he didn't feel comfortable going to his mother. Joe couldn't deny that he missed that.

"You're right," he finally admitted, snapping out of his musings. "I would never want him to think that. I can deal with his trifling-ass mama if it means helping him out."

· · · ·

LATER ON THAT EVENING, Joe went to Tanisha's, eager to spend some time with his daughters, Jillian and Tara. They were always able to take his mind off of everything and cheer him up, and after the long day he had at work on the construction site and then giving himself a headache talking about his ex, that was just what he needed.

But that was all shot to hell when the girls started asking about Van, too.

"I miss her," Jillian announced, pouting slightly.

Telling himself to keep his patience in check, he replied, "I know you do."

"Can you take us to go see her, Daddy?" Tara asked, linking her arm through his.

"Not now, baby."

"*When*, then?"

"Y'all, I know you miss Van, but I told you, she's moved and doing her own thing now," Joe told them for what felt like the hundredth time. "I don't even know where her house is."

"Can't you call her and find out?" Jillian pressed.

Joe felt his frustration rising despite himself. He hated being in this position, having to repeatedly explain to his daughters why Van was no longer in their lives. They had grown to really love her, and had not taken it well when Joe first told them that he and Van were no longer together and they wouldn't be seeing her anymore. He tried to explain it as nicely as he could while still being clear, but that didn't stop the questions or requests to see her. They just didn't understand why they couldn't, and Joe resented Van for evidently not even considering the effect her actions would have on his girls, also.

"No, we can't call her right now," Joe replied patiently.

"Awww," they whined.

"Is she mad at us?" Tara asked.

"Of course not; y'all didn't do anything wrong. Things are just different now, that's all. But you still have me, you have your mama..."

"Mama isn't as nice as Ms. Van was," Jillian interjected. "Ms. Van actually spent time with us when we were over there. Mama stays in her room all the time, like she is now."

Joe couldn't dispute that. He had always told Tanisha that she didn't spend enough quality time with the girls, and it apparently was still falling on deaf ears.

"We just miss her, Daddy, that's all," Jillian continued, regarding Van. "Cassie and Canton, too."

They both started looking sad, and Joe knew he had to do something quickly to lighten the mood. He didn't want to spend his evening with his daughters talking about his ex.

"What, y'all aren't having fun with me or something?" he teased, ticking them. They both broke into fits of giggles, and Joe managed to keep their minds off of Van until it was time for them to go to bed. He waited for them to take their showers, put on their night clothes, and hugged and kissed them both before tucking them in. He was glad they even still wanted him to do that, considering they were getting older now; Jillian was almost thirteen and Tara was eleven. But they were still his little girls.

"Will you be here when we get up in the morning, Daddy?" Tara asked.

Joe hadn't planned on staying the night, but he couldn't say no. "Yeah, baby, I'll be here."

"Good," both Jillian and Tara chorused with smiles before dozing off to sleep. Joe stood there gazing at them for several moments with his own smile on his face before leaving the room and quietly closing the door behind him.

He went to Tanisha's room, only knocking once before easing the door open. She was sprawled across her bed, watching *Real Housewives of Atlanta* on her twenty-four-inch television.

"They in the bed yet?" she asked, her eyes still glued to the TV screen.

"Yeah," Joe grunted, shaking his head as he closed the door behind him. "Why did you stay in here all this time?"

"I wanted to watch my show."

"And that's more important than spending time with your daughters, huh?"

Sucking her teeth, Tanisha rolled over to her side. "Don't start with that."

"Why shouldn't I? You never spend any time with them, and just being in the same apartment at the same time doesn't count."

"You ain't here all the time. You don't know."

"Am I lying?"

Tanisha looked at him, then sucked her teeth again. He wasn't lying and they both knew it. "I don't need no parenting lesson."

"You need more than that. I just want you to remember how you treat them later on down the line when you need something and they're not trying to hear it. Maybe you can call one of those so-called housewives you're always watching, since you probably know more about them than you do Jillian or Tara."

"Whatever."

"Yeah, whatever." Joe turned to leave the room.

"Where you going?" Tanisha exclaimed, sitting up.

"The living room."

"Why?"

"Because I want to."

"You can stay back here," Tanisha suggested, looking at him seductively as she rose to her knees.

"I'm straight. I don't even like that show."

"We don't have to watch that," Tanisha quickly declared. She grabbed the remote and switched the channel to ESPN. "There."

"I'm not trying to watch TV at all, Tanisha. I'm tired."

"The bed is back here. And I'm not trying to watch TV, either."

Joe watched as Tanisha slid off the bed and strutted on her bowlegs over to him. Grabbing the front of his t-shirt, she stood on her tiptoes and kissed him, sliding her tongue into his mouth. Joe let it happen, even returning the kiss, but he wasn't really in the mood for this tonight. It had been a long day and he just wanted to go to sleep.

When he felt Tanisha's hands start unbuckling his belt, he broke the kiss and stepped back.

"Not tonight."

Tanisha frowned breathlessly. "Why not??"

"You know I don't get down with you like that while the girls are here."

"What difference does it make? They 'sleep!"

"I don't care."

"How 'bout if I just break you off, then?" Tanisha offered, sliding her small hand down his pants.

Joe grabbed her wrist. "No, Tanisha."

"So we're not gonna have a relationship now?"

Joe's face screwed in confusion. "What? How did we even get on *that*?"

"I'm saying I want you to be my man again. We might as well."

"We might as well? Why, because we have kids together? That doesn't mean anything."

"That ain't the only reason. We're feeling each other, too."

"Are you smoking again?"

Tanisha sucked her teeth. "I'm serious, Joe."

"I'm serious, too. We've tried being together, several times, and it doesn't work. We need to just be glad we can tolerate each other and leave it at that."

"I want more than just sex."

"We don't have to have *that*."

Tanisha shut her mouth. She knew Joe would have no problem cutting her off if he chose to, and she didn't want to lose that on top of everything else.

Just then, Joe's phone chimed. He fished it out of his pocket and smiled when he saw a text from Raven:

Just got home and I need a few rounds of that lovin'. Can u come over?

"Who is that?" Tanisha demanded.

Joe ignored her as he typed out a response:

I told my girls I'd be here when they got up in the morning. Can you keep it hot 'til 2morrow night?

In no time, Raven responded:

I STAY hot.

"You sure are smiling hard at whoever that is," Tanisha griped, folding her arms. "I like your nerve to be texting other chicks right in my face."

"I'll go to the living room, then." Joe grabbed the doorknob.

"Joe!"

"What, Tanisha? Look, I'm only staying here at all tonight because I told the girls I would. I'm not trying to mess with you. So just keep watching your show and let me get some rest. Some of us actually *worked* today."

"Why can't you sleep back here, though? I ain't gon' try nothing."

"And if I believe that, then I believe in Santa Claus and Tinkerbell and unicorns made out of glitter, too."

Tanisha sucked her teeth as she stomped back over to her bed. "You always gotta be such a smart ass."

"I'm good at it," Joe retorted as he opened the door and walked out. He could still hear Tanisha fussing as he headed back to the living room. It was time for him to officially get his own place.

Chapter 7

• • • •

JOE TONGUE-KISSED RAVEN'S neck before starting to roll off of her, but Raven stopped him.

"Not yet," she whispered, tightening around him. She smiled when Joe groaned and bit his lip.

"Tryin' to go again?" Joe asked her, his hips easing back into a smooth grind.

It was Raven's turn to groan. "If you keep doing that, I am."

Joe grabbed her thigh and lifted it higher around him so he could get deeper, and Raven cursed under her breath in pleasure. In no time, they were going at it again, grinding against each other as if it would be their last time doing so. They whispered sexual trash talk against each other's lips as they worked up yet another sweat, Joe holding Raven's arms over her head by the wrists. Time stood still as they rolled around on Raven's bed, neither being able to get enough of the other.

Finally, they lay side by side, both panting and smiling.

"You are something else, Mr. Miller," Raven complimented, looking over at him with a hand on her stomach.

"You're not so bad yourself, Ms. Flank," Joe replied, winking at her. He rubbed his rough hand across her smooth thigh.

Raven grinned. She liked when he touched her. "You want something to drink? I've got wine, juice, sparkling water..."

"Water is fine for me, but stay here...I'll get it," Joe said as he sat up. Raven looked at him in surprise. He gave her thigh a little squeeze as he asked, "What do you want?"

Raven started to say "You,", but thankfully stopped herself. She didn't even know where that came from. It was probably just her sex high.

"Some orange juice would be great. The glasses are in the cabinet by the stove."

"I got you."

Joe stood and walked out of the room, and Raven automatically bit her lip and squeezed her legs together at the sight of his beautiful bare behind leaving the room. She flopped onto her back and mindlessly bit her nail, hearing him move around in her kitchen and thinking about what he had done to her body just now. Remembering how he licked, caressed, sucked, and stroked her made her body rev back up all on its own. Her legs were still rubbing together when he came back into the room, a glass in each hand.

"Thank you." She smiled at him as he handed her a tall glass of orange juice.

"No problem."

"You didn't see the bottled water in there?" she asked, motioning towards his glass of water.

"I don't need all that. Tap water is fine for me," Joe shrugged, taking a long sip.

Raven chuckled as she brought her glass to her lips, eyeing Joe as she did so. He was so unpretentious and easy to please, and that was something new for Raven. Most of the men she dealt with were spoiled, arrogant jerks; she couldn't recall any of them ever offering to get her anything to drink after a roll in the hay. They always expected *her* to get it, and it was something she never really thought much of because it had never been any other way. But Joe was a refreshing change from all that.

When they'd had enough of their drinks, Joe set the glasses on the nightstand and gently grabbed Raven's foot, bringing it to his lap. Raven looked at him in surprise, but when he began massaging her foot, her eyes slid closed and her head fell back in pleasure.

"Oh my *god*," she moaned. "Joe, that feels *so* good..."

"Glad you like," Joe replied with a lopsided smile. It was then that Raven noticed he had a dimple.

"You know you don't have to – *oooh*," Raven's voice caught in her throat when Joe dug his thumbs into her sole.

"I don't have to what?"

"Do this...what you're doing..."

"You like it, though, right? You want me to stop?"

"No...*hell* no..."

"Then be quiet and enjoy it."

Raven did just as she was told, leaning back on her elbows as she let Joe massage her foot as much as he wanted. It was clear he knew was he was doing, and the rough texture of his hands made it feel twice as good. He spent a good twenty minutes on one foot and Raven felt like she was melting into the bedspread; she almost forgot he had another foot to go.

She had received her share of foot rubs over the years, but Joe's was almost orgasmic. She was actually writhing and her body was on fire. Everything in her wanted him on top of her and inside of her again. She attributed it to the foot rub; he must have done some kind of reflexology magic on her and pressed on a spot that was directly connected to her vagina.

After a while, she couldn't take it anymore.

"Joe."

He looked over at her.

"Come here."

The lust in her eyes was clear. Joe asked no questions as he laid her foot down and yanked her by the legs closer to him, eliciting an excited shriek from Raven. He lowered his body onto hers, kissing her deeply. Raven enjoyed that for several moments before pushing him onto his back. She grabbed a condom from the pile on the nightstand, covered him as she looked right into his eyes, then slowly lowered herself onto him, biting her lip as she did so. Joe whispered how good she felt as he grabbed her hips, bringing his to meet hers in a steady and sensual rhythm.

Raven cursed repeatedly as the pace increased, both of them losing control; Joe felt sinfully good. They urged each other on, trading sexual banter and trash talk. She braced her hands on his granite-like pecs and worked her hips until ecstasy hit her with both fists, leaving her screaming then reeling in a sweaty, sex-satisfied stupor as she collapsed on top of Joe.

"Damn!" she exclaimed breathlessly, pushing her sweaty bangs away from her face.

"I know, right," Joe concurred with her implied appreciation. "You got some skills, girl."

"Well, ya know...I try to make memories," Raven teased.

Joe chuckled as he slid his fingertips up and down her back. "You do *that*. You want your juice?"

"Yeah."

Joe reached over and got her glass from the nightstand, and waited for her to sit up before he handed it to her.

"Thank you," she said, her eyes lingering on him before she realized it and made them stop. She suddenly felt unexpectedly and inexplicably nervous as she sipped her juice, looking at the perfume bottles on her vanity as if they were speaking to her. What was up with her all of a sudden?

Thankfully, Joe broke her out of her reverie.

"Van called me."

Raven didn't really want to talk about Van, but figured that was better than the uncharacteristic awkwardness that was starting to creep up on her.

"Again?"

"Well this time, she made it about Canton."

"Ahh." Raven didn't want to reveal that Van had told her she was going to do that. "She did mention that he hasn't been himself lately."

"Yeah. I'm not gon' lie; I'm worried about him."

"Me too. I don't like to hear about him hurting like he is. He misses you."

"I miss him, too."

"So when are you gonna call Van back?"

"I don't know," Joe sighed, running a hand over his head. "I don't wanna be overly petty but I just do not want to talk to Van. About *anything*."

Raven rolled over onto her stomach and played with her nails thoughtfully. Joe looked equally as thoughtful from his seat with his back against the headboard, gently tapping his empty water glass against his thigh. He seemed genuinely conflicted, and Raven knew he still cared about Canton as much as he always did. The fact that he didn't automatically declare that Van's kids were no longer his problem just because Van dumped him endeared him to Raven.

"You don't think she's just using this as an excuse to get you to talk to her?" she asked softly, still playing with her nails as she looked at him.

"I think it's probably both; she wants to talk but she's more worried about Canton. Van wouldn't use her kids like that. At least, I don't think she would." *But I didn't think she would cheat on me and leave me for another man, either, so what do I know*, he thought to himself.

"You know you don't necessarily *have* to go through Van to talk to Canton, right?" Raven reminded him. "I *am* his cousin, too."

Joe's eyes brightened. "True; I didn't even consider that."

"But you don't need to let Van know anything about it, though," Raven quickly added. "Let her think you're just ignoring her. Drive her crazy for a minute."

Joe looked at her in amusement. "Damn, Raven. For real?"

"What? Don't act like you wouldn't love that."

"I'm just surprised to hear that coming from you. I thought you had forgiven her."

"I thought I had...I thought I *could*. But the more I thought about it, the more incensed I got, especially after

Donald dumped me. I mean, yeah, I know Grant and I were never in love or anything but he *was* somebody I was dating; who knows how long it was that they were making eyes at each other or having private conversations during the time he and I were going out. She knew how much I was into Grant. And Van never even hinted about having any feelings for him, even a little bit. Then she just up and announced they were together, shocking me right along with you. As close as we were, that's just some shit you don't do."

Joe just looked at Raven intently, taking in her words. "*Did* you love him?"

Raven shrugged. "Probably not, if I'm honest. But I could've eventually; I definitely had feelings for him. But apparently he was only seeing me at all so he could get closer to her; he was never really interested in me like I thought he was. I was just...a pawn to get what he wanted. It's actually kind of humiliating, when I remember that part of it."

That was new information to Joe, that Grant only dated Raven to get to Van. "So they're both shady. Let 'em have each other."

"I guess." Raven shrugged again, turning her attention back to her nails. "It just doesn't seem fair, though, you know? For them to do this to us and get to live happily ever after, with *no* consequences or anything?"

"Everything comes back around. If they're not feeling the consequences now, they will. You don't just dog people and not have it come back on you at some point."

Raven smiled at that. "True."

Just then, Raven's phone rang. It was the *Laverne and Shirley* theme so she knew it was Van.

"I really need to change that ringtone," Raven muttered.

"You gonna get that?" Joe asked.

"Should I?"

"Why not? See what she wants."

Raven looked at him curiously as she pushed herself up to get the phone. She had just planned on ignoring it and *maybe* calling Van back the next day, if she felt like it. She was curious as to why Joe was encouraging her to take the call.

Joe eyed her as she got up to get her iPhone from the dresser, silently admiring her long, lithe body. Her just-big-enough breasts, her long, toned torso, her cute ass and her long legs that he loved the most...Joe usually preferred a little more curves, but Raven's body was soft, smooth, and proportioned. And she could bend those legs of hers back like no other woman he had ever been with.

"Van, what's up?" Raven answered the call, a distracted frown marring her brow. "Yeah, I *am* in the middle of something, actually...no, I'm not *always* busy..."

Joe motioned for her to come back to bed, and Raven shot him another curious look but complied. She sat with her back to him, and he crawled over and began licking her neck from behind, one hand snaking around and fondling her left breast. He smiled when she almost dropped the phone.

"H-huh? What?" Raven stammered into the phone distractedly, clearly thrown off. A tiny moan escaped when

Joe began sucking her neck, and he wondered if Van had heard it. "Yeah...um, yeah, I'm listening..."

With his other hand, Joe reached around and pushed Raven's thighs apart before slowly teasing her clit with his fingers.

"Shit!" Raven exclaimed, a hard shudder rippling through her body. She tried to look back at Joe but he quickly grabbed her chin and turned her head facing forward, holding it there while the other hand continued to tease her center. Raven felt like she was about to lose her mind and for a few seconds, she forgot that Van was still on the phone.

"Raven! What's going on over there?" Van was shrieking.

"Keep talking," Joe whispered in Raven's ear, his hand still holding her face in place.

Raven couldn't speak, though; Joe had eased two fingers inside of her and she automatically started slowly grinding his hand, closing her eyes and leaning back against Joe in pleasure.

"Raven!" Van called out.

"I'm here," Raven managed to say. Her mouth fell open when Joe changed the angle of his fingers and pushed a little deeper; it felt like her body was about to shatter into pieces.

"Are you having *sex*??" Joe heard Van ask through the phone.

"Say yes," he instructed Raven in a whisper, his lips brushing her ear.

"Yes," Raven moaned, as much in response to Van as in reaction to what Joe was doing to her. Her hips grinded a little faster against Joe's hand. "*Hell* yes..."

"Now hang up," Joe ordered.

"Bye, Van." Raven ended the call right when Van was asking, "With who?" Dropping the phone on the floor, Raven opened her legs wider for Joe. He continued to sexually torture her, one arm holding her tight against his chest while the other hand drove her quickly and steadily up the mountain of pleasure until she careened off the top. Her body jerked repeatedly as she screamed, the orgasm sending jolts through her as if she had stuck her wet finger in a light socket.

"Joe!" she exclaimed, blindly reaching back to clamp the back of his neck.

"Don't stop...I want all of it," Joe urged, his fingers still pleasing her. He nipped her neck with his teeth, something he had discovered she liked. "Give me all of it, Raven."

Biting her lip, Raven opened her legs even wider, not knowing how she was possibly going to be able to handle any more but more than willing to find out. When Joe ducked his head under her arm and tongued her breast, she thought she was going to pass out. And when he jumped in front of her and dove his head between her legs, she was certain he was trying to kill her.

"Yes...yes...yes," she whimpered, collapsing onto her back because she just couldn't hold herself up anymore. She grabbed a pillow and put it over here face, muffling the increasingly-loud screams of pleasure that she wasn't able to help making. When another orgasm hit her, Raven saw stars flicker and dance in front of her eyes. Every inch of her body tingled so much it almost burned.

Joe wordlessly kissed up the length of her body as he climbed back onto the bed, resting beside her. He slid the pillow away from her face, moving her hair out of her eyes and gently wiping her sweaty forehead with his fingertips as she caught her breath.

"You good?" he eventually asked her when it seemed she had calmed down.

Raven looked up at him amusingly. "I don't know who taught you how to do what you do," she breathed, a hand on her stomach, "But I will personally cook a four-course meal for them, using my good plates and everything."

Joe laughed heartily. "Wine, too?"

"The best I got."

"You're a mess, girl," Joe chuckled, running his hand up and down her long torso. He swirled his finger in her bellybutton. "I just pay attention to women's bodies...get in tune with what they like, how they respond, how they move. Give 'em what they want."

"You might need to teach a class."

"Dudes wouldn't take it. They think they know already."

"Trust me, you're a rare breed, Mr. Miller."

"'Preciate the compliment. As long as you're getting what you need."

Raven looked up at him thoughtfully. His eyes were watching his fingers playing on her stomach. He seemed to really and sincerely be all about pleasing the woman he was with. Raven noticed that not once did he ever ask her to return the favor on anything he did to her. Raven was used to men trying to push her head between their legs after a couple of kisses, but not Joe; he got his pleasure from pleasing.

"And what is it *you* need, Joe?" she couldn't resist asking.

He looked at her. Raven could tell he was pondering her question, but he eventually just shrugged.

"Still figuring that out, I guess."

"Hmm."

Joe scooted closer to her and rested his head on his hand. "You think Van had any idea it was me making you lose your mind like that?"

Raven's grin was automatic. "I wish I knew. I'd love to see her face if she did."

They both laughed.

· · · ·

VAN WAS STILL LOOKING at the phone, wondering if she was in some kind of alternate universe.

Raven had just brushed her off, again, because she was with a man. Van could hear him whispering to Raven in the background, even though she couldn't quite make out what he was saying. What Van couldn't understand was why Raven kept answering the phone if she was in the middle of that, but more so, why Raven kept brushing her off at all if she was really trying to forgive her like she claimed. Once upon a time, Raven would stop just about whatever she was doing to talk to Van, even if it was only for a couple of minutes. There had been plenty of times when Van would call Raven while she was out or with someone, and Raven would take her call and let her know she'd call her right back with all the details. And she always did. Van still wasn't used to that not being the case anymore.

Really, there were times when Van wondered if she and Raven's relationship would *ever* recover. Raven had already told her that she would never look at Van the same anymore, and sadly, Van didn't think there was anything she could do to change that. Even if she were to go so far as to break up with Grant, that might help *some*, but it would probably be in the back of Raven's mind that Van might do the same thing again with another man. It killed Van that she might never fully get Raven's trust back.

And what was worse, she didn't really feel she had anybody she could talk to about this. Raven had always been her go-to confidant. Of course she no longer had Joe. Her parents still didn't know anything about the situation...that left Grant. Maybe she *should've* been able to talk to him about anything, but for whatever reason, she couldn't. And since he was at the center of her and Raven's rift, she didn't think he could be totally objective.

In what probably should have been the happiest time of her life, Van had never felt more alone.

Tears were welling in Van's eyes when her phone rang in her hand. She hastily swiped them away as she anxiously looked down at the screen, hoping it was Raven calling her back. She automatically tensed up when she saw it was her mother.

It took several rings, but Van finally hesitantly answered. "Hey, Mama."

"Hey, sweetheart," Van's mother, Florence, greeted warmly. "Were you asleep? I know it's a little late..."

"It's nine o'clock," Van reminded amusingly.

"That's late for me. I'm usually in the bed by now. But it was on my heart to call you tonight."

"Really?" Van shifted uncomfortably, as if her mother knew what she had been thinking about right before her call. "Why is that?"

"You tell me. Is everything going okay down there?"

Van's parents lived in Ohio, and Van was especially glad about that now. "Everything's great."

"Really?"

"Absolutely."

Florence was silent, and Van knew she probably wasn't buying Van's act. Florence always had a way of being able to pick up on Van's facades, even if she didn't know the exact reason behind them. Van was always rather proud, and Florence worried that it was sometimes to her detriment. While she might not have known exactly what was going on with her daughter, she knew all wasn't as peachy as Van always made it out to be.

"My grandbabies doing all right?" Florence asked, choosing to let Van think she took her at her word that all was well.

"Oh, they're wonderful," Van replied. Not having the energy to get into Canton's troubles, she continued, "I let Cassie talk me into letting her enter another modeling competition."

"I think that's a good thing, if that's what she still wants to do with her life. And as long as her grades stay up. How did she do?"

"Well, she won this one. So now it's even harder to tell her anything."

Florence laughed. "I can only imagine. I hate I wasn't there to see that."

"I recorded it, and I have pictures. You know we'd never hear the end of it if we didn't take lots of pictures."

"Well, I can't wait to see 'em. What did she get for winning?"

"Five hundred dollars, some professional headshots, and a meeting with a talent agent. She wasn't too happy with me, though, when I said that she still had a while before I'd let her really jump into all this."

"Why's that?"

"I want her to have a childhood. She won't be able to get this time back and I don't want her to regret anything by growing up too fast."

"Is it that you don't want her to regret anything by growing up too fast, or that you aren't quite ready for her to grow up?"

That stumped Van momentarily. "What do you mean by that?"

"As smart as you are, I'm sure you know full well what I mean but I'll say it, anyway. Cassie can't stay your little girl forever, baby. Eventually those children are gonna wanna get out from under you. Before you know it, she'll be a teenager...she's been saying what she wants to do for years and she hasn't wavered from what she wants. She certainly seems serious about it. It might not be the worst thing to let her really start getting her feet wet, provided she stays on top of her grades."

Van pondered her mother's words. Was she really trying to keep Cassie from growing up? She couldn't deny that she wasn't looking forward to her twins getting to the point where they didn't feel like they needed her as much anymore. And especially with everything going on with Canton and him not thinking too highly of her these days, was she unconsciously trying to keep Cassie from breaking away from her, too?

"You can always monitor what she does," Florence continued, regarding Cassie. "She's only eleven so everything would have to go through you, anyway. And you know you and Joe would be right there looking after her."

The mention of Joe's name only reminded Van that her parents still had no idea that he was no longer in the picture. "Right..."

"How *is* Joe, by the way? I haven't talked to him in a long while."

"He's fine," Van managed to say.

"Is he there? I sho' would like to speak to my future son-in-law."

Van's face was on fire. Chuckling nervously, she asked, "Wh-what? Joe and I aren't engaged...kinda jumping the gun, aren't you?"

"Just trying to speak it into existence. You know we love Joe. He would make a wonderful husband to you and father to my grandbabies. And y'all certainly have been together long enough; that man ain't goin' nowhere. I'm surprised he hasn't proposed already, as much as he adores you."

Van knew she needed to tell her mother the truth. She needed to admit that she broke up with Joe almost a year ago and is now engaged to another man.

But when she opened her mouth to say the words, she couldn't make herself do it. She had always been so close to her mother, but she still couldn't bring herself to tell her about all of this. Was she ashamed?

"Yeah, well..." Van hedged after a moment, "I guess we'll see. But no, Joe isn't here...working late. But I'll try to remember to let him know you called; I might be asleep when he gets in."

"Oh, okay. Well, let me get on in this bed...I'll talk to you later, baby."

"Okay, Mama. Love you."

"I love you, too."

Van ended the call and buried her face in her hands. She hated lying to her mother like that, and she wondered how much longer she was going to be able to continue this charade of her and Joe still being together. *She* had been the one to end the relationship, for what she had considered to be good reasons, so why couldn't she just be honest with her parents about it?

One thing she could agree with her mother on; Joe *would* make a wonderful husband.

Chapter 8

• • • •

A COUPLE DAYS LATER, Van, Grant, and the twins were sitting down to dinner. Van hadn't felt like cooking so she ordered in a meal of steak, asparagus, sweet potatoes, biscuits, and apple pie. Grant had offered to hire a personal chef if she wanted, but she declined, feeling it was too extravagant and that they were more than capable of cooking themselves. But she'd mindlessly gotten used to the convenience of ordering in when she felt like it, which was a luxury she didn't have before. It wasn't too long ago that she would've had to cook whether she felt like it or not.

Joe cooked plenty, her mind reminded her. *He helped you with that just like he did everything else, and without complaint. Even when he was as dog-tired as you.*

Van hastily pushed those thoughts from her mind.

As they all sat down to eat, no one was doing that much talking...except for Cassie, that is.

"So my friend Neicy tried to say that I only won that modeling competition 'cause I'm light-skinned and I have long hair, but I told her I'm not even light-skinned, and even if I *was*, that wouldn't have nothing to do with it," she rambled on. Van didn't even bother correcting her grammar. "She just mad 'cause she couldn't have won it and her hair ain't as long as mine. You know she tried to say I had a weave, right? All my hair is *natural*!"

Van sighed and Grant looked at her in amusement; he always seemed to get a kick out of Cassie.

Figuring her daughter wanted some kind of response, Van droned, "I know that, Cassie. And don't say *ain't*."

"I'm just sayin', she's always tryin' to talk about somebody."

"Why are you friends with her, then?" Grant asked.

Cassie paused, the simple question momentarily stumping her. "I don't know..."

"Real friends don't spread rumors and talk about you behind your back. You know that, right?"

"You're right. And she's *always* doing that! Well, she's deleted."

Grant chuckled at this but Van didn't care for the haughty tone Cassie was using. She made a mental note to address that with her later.

Canton just continued to eat his food, totally disinterested in the conversation. Van pursed her lips as she looked at him, wishing there was something she could say to get him more engaged. There was a time when he would have been taunting Cassie or debating with her about the frivolity of worrying about what someone said about her hair, but he wasn't uttering a word. He might as well have been at the table by himself.

"Did y'all see the new iPhone that came out?" Cassie asked, spearing a stalk of asparagus with her fork. "They come in all those pretty colors. Can I get the pink one?"

"There's nothing wrong with the phone you have, Cassie," Van replied.

"Yeah, but it's not the best one."

"Girl, be glad you have a phone at all. You're just eleven."

"But I'm *sayin'*, if I'm gonna have one, shouldn't I be able to get the one I want?"

Van cocked an eyebrow. "Oh, really?"

"I just don't see what the big deal is. It's just a phone. And it's not like we have to worry about how much it costs."

"Cassie!" Van couldn't believe she just said that.

"What?" Cassie replied innocently.

"I can get the phone for her tomorrow," Grant offered, seemingly oblivious to Van's ire. He looked over at Cassie. "The pink one, you said?"

"Yes yes yes! Thank you, Grant!!" Cassie cheered, bouncing in her seat and clapping her hands excitedly.

"Hold it! Little girl, I said you don't need a new phone and I meant it. You don't get stuff just because you think you should have it!" Van informed Cassie angrily.

"But *Grant* said I could have one!" Cassie countered, looking at Grant to help plead her case.

Glaring at Grant momentarily, Van retorted to Cassie, "What did *I* say, though?"

Huffing angrily, Cassie folded her arms. "That's not fair!"

"Why, because you're not getting your way? I've told you, you're not gonna get every shiny new thing you want. You need to be grateful for what you already have."

"How come I can have an iPhone but can't get it upgraded when I want to?? That doesn't make any sense to me!"

"Keep talking and you won't have that, *either*! You know better than to question me, little girl!"

"Ugh!" Cassie exclaimed angrily, banging her hands on the table before getting up and running out of the room.

"Cassie!" Van called after her.

Cassie ignored her and stomped up the stairs to her room. Van looked over at Grant, shocked. Cassie had always been outspoken and a little sassy, but she was never outright disrespectful. Van had noticed that ever since they moved in with Grant, Cassie had become increasingly more spoiled and entitled. Grant obviously had no problem buying the twins whatever they wanted, but Van didn't want them to think they could just snap their fingers and make their wishes commands. And it didn't help when Grant caved in to their requests so much; he didn't seem to like telling the twins no, regardless of what Van had already told them.

Joe never would have done that; he always backed Van in front of the twins, and if he happened to disagree with her, he'd talk to her about it in private. Van would have to get Grant to do that.

"Van, I didn't think-"

"Can we talk about this later?" Van hissed at Grant, motioning towards Canton, who was still in his own little world.

Grant looked at Canton then back at Van, his expression a mix of frustration and concern. But he just nodded and went back to his meal.

Canton finished eating and pushed his plate away. "I'm done. May I be excused now?"

Van looked at him helplessly. It broke her heart that he was so detached from her, and even more so that there didn't seem to be much that she could do about it. He never did apologize for the comment he made about her leaving Joe because he wasn't good enough, and had barely had any words for her since.

"You don't want any pie, baby? You know how much you like apple pie," Van suggested. She knew she sounded desperate. Grant glanced at her, apparently noticing it, too.

"No, thank you. I don't want any pie right now. May I go?"

Van looked at Grant as if expecting him to do or say something to get Canton to change his mind, but Grant didn't have the solution any more than Van did. Finally, Van just sighed, defeated.

"Go ahead."

Canton wordlessly got up from the table and left the room, not looking at either of them. Van rubbed her temples, feeling another headache coming on.

"You okay?" Grant asked her.

"No," Van wasted no time responding. "I'm not."

Grant hated seeing Van so stressed out; it was a state she seemed to be in a lot recently. He considered it part of his role as her man to remove all of her worries, but apparently he wasn't doing a very good job of that.

"Why don't you go on upstairs, take some Tylenol, and I'll clean up the dishes," Grant suggested. "Just go chill out for a while; I'll be up when I'm done."

Van just nodded, not having the energy or desire to protest. "Thanks," she mumbled before turning to head upstairs.

Once in their bedroom, she took the Tylenol, then laid down on the bed, burying her face in one of the super-soft pillows. She knew she probably needed to go and deal with Cassie, but she just didn't have the energy for it. But she knew she would need to get a grip because it really felt like she was slipping when it came to her kids. And this wasn't something she could blame on hormones or them just getting older; this was a direct result of the decision she had made to be with Grant.

About a half hour later, Grant entered the bedroom. Van was still lying down.

"Feeling any better?" he asked her.

Pushing her hair out of her eyes, Van rolled onto her back. "The headache is, a little."

"That's good. You need anything?"

Van sat up. "I need you to not go against what I say in front of the twins."

Frowning, Grant turned to her. "I beg your pardon?"

"You know what I'm talking about, Grant. You heard me clearly tell Cassie she couldn't have that new iPhone, and then you announce that you'll get one for her tomorrow. That doesn't do anything but make her think she can come running to you every time I tell her something she doesn't like, because she knows you'll indulge her. *And* it makes me look like the bad guy. Don't do that to me."

Grant sat down next to her on the bed. "I apologize. I wasn't blatantly trying to go against your word...guess I just wasn't thinking." He placed a hand on her leg. "You know I'm on your side."

"*They* need to see that, Grant. We need to have each other's backs when it comes to the twins. If you don't agree with something I've said or done, then talk to me about it, privately. But don't just overrule me. If they know you'll do that, they won't take anything I say seriously."

"You're right."

"And please, please stop giving in to them so much," Van continued. "I know you want to give them things they never had and I appreciate it, but I don't want them to be spoiled. Cassie apparently already has it in her head that she's entitled to whatever she wants."

"Van, look, I know I have a lot to learn when it comes to raising kids, but please know that I love Canton and Cassie and whatever I do is because of that. Maybe I go a little overboard with it at times and I'll try to rein that in...but I spoil the people I love. I just can't help it. I'm so blessed to have everything I have that it only feels natural to share it with my loved ones."

Van smiled at him; Grant was such a generous man, and she knew by the way he took care of his mother and little sister that he spoiled his loved ones. She couldn't help but appreciate him wanting to take care of her and the twins so much; they just had to find a balance.

She scooted closer to him, sliding her leg over his lap and taking his handsome face in her hands. "Sweetie, I appreciate *everything* you do for us. I hope you know that."

"I do. It's part of what makes me want to do even more for you."

"And I love you for that. But we're used to not having a lot...I want the twins to stay grounded. Let's just make sure they have everything they need and ration the wants, especially with Cassie. I don't mind them having things, but I need you to be able to tell them 'no' sometimes, too."

Grant nodded. "I understand that. I'm sorry for making it seem like I was going against you."

"It's okay; I know you meant well." Van smiled, bringing his face to hers for a kiss. They enjoyed it for several moments before pulling back, Grant caressing the side of her face as he looked at her in concern.

"I don't like seeing you stressed out," he commented.

Van sighed, leaning her head on his shoulder. "I'm worried about the twins, Grant. They never used to act like they've been acting lately."

Grant wrapped an arm around her comfortingly. "It's just growing pains, baby, that's all."

Van disagreed, but she couldn't tell him that they didn't start acting like they were until she left Joe to be with him. "Whatever it is, we need to figure out how to fix it."

"I can talk to them," Grant offered.

"That's okay," Van declined. "You don't have to do that."

Grant pulled back so he could look her in her face, a slight frown marring his brow. "What's wrong with me talking to them, Van?"

"Nothing," Van replied quickly, realizing she may have offended him. "I didn't mean it like that...I just-"

"You don't have to do everything by yourself anymore," Grant interjected gently. He kissed the tip of her nose. "I'm right here with you. Let me help you with the twins; I *am* about to be their father, after all. They need to get used to dealing with me for more than just when they need or want something."

Van nodded. She tended to still think of the twins as only hers; she knew she would have to start thinking of them as Grant's, too, even though it still didn't quite feel like they were yet.

"You're right." She kissed him. "I'm sorry."

Grant took her face in his hands and deepened the kiss, eventually ending up on top of her on the bed. He slid his hand under her shirt and squeezed her breast before gripping the waistband of her pants.

"You don't mind if I take these off, do you?" he asked between kisses.

"Be my guest," Van replied flirtatiously.

Grinning, Grant began to undress her before removing his own shirt. They slid under the covers and began making love, kissing and whispering to each other quietly. Their lovemaking had only gotten marginally better over the months they'd been engaged, and while Van enjoyed it, she couldn't deny that Joe still held the title of the best lover she ever had. She hated comparing Grant to him, but she couldn't seem to help it. Grant was so careful and polite and low-key, and there were times when Van missed Joe's aggressiveness and intensity in the bedroom. He would've just torn Van's pants off instead of asking first. Van wished Grant would be a little more animalistic, but maybe that just wasn't his nature.

She knew it wasn't all on Grant, though...she still didn't feel as comfortable with him sexually as she had felt with Joe, either. She and Joe certainly never wasted time getting under the covers; they just did it wherever. There were plenty of times when she and Joe just walked around their house naked when the twins weren't there, but she wouldn't do that now. Just like she didn't have the nerve to be as vocal during sex as she had been with Joe. For whatever reason, she still just couldn't fully let go.

Afterwards, she laid in Grant's arms, snuggled against his chest. Instead of reveling in the post-coital bliss she should have been feeling after making love to her fiancé, all she could think about was that Joe still hadn't called her back yet.

Chapter 9

• • • •

GRANT KNEW VAN WAS still holding back from him, but what he didn't know was why. He didn't know what he had to do or say to get her to open up to him and fully give herself over, but if they were going to last, she had to.

He knew she was concerned about the twins, but something told him there was more to it than that. She just didn't seem happy lately. He had a lot going on with work, but he knew he was going to have to figure something out.

He was sitting in his office deep in thought when Lee, one of his main assistants, knocked on the door.

"You got a second, boss?"

"Yeah, come on in."

Lee entered the office, closing the door behind him. His long dreadlocks were secured in their usual ponytail and his ever-present iPad was in his hand as he took a seat in one of the chairs in front of Grant's desk.

"I wanted to go over your itinerary with you for next week; you're gonna be going pretty much non-stop so we'll need to stock up on your Red Bull."

Grant chuckled, scooting closer to his desk. "All right, hit me...I'm leaving out for Miami Friday night, right?"

"Actually, I had to change your flight to Friday morning. Mr. Douglas needed to move up your meeting."

"Great," Grant said glumly.

Lee chuckled. "Then you'll go to Chicago Sunday, D.C. on Tuesday, then you have meetings all day Wednesday in Boston..."

Grant listened as Lee ran down the rest of his schedule, and he knew he wasn't going to be getting very much sleep over the next few days. He delegated whenever he could, especially after Van and the twins moved in with him, but there were certain times when that just wasn't an option. With everything going on at home he hated to be going out of town, but this was one time it couldn't be helped. Running Fortune 500 companies required a lot of his attention, regardless of what he had going on at home.

"Sheri's going to be going with you," Lee continued, referring to his sister and Grant's other main assistant. "I'm gonna help hold down the fort around here. Did you think of anything else you needed me to do while you're gone?'

"Yeah, get in touch with my contact with the Hawks and see about securing a hundred tickets for the opening night game," Grant instructed. "I want to surprise the kids at the Boys and Girls Club."

"Aww," Lee grinned, glancing up at Grant before putting the note into his iPad. "That's cool of you; they're gonna love that. Any special reason, in case they ask?"

"Nope; just because. I probably won't get to make it to many games myself this season," Grant chuckled. "Just be sure that when you inform the Boys and Girls Club of all this, my name isn't mentioned. If they need to know who it's from, just say the company, not me personally."

Lee nodded, the smile still on his face. "Got ya, boss."

Grant wasn't kidding when he said he loved to give; he often donated to many charities and organizations, and unless it couldn't be helped, he always did so anonymously. He didn't want or need recognition or publicity; he did it because he genuinely wanted to. Van had said that she and the twins were used to not having a lot, but he hadn't exactly grown up with a silver spoon in his mouth, either; he worked for everything he had.

Speaking of Van, a thought popped into his head. Maybe they could use some time away together, alone. They hadn't been anywhere since they got together and Grant figured it would do them some good to get in some uninterrupted quality time.

"Lee, clear whatever I have going on weekend after next. I want to take Van somewhere special."

Pulling up Grant's calendar, Lee did a quick check of the schedule. "Not a problem; you didn't have a lot going on, anyway. And whatever you did have can be postponed or moved."

"That's what I wanna hear."

"Where do you want to take Van? I'll make all the arrangements."

"Sadly, I'm not sure...it's been a while since I've taken a lady away for the weekend," Grant admitted with a smile.

"Yeah, it's about time you're off the market," Lee joked. He and Grant shared a chuckle.

"All I needed was the right woman. And I have that in Van."

"Hey, no arguments here. I think she's awesome," Lee agreed. "You don't meet too many women that naturally beautiful who are also as nice as she is. I'm still tripping over that time she brought us brownies; you know me and Sheri actually fought over the last one?"

Grant laughed. "I can't say I'm surprised. But I'm sure Van would make you all some more, if you asked her. No need to fight."

"I need my own batch," Lee grinned. His dark, handsome good looks drew a lot of attention whenever he and Grant were out and about. "So about this romantic weekend...Vegas, New York, Miami?"

"Nah, needs to be somewhere relatively close...she probably won't want to go too far from the kids right now. Plus she's not terribly flashy so she'd love a simple bed-and-breakfast somewhere, or maybe a cabin."

"Say no more." Lee made a note into his iPad. "I know just the place. Leave everything to me. I got you, boss."

"All right. I trust you." And Grant did; Lee and Sheri had been with him so long that they both knew what he went for and what he didn't, and they were both excellent at anticipating his needs and making sure things were done to his satisfaction. He dreaded the day when either of them came to him and said they wanted to move on.

"Excellent; just send me the information once the arrangements are made."

"Consider it done. Now, your meeting with Marty and the legal team is in thirty minutes in conference room C; I emailed you the agenda. You have a breakfast meeting in the morning at seven at Stone Soup Kitchen; Tommy will pick you up at home at 6:15. Your dry cleaning will be in your closet here by the time you get back; I noticed you only have two suits left in there."

"Thanks, Lee." Grant liked to keep suits at his office for when he was able to get in a workout during the day, or spilled something on himself.

"You want me to order some dinner for you?"

Grant looked at his watch. "Nah, I'm gonna be heading home in about another hour. I think I have some chips or something in my desk if I get hungry before then."

"Chips? You can't be eating like that if you want to look good for your weekend away with your lady. I'll bring you up some fruit from the café," Lee offered, standing up.

Grant just shook his head, smiling. "Yeah, thanks."

Lee left, and Grant looked over the agenda Lee emailed him for his upcoming meeting for a few minutes before standing and putting his suit jacket on. Glancing at his watch again, he sent Van a text letting her know he would call her when he was on his way home, then grabbed some files and headed for the conference room.

It turned out to be another couple of hours before Grant headed home. He was anxious to see Van and broach the weekend getaway idea to her; he hoped she'd be as excited about it as he'd been since he thought of it. They needed some one-on-one time, to get a break from everything going on but also just to get to continue getting to know each other better.

When he got home and upstairs, Van was just coming out of Cassie's room with a not-so-pleasant look on her face.

"Uh-oh. What's wrong?" Grant asked, stopping in his tracks.

"That little girl is gonna drive me insane," Van muttered, stalking past him towards their bedroom. Grant followed her and closed the door, placing his briefcase next to it. Van removed her small diamond earrings that Grant had bought her and practically threw them into her jewelry box. "Every day it's something else with her."

"What's wrong?" Grant asked again.

"She's calling herself mad at me for not letting her get that stupid pink iPhone. Actually had the nerve to talk back to me! And *then*, she has the audacity to ask if she can go to some sleepover at her friend's house, and act surprised when I said no!"

Grant shook his head, not wanting to admit he found the situation kind of amusing. He thought Cassie would be perfect for television because she definitely had the personality for it; she always amused him, even though Van didn't always find her actions as funny as he did.

"Van, baby, come here." Grant held his hand out to her.

Van looked over at him for a second before crossing over to him, putting her hand in his and letting him pull her to his chest.

"What can I do?" Grant asked, his cheek resting on the top of her head.

"Nothing, it's just..." Van shook her head and sighed. "Cassie being Cassie."

"Maybe we need to try a different approach."

"Like what?"

"How about if we make Cassie work for the iPhone, or whatever else she wants?" Grant suggested. "If she has to earn the money herself as opposed to it just being given to her, she'll appreciate it more and start learning the value of a dollar; she'll realize that money comes from working, not privilege. Either that, or she'll realize she doesn't really want it that badly after all and stop asking for it."

Van thought about his suggestion, and looked up at him with a smile. "I *like* that idea! But we need to make working for it a requirement and not an option. She'll just choose not to do anything, if we leave it up to her. I don't want her to be lazy on top of everything else."

"You never know; she may surprise you. I was younger than her when I started trying to make my own money. Cassie is pretty determined, and if she wants something bad enough, I think she'll do what she needs to do to get it."

"Well, yeah...that's true," Van admitted.

"It'll be good practice for her. She needs to get used to working hard now, anyway, if she plans to do *anything* in the entertainment business. I think she might have the wrong idea of what it takes to really be successful and needs to know it's not going to come to her as easily as she might think it is."

"I can agree with you on that, too." Van smiled at him again, and Grant was relieved to see she was feeling a little better. She leaned up and kissed his lips, squeezing him around his waist. "Thank you so much; that's a great idea, sweetie."

"No need to thank me. We can talk about all the particulars later but right now, I need a *real* kiss."

Giggling like a schoolgirl, Van turned her face up to Grant's again and let him lay one on her. He kissed her gently but deeply, the intensity building just slightly as the moments wore on, his hands sliding down to her round backside and caressing it lovingly.

After the kiss broke, Grant tweaked her chin. "Hey."

"Yes?"

"I want us to go away together."

Surprised, Van leaned back a little. "Really? Just the two of us?"

"Yeah."

"Oh, Grant, I don't know," Van replied hesitantly. "With everything going on with the twins, I just don't think it's a good time. I just put Cassie on punishment; I can't turn around and leave right after that."

"I'm not talking about tomorrow, Van; it'll be weekend after next. I'm gonna be all over the place next week out of town and I'm going to need some rejuvenating when I get back, but more importantly, you and I need some time alone. We haven't been anywhere since we've been together and it will do us both some good." He squeezed her, his eyes looking right into hers. "Come on...do I need to say please?"

Despite herself, Van chuckled, shaking her head. "Okay, maybe you're right; it *would* be nice for us to spend some time alone for a couple of days. I don't want to go too far, though."

"I figured that."

"Okay. Thank you, for suggesting it; it's really sweet of you." Van grinned up at him, melting his heart like she always did. "I'll see if Raven minds watching the twins while we're gone."

"All right. Just let me know what she says."

"I'll call her in a minute. Are you hungry? I can fix you something to eat. Or I can run you a nice bath…" Van slid her hands up his chest, looking at him seductively.

Groaning, Grant lightly grasped her wrists. "Damn baby, as much as I'd love that, I have some stuff I need to look over for tomorrow. I have a breakfast meeting first thing in the morning."

"Aww," Van pouted playfully, causing Grant to chuckle. "Can't blame a girl for trying. I'll bring you something to your office, then. What do you want?"

"A sandwich is fine. I'm not terribly hungry."

"No problem."

"Thanks, baby. I'm gonna go speak to the kids real quick while you're down there."

"Okay, good."

Van headed downstairs to the kitchen and started gathering the fixings for Grant's sandwich. When she reached for the meat, she paused, unable to remember if he preferred smoked turkey or roast beef, or hummus or Dijon mustard. And was it ciabatta or multigrain bread? Or rye? She bit her lip, racking her brain…she was actually feeling a little embarrassed that she couldn't remember. After all this time, what Grant liked on his sandwich was something she should have known by then.

Joe was easy to please; ham on white, with mustard.

Van shook her head, clearing it of the thought. The last thing she needed to be doing was thinking about Joe right then. He still hadn't called her back after the message she left about Canton, and that had been almost a week ago.

Figuring Grant would be satisfied with whatever she made, she grabbed the multigrain bread, the hummus, and the turkey, along with prosciutto, lettuce, and tomato, and proceeded to make the sandwich. She also rinsed off a few green grapes and put those in a bowl, grabbed a couple of bottles of sparkling water, put everything on a tray, and headed up to Grant's office. He was already hunched over some papers on his desk, his brow furrowed in concentration.

"Thanks, babe," he said, flashing her a brief smile before turning his attention back to the papers.

Van hesitated, not wanting to bother him but also feeling the need to make sure he was satisfied with what she brought him. "I hope this is okay..."

"Yeah, it's good," Grant confirmed, not even looking up.

Van wanted to ask if he would prefer roast beef, but figured she'd leave well enough alone. Grant had their groceries delivered and she was sure the turkey wouldn't be in there if he didn't like it.

Placing a light kiss on the top of his head, Van turned and left him to his work, closing the door behind her. She went back downstairs and curled up on the couch in the living room, taking her cell phone out of her pocket. Dialing Raven's number, she prayed her cousin was alone this time and actually able to talk.

No such luck. Raven was giggling when she answered the phone. "Hello?"

"Raven; hey, girl," Van tried to sound casual, even though she was in explicably nervous. She propped her foot on the couch and rubbed the front of her leg.

"Hey," Raven replied, then giggled again. It almost sounded like she was being tickled.

"Let me guess; you have company again?"

"Yeah, something like that."

Van sighed. "Well, look, I don't want to bother you. I mainly called to see if you would be able to watch the twins weekend after next." She stopped short of saying the reason was her and Grant wanting to take a romantic weekend together.

Raven whispered something to whoever she was with, then replied, "I might be able to do that; you said weekend after next?"

"Yeah."

It sounded like Raven put her hand over the phone because her voice became muffled as she spoke again to her mystery companion. If Van didn't know any better, she'd think Raven was conferring with them first. But since when did Raven ever need to do that when it came to spending time with her own cousins?

After a few moments, Raven came back on the line. "Sounds like a plan. Just bring them by that Friday afternoon. Be sure to let me know when you're on your way, though, so I can make sure I'm here."

Van wanted to let it go, but she couldn't resist asking, "Raven, did you actually *check with your man* before agreeing to watch Canton and Cassie?"

Pause. "What makes you say that?"

"Because I have ears and I'm not an idiot."

"I don't know what you're talking about."

"Then what was all the mumbling to him about before you actually agreed to it?"

"Van, as much as I would love to sit here and go back and forth with you about this nonsense, I have to go," Raven evaded. There was whispering in the background and Raven giggled yet again. "I can't wait to see my babies. Give them a kiss for me and I'll see y'all that Friday."

"Fine. I appre-"

Raven had already hung up.

• • • •

AFTER A COUPLE OF WEEKS, Van and Grant were finally checked into a cozy bed and breakfast down in Savannah. Van grinned when they were shown to their corner room, loving the king-sized English-canopied bed, black and tan toile printed wallpaper, and period boarders. It even had a sitting area, a fireplace, a flat-screen television, and a balcony overlooking Olgethorpe Avenue. Van immediately felt more relaxed.

"Oh Grant, this is beautiful," she gushed, setting her purse on the writing desk and turning to him with a huge smile on her face. She slowly wandered around the room, running her hand over everything in admiration, and Grant couldn't resist the smile that came to his face as he watched her. He loved how she appreciated even the smallest things he did for her.

"I'm glad you like it," he said, tipping the bellboy before closing the door.

"I love everything about it," Van confirmed, her hands on her chest. She shook her head as if in awe. "Thank you *so* much for this; this is just what we needed."

"Yeah, I feel relaxed already. And you know you're welcome." Grant placed his leather duffle bag on the smoke-gray couch in the sitting area and walked over to her, wrapping his arms around her waist. "I'm just glad you're happy, babe."

"Of course I am," Van verified, smiling up at him.

Grant really wanted to talk to Van about his concerns about their relationship, but decided then wasn't the time to do it. He figured they could just chill with each other for the rest of that night and he could talk to her about all of that the next day.

"You want something to eat?"

"Ehh...not really. But I can- *oh*! They have champagne and white chocolate-covered strawberries!" Van exclaimed excitedly, just noticing the complimentary offerings.

Grant chuckled, glancing at them over his shoulder. "Yeah, and I see some kind of pastries, too. I take it you're good with that?"

"I'm *great* with that!" Van replied with a grin, scurrying around Grant to get to the goodies. Grant chuckled again as he followed her to the sitting area, and they both sat down and helped themselves to the treats. They talked about various things, like the drive down there, how long it had been since either of them had been to Savannah, how great the weather was...it was like they were each trying *not* to bring up anything about home or their relationship.

After they ate, they each took showers, then climbed into bed. Neither was very tired, so they spent the remainder of the night kissing and holding each other. Van went to sleep that night wishing every night could be as stress-free and peaceful as this one had been, and looked forward to the next day being a repeat of this one.

But Grant had anything but peace on his mind when he confronted Van during breakfast in their room the next morning.

"What did you just ask me?" Van asked in shock, almost dropping her fork.

"I asked if you wanted out of this," Grant repeated calmly, pushing his scrambled eggs around on his plate. His eyes were on the action, as he couldn't look in Van's face and ask her such a question. He wouldn't even know how he would react if she said yes, but he couldn't make himself hold his tongue any longer. "There has to be a reason you've been acting the way you have, Van. You're holding back from me, and I don't think it's just you worrying about the twins or stress from work."

"Grant..." Van carefully placed her fork beside her plate and looked out the window nervously. "I-I don't know what to say to that."

Grant felt his chest tighten. "Just be honest with me, Van. That's all I've ever asked of you."

Van's eyes turned to him briefly before falling to her lap. "You're right."

"You don't seem like a woman who is looking forward to getting married," Grant informed her, putting down his own fork. He made himself look at her, and she was thoughtfully gazing back at him. "You hardly ever even talk about the wedding anymore. There are plenty of times when it seems like you're just not all the way with me; I can see it in your eyes sometimes that your mind is somewhere else, yet you always insist it's nothing. And then there's still the matter of you not telling your parents about our engagement yet...all of that is adding up to doubt to me."

Blinking back tears, Van took a moment to dab her eyes with her cloth napkin. The guilt felt as warm on her as the morning Georgia sun. "You're right," she agreed again softly.

All the air went out of Grant's chest. "I am?"

"Yes. I haven't been fair to you when you've been nothing but wonderful to me," Van replied. "Other things have been getting too much of my attention, and I do apologize about that. But it has nothing to do with me not loving you or not wanting to be with you."

Grant's facial expression didn't change, but he was breathing a huge internal sigh of relief. While he would have let Van go if that's what she wanted, it would've killed him...he had never loved a woman like he loved Van. If he had a soft spot outside of his mother and sister, it was her.

"I'll admit I'm scared, Grant," Van continued, momentarily placing her hands on her chest before dropping them back to her lap. "Everything just came about so fast and I guess I didn't even realize that I needed to slow things down a little bit to get my bearings. All those things you pointed out; I didn't even realize that's what I was *doing*. And I've just...I've let other things take precedence when I shouldn't. But that's absolutely not fair to you, and I am so, so sorry."

Eyeing her, Grant sat forward in his chair, leaning an elbow on the table. "I don't want to lose you, Van..."

"I don't want to lose you, either."

"But I also don't want to waste my time. If you've changed your mind, or you're not sure I'm the man for you, or-"

"Stop," Van interjected, shaking her head adamantly. She stood from her chair and went over to sit in his lap. Looking right into his eyes, she felt her heart swell...the love she had for him warmed her, and the thought of losing him was frightening, especially after everything that had already happened. Her hand caressed his face. "You don't even have to finish that sentence. I haven't changed my mind about anything, and you *are* the best man for me. I am so sorry for doing anything to make you question that. I promise to do better."

Leaning down and kissing him deeply, she wrapped her arms around his neck. She felt encouraged when she felt his arms tighten around her, and he returned her kiss with equal feeling and intensity. She straddled his lap, and his hands immediately slid under the hem of her short silk nightgown. He squeezed her warm, bare skin when she began to subtly grind on him.

"Make love to me," she whispered against his lips.

Grant moaned as he continued to kiss her, pulling down the straps of her nightgown. He palmed one bare breast as he helped himself to the other. Van threw her head back in pleasure.

"Grant...yes..." she panted.

Fueled by her reactions, Grant moaned again, loudly, as he sucked her breasts a little harder, running his hands up and down her now-bare back. They were now full-on grinding, and after a while Grant couldn't take it anymore and stood, picking Van up with him. She clung to him as he carried her to the bed, their kiss never breaking, before he practically threw her on top of it. She looked so beautiful and so sexy to him, and it was a reminder of how much he didn't want to lose her. Quickly and eagerly pushing his pajama bottoms down, he tossed her nightgown out of the way before climbing on top of her and pushing himself inside immediately. His actions were sensual, but almost desperate; the emotion from the thought of Van not being in his life was overtaking him and causing his intensity to double.

Van could tell something was different about Grant; he had never been so fervent and intense as he was being then, and Van loved it, because she was feeling the same way. She had to show Grant that he was the man she loved; *he* was the man she wanted; *he* was the man she still planned to spend the rest of her life with. With everything that had been coursing through her mind and heart the previous weeks, including her self-admitted doubts about her decision to leave Joe for Grant, the thought of Grant walking away from her made her realize just how much she didn't want that to happen.

"I love you so much, baby," Grant panted, his voice breaking, as he pumped into her relentlessly. "Van..."

"Oh Grant, I love you too," Van assured him breathlessly, meeting him stroke for stroke. Her hands clawed at his back and she spread her legs wider for him. "Oh my god..."

"Are you mine, baby?" Grant asked, lifting his head to look into her eyes. Their now-sweaty bodies continued to move against each other, but his eyes were focused. "Say you're mine."

"I'm yours, baby," Van assured him in a whisper.

"Tell me again."

"I'm yours."

"Louder, baby."

"I'm yours!"

"Forever? Say yes!"

"Yes!" Van exclaimed as the orgasm ripped through her body without any warning. Her shocked eyes widened then squeezed shut in pleasure, and she tightened herself around him, unable to move.

Grant continued to move inside of her, though considerably less feverishly, and repeatedly planted kisses all over her face and neck. He didn't know what had gotten into him, making Van promise herself to him like that as they made love...he sounded desperate, even to himself. But he hadn't been able to help it. Even if it *was* said during sex, he needed to hear Van reassure him that she was his and would remain his.

Van wrapped her arms around Grant's neck, her hand languidly caressing his smooth bald head. She actually wanted to purr in contentment, she felt so good. That was officially the best sex she and Grant ever had, and even though that hadn't even been her main concern about their relationship, it somehow renewed her focus and hope about it.

She knew she needed to check herself. Here she had a gorgeous Boris Kodjoe-lookalike millionaire fiancé who adored her, loved her children as his own, and wanted to make her life as easy as possible. What in the *world* did she have to complain about?? How big of an *idiot* would she have to be to lose a man like that because she was too worried about other things she shouldn't even be thinking about? And it wasn't even as if she was only with him because it would be stupid not to be; she actually and sincerely loved and was *in* love with Grant. She needed to get her act together before she blew another one of the best things that ever happened to her.

"Hey," she said softly, biting her lip as he leaned back slightly to look down at her.

"Yeah?"

"What about January eleventh?"

Grant frowned slightly in confusion. "For?"

"Me becoming your wife."

Grant's hips stopped moving as his eyes brightened in realization. Then they turned serious as they locked on hers. "Are you sure?"

"Yes," Van verified, resuming their grinding. Unable to help himself, Grant joined her, their intensity slowly warming back up to a boil. "Yes, baby, I'm sure. I'm ready to set a date for our wedding."

Thrilled beyond description, Grant dove down and claimed her mouth with his, kissing her so deeply and intently that her head was burrowed into the mattress. Part of his brain told him that Van's sudden readiness to set a date for their wedding was probably mostly fueled by being caught up in the emotion of the moment, but the hopeful part of him pushed that thought aside. He continued to make love to his fiancée, finally feeling like he actually had one.

Chapter 10

• • • •

RAVEN COULD SEE THE surprise in the twins' eyes when Joe showed up to her apartment.

"Joe!" Canton and Cassie screamed, running over to him and practically tackling him as they jumped into his arms, actually knocking him back a few steps. Raven grinned at the sight.

"Hey!" Joe replied, hugging them back, clearly as glad to see them. "I miss y'all!"

"We miss you, too!" Canton replied, exhibiting uncharacteristic excitement. When Cassie let go of Joe, Canton hung on, the side of his face plastered to Joe's chest, his arms clamped around his waist. Joe just wrapped his arms around him tighter and rested his cheek on the top of his head. Raven placed a hand on her chest, touched. She knew Canton missed Joe, but Raven hadn't known just how much until that moment. He didn't want to let Joe go.

"Come on, man; it's okay," Joe said to him softly after several moments as he clamped a hand on Canton's shoulder and led him over to Raven's couch. Cassie bounced down beside them, on the other side of Joe. Raven curled up in her beige armchair, her bare feet tucked under her.

"Raven, sit over here!" Cassie pleaded loudly, patting the cushion next to her. Raven chuckled as she got up to go sit by her cousin as requested. Cassie immediately lifted Raven's arm and snuggled under it, wrapping her arms around Raven's waist.

"Can we order some pizza?" she asked excitedly.

"Maybe, a little later. You want some pizza, baby?"

Joe immediately started to answer Raven, and actually blushed when he realized she was talking to Canton. He was glad he was too dark for anyone to notice. *Man, I am trippin'*, he thought to himself, actually a little embarrassed.

"That's fine," Canton shrugged.

The four of them chatted for a little while before Joe suggested he and Canton go to another room to talk in private. Cassie and Raven remained in the living room.

"Raven, you have *got* to see these shoes," Cassie boasted, pulling out her phone. She pulled up the picture of her new hot pink-and-black sneakers, grinning with pride. She eagerly held it up for Raven to see.

"Yeah, girl, those are fierce," Raven concurred, peering at the picture. "When did you get those?"

"Grant got them for me a couple of months ago. *Custom-made*; nobody else has 'em but *me*! He got me this phone, too, even though I *wanted* that newer iPhone in pink and he woulda got it for me but Mama said I couldn't have it. She be trippin.'"

Raven frowned, not liking her tone. "Excuse me?"

"She said I should be grateful for the phone I already got. But I don't see what the big deal is. Grant's got enough money; he can buy us whatever we want. It's not like *she's* paying for it."

"Cassie!" Raven scolded. "Girl, you better *watch* yourself!"

"What?" Cassie replied innocently. "I'm sayin', we're not broke anymore. When she was with Joe she couldn't buy us stuff 'cause she was always spending her money on bills, but Grant is paying all her bills now and she *still* says no when I ask for something! And it's not even really *her* money! I don't get that!"

Raven actually popped Cassie lightly on the mouth then harder on the leg, and Cassie looked up at her with as much fear in her eyes as when Van was angry with her.

"Let me tell you something, little girl," Raven pointed a finger at her. "I see you've gotten a little too spoiled since you've been over there at Grant's and you need to check yourself. Just because Grant has money doesn't mean you're gonna get every little thing you want, and if *this* is the attitude you've been having at home, I don't blame Van for telling you 'no' when you ask for something!"

Cassie immediately opened her mouth to protest but Raven held up a hand. "Don't even try it. There isn't anything you can say!"

Cassie clamped her mouth shut and looked at Raven timidly. She never did like for her older cousin to be upset with her; she often looked at Raven as her big sister. And Raven couldn't deny that part of Cassie's sass came from her.

After several moments, Cassie looked up at Raven cautiously before venturing, "I thought Mama said we moved in with Grant so we can live better."

Raven chose her words carefully; she would never want to say anything disparaging about Van in front of the twins. "Even still, Cassie, 'living better' doesn't just mean you getting cool shoes and phones and whatever else you think you want. It's *everything*. Your mama isn't all stressed out like she used to be from trying to figure out how she was going to keep a roof over your heads and food in the refrigerator, and making sure you and Canton had everything you needed. She can spend more time with the two of you...you like that, right? When she was working two jobs, she was tired all the time."

"Yeah, she was," Cassie agreed. "We do more fun stuff now, like going to the hair salon together and having movie nights on Saturdays."

"See there? You didn't get to do those things before. That's way more important than the stuff Grant can buy you, Cassie...there's always gonna be some new phone coming out or some hot new dress or whatever, and you're never gonna be satisfied if that's all you're worried about. Your mama is right; you *do* need to be grateful for what you have. There are plenty of kids who would *love* to have this phone you have right now."

Cassie glanced down at her phone, turning it over in her hands. Raven could tell she was pondering what she said.

"But even more than all that..." Raven made herself continue, "Your mama is happy with Grant. She didn't *just* move in with him for y'all; she actually loves him. And he loves her."

Raven thought she deserved an award for saying that without throwing up.

Cassie looked at Raven thoughtfully. "But I thought she loved *Joe*. How come he lived with us all those years and then we just up and moved in with Grant like that?

Does she love both of them? And how come Joe is over here?"

Raven pursed her lips. "Van *did* love Joe; very much. But sometimes...things just don't work out."

"Did he cheat on her or something? My friend Qiana said her mama put her boyfriend out 'cause she caught him-"

"Cassie!" Raven stopped her. "That's not your business to tell. And Joe absolutely did *not* cheat on Van; he didn't do *anything* wrong!"

Raven felt the strong need to defend Joe, even though he wasn't *really* being accused of anything. She just didn't want even the inkling of a negative thought towards him in Cassie's head. As to why that was so important to her, she didn't want to think about. "And as for the rest of the stuff you asked, that's grown folks' business. Just be glad your mama is happy, all right?"

"All right," Cassie shrugged. "Can we go ahead and order that pizza now?"

Raven couldn't help but laugh. She playfully nudged her little cousin in the shoulder. "Fine, but you're doing the dishes afterwards."

• • • •

MEANWHILE, JOE AND Canton were in Raven's bedroom talking.

"You been doing all right, man?" Joe asked, not wanting to mention Van's message about him.

"I guess," Canton replied nonchalantly. He pushed his glasses further onto his nose and played with the seam on his jeans.

"Talk to me, Canton...what's on your mind? You don't even seem like yourself."

After a couple moments of looking like he was working up the nerve, Canton blurted out, "I want you and Ma to get back together."

Joe pursed his lips, trying to choose the right response. "That's not gonna happen, man; I'm sorry."

"Are you still mad at her for leaving you for Mr. McCallister?"

Slightly taken aback, Joe asked, "Where did you hear that?"

"I didn't hear it. I just pay attention."

Joe had to resist a smile at that. Canton had always been wise beyond his years and way more intelligent than most boys his age. It didn't surprise Joe at all that he had seemingly figured out what had really gone down between him and Van.

Not bothering to try and deny the fact that Van left him for Grant, Joe replied, "Well, mad or not, your mama is with Grant now, man. There's nothing I can do about that. What, you don't like him?"

"He's all right," Canton said dismissively. "But you're like my dad. And I miss seeing you every day."

Joe couldn't help being touched by that; he definitely missed seeing Canton and Cassie every day, too. He reached over and clamped a hand on Canton's shoulder. "I miss you too, man," he replied with a small smile. He looked him in his eyes. "But just because I'm not in the same house as you anymore doesn't mean we can't still be tight. As far as I'm concerned, you are still my son. I'm *always* gonna be here for you, okay? Whenever you need me, even if it's just to talk, all you gotta do is call."

Canton looked at him and beamed, and it melted Joe's heart a little bit. He hadn't even realized how big of an impact he'd made on Canton's life until he started hearing about Canton misbehaving due to missing him. Treating Canton as if he was his own flesh and blood had just been the natural thing to do after he and Van got together.

"Anytime?" Canton verified.

"Anytime."

"Good. Mr. McCallister got me my own phone, but I don't use mine as much as Cassie uses hers. She's on hers all the time."

"I'm not surprised," Joe chuckled. "You have my number in your phone?"

"Yes, sir. But I didn't know if it was okay to use it, you know, since you and Ma aren't together anymore."

"It's most definitely okay. And maybe, if it's cool with your mama, I can come get you sometimes and we can hang out. I'll bring you over to the construction site; you know you've been wanting to do that for a while and I was waiting until you got a little older."

"That sounds great!" Canton grinned.

"Yeah, we can do that. As long as your school stuff is on point. It *is* on point, right?"

Canton's smile faded slightly and he looked away, pushing up his glasses. "Umm..."

"Canton."

Canton sheepishly turned his face back to Joe.

"Since when do you not stay on top of your schoolwork? You used to knock everything out of the park when it came to that. Don't start slippin' now."

Looking down at his lap, Canton just nodded. "Yes, sir."

"I know there's been a lot going on, but your education is too important, man," Joe continued. "I've always been proud of you 'cause I like how you actually *want* to learn everything you can; most kids don't care about that. I know *I* didn't when I was your age. You're miles ahead of where I was."

Canton smiled, seemingly flattered by the compliment.

"So get your act together in that school, man," Joe ordered sternly. "The next time I ask you about all this, I want to hear a good report. You got me?"

"Yes, sir."

"That's what I wanna hear."

They talked for a few more minutes before rejoining Raven and Cassie in the living room. The four of them ate pizza, watched movies, told jokes and played games, and both Canton and Cassie were looking a lot happier than they were when they arrived. When one of them mentioned Van, Joe immediately felt his annoyance flare up. Hers was the *last* name he wanted to hear and he had to fight to keep his good vibe from being ruined. Raven seemed to sense his agitation and placed a hand on his arm, giving him a reassuring smile. He looked at her gratefully, feeling himself calm down.

Joe didn't like being this angry towards Van. Breakups happened; he thought he'd be past it by now. He *wanted* to get past it. But it burned him that Van was with Grant, for no other reason than there were still a lot of memories of him and Van that he couldn't make himself forget. He had honestly gotten past the point where he missed her and wanted her back; he no longer did. Now, all that remained was anger, and he hated that she had that kind of power over him. It wasn't something he was proud of, but he really just wanted to hurt her even a fraction of how much she had hurt him.

She still called him at least every other day, and he ignored all of her calls. They didn't have anything to talk about, as far as he was concerned. She just wanted to clear her conscience so she could go on and live happily ever after with Grant. Maybe it was petty, but Joe wasn't about to make that easy for her.

He hoped the twins mentioned his presence at Raven's when they recounted their visit to Van; *that* would really mess with her.

Chapter 11

• • • •

AFTER SHE AND GRANT returned from their weekend trip to Savannah, Van dove headfirst into planning their wedding. She was actually excited about it, looking forward to the look on Grant's face when he saw her walk down the aisle. Every single time she imagined that, it automatically brought a huge smile. She finally felt like the happy, blissful fiancée she should have been ever since Grant proposed to her.

As if that wasn't great enough, Van also noticed a difference in the twins. Ever since their weekend at Raven's, both Canton and Cassie had renewed and improved attitudes. Cassie had far less entitlement and sass and was actually saying 'thank you' more than she usually did, even for little things. And Canton was considerably less moody and standoffish; he wasn't so quick to retreat to his room when he was home, and though he still wasn't saying all that much to Van, he did smile at her a couple of times. But Van got a call from one of his teachers saying that his attitude and performance in class had greatly improved, which Van was thrilled to hear. She figured maybe Grant had spoken to them as he offered; she didn't know what he said to cause such a sudden turnaround in both of them, but she was certainly grateful for it. It only reminded her that when it came to the twins, she wasn't by herself and could trust him more than she had been.

Things were finally looking up. Van of course remembered that Joe still hadn't called her back regarding

Canton or accepted any of her subsequent calls, but maybe it was a moot point now; she had apparently underestimated Grant's influence over Canton. Clearly Joe wasn't the only one that could get through to her son. Yes, it would have been nice if he had shown her the courtesy of acknowledging at least one of her messages, but maybe it was for the best. Joe obviously didn't want to talk to her, and maybe it was time to just leave well enough alone.

She still wanted them to have a *real* talk because she cared about him, and wanted to better explain why she did what she did, in regards to ending their relationship. Because regardless of whether she *should* care whether he did or not, she didn't want Joe to hate her. But maybe if she backed off for a while, he would come around.

Grant was working a lot again and was in and out of town, so that left Van to do most of the wedding planning herself. She hadn't really expected him to do that much, anyway; she knew he was a busy man. He was incredibly happy, though, that they were finally making actual progress towards getting married, and she was glad that she could put that smile on his face.

"Vanetta McCallister," he mused one morning as they were both getting ready for work. He looked over his shoulder at her, smiling as he put on his tie. "I am loving the sound of that."

Van grinned from her seat on their bed, where she was rubbing lotion on her legs. "Me, too. Even though you know I hate my full first name and I thought we agreed you would never call me that."

"Hey, just stating it as it will appear on the marriage certificate," Grant teased, securing his tie. He grabbed his silver Rolex from the dresser and slid it onto his wrist. "I know January is a ways away, but I can't wait, baby, for real."

"Me, either." Van rubbed the excess lotion into her hands and looked at him thoughtfully. "Are you sure you don't mind waiting so long?"

Grant peered at her for a moment before answering. "I'd marry you today, Van, you know that. But since I plan on this being the only marriage either of us will have, I want you to have the wedding you want. And if it takes months to plan, then I'm fine with that."

"Good. I'm sure that the time will fly by. The January after next will be here before we know it."

His smile faded. "I beg your pardon? January *after* next?"

"Yes..." Van's hands gripped the comforter. "I thought I told you that."

"No you didn't."

"It doesn't make any difference, does it? We're still going to be together in the meantime. And wedding planning takes time."

"Not *that* long, Van. I know I said I want you to have the wedding of your dreams but that's damn near two years from now."

"It's more like eighteen months..."

"Van, I do not want to wait that long," Grant stated firmly, folding his arms. "There's no reason we should. What aren't you telling me?"

"Grant, please don't start getting suspicious," Van pleaded, clasping her hands together. "There's nothing untoward going on, nothing I'm not telling you, nothing for you to be worried about. I swear. I'm committed to you and want to be your wife; I want to spend my life with *you*. Isn't that more important than what date we choose to make it official?"

Grant eyed her. His gut told him there was more behind her choosing such a faraway date than she was letting on, and part of him wanted to press until he got a more concrete explanation. He sensed Van's choice was deliberate, and he sensed he wouldn't like the reason behind it.

But as she sat there looking at him pleadingly, he sighed and dropped his arms. He didn't have the energy for this.

"Fine, Van," he finally relented. "I'll leave it alone. For now."

She peered at him. "Are you upset with me?"

"I'm not thrilled about the curveball you just hit me with. But I'm making myself focus on the other things you said. We *are* still going to be together in the meantime. As long as you're my wife at the end of it, I'm good."

Van couldn't resist blushing; she loved when Grant said things like that to her. She stood and walked over to him, wrapping her arms around his neck.

"How did I get so blessed?" she dreamily mused as she gazed at his gorgeous face. "Honestly, there are times I still really can't believe all this."

His frown melted some as he looked down at her. He wasn't over his frustration by any means, but he made himself tuck it away for the time being and just enjoy the moment with his fiancée.

"You're not the only one," he replied, lacing his fingers across the small of her back. "I was at the point where I wondered if I would ever find the woman I wanted to marry. But as soon as I met you, I *knew* you were it for me. And you still captivate me now as much as you did then. I am truly, truly grateful for you, Van."

"Baby! You're gonna make me cry!" Van whined, grinning. Grant had a way of melting her heart and making her feel like the only woman on earth. There were times when she worried that she simply wasn't good enough for him, being a simple woman who didn't have much, but he always assuaged those silent fears. He made her feel cherished, like a priority...he never judged her or made her feel less-than. Even though she was working a second job flipping burgers and driving an old station wagon when they met, he didn't care. He had always been interested in *her*, not what she had. And all he ever tried to do was make her life easier so she could actually enjoy it and not work and worry so much.

Grant leaned down and kissed her tenderly, cupping her face in his hand. Her kisses still lit the same fires in him as they did the first time he kissed her in his car in the Krystal's parking lot the night he impulsively showed up at her night job. He hadn't been able to resist then, and he was even less able to resist her now.

Van really was the woman he'd been waiting all these years for; there wasn't a doubt in his mind about that. She was so caring and humble and sweet, and appreciative of everything. He had given her access to his account as well as giving her one of her own with thousands of dollars in it, but she never touched his money and he could tell by the minimal movement on the account he opened for her that whatever she bought, she did with money from her own salary as a recruiter. She liked and appreciated nice things, but she wasn't extravagant; she still tried to save money when she could, even clipped coupons at times, and Grant appreciated that. Most of the women he dated before her wouldn't have cared about such things, and would have spent his money without thinking twice about it. Really, most of them wouldn't even still be working at all, but Van hadn't wanted to quit her job, even though Grant had long since told her she could.

They kissed for several long moments before Grant reluctantly pulled back. "You're gonna make me late, woman," he smirked, resting his forehead against hers.

"Hey, *I'm* the one that needs to be worried about that; at least you're the boss where you work," Van reminded with a smile.

"Touché." He stole another quick peck before stepping back, but Van grabbed his tie and pulled him back to her.

"Where do you think you're going?" she asked, looking up at him with seductive eyes. She was suddenly very turned on, and hoped they'd be able to have their first pre-work quickie. Really, she would have preferred them to both skip work altogether and spend the day in bed, but she knew that was a long shot. Those kinds of days were few and far between.

Grant recognized the darkened desire in her big brown eyes and bit his lip. "I thought you had to go."

"I never said that, did I?" Van boldly slid her hand between them and squeezed his hardening erection through his slacks. "I can call in sick if I need to."

Moaning, Grant closed his eyes and leaned his head back as Van stroked him. "Van..."

"Call Sheri or Lee and tell them to push back whatever you have this morning," Van instructed, continuing to drive him crazy. Her free hand was slowly starting to pull his crisp white shirt from his slacks. "Can you do that?"

Taking a peek at his watch, Grant licked his lips. "Where is my damn phone??"

Grinning triumphantly, Van reached around him and grabbed his phone from the dresser, handing it to him. She began to unbutton his shirt as he called his assistant Lee and told him to reschedule his morning meetings, eyeing her the entire time. Van giggled when he practically tossed the phone aside and grabbed her by the waist, kissing her passionately as he groped for the side zipper of her skirt.

They were both only partially undressed when Van pushed Grant onto the bed and yanked his pants and briefs down to his ankles. She dropped to her knees between his legs and grabbed him in her hands, stroking only a few times before sliding her mouth over him, causing him to hiss loudly in pleasure. When she looked up at him she could tell he was surprised, probably wondering what had gotten into her, but she felt this was something they needed to do. They needed to be more free and spontaneous with each other, like she had been with...

Mentally scolding herself for thinking of her ex at a time like this, Van concentrated on giving Grant the best head of his life. She ran her hands up and down his taut thighs and abdomen, moaning and grunting as she savored him, and she could tell he was getting close. He lifted his hips, his hands gripping the comforter on the bed, whispering about how good she felt. Van wanted him to get loud, yell obscenities, grab her hair, get aggressive...she yearned for that. But she couldn't very well stop and *tell* him to do those things. It just seemed like he was holding back, like he didn't want to get too loud, even though the twins had already left for school. Even though she should have, Van couldn't say she felt *entirely* comfortable herself, but she was acting like be the seductress she knew she could be; she didn't want the great sex they shared in Savannah to be a one-time or even just once-in-a-while thing.

After a while, Grant still hadn't orgasmed and Van was *sure* he was refraining; it normally didn't take him this long. Her jaws were starting to cramp.

"Baby, what's wrong?" she finally panted, looking up at him.

Grant opened his eyes. "What do you mean? Why'd you stop?"

"You usually would have come by now...you don't like it?"

"I *love* it! It's not that at all."

"Then what *is* it?"

Hesitating, Grant looked away momentarily. "*Please* don't take this the wrong way..."

*Aww hell...*Van quirked a suspicious brow.

"But I just remembered something important I needed to do this morning at the office, and-"

"Are you *serious*??" Van exclaimed, pushing away from him. "My head is between your legs and you're thinking about *work*??"

"Baby, please don't take this personally!"

"Don't take it personally?? I'm trying to seduce you and your mind isn't even *on* me! How can I *not* take that personally??"

"Van-"

"Forget it, Grant!" Van stood and yanked her bunched skirt down, feeling angry and foolish. "Just forget it!"

Grant stood and reached for her, but she jerked away. "This doesn't mean I wasn't enjoying it, Van!"

"But obviously it wasn't good enough to keep your attention, right?"

"I didn't say that-"

"You didn't *have* to say it for it to be true. I guess I should have known better. Next time I want to make love to you, I'll be sure to check your schedule first."

"Van!"

"What else is there to say? Go on to work; don't let me hold you up anymore," Van huffed, re-buttoning her blouse and turning away from him. She wanted to cry but she told herself not to, at least not until he left. She felt silly enough as it was.

Grant was quiet for a moment and Van knew he was waiting on her to turn around. She wouldn't.

"I don't want to leave things like this," he finally said from behind her.

"I'm fine, Grant. That's obviously more important to you. Go on and handle your business."

Grant immediately closed the distance between them and turned her around to face him. "What do you mean by that?"

Van sighed as she finished with her blouse. "Clearly, being second to your work is the kind of thing I'll need to get used to if I'm going to be with you. It didn't really hit me until this moment but I guess I'll just learn to live with it."

"Listen to me," Grant said sternly, grabbing her by the arms and pulling her closer to him. "Don't *ever* say that again, baby. Is my work important to me? Of course it is. I've worked my ass off for years to get where I am. But it is absolutely *not* more important to me than you are. And I need for you to believe that. Okay?"

Van just looked at him, her eyes moist with embarrassed tears. His face was the picture of pleading sincerity. She knew she was probably overreacting; Grant was the owner of major companies, not to mention other ventures he had a hand in. She couldn't very well expect him to just forget about everything he was responsible for just because she was spontaneously horny.

Sighing again, Van nodded. "Okay," she conceded softly. "I *do* believe that. I'm sorry for overreacting...you are more than good to me and you have definitely proven that I'm a priority to you. I guess my pride was just a little bruised, that's all. I really wanted to...just...I just wanted to make you feel good..."

Grant lovingly gathered her into his arms, holding her close to him. "You make me feel good every single day."

He didn't get it. And Van didn't know how to express to him exactly what she meant without feeling even sillier than she already did. How could she tell her fiancé that she wanted him to be less 'gentleman' and more 'roughneck' in the bedroom? That she wanted them to have spur-of-the-moment fun and heat-of-the-moment quickies? Why couldn't she express this to the man she was planning to marry?

"Go on to work," Van instructed after a few moments, gently pulling back. She gave him a small smile. "We're fine. Really."

Looking relieved, Grant leaned down and placed a tender kiss on her lips. "I love you, baby," he expressed, looking right into her eyes.

"I love you, too."

"I'll be home as early as I can."

"Okay."

Grant went into the bathroom to fix his clothes and freshen up, then left a few minutes later. Van contemplated not going to work, preferring to just stay home and mope, but knew that wouldn't do her any good. Still needing to take the edge off, she retrieved the small bullet vibrator she kept in her purse, reclined on the bed, and brought herself to a much-needed orgasm before she went and fixed herself back up and headed out the door.

• • • •

A FEW HOURS LATER, Van was just going through the motions at work when she got a text from Grant:

If it'll make things easier on you, why don't you just hire a wedding planner? I know some excellent ones.

Van couldn't help but smile at his thoughtfulness. She had toyed with the idea of hiring a planner a while back, but things were so up-in-the-air between them at the time in regards to the wedding that she didn't want to be bothered. But really, the plan was always for Raven to help her. She knew things weren't like what they used to be between them, but she hoped that was still the case.

When she got off work for the day, she called Raven to ask her about it.

"You can't be serious," Raven scoffed immediately.

Van figured she shouldn't have been surprised by that reaction. Still she replied, "Yes, I'm serious. You know we always talked about helping each other plan our weddings; why would it be any different now?"

"Because I used to date your damn fiancé, that's why. Because he only pretended to like me in the first place to get next to you, lying to me and leading me on for months. Because you never even told me you had feelings for him while he and I were seeing each other. Because you didn't even mean for me to find out about the two of you when I did...I just happened to be in the wrong place at the right time and overheard it. Need I go on?"

"Raven, come on..." Van found herself pleading, guilt pricking her at her cousin's words, all of which were true.

"I know this isn't an ideal situation, but I still consider you my best friend. There's nobody I would want to share this experience with more than you. It just wouldn't feel right."

Raven sighed. "Van...look, I appreciate that. And it's not like I just don't want to help you. But...can't you at all understand how awkward that would be for me?"

"Of course I do," Van replied softly. "I get it. And I'm not trying to be insensitive by asking this of you. I guess I was just hoping that we could all just...move past what happened somehow. This is supposed to be one of the happiest times of my life and I want you with me."

"This is going to sound way bitchier than I mean it to, but just because it's the happiest time of your life doesn't mean it's the same for everybody else. It's easy for you and Grant to be walking on air right now but y'all forgot about those that you stepped on to get up there."

Despite herself, Van felt tears come to her eyes. "I guess I deserve that. But Raven...are you ever going to forgive me for this? Isn't there any way you can find it in your heart to be there for me right now? I don't know if I can do this without you."

"You don't need me now that you have Grant, though, right?" Raven immediately sniped. After a moment of shocked silence, Raven conceded, "Okay, I admit that was uncalled for. I'm sorry for that."

"I understand."

"Van, this is not easy for me. At all. But if it's really that important to you, then of course I'll help you plan your wedding. And I'll try to leave the snide comments at the door."

That was music to Van's ears. "Really??" she grinned into the phone.

"Yes, really. I don't want to be upset about this forever; it's not like I don't have anything else to think about other than what you and Grant did."

Van started to ask for her to elaborate on that, but figured she'd better quit while she was ahead.

"Thank you *so* much, Raven! We're gonna have so much fun doing this together...remember all the stuff we used to talk about? Trying on dresses, staying up late planning out every detail, getting to have all those wedding cake samples..."

They shared a giggle, and for a brief moment it felt like old times between them. "Yeah, it'll be fun. We'll *make* it fun."

"Absolutely!"

"So when are you trying to get started on all this? When is the date?"

"January eleventh. Not next year, though; the following year."

Raven paused. "Why are you waiting so long?"

"It's not that long."

"You've already been engaged over seven months. I thought y'all were so anxious to get this show on the road."

"I..." Van didn't want to admit she had no real reason for choosing that date other than because it was a ways off. "I just like the idea of a January wedding, that's all. And a lot of the ideal venues have long waiting lists."

Raven didn't really buy that reasoning, but she chose to let it go. "If you say so."

"Yeah, so...how 'bout you come by the house this weekend and we can get started? I've already earmarked a few dresses and I can't wait for you to see them."

"No can do," Raven replied immediately.

"What? What do you mean? I thought you said you were helping me."

"Yeah, I am. But I'm not coming to your house to do it."

Van sighed, not having even considered that. "Raven..."

"Van, forget it. I'm unyielding on this. I'm willing to help you and all, but I do not want to be in Grant's house and I'm sure he probably doesn't want me up in there, either. We're just gonna have to meet up somewhere else."

"Raven," Van began, telling herself to choose her words carefully, "I get why you feel that way. I really do. *But*, at some point you and Grant are going to have to learn to be around each other again. I mean, we're family. And you two can't avoid each other forever if he's gonna be my husband."

Raven was quiet.

"I'm not saying you two have to be best buddies and act like the past never happened," Van continued carefully, praying she wasn't just pissing Raven off more. "But after all these months, I would think the two of you could at *least* be in the same house with each other, if not the same room. I think both of you are mature enough for that and it would just make things so much easier."

After a few more quiet moments, Raven finally spoke. "Once again, it's easier for you to say that. Maybe if you were on the other side of all this, you wouldn't expect everybody to be ready to hold hands and sing just because you think it's time to. You're right; at some point, I'll have to be around Grant again. But that point hasn't come yet. So like I said, I'll help you plan your wedding but I am *not* coming to your house and that's all there is to that. So I suggest you take it or leave it."

"Okay, okay. How 'bout I come by your place tomorrow, then?"

"Uh, I can't tomorrow. I've got plans already."

"Raven-"

"Look, I've gotta go," Raven interjected. "Maybe we can set up a time next week for you to come over, or we can meet up somewhere else. Talk to you later." She hung up.

Upset, Van groaned in frustration as she hung up the phone and tossed it onto the passenger's seat of her car. She was frustrated, but she figured she shouldn't be too surprised about Raven not wanting to come to the house she shared with Grant to plan Van's wedding to him. The same house that Raven had been in on a date with Grant before, herself. So that was understandable, even though it was something of a headache for Van.

When she thought about it, she knew Raven's points were valid, though...yes, months had passed, but that didn't make this situation any less awkward for her. She was sincerely into Grant when they were dating; she'd told Van so many times. Even though Raven had ultimately been the one to end things between them by foolishly believing the lies of one of Grant's jilted exes about his sexuality, Van imagined that it couldn't have been the easiest thing for Raven to see her cousin and her ex together. And everybody knew it was only a matter of time before Grant would have ended things with Raven, anyway, since it was also true that his only motive for dating her at all was to get closer to Van.

Van knew she had to consider how she would feel if she were in Raven's shoes, and she honestly didn't know if she would be any more over it than Raven was. But even still, she thought she and Raven's bond should have been strong enough to withstand a little awkwardness. Raven could have sucked it up and dealt with it if she really wanted to. Van just wanted everyone to get along and leave the past in the past, and yes, maybe it *was* easier said than done for her, but that didn't mean it was impossible. Both Raven and Grant were important people in her life, and they were simply going to have to learn to get along with each other, and the sooner the better, as far as Van was concerned.

She was still mulling over all of this when she pulled up to the house, surprised to see Grant's Benz in the garage.

"Hey, baby," Grant greeted her as soon as she entered the house.

"Hey." Van smiled as she accepted his quick peck on the lips. "I thought you'd be working late."

"I told you I'd be home as soon as I could. You apparently didn't believe me," Grant reminded amusingly.

"It's not that. I just know how busy you are and everything..."

"Van," Grant looked at her, his expression turning serious. "Are you still upset with me about this morning?"

"No, sweetie, I'm not. I told you we were fine."

Grant eyed her. "You sure?"

"Yes. I was a little embarrassed, I admit, but I'm not going to hold a grudge about it."

"I am so sorry," Grant said sincerely, taking her into his arms. "The last thing I want to do is embarrass you."

"I know."

"Will you give me a chance to make it up to you later?" Grant asked, his voice dropping as he leaned down to nuzzle her neck.

Van couldn't resist grinning as she enjoyed the feeling of him. She wrapped her arms around him tighter, giggling when she felt his tongue tickle her skin. "I think I could be convinced..."

Grant moaned and began sucking her neck before suddenly picking her up and setting her on the marble kitchen island, causing Van to squeal in delight. They kissed deeply for several moments, Grants fingers inching underneath the hemline of her skirt. Van caressed his face, reveling in the spontaneous moment, then she pulled back, remembering something.

"Baby, where are the twins?"

"Upstairs," Grant muttered, leaning in to resume their kiss.

"We should probably stop, then...I wouldn't want one of them to walk in here and see us like this." She gently pushed at his chest.

"I'm sure they've seen worse," Grant joked, even though he wasn't entirely kidding. He tried to kiss her again.

"Grant!" Van giggled, leaning back to evade his lips. "Come on..."

"Okay, fine."

"I promise, though, you can have me all to yourself later," Van informed him seductively, placing a playful finger to his lips. "For as long as you want."

"Oh yeah? I think I'm ready for bed *now*, then," Grant teased, grabbing her as if he was going to pick her up off the counter.

Van squealed again with laughter, causing Grant to laugh, himself. She absolutely loved it when they had fun together like this.

"You want something to eat? The twins had dinner already," Grant informed her as he helped her down off the island.

"Already? What did they eat?"

"I made some pork chops and rice pilaf. They gobbled it up, too."

"*You* made it? How long have you been home??"

"A couple of hours. I came home and worked for a while until the twins got in from school, then we just hung out. They said they were hungry so I made them some dinner."

"I almost forgot you could cook." Van smiled at him. "Where is it, in the refrigerator?"

"Yeah, but I'll get it for you. Go on and sit down."

"Thank you, sweetie." Van flashed him an appreciative smile as she quickly washed her hands in the kitchen sink and took a seat at the table. Grant warmed her plate of food and set it in front of her, along with a bottle of her favorite red grapefruit juice.

"Grant, this is so good!" Van gushed after taking a few bites. "How did you get these pork chops so moist? And what is this seasoning you have on here?"

"I can't reveal my secrets." Grant winked at her as he sat down in the chair beside hers, scooting it closer so he could run his hands along her leg. "Let's just say my mother taught me well. So how was your day?"

"Work was work," Van shrugged, taking another bite of the fluffy pilaf. "I might have to go out of town myself soon, though I can't say I'm looking forward to it."

"Baby, you clearly don't like your job anymore. Why are you still doing it?"

Van looked at him. "It's my *job*, Grant. I can't just quit."

"Why can't you?"

"And what am I supposed to do with myself if I do? I can't sit around here all day doing nothing."

"Well then find something you love to do. You should enjoy what you do every day, baby. And it's not like you're staying there because you *have* to anymore. Take your time with it."

"We've talked about this, sweetie...I just don't feel comfortable being totally dependent on you like that," Van replied carefully, putting down her fork. "I have to have something for myself."

"I get that, even though I'm about to be your husband so there's nothing wrong with you depending on me. I'm not asking you to be a housewife. I'm just telling you that you shouldn't stay at a job you're clearly not feeling anymore when you don't have to. That's all."

"I get it. I'll think about it."

"That's all I'm asking. What else went on today?"

Van remembered her conversation with Raven and hesitated; she picked up her fork and raked it through her remaining pilaf. "You wouldn't want to hear it."

"Try me."

Van hesitated again, then again put down her fork. "I talked to Raven about helping me plan the wedding."

"Okay..."

"See? I told you you wouldn't want to hear it. Never mind."

"Van," Grant sighed. "I wish you would stop doing that."

Van looked at him, confused. "Doing what?"

"Always trying to pick and choose what to tell me and talk to me about. How many times do I have to remind you that I am your fiancé and there's *nothing* you have to keep from me? If it's uncomfortable, it's uncomfortable; I can handle it. But you can talk to me about anything."

"I just know this is still kind of a touchy subject."

"For whom?"

"Grant, come on. You can't say that Raven is one of your favorite topics of conversation. I can't imagine you want to talk about her any more than she wanted to talk about you."

"Well, I'm sure you can understand why that is. But I have no problem talking about her if there's something about her you need to discuss. So she's going to help you plan the wedding, huh?"

"Yeah," Van sighed, "Even though I had to kind of twist her arm to get her to do it. That was what we had always talked about, ever since we were kids; helping each other plan our weddings. And I was looking forward to having this experience with her."

"Was? I thought she agreed to help you."

"Eventually, yeah. But when I invited her over here to get started, she refused to come. And insisted she wasn't going to change her mind. It's just so frustrating."

"Van, baby," Grant turned her chair to face him and took her hands in his. "I *know* you can understand that, though, right? I'm sure if you were marrying anybody else, it wouldn't be an issue. But Raven and I have something of a history, and not a very pleasant one...of course she's not going to want to be in my house. A house she and I have been intimate in, I might add."

Van cocked a brow at him. "You don't have to remind me about that."

"I'm just saying. I've told you all about it; I don't have anything to hide."

"Yes, I know. You still could've spared me those details."

"Van," Grant chuckled, shaking his head. "So you're just going to do all the planning at her place, then, I take it?"

"Yeah. Or we'll meet up somewhere else." Van ran her hands through her hair and looked at her future husband. "I mean, is it really *that* unrealistic for me to want all of us to leave the past in the past and move on?"

"It's not necessarily unrealistic for you to want it but it *is* a little unrealistic for you to expect it, at least on your timetable," Grant replied. "You've gotta remember, baby,

Raven feels both of us dogged her. And she's not entirely wrong. I'm not proud of my part in all this...I knew all along that her feelings for me far exceeded mine for her, and it can't be a good feeling finding out she was nothing but a pawn in my quest to get with you. I'll never apologize for wanting you, baby, but I certainly understand her position and I can't even say I don't deserve her animosity."

Van nodded. "You're right," she admitted softly.

"Of course it would be ideal for all of us to get along, and hopefully we will one day, but I can't expect her to just forget about what happened because some time has passed," Grant continued. His hands squeezed her legs. "You shouldn't, either."

Van just looked at him for another moment or two before looking at the ground in shame. He was right. Maybe it *was* unfair for her to expect Raven to be over everything just because Van thought she should be by now. It was just another reminder of how her actions had hurt the people she loved, and she started to feel those all-too-familiar prickles of guilt.

"I just don't know how I can make all this right with her, baby," Van admitted, willing herself not to cry. The thought of losing Raven from her life always brought tears to her eyes. "Sometimes I really wonder if she'll *ever* fully forgive me. Or trust me again."

"I'm sure she will," Grant assured her, brushing some hair out of her face. "But you have to be patient. And you can't push her. Everybody handles things differently; just because you might be past something like this by now doesn't mean she should be. She's just hurt, and maybe still a little angry, but her agreeing to help you plan the wedding says that she's at least willing to start mending the relationship between the two of you. You're just going to have to do it on her terms."

Van knew he was right. She would have to continue to be patient with Raven and give her time to come around at her own pace.

• • • •

EVEN THOUGH VAN CAME to that realization, she couldn't resist wanting to see Raven and talk about all of this face-to-face. Grant had been absolutely right about her needing to be patient with Raven, but Van hated the awkwardness between her and her cousin/bestie.

So the next day, Van decided to pay Raven a visit. She recalled Raven mentioning having plans, but hopefully she would give Van a few minutes to talk. During the drive over to Raven's apartment, Van reminded herself not to push Raven or say anything to set her off; she just wanted to spend a little time with her, hang out for a little bit, talk about safe subjects like how things were going at the restaurant Raven worked at as a chef or even maybe try to get some details out of her about this new man she had been so tight-lipped about. Van wondered if that was who Raven's plans were with as she turned onto Raven's street, and decided that it was good if it was. Maybe if Raven was getting serious with this new guy, it would help her get over the whole situation with Grant sooner. Van couldn't wait to grill her cousin for some details, and even encourage her to take things to the next level with this new man, since

Raven always raved about him despite being so secretive about who he was.

When Van pulled up to Raven's building, though, she just knew her eyes were playing tricks on her. She actually almost ran into another car because she simply couldn't believe what she was seeing.

She'd know Joe's truck anywhere. And that was definitely Joe, pulling a duffel bag out of the front seat before locking the door and heading right up to Raven's apartment.

Chapter 12

• • • •

"WHAT THE *hell*??"

Van was absolutely reeling. What in the world was Joe doing at Raven's apartment?? He was walking up to her place like it was something he usually did; he didn't look unfamiliar with where he was going at all. And he had a *duffel* bag! Were they...

Van grabbed her stomach. Surely, she must be delusional. There had to be a perfectly reasonable explanation for Joe being at Raven's, but something in her gut told her this wasn't just a random, casual visit. Had they become friends after Raven helped Joe plan Van's proposal? It wasn't impossible. But why hadn't Raven ever mentioned that she and Joe were hanging out? Would Van have even wanted to hear that? Raven never wanted to talk about Grant; maybe she figured Van wouldn't want to talk about Joe.

But that didn't make sense, considering Raven knew Van had been wanting to talk to Joe for month; had even confessed to missing him. Why hadn't Raven mentioned being in contact with Joe any of the hundred times Van mentioned that? Exactly how long had they been hanging out? Was *Raven* the reason Joe hadn't been returning Van's calls? Van's head was swimming with all these questions.

Parking her car and turning off the ignition, Van tried to gather her thoughts. The idea of Raven and Joe together did not sit well with her at all, and the more she thought about it, the more she felt herself getting upset. Even if

Van *was* with Grant, she didn't want her cousin and her ex together. That was just...sick. Not to mention disrespectful.

"Okay, I'm losing it," she muttered to herself, trying to shake those thoughts. There was no way that Raven and Joe were anything other than friends, if that. Surely, they wouldn't do that to her. It would just make an already messy situation even messier; they *had* to know that. No, they were just hanging out together, or maybe Joe was coming over to fix something of Raven's, since he was such a whiz at that kind of thing. Van could even accept that they had bonded over the whole ordeal of finding out about her and Grant the way they both had and were obliging each other polite comfort. That had to be it.

Now Van didn't know what to do. Should she leave or go knock on the door and surprise them both? She was dying to know what was going on with them and knew she wouldn't be able to rest until she did, so she grabbed her purse before grabbing the door handle, but hesitated. What if she saw something she didn't want to see? Van honestly didn't know how to prepare herself, but she knew if she drove away from there right then, the speculation about the nature of Joe and Raven's relationship would drive her crazy. She had planned on visiting her cousin, anyway; that didn't have to change just because Joe was there. Maybe he wasn't even going to be there that long.

But when Van sat in her car for another fifteen minutes and Joe never emerged from the building, she figured that wasn't the case, either. There was no way she could keep sitting out there guessing. Before she totally lost her nerve, she pushed open the door, hopped out of her car, and hurried to Raven's door, her hands shaking with nervousness as she reached up to knock on it. Hearing footsteps, she took a deep breath and braced herself.

"Who is it?" Raven called out.

"Hey girl, it's me." Van tried to sound casual. She didn't even realize how hard both hands were gripping her purse.

"Van?" There were some muffled sounds, and Van imagined Raven telling Joe to go hide in her bedroom or something until she could get rid of her nosy cousin.

It took a few moments before Raven finally cracked open the door, peeking out at Van with a distracted expression. Van's eyes did a quick sweep and Raven was fully dressed in a ribbed fitted tee and tight skinny jeans, and she didn't look disheveled. Nothing was askew or haphazardly put on backwards. Her shiny, shoulder-length black hair was in place and not mussed at all. Her face wasn't flushed, with embarrassment or anything else. Her feet were bare. She looked perfectly put together for a casual afternoon at home. Van tried to peer past her into the apartment, but Raven's body was blocking her view.

"What's going on?" Raven asked.

"Nothing; just wanted to stop by and see you since I was over this way," Van lied. She had come specifically to see Raven but that was neither here nor there. "I know you said you had plans today..."

"Yeah; yeah, I do," Raven confirmed, her voice holding just a tinge of annoyance at being dropped in on unannounced.

"I thought maybe they were over with by now or something."

"No, not yet. You could've just called."

"We haven't hung out in forever. I can't come in just for a little while?"

Raven didn't move. "Now's really not a good time, Van."

A cold wave shot through Van's body. "Why not?"

"I have company."

"Anybody I know?"

Raven just stared at Van, and with every second that ticked by, Van was losing hope of the possibility that *maybe* Joe had been coming to see somebody else, or was just there to fix Raven's sink.

"Go home, Van," Raven finally ordered, her voice firm and even.

Swallowing, Van gripped her purse even tighter. "Why?"

"Umm, because I asked you to? Because I told you I have company? Because it's clear that I'm busy?"

"Let me in, Raven."

Frowning, Raven stood up straighter; she towered over Van by a couple of inches. "What part of *I have company* don't you get??"

"I want to meet whoever it is you have in there," Van persisted, her voice rising slightly as if giving her "company" a heads-up that she was about to barge in. "It won't take all that long."

"It's not happening."

"Is there some *reason* I shouldn't meet him? You're acting as if you have something to hide. If you have nothing to hide, it shouldn't be a problem, right?"

"Van, I don't know what's up with you right now, but you are really starting to piss me off," Raven warned her. "Go *home*, and I will talk to you later."

Van wasn't trying to hear that. Clenching her jaw, she pushed past Raven, managing to get by her after a brief arm-tangling scuffle. Upon seeing Joe sprawled out on the couch as if he lived there, shoes off, the television remote in his hand, Van couldn't tell if her heart had sped up to an indecipherable rate or had stopped altogether.

"Oh my god," she gasped, a hand on her chest. She gaped at Joe, then glared at Raven, who had moved over by the couch. "What the hell is going on??"

"We *were* binging *Game of Thrones*," Raven informed her, dropping onto the couch next to Joe and casually tucking a leg underneath her. It wasn't lost on Van how close she sat to him, and she wondered if that was done on purpose to goad her. "I'd invite you to join us, but I know you don't like that show."

Any idiot could see that Raven was being sarcastic. The amused smirks on both her and Joe's faces were undeniable. Van tried to get her breathing under control, but wasn't quite able to do it. "S-since when do you two hang out?"

"For a while now," Raven shrugged casually, taking the remote that Joe handed to her and winking at him. He winked at her in return.

Van felt her blood boil. Were they actually dating, or were they just trying to get a rise out of her? Either way, Van didn't like this whole situation. She didn't like it one bit.

"What *is* this?" she demanded, waving a hand between the two of them. Her face felt like it was on fire. "What the *hell* is going on between you two??"

Joe just peered at her before looking at Raven. "You want me to check on the chili?"

"Nah, I just stirred it...it needs a little while longer," Raven casually replied, as if Van wasn't even standing there. "But if you can't wait, there's still some pot roast from the other day. I can make you a sandwich or something."

"Yeah, your pot roast *is* something serious," Joe confirmed, essentially letting Van know that this little hang-out wasn't a first-time thing. His fingertips brushed Raven's shoulder. Van felt like there was steam literally coming out of her ears. "You know you can cook your ass off, girl."

"Aww," Raven grinned, playfully nudging him. "You know I try put it down when I can."

"Oh, you most *definitely* do that," Joe confirmed emphatically. He smirked at Van when he added, "Best I ever had."

Before Van could stop herself, she was lunging for her cousin. Raven, who had still been grinning at Joe's statement, was caught completely off-guard and screamed, trying to move out of the way. But before Van could lay a finger on Raven, Joe jumped up and caught her by the waist, picking her up with ease and turning her away from her cousin. The fact that Joe was protecting Raven only infuriated Van more.

"You need to calm yo' ass down!" he growled at her.

"Put me down!" Van screamed. She knew her face was as red as a beet, and tears were flowing like streams. "I cannot believe you! You broke the girl code, Raven! Getting with my *ex*? That I was in love with – and *lived* with - for years??"

"And yet you *still* dogged him and left him for someone else," Raven snapped, no remorse to be found. "Not to mention how you kept shit from *me*, too. And you seem to be conveniently forgetting that I dated Grant first and then you got with him, but there's nothing wrong with *that*, right? It's okay for *you* to break the girl code when you're *doing it for your kids*? Isn't that the bullshit justification you gave for cheating on your man with a millionaire?"

Van flinched at her words. "That was a low blow, Raven."

"But it was a true blow, *Van*. You wanna come in here playing the victim when you're guilty of much worse shit than Joe or I did. We were single when we hooked up. Your ass was still with Joe when you were creeping around with Grant. But *we're* wrong? You can get the fuck on with that."

"How could y'all betray me like this?? Were you even gonna *tell* me??"

Both Raven and Joe scoffed. "*What??*" Joe asked incredulously.

"Are you serious??" Raven asked, equally aghast. "You have the *audacity* to ask that after what you did??"

"This doesn't have anything to do with that!" Van declared angrily. "Or *does* it?? Is this just some kind of revenge to get back at me? Are y'all really that petty??"

"Take her ass outta here!" Raven ordered, standing from the couch and placing her hands on her hips.

"I'm not going *anywhere*!!"

"Oh okay then, but know *this*; if Joe lets you go, it's *on*! You won't be catching me off-guard no more and you *know* you've never beat me in a fight! Try to run up on me again!" Raven challenged, looking every bit as angry as Van. They were both breathing fire, glaring at each other.

"Raven-"

"This is ridiculous!" Joe declared, carrying Van to the door with one arm like she was a sack of groceries. She tried to free herself, but his arm was like steel.

"Joe, let me go!"

"Yeah, you better go on outta here before you make an even *bigger* ass outta yourself!" Raven taunted from behind them. Van tried to turn and glare at her, but Joe had her out of the apartment by then, closing the door hard behind them with his free hand.

He carried Van out of the vestibule and into the parking lot, a ways from Raven's apartment door, before he finally set her down. When she tried to run past him back to the apartment, he easily restrained her.

"What the hell is your problem??" he demanded. He stood right in front of her, glaring down at her furious face. "Do you have any idea how crazy you look right now?"

"I don't care, Joe! I cannot believe y'all were in there carrying on like that right in front of me!!"

"I don't know what you're talking about."

"The hell you don't! Don't think I don't know that little show in there was for my benefit. You were *clearly* trying to rub your friendship or relationship or whatever the hell it is you have right in my face!"

Joe crossed his arms over his muscular chest. "So?"

"What do you mean, *so*??"

"Even if Raven and I ran off and got married this morning, that's our business. I'm single and so is she. We can do whatever the hell we want."

Van's mouth fell open. "How can you say that to me??"

Joe dropped his arms. "Van, for real, you have a lot of nerve barging up in here questioning us about *anything*."

"Joe-"

"You and I are no longer together, remember? Or do you not recall interrupting my marriage proposal to you to let me know you were leaving me for another man with more money because 'love doesn't pay the bills'?"

Hearing her words from that awful night immediately calmed Van down, but her face still burned. It was then that she realized she was face-to-face with Joe like she had wanted to be for months, but now that she was, she didn't quite know what to say. Especially after his harsh reminder of how she ended their relationship.

"Joe, I..." Her voice broke but she silently told herself to keep it together. She extended her hand towards Raven's building. "All I'm saying is, how can you not see anything wrong with this?"

Joe glared at her. Then as if he couldn't stand the sight of her anymore, he turned away. "Go home, Van."

"Can we please talk?" Van quickly pleaded, lightly grabbing his arm. "Please?"

"We don't have anything to talk about," Joe retorted in a low voice, still not looking at her.

"Yes, Joe, we do. I don't want to leave things like we left them in the restaurant that night. We've known each other too long for that."

"And whose fault is *that*, Van?" Joe asked angrily, snatching his arm away from her.

"I know you're angry at me, and you have every right to be," Van persisted. "I just want the chance to finally explain myself to you. That's all I'm asking."

"I don't see what you think you could possibly say to explain yourself."

"Let me try, though." Van stepped in front of him, trying to get him to look at her. Her eyes begged him. "Joe...please?"

Joe cut his eyes at her before finally sighing in frustration. "Fine, whatever. Meet me at the Waffle House down the street at one tomorrow."

Down the street? Are you planning on spending the night over here? But Van knew better than to ask that out loud.

"One o'clock?"

"If that time doesn't work for you, then forget it."

Van would have to shift some things around, but she knew she would be there. And part of her was surprised he was so inflexible; the old Joe would have asked what time would work for her if that one didn't. "No, no...one is fine. I'll see you then. Thank you so much, Joe."

"Yeah. Bye." Joe turned and headed back into the building without waiting for a response.

Van stood in the middle of the parking lot, looking after him until he was out of sight. Her mind was still trying to process the past half-hour or so. Were Joe and Raven really a couple? Or were they just messing with her? She had no idea, but they were definitely more familiar with each other than Van liked. Whether she had a right to feel this way or not, Van couldn't help being upset about this whole situation. But the bright side was that Joe had finally agreed to talk to her.

• • • •

THE REST OF VAN'S DAY was shot, as far as concentrating on anything else. Her mind kept straying to the scene in Raven's apartment, and wondering what they were doing at any given moment. She didn't even want to *think* about them sleeping together, but given their current anger towards her (not to mention them both having sex drives that were through the roof), she wouldn't put it past them. She could only hope that they were just trying to get under her skin and that was the extent of it.

"You all right?" Grant asked her later that evening, in their bedroom. They had just finished dinner a little while earlier.

"I'm fine," Van muttered unconvincingly, her back to him.

"You seemed like you were in a bad mood or something at dinner. You practically bit Canton's head off when he asked you to pass the salad dressing."

"No, I didn't," Van automatically dismissed, then turned to him as if his words just registered. "Did I, really?"

"Yeah, you did. What's going on?"

"Nothing."

"Why are you lying?"

"I just don't feel like talking about it, Grant."

"All right, I'll respect that. But I'd prefer it if you didn't take your bad days out on all of us and then act like you didn't. Especially when work is a headache you don't have to have."

Van sighed. She'd been snippy ever since she came home from going to see Raven, and she knew she'd been taking her aggravation out on Grant and the twins. But she was glad Grant was assuming it was about work because she certainly wasn't about to tell him the real reason for her attitude.

"I'm sorry," she said simply. "I know I've been acting like a bitch this evening."

"I never said that."

"But I was."

"You need to relax," Grant advised, walking over to her and rubbing her shoulders from behind. "I don't like seeing you so stressed out, babe. What can I do to help?"

Van closed her eyes and leaned back against Grant, wishing there *was* some way he could erase what happened earlier from her mind.

"You being so concerned is enough, sweetie," she sighed.

"Always. Wow, you really are tense..."

"Mm-hmm."

"Why don't you go take a long, relaxing bath, then I'll give you a full-body massage. You feel like you need one," Grant suggested.

"That sounds good."

"I'll go run it for you."

"Thank you, sweetie."

Grant planted a kiss to her temple before going into their bathroom and starting the water in the huge soaking tub that Van loved, adding her favorite foaming bath salts. Van proceeded to get undressed and put her hair up, trying to clear her mind, but it wasn't quite working. She was just too wound up and she knew that wouldn't be relieved until she talked to Joe the next day.

She went and got in the tub, exhaling as she sank into the hot water. Leaning her head on the lavender bath pillow, she tried her best to relax. But every time she closed her eyes, she got an image of Joe and Raven together, and the tension automatically returned. Maybe she should have asked Grant to join her in the tub for a distraction; she knew she wasn't going to be able to think about anything else other than Joe and Raven as long as she was in there alone. She remembered how Joe always used to run her baths after long days; did he do that for Raven? Did they take baths together?

Giving up on the relaxation mission, Van got out of the tub and wrapped herself in a large, fluffy towel, padding back into the bedroom. Grant motioned for her to get on the bed, where he proceeded to rub her down with sweet almond oil. Thankfully he didn't try to hold a conversation, even though part of Van would have welcomed the distraction. When things were silent, her mind just wandered back where she wished it wouldn't. She just couldn't stop thinking about Raven and Joe; wondering if they were still together right then, and what they were doing if they were.

If Van was honest with herself, she was jealous. And angry. Of all the people in Atlanta and beyond, why did they have to choose *each other*? Van still didn't know if they were an actual couple or just friends or what, but it almost didn't matter; she didn't think they should be as close as they appeared to be. And something told her it wasn't all just an act for her benefit, if it was an act at all. The way Raven was grinning at Joe was sincere; Van could tell. And Joe wasn't *that* good an actor.

"Are you okay?" Grant murmured as he massaged her lower back.

"Mm-hmm," Van moaned, her eyes closed. What he was doing felt good, but Van knew there wasn't a massage invented that could make her stop obsessing.

"I just want you to feel better," Grant said, his hands sliding up her back and across her shoulders. "I hate seeing you like this."

Van hated it, too. In the back of her mind, she knew she had no business being so concerned about what her ex and her cousin were doing together. Joe was right; they were both single and could do as they pleased. But that didn't mean Van had to like it. Even if she *did* break up with Joe for Grant, that didn't mean that she wanted him to go and get with Raven. That just didn't seem right to her.

For a brief moment, Van thought about getting Grant's take on the situation. Maybe she needed another perspective. But she stopped herself. She had a pretty good guess what he would say; he'd probably just agree with Joe that it was none of Van's business. Maybe even say that it was a good thing; that Raven and Joe were helping each other through a tough time and that might help them get over their anger towards Van faster. Even if that were true, it still didn't make Van feel much better about the situation. Van had almost six years' worth of memories with Joe; he had treated her like a queen the best he could. Cooking for her, washing her hair, fixing anything around her that needed to be fixed without her having to ask, giving her amazing foot rubs, being her best friend, coming into her life and helping with the twins at a time when she honestly didn't know how she was going to make it on her own...and there was no way she could forget Joe's lovemaking. It wasn't hyperbole to say he was the absolute best she ever had. He didn't have one flaw when it came to that. And maybe it was silly, but she didn't want Raven experiencing that. She and her cousin had never shared men before and she didn't want to start with Joe.

But then she remembered, it had kind of already started with Grant.

Van ended up not telling Grant about anything that happened at Raven's apartment that day, nor did she tell him about her upcoming meeting with Joe. She didn't know why; it wasn't like she was doing anything wrong or that she felt it was something she needed to hide. Grant was well aware of her desire to clear the air with Joe. She couldn't imagine he would have a problem with it if she told him. But she didn't. For the time being, Van just wanted to keep it to herself.

Van realized that she was developing a habit of keeping things from her fiancé; and worse, it wasn't that hard for her to do. She couldn't even explain herself; Grant had always encouraged her to be up front with him, and she knew from the whole situation about her not telling her parents about their engagement that he detested secrets. Van kept very, very few secrets from Joe when they were together...what did it say about her and Grant's relationship that it was so easy for her to keep them from Grant?

Chapter 13

• • • •

VAN COULDN'T REMEMBER the last time she was so nervous. She had been anxiously anticipating this talk with Joe all morning, and the closer it got, the more her nerves went into overdrive.

Knowing Joe probably wouldn't hesitate to leave if she was even one minute late, Van made sure to be at their agreed-upon location early. She actually beat him there; he strolled into the Waffle House down the street from Raven's apartment at a quarter after one. Van didn't comment on his tardiness; she figured he might have been late on purpose either in an attempt to annoy her or let her think he wasn't coming, but Van would have waited an hour if she needed to. This was something she felt was long overdue and there was no way she was going to miss it, if she could help it.

"Hi," she greeted Joe shyly as he approached the booth she was sitting in.

"Hey," Joe grunted, taking a seat across from her.

"Thank you for coming," Van said, noting that he wasn't really looking at her. She nervously played with her fingers. As much as she had wanted and anticipated this meeting, her mind had gone blank now that Joe was in front of her. "I, um...I got you an orange juice. Are you hungry?"

"I don't want anything."

"You sure? I know you like their patty melts-"

"Look, how 'bout we get to the point of this little talk you just had to have so I can go on about my business?" Joe interrupted. "And I ate already, anyway."

It was on the tip of Van's tongue to ask if he was just coming from Raven's, but kept that question to herself; she wasn't about to upset Joe any more than he already was. He clearly didn't want to be there.

"All right, then," Van conceded, pushing away her own glass of juice. "I appreciate you coming."

"Uh-huh. You said that."

"Okay, Joe, look," Van hedged, leaning forward slightly. "It's obvious you're not in the mood for preamble or pleasantries so I'll just get right to it. I owe you a huge apology. Really, 'I'm sorry' doesn't feel like *enough* for how much I hurt you. But I really, truly am, Joe...I don't think I'll ever forget the look on your face when I walked out of the restaurant that night. It's haunted me ever since."

"Yeah. But I see you got over it," Joe noted pointedly, glancing at Van's large engagement ring.

Swallowing nervously, Van eased her hand under the table out of sight. "Joe...I know there's really nothing I can say. I should have handled everything *way* better than I did. You didn't deserve that, and...it really just breaks my heart that I caused you so much pain. You were always so good to me and the twins..."

"A lot of good it did."

"Please don't do that. Don't discount everything we shared together just because I did...what I did."

"I didn't *discount* anything. You're the one that did that when you threw our relationship away like it was nothing."

"Joe, our relationship was anything but *nothing*!" Van insisted emphatically. She could feel the tears coming but willed herself not to break down. It shocked her how important it was for Joe to see where she was coming from. "You meant the *world* to me; I still care about you, *so* much. None of this is because of anything you did-"

"Yeah, you can save that," Joe interrupted her. "Don't try to sell me that bullshit, Van. If it wasn't about anything I did then that would be *my* engagement ring on the hand you're trying to hide under the table instead of that rich dude's. I didn't have enough money for you, and you weren't woman enough to just break up with me *first* instead of messing around with him behind my back while I broke my neck trying to do better for you. If we're gonna talk, let's be real about it."

"Joe, okay, you're right. I was dishonest and I was wrong for any time I spent with Grant behind your back; there's no excuse for that," Van admitted truthfully. "But that was only because I couldn't bring myself to end things with you, Joe. Just the *thought* of that tore me up."

"Right," Joe scoffed.

"It *did*! You don't know how many times I agonized over that decision; how many times I went back and forth and tried to rationalize going one way or the other. This wasn't easy at *all* for me. But I was just tired, Joe...I just got tired of the way things were."

"You don't think *I* got tired? You think I was *satisfied* with the way things were? Hell no, I wasn't. That's why I went back to school and applied for a better job, all because I knew you needed more from me. I would've done anything for you, Van; I would've worked four jobs if that's what it took. But nothing I did turned out to be good enough for you because it still couldn't measure up to what *he* had."

"Joe, *why* didn't you just tell me about everything you were doing??"

"Would it have mattered?"

"Yes! I mean, maybe...I don't know! But at least I would have known you were trying-"

"What the *fuck*? You don't think I was *trying* the whole time we were together?? What do you think I was doing every damn day for twelve or thirteen hours? Shopping??"

"Joe, I didn't mean it like that-"

"Yeah, you did, Van. You said exactly what you meant, just like you meant everything you did when you were cheating on me with Grant, and the night you dumped me and told me you were moving in with him. I know I wasn't perfect and I ain't never claim to be, but I always did right by you; I *never* would have stepped out on you like you did me. You were all I wanted and needed, but you can't say the same about me, can you?"

Despite herself, a tear rolled down Van's cheek and she quickly wiped it away. "Joe, please don't say that."

"Why shouldn't I say it?"

"Because it's not true!"

"Oh it's not? Then what did you cheat on me for? Huh? Why did you dump me and tear my heart out like you did? Why did you move out of the house we shared and move you and your kids in with Grant? Why did you agree to be *his* wife but cut me off when I was about to ask you to be mine? Tell me *that*!"

More tears. Van wiped them with the back of her hand, noticing the waitress peering at her in concern. She tried to smile at her reassuringly, wishing she and Joe had met somewhere with more privacy.

"Joe, I know you probably won't believe this but I'll still say it; I have never loved another man like I loved you. You were a godsend to me and the twins, and no one can replace you in my heart. And I mean that with everything in me."

"Uh-huh." Joe's expression was hard and disbelieving. His chest heaved with barely-caged anger.

"Joe?"

"What?"

"Is there *any* way you can forgive me for this? You have no idea what it did to me to hear you say you hated me. To know I brought you to that...Joe, I just...I can't apologize enough. If there was *anything* I could do to fix things between us-"

"Leave him and come back to me."

Van's jaw dropped. "Wh-what?"

"If you're serious about *fixing things* between us, leave Grant and come back to me."

Van was literally at a loss for words. She didn't even know what to say, as that was the *last* thing she expected to come out of Joe's mouth. The fact that he even *wanted* her back was shocking enough...could she do that??

"Yeah, that's what I thought," Joe shook his head with a spiteful smirk. "You ain't gotta try to think of a polite way to say no 'cause I didn't mean it, anyway. I don't *want* your ass anymore. I was just calling your bluff since you keep saying how *sorry* you are."

Still reeling from Joe's *leave him and come back to me* statement, it took Van a moment to get her bearings back. She felt like the rug had been yanked from under her. Joe telling her he didn't want her anymore was almost as jarring as him suggesting they get back together. She still didn't even know what her answer would have been if he'd been serious.

"Joe, I *am* sorry," she finally insisted, looking at him pleadingly. She glanced at his rough hands on the table and wanted to reach across and grab them, but she knew he wouldn't go for that. "Maybe it just...wasn't our time."

"Oh, so now you're gonna try *that*, huh?" Joe shook his head again. "Whatever you need to tell yourself to rationalize it, I guess."

"No, no, you're right; that's a cop-out and it's beneath everything we shared together," Van quickly agreed. "I just don't want you to hate me."

Joe just glared at her.

"Joe, is there anything I can say or do-"

"Don't ask me that bullshit again."

"Please," Van knew she was begging but she didn't care. It hadn't hit her just *how* important it was to her to get Joe's forgiveness until he was sitting right there in her face. The way he looked at her, with such indifference one minute and disdain the next, tore at her insides. She couldn't deny that she missed when he would gaze at her with unbridled admiration, like she was the only woman on the planet to him. But those days were gone, and she knew it. But that didn't mean she couldn't try to at least get him to care about her again.

"Please," she pleaded again. "I don't want to lose you from my life, Joe. I mean that. What has to happen for us to be on good terms? We just have so much history..."

Joe actually laughed in her face. "This ain't got nothin' to do with history. You know you did something foul and now you're trying to clear your conscience so you can go skipping off into the sunset with Grant without any guilt. Well, damn if I'm gonna make it easier on you to do that."

"That's *not* what I'm doing!" Van protested, even though she knew there was *some* truth to that. "Joe, you're acting like I just up and left you for no reason. I told you, I was tired of struggling and wanted a better life for my kids...can't you understand that?"

"Boy, you're *really* trying to piss me off, huh? If that was all it was about, Van, you wouldn't have dumped me; once I told you about everything I had been doing, everything I had been planning, that should have been enough to make you stay. But even after I told you about all that, you *still* left. So as far as I'm concerned, you just wanted to leave."

"No!"

"You know what, Van? I might not like you, but I'd respect you a whole lot more if you'd just admit that. Be real with me, for *once*. Because apparently everything you've ever told me about how you felt about me has been a lie."

Van's hand flew to her chest in shock; she didn't know if Joe was just being mean to hurt her or if he really believed that. But hearing him say it truly made her heart hurt. "How can you possibly say that to me? After everything-"

"I don't have no more time for this," Joe declared, standing up and starting to walk off. His expression was one of disgust, but Van could see the hurt, too. He just didn't want her to see it.

"Joe, no! Please! Please don't leave!" she pleaded, grabbing his arm with both hands. She was full-on crying; she couldn't help it and she didn't try to stop it this time. She hadn't realized just how much she had hurt Joe until then, and she hated the thought of him leaving there with an even worse opinion of her than when he came.

Joe just glared down at her.

Van sniffed, tears running down her face. "Please don't leave like this," she whimpered, looking right into his eyes. "I am so sorry if I upset you; I know I'm probably messing everything up even more but please don't go. Please?"

Joe turned his face away from her. He hated himself for caring, but he could never stand to see her cry when they were together and apparently he still couldn't. The sight of it caused a pang in his stomach that he didn't want or like. He wanted to wrench himself free from her tightening grasp and leave her crying ass sitting right there in the restaurant like she had done to him that night.

But despite himself, he slowly lowered himself back down into the booth and folded his arms across his chest, looking at her with a slightly raised and expectant brow.

Van was surprised yet grateful that he stayed, but she really had no idea what to say now. She didn't know what she had expected exactly when she asked Joe to meet her;

maybe it was naïve, but she really thought he might forgive her if she apologized face-to-face. It's not like she wasn't sincere. But she realized that one conversation wasn't going to help Joe get past his anger towards her. Only time could do that.

Opting to just change the subject off of them altogether, she took a calming sip of her juice before tentatively asking, "How are the girls?"

Joe seemed to relax only slightly at the mention of his daughters. "They're fine."

"I miss them."

"Yeah." Joe didn't want to mention that they missed her, too, and asked about her every chance they got.

"Is, um, is work going okay?"

"Yep."

"You made head foreman, right?"

"Yep."

"That's so great, Joe. I'm proud of you."

"Thanks."

"And you got your degree..."

"Uh-huh."

"Is Tanisha still giving you a lot of trouble?"

Joe just shrugged, certainly not going to tell Van about briefly getting back with her or still sleeping with her when he felt like it. "She's still Tanisha."

"I bet." Van took another sip of juice, hating the awkward small talk but glad Joe was at least entertaining it, even if he was giving short answers. She licked her lips, wanting to ask something in particular but knowing it might set him off again.

Eventually, though, she couldn't resist anymore. "Joe...what's going on with you and Raven?"

Joe shook his head. "Now we're getting to the real. I knew that's what all this was really about."

"No, Joe, it's not, but...come on, you must understand why I'm so curious about it. I mean, it's not every day your ex and your cousin..."

Joe cocked a brow. "Your ex and your cousin what?"

Van hesitantly lowered her head towards her shoulder. "You know..."

"Why don't you enlighten me, since you apparently think you already have an idea."

"Are you a couple? Friends? Just sleeping together? What?"

Joe peered at her for a moment. "Why do you wanna know so bad? You dumped me for another man but think you're entitled to details about what I'm doing? Don't you have enough of your own stuff to be worried about, *Mrs. McCallister*?"

Pursing her lips, Van straightened in her seat. "Why can't you just tell me?"

"Because it's none of your damn business, Van, that's why. I don't have to tell you anything."

"Joe-"

"Nah, you know what? I'm done. I hope you got out everything you needed to say 'cause I'm over this," Joe announced, standing from the booth. He looked down at her with hateful eyes. "Get this through your head: I am *not* over what you did, and I have *not* forgiven you. I'm sure I will one day, but I have no idea when that's gonna be. So how 'bout you just leave me alone and let me stay pissed for as long as I need to stay pissed at you, because just like I'd never loved another woman like I loved you, I've also never been as *gutted* by another woman as I was by you."

Hearing that caused literal pain in Van's chest. She opened her mouth to speak, but nothing came out.

"And anyway, don't you have a wedding or something to plan?" Joe spat before stalking out of the restaurant. Van just looked after him, then down at her hands sadly. If at all possible, she knew she had just made things worse.

"Are you ready to order?" the waitress tentatively asked, coming to Van's side.

Hastily wiping her eyes and running her hands through her hair, Van shook her head. "Actually, um, I'll just take the check, please."

"Don't worry about it; it's on me," the waitress said, placing a brief comforting hand on Van's shoulder. "I got it."

"Oh, you don't have to-"

"I insist," the waitress interrupted. She winked at Van like they shared a secret.

Van knew the waitress (and everyone else sitting around them) had overheard her entire conversation with Joe and just felt sorry for her, but she didn't have time to worry about being embarrassed. Not even when she realized that someone had not-so-discreetly been recording them. She just muttered her thanks to the waitress, grabbed her purse, and scooted out of the booth, knowing she wouldn't be coming back to that particular Waffle House any time soon. She had been listening to the waitresses gossip while she waited for Joe so she could only imagine what would be said about her once she left.

As soon as Van was back in her car, she pulled out her cell phone and tried to call Raven. But of course, it went straight to voicemail. Van couldn't help but wonder if Joe had gone straight to Raven's after leaving there, and part of her wanted to go by Raven's apartment and look for his truck, but she figured she better leave well enough alone, for now. If Joe was in fact there and happened to see her, it would only make him angrier at her, and she didn't want to come across like some crazy, obsessed ex.

Van headed home, her whole body a tight ball of nerves. Even though Joe hadn't confirmed one way or the other, she just knew he and Raven were together. Call it a gut feeling, but something told her they were a couple.

And Van hated that.

• • • •

A WHILE LATER, VAN was back home, alone in the house. Grant was still at work and the twins hadn't gotten home from school yet, and Van knew she needed to clear her head before they all returned. Try as she might, though, she couldn't keep her mind from straying back to the conversation with Joe.

Of course she knew she hurt him when she left him for Grant, but now she had an idea of just how much. Part of her really thought he would be over it by now; or at least to the point where he could be cordial with her. He was still so angry and so bitter, and Van had no idea what it would take for him to get past all of that. She knew it sounded cliché, but she really did want her and Joe to be friends; maybe he would consider that an insult, considering the way their relationship ended, but Van just couldn't fathom the idea of Joe not being in her life at all. She wasn't lying when she said she still deeply cared about him, and she knew she always would.

Leave him and come back to me.

At the time, Van's mind had gone blank and she hadn't known how to respond, but what if Joe had actually meant it? What if he really *did* want her back? Would that even be an option for her? He was certainly in a better position financially than when they were together, and that had been her main complaint...they could all be even happier than they were before.

But how would that make her look, going back and forth between Joe and Grant with money being the main string pulling her? Van had always prided herself on being independent and not needing a man just for his money...and while she did love Grant very, very much, Joe was and always would be the love of her life.

What if...

Her ringing cell phone broke through her thoughts, and she actually blinked a few times before her eyes darted around, trying to remember where she was. She quickly went over to get her phone from the counter where she'd left it. She groaned when she saw it was her mother, not really in the mood to talk to her right then but knowing she couldn't ignore her call like she wanted to.

"Hey, Mama," Van greeted after a fortifying breath.

"Hey, sweetheart. You all doing okay down there?" Florence asked.

"Yes, we're fine. Why?"

"I was just getting that feeling again that something wasn't right."

"Mama, I think you've been watching too much of that show with the lady who thinks she can read minds," Van joked nervously, tucking some hair behind her ear. She stood up and started pacing anxiously. "There's nothing going on down here."

"Really?" Florence sounded suspicious. "My grandbabies aren't in any trouble?"

"Of course not; you know I would have told you about that if they were."

"And nothing is wrong with Joe?"

Van bumped into the end table and had to quickly catch the lamp that was sitting on it before it fell crashing to the floor. Silently telling herself to get it together, she replied as casually as she could manage, "Nope, nothing is wrong with Joe."

"You sure?"

You mean other than him hating me with the fire of a million furnaces? Yeah, I'm sure. "Yes, Mama. You worry too much."

"I ain't crazy, child...I *know* something isn't right," Florence insisted. "I just don't know *what*. So either you're just not telling me or it ain't happened yet."

Van bit her lip so hard she actually winced in pain. Her mother had always been frustratingly intuitive, but she usually wasn't this persistent about it; usually all it took was Van saying everything was fine for her to drop it. But Florence must've sensed it was something pretty major this time, because she mentioned this "feeling" she had every time they talked lately.

Van knew she needed to bite the bullet and just tell her mother the truth about leaving Joe for Grant. It just didn't make sense that she was still so hesitant to be up front about that; if she was woman enough to make the decision, she should have been woman enough to tell her mother she did it. But for a reason she had yet to figure out, she still couldn't make herself do it. And she wondered just how long she would be able to keep this up before she either cracked or it all blew up in her face.

"You don't have to worry about me, Mama; I'm good," Van insisted weakly. Before her mother could respond, she quickly continued, "You know the twins are going to be twelve before we know it. I'm thinking about what to do for their birthday."

"Time sure does fly, doesn't it? Seems like they just turned eleven."

"I know we still have a while but I like to start thinking about that kind of stuff early. You know Cassie has a notebook full of stuff she wants."

"I bet she does. Maybe we can come down for their birthday this year."

Van's head snapped up and her pacing stopped. "Are you serious?"

"Yeah, I'm serious. We missed their last two birthdays; plus, we haven't been down there to see y'all in a while. And it'll be good to get out of Ohio for a little bit."

"Right..." Van didn't know how to tell her mother not to come visit. There was no way she would be able to hide her situation in person. "But you know Daddy doesn't like to fly, and that's a long drive...maybe we can just Skype or something."

"We don't mind the drive, but he'll get on a plane if he needs to," Florence assured, referring to her husband. "And I don't know what *Skype* is."

"It's video-messaging...we can see and talk to each other through the computer."

"Oh. Well that's nice and everything but that ain't the same as seeing y'all in person. I want to hug on my grandbabies and I can't do that through a computer."

"Right," Van muttered again, biting her nail nervously. Her mind raced. "Well, you might not even need to bother; given the way the twins have been acting lately, they might not even *get* a party or anything else. So you'd be coming for nothing."

"It wouldn't be for *nothing*; I'd still get to see y'all. What, you don't *want* us to come?"

"That's not it at all," Van insisted, even though that was exactly it. "I just don't want you to go through any trouble, that's all."

"Why would you think it would be any trouble for us to come see our family?"

Van hesitated before shrugging her shoulders in sudden exhaustion. She so wished she could just hang up and blame it on a bad connection. "I don't know...I'm sorry, Mama. I'm a little distracted right now."

"What's wrong?"

"Honestly, nothing I have the energy to get into. But it's nothing for you to worry about."

"Hmm." Florence paused, and Van prayed she would just leave it at that. Thankfully, her prayer was answered. "All right then...I'll go on and let you go. I've gotta make my biscuits for dinner."

"Okay," Van said, relieved. "Give Daddy a kiss for me and I'll talk to you later. Love you."

"Love you, too. And I'm praying for you."

Van ended the call without responding, though she knew she certainly needed all the prayers she could get.

Van felt ridiculous. She knew there was no excuse for keeping something so huge from her parents; they were up in Ohio thinking she was still living in bliss with Joe while in fact she was planning her wedding to another man they had probably never even heard of. The fact that she'd kept it from them at all was bad enough, but the fact that she continued to essentially lie to them for months was just inexcusable. Even knowing that, though, she didn't pick up the phone and call her mother back to tell her the truth about everything.

Dropping onto the couch, Van buried her face in her hands. Maybe there was more to it than just not wanting to disappoint or upset her parents by telling them the truth about Joe...maybe telling them would also sever the last small tie she had *to* her relationship with Joe. There were still two people that thought they were still together and happy, and maybe Van didn't want to lose that, even though she was happy with Grant.

Wasn't she?

Did you ever think that maybe, deep down, you just miss being with Joe?

Van immediately shook that thought from her head. That couldn't be it. Grant was everything she could ever want or need in a man, and he treated her like gold. He treated her kids like his own. He made it so she didn't have to worry about anything, or at least he tried to. Joe had been awesome to her, but she definitely had more stress in her life when she was with him than she had now.

*Oh yeah, you're **totally** stress-free now, right?*

The thought jarred Van. If she was honest, she might not stress about the same things now as she did with Joe but she was still stressed. And a lot of her current stress stemmed from her breaking up with Joe. But that didn't mean they needed to be together....did it?

Joe treated you like gold. He treated your kids like his own. He tried to lessen your worries. Be real; the only difference between Joe and Grant is that Grant is a millionaire and Joe isn't. Whatever you might feel for Grant can't come close to what you felt for Joe, and you know it.

Just face it; you chose money over love. And what's worse, you used your kids as an excuse to do it.

The internal reminder stung so much it actually made Van flinch. She rubbed her arms self-consciously as she glanced around her, even more relieved that she was home alone. She'd gotten good at justifying her actions, but she had to accept that she'd shown herself to be the kind of woman she always despised, and that she preached against to her daughter. Shame made tears spring to her eyes and blur everything around her.

Slowly easing onto her side on the couch, Van just stared ahead of her, her hand gripping the decorative couch pillow under her head. She'd made such a mess of things, and something told her that no matter how much she apologized or how much time passed, not all of it could be cleaned up.

Chapter 14

• • • •

GRANT COULDN'T REMEMBER the last time he'd had a more frustrating day. So many things had gone wrong, and it wasn't even noon yet.

"Mr. McCallister, Marty wants to speak with you and he says it's urgent," Rita, his secretary, announced over the intercom.

Resisting the urge to groan out loud, Grant sighed as he pressed the button to respond. Marty was the head of his legal team so he knew whatever this was about couldn't be good. "Go ahead and put him through, Rita."

"Grant, I hope you have some time because there's something we need to make you aware of," Marty announced as soon as he was connected.

"Where are you?" Grant asked.

"I'm on my way over there now. I'll be there in ten."

"I'll be in my office."

Briefly rubbing his temples, Grant braced himself for whatever this latest urgent issue was just as his business cell phone rang.

"Yeah, Sheri," Grant answered, turning to his computer as it pinged multiple times with incoming emails.

"We have a little problem," Sheri greeted him.

"Of course," Grant muttered. "What is it?"

"Mr. Benton's flight from Japan was delayed. I just found out when I came to pick him up from the airport. And Mrs. Perry refuses to reschedule the meeting because of it."

Resisting the urge to curse out loud, Grant just shook his head. "I'll deal with her. Thanks for letting me know."

He disconnected the call with Sheri with one hand and reached for his desk phone with the other.

"Rita, get me Mrs. Perry on the phone," Grant ordered.

"Right away, sir."

Grant had a huge deal riding on this meeting and he wasn't about to see it fall through just because some entitled executive's wife was feeling herself a little too much and being stubborn. Her husband had only given her an executive position because she was bored and wanted something to do with herself. Grant wasn't about to tolerate her wasting his time like this.

"Mrs. Perry," Grant greeted once Rita connected their call. He paused, listening. "Oh, you won't think it's very good to hear from me if we can't work out this little issue I hear you have with our meeting later today."

The rest of Grant's morning went like this, with one crisis after another, and it only died down marginally as the day progressed. Days like this certainly weren't anything new, but today everything just seemed to aggravate him more than usual. But a much-needed bright spot came when he got a call from his mother.

"Mama, you are right on time," Grant breathed as soon as he picked up his phone.

"Why you say that? What's wrong?"

"Ugh, nothing for you to worry about. Just one of those days at work, that's all. No sense in complaining."

"You sho' right about that, baby. You the big man in charge so all that headache comes wit' it. But you tough; you can handle it."

"True enough. So what's going on; how are you today?"

"Just got back from getting some groceries; about to put my greens on."

"Aww man! I sure miss your greens," Grant mused, sitting back in his chair and rubbing his bald head. His stomach growled and he remembered he hadn't had anything to eat other than the apple he grabbed on his way out the door that morning. "Can you mail some to me?"

"Or you can bring your behind on up here to South Carolina and get some," Bernice scolded, though Grant could tell she was smiling. "It's been too long since you came up here for a visit."

"I know you're right. I'm gonna have to fix that. But on another note, I do have some good news."

"Yeah? What's that?"

"Van and I have set a date for the wedding."

"Oh that *is* good news! When is it?"

"January eleventh. The year after next."

"Hmm."

"What?"

"Seems mighty far off. Is there a reason you're waiting so long?"

Grant didn't want to reveal his frustrations about the long wait to his mother, especially since he still believed there was more behind Van's choosing that date than she let on. "Van chose it, actually. I don't know her reasoning. Why do you ask?"

"Something is pricking me about that...like there's something behind that choice that shouldn't be. But if that's what y'all want, I'm happy for you."

Grant frowned, but quickly cleared it. He figured his mother found Van's choice as suspicious as he did. But that was a road he wasn't ready to venture down at the moment. "The date doesn't matter to me; I'd marry Van tomorrow. But I know she wants a nice wedding so I can wait. I'm just glad we're moving towards it."

"You certainly sound happy about this one. I don't even remember the last time I've met one of your lady friends, let alone heard you even mention marrying one of 'em. Now you're all over the moon about this Van."

"Hey, what can I say...she's the one," Grant admitted with a smile. "I knew it as soon as I saw her."

"She must be pretty."

"She's beautiful, but that wasn't all that attracted me to her. She just had this aura...almost a glow around her. And she was so shy and hesitant to get to know me at first..."

"She was playing hard to get?"

"No, not at all," Grant quickly clarified. He didn't want his mother thinking Van was the type of woman to play games. "Nothing like that. Truth be told, she was with her cousin the night we met, and her cousin took quite a liking to me...she didn't want to step on her toes."

"Oh. Okay well yeah, I can understand that."

Grant knew he was leaving quite a few things out, like the main reason Van was hesitant towards him at first. She was with Joe, but Grant had pursued her, anyway. And he used her cousin Raven to help him get closer to her. Grant knew his mother wouldn't approve of his methods to get with Van so he chose to keep that to himself. He knew he'd never hear the end of it.

There was a brief pause before Bernice spoke again. "Baby, I wanna ask you something..."

"What's that?"

"Are you absolutely sure you're ready for all this? Getting married, being a father to kids that ain't yours-"

"As far as I'm concerned, they're mine," Grant interjected. "It's not like their biological father is in the picture; he passed away years ago. They barely remember him."

"So Van's been raising those babies by herself all this time up until she met you? Wow, me and her got more in common than I thought."

Grant felt horrible. He hated lying to his mother, even if it was a lie of omission.

"I wouldn't say she was *totally* by herself," Grant replied, figuring he should give Joe his due credit even if he wasn't naming him directly. "She had some help. But they've got me now and I've got them, and honestly Mama, I couldn't be happier. So in answer to your question, yes, I'm absolutely sure I'm ready."

"I know you usually make good decisions, baby, so don't get upset with me..."

"Of course not."

"But I just want you to be absolutely, *positively* sure. Without a doubt in your mind. Marriage is supposed to be a serious, lifelong thing and folks today don't respect that; the slightest little bump in the road and they're running to divorce court. Or, they don't take the time to get to know each other and build a foundation before rushing down the aisle, not knowing the difference between infatuation - or just plain lust - and real love. All of this just seemed to come out the blue; I had never even heard of Van, then you up and call me one day sayin' you about to marry her. I'd like to think you know what you're doing; I just had to be sure you know what you're getting into."

"I know, Mama. And I do appreciate your concern but believe me, I would never have asked Van to be my wife if I wasn't sure she was the one I wanted to spend the rest of my life with. Trust me, I absolutely take marriage seriously. *That's* why you haven't really heard me mention anyone over the years; if I know a woman isn't the one, I'd rather not waste my time. But Van is."

"She ain't pregnant or nothin', is she?"

"No, ma'am," Grant replied, trying to hide his amusement to what he knew was a serious question.

Bernice was quiet for a few moments, as if she was pondering his words. Of her two children, Grant was the one that tended to think first and act second, as opposed to his younger sister Gabrielle, who was pretty much the opposite. If Grant said he was sure, Bernice knew she could take that to the bank.

"Well that's all that needs to be said, then," Bernice concluded with a smile in her voice. "I'm so happy for you, baby...your voice just changes whenever you talk about her. I can tell from up here she got you."

Grant laughed, unable to deny it. "Guilty as charged."

"Well I know it's the middle of the day and you need to get back to work, so I'm gonna let you go now," Bernice said. "Don't let those folks upset you so much...whoever gets on your nerves for the rest of the day, fire 'em."

Grant laughed louder at that. Talking to his mother had been just what he needed; she always cheered him up.

"If I did that, I wouldn't have much of a business left, Mama," Grant finally replied when he calmed down. "I can't just fire everybody who annoys me."

"Why can't ya? You the boss, ain't you?"

Grant shook his head, still chuckling. "I love you, Mama."

"I love you too, baby."

"You need anything?"

"No, I'm okay."

"You been taking your medicine?"

"Yeah, I took it."

"Good. Well, I'll talk to you soon; I have a meeting coming up in a few minutes."

"Okay. Oh, before I forget, make sure you call your sister sometime soon to check on her; she was crying 'bout that boy again."

"I'll try to give her a call tonight," Grant assured her, making a mental note. "Bye, Mama."

"Bye, baby."

Grant didn't leave the office until after six in the evening, delegating several things to his staff. He just wanted to get home to his family and forget about his horrid work day as much as he could. He had gotten Mrs.

Perry to reconsider about rescheduling their meeting, and it was going to be first thing in the morning. He would have to do a little work in his office at home, but he was anxious to spend a considerable amount of time with Van and the twins. His body was already starting to relax when he got a call from one of his finance executives that killed any good mood he had generated.

"Someone is embezzling money."

"What?!?"

Grant's rage flared the more he listened to how it had been discovered that day that over the past several months, money had been siphoned into some kind of offshore account, going unnoticed due to the small amounts of the transactions. He was assured that they would get to the bottom of who was behind it and contact the proper authorities, but that didn't do much to assuage Grant's anger. He always tried to be good to his employees so to hear that someone was trying to take advantage and steal from him was infuriating.

This was still heavy on Grant's mind when he made it home. He sat in his car for several minutes once he pulled into the garage, trying to clear his head best he could. No matter what went on at work, he always tried to *leave* it at work; he didn't want to bring his problems home with him, especially now that he had a family to come home to. This was often easier said than done considering he was the boss, but he knew it was necessary.

Taking a deep breath, he got out of the car and went on into the house. Cassie and Canton were in the living room; Cassie was watching television and Canton was surprisingly talking on his cell phone, something Grant hadn't seen him do since he bought him the phone months earlier.

"Hey guys," he greeted them. He leaned down and planted a kiss on Cassie's forehead and patted Canton on the shoulder.

"Hi," they chorused obligingly.

"How was your day, Cassie?" Grant asked, since Canton seemed pretty engrossed in his phone conversation. "That's an interesting hairdo."

"Yeah, I was trying something I saw on YouTube," Cassie informed him, patting her long, thick natural hair that was more crinkly than usual and swept to the side, held in place by several sparkly barrettes. It reminded Grant of how some female musicians wore their hair in the 80's. "I don't really like how it turned out, though. I don't think I wet it enough first. And I twisted it too big."

"Yeah? It looks fine to me."

"It's too puffy. Mama already said I'm not wearing it out in public like this."

Grant chuckled. "So you're interested in doing hair?"

"Just *my* hair; I don't want to work in a salon or anything. If I'm gonna be a model and an actress, I'm gonna need to know how to do my own hair, in case those other stylists don't know how to do it right," Cassie declared confidently. "Don't you think so?"

"I suppose," Grant replied amusingly. He loved Cassie's confidence and drive, even though he knew it annoyed Van at times. In a lot of ways, Cassie reminded Grant of himself when he was younger, as far as his determination went. He knew she was going to be successful at whatever she tried to do.

He talked to Cassie for another few minutes before heading upstairs. Once in his bedroom, he sat his briefcase down and was just starting to remove his tie when Van entered.

"Hey, baby; I didn't hear you come in," she greeted him with a smile, immediately going to him and wrapping her arms around his neck.

Grant leaned down and kissed her. "I got here a little while ago. Was downstairs talking to Cassie."

"Oh, you mean Ms. Purple Rain down there? Yeah, she's been experimenting again."

"So I saw," Grant chuckled. "I kind of liked it."

"I bet you did," Van smiled, rubbing her hand over his bald head. "There's no way she's wearing it to school like that. But I don't mind her playing around with it, within reason. Of course she asked if she could experiment with makeup, too."

"And you said no?"

"Of course I said no. She's too young to be wearing makeup."

"Even if it's just around the house?"

"Then she'll be trying to post it on Instagram and all that."

"But you monitor all that, I thought."

"I do. But still. Trust me, you give Cassie an inch with some things and she'll try to take two miles. You have to keep her reined in."

"Hmm." Grant thought that Van was being a little too restrictive with Cassie, as he did on several occasions, but he didn't feel like getting into it right then.

"Was Canton still on the phone when you came in?" Van asked him, loosening his tie the rest of the way and sliding it off.

"Yeah."

"He's been on there more than usual the past couple of days. He used to hardly ever talk on the phone."

"Who is he talking to?"

"He just says it's a friend of his. He never tries to leave the room or anything and the conversations seem to be a lot about school and college and other generic or boy-type stuff so I don't think much of it. It's just interesting to me, is all."

"He's growing up," Grant shrugged. "Before you know it, he'll be bringing some girl home to meet you and asking to borrow my car."

"Ugh, don't even say that!" Van scoffed, but she was smiling. "I can't even imagine my baby doing that because that'll mean he's closer to moving out on his own. I *hate* that thought."

"Well, baby, I hate to say it but it's coming," Grant informed her, tweaking her chin.

"At least Canton will ask to *borrow* your car. Cassie will want us to buy her one of her own as soon as she turns sixteen." They shared a laugh at that, knowing it was the truth.

"The good thing is that then it'll just be the two of us and we can just focus on each other," Grant pointed out, gazing down at her.

Van grinned at him, sliding her arms around his neck again. "Well, that *is* one good way to look at it, huh?"

"I'd say so."

"What if we have another one of our own? Would you want that?"

Grant gazed at her adoringly for a moment before replying, "Creating a child with the woman of my dreams? I'd love nothing more, Van."

He moaned as he claimed her lips again. The kiss was longer and deeper this time, with Grant gathering her tightly in his arms. When they heard Cassie come down the hall, evidently talking to someone on the phone, Van immediately backed up. Grant looked at her curiously but chose not to comment on it, even though he had noticed that Van didn't seem to ever want the twins to see them being affectionate towards each other.

"I left you a plate in the refrigerator, if you're hungry," Van informed him, moving away. "Did you have a good day at work?"

Grant continued to eye her for another moment or two before finally answering, "Uh, it was just another day; nothing to write home about." He didn't feel like getting into everything that happened that day, especially right then. "What about you?"

Van looked at him thoughtfully, then crossed over and closed their bedroom door. "Well...I finally talked to Joe."

Grant was just about to enter their walk-in closet and stopped, turning to look at her with raised eyebrows. "Oh yeah? Today?"

"Earlier this afternoon, yeah."

"How did that go? I'm glad he finally agreed to sit down with you; I know you've wanted that for a while now."

"Well, to be honest, baby, it didn't go as well as I had hoped," Van admitted, taking a seat on the chaise lounge, her leg tucked underneath her. She brushed her bangs out of her eyes. "He's still so angry with me, and I probably didn't do much to help that."

"Wow."

"I mean, am I tripping? Would *you* still be this upset over a breakup after this long?"

Grant removed his cufflinks and set them on the dresser before going to join her on the chaise. He lifted a thoughtful shoulder as he answered, "It's hard to say, Van. Everybody handles and reacts to things differently."

"Grant, it was like he could barely stand the sight of me. I honestly wasn't expecting that."

"Well, babe, he *did* say he hated you."

"But that was *months* ago! I thought he would at least have cooled off *some* by now. It just hurts that he thinks so poorly of me."

"Van, I think you might be underestimating how much he loved you, and how hurt he is," Grant informed her. "And I'm sure the fact that you've moved on so quickly, not to mention that you're *engaged* to the man you left him for, doesn't help things any. Honestly, if I was in his shoes, I can't say I'd be much different. I love you just that much and I can't stand the thought of you being with another man; I'm sure Joe feels the same way."

Van slumped down a little bit. "You mean he *did*. He made it perfectly clear that he doesn't want me anymore."

Grant eyed her. "And you have a problem with that?"

"I can't say I loved hearing it."

"Sounds like you want him to still want you while you get to move on from him."

"No!"

"Then what is it, Van?"

"Grant, I've told you that I'm gonna always love Joe; he was more than just my man, he was my best friend in the world, besides Raven. So I'm sorry if I didn't enjoy hearing him tell me he *doesn't even want my ass anymore*."

"That's what he said?"

"Yes!"

"How did that even come up?"

Van hesitated slightly. "I was asking if there was anything I could do to make things better and mend the rift between us, and his response was for me to leave you and come back to him. Turns out he was just calling my bluff and made sure I knew he didn't really mean it."

Grant frowned, pondering this. He wasn't so sure Joe didn't really mean it; he had a feeling that if Van *really* wanted him back, Joe would take her back, at least eventually. "I see."

"But that's not even the worst thing," Van continued, playing with her nails. "I think he's with somebody else."

Grant's frown deepened. "How is that the *worst* thing?"

"Because I think he's with Raven."

That cleared Grant's frown. "Really? What makes you think that? You saw them together or something?"

"I had gone to see Raven the other day and Joe was there," Van informed him. "And he looked quite comfortable. Neither of them would really tell me anything about the nature of their relationship, but I feel it in my gut that they're more than just friends." Van left out the part about trying to attack Raven and how conflicted she had been about the whole situation ever since.

"I guess I can understand how that might be weird for you, but I think it's a good thing that they have each other."

It was Van's turn to frown. "Well, I'm sorry but I don't think it's a *good* thing. Raven is like a sister to me, and Joe is my ex. That's a *major* girl code violation. You just don't do that."

"Van, they can do whatever they want. And I'm sure you don't want to hear this, but you're really not in much of a position to say anything about it. Especially since you essentially did the same thing when you got with me after I dated Raven."

"So you're saying I'm a hypocrite?"

"Do you think you're wrong for getting with me?"

"No..." Van mumbled, her face flaming slightly.

"Then yes, you're a hypocrite. You're upset at them for doing something you did first."

"Thanks a lot."

"It's just facts."

Van sucked her teeth and looked down and away, her knee bouncing rapidly. "I don't expect you to get it."

"Nah, I get it. What I *don't* get, though, is why it bothers you this much."

"Who said it bothered me?" Van quickly asked, her head snapping up.

"Um, you just called it the worst thing, plus I'm looking at you..."

"Well, you're wrong. No, I don't *like* it, but it's not like it's consuming me. I have other things to worry about. They're just gonna do what they want, anyway. I'm fine, regardless," Van rambled on, averting her eyes.

Grant raised a suspicious brow. "Hmm. If you say so."

"I *do* say so. I mean, I'm sure they had to know that it would upset me a *little*, but whatever. They obviously didn't care. So why should I?"

Grant hoped Van wasn't expecting him to buy this little nonchalant act she was putting on. Any idiot could see that she was bothered about the idea of Joe and Raven being together. And on some level, Grant could understand it. But what worried him was just how deep her concern about it ran, not to mention how hard she was trying to convince him that she *wasn't* concerned. Did seeing Joe with another woman, especially if that woman was her cousin, just make Van miss Joe more? Would it get to the point where she actually wanted him back, if for no other reason so that Raven couldn't have him? Grant knew he was reaching and jumping to some premature conclusions, but he couldn't help it. And he hated this insecure feeling that was suddenly spreading over him.

And he also wondered what Van's response had been when Joe suggested that she go back to him, but surprisingly, he didn't have the nerve to ask.

· · · ·

A FEW HOURS LATER, Van and the twins were asleep and Grant was in his office. He tried to get some work done but couldn't make himself concentrate, which only frustrated him more.

Suddenly remembering he was supposed to call his sister, he glanced at his watch before reaching for the phone. It was rather late but he knew Gabrielle was a night owl.

"Hey, Grant," Gabrielle answered, sniffling.

Grant frowned. "Hey...are you crying?"

"No."

"Don't lie to me."

"Okay, yes."

"What's wrong? Is it because you broke up with your boyfriend?"

"I swear, Mama can't hold water," Gabrielle muttered. "It's a little more to it than that, though; I didn't tell Mama the whole story. He, um...he cheated on me."

"Aww, damn," Grant muttered, instantly infuriated. He hated the thought of anyone mistreating his little sister. "I am so sorry, baby girl. What happened? How did you find out?"

"My girl had shown me some pictures on Instagram of him with some other chick and I confronted him...he tried to play it off but he eventually admitted that they had been fooling around for a while now," Gabrielle tearfully admitted. "Then he said he was sorry but he'd rather be with her."

"And his punk ass couldn't have told you that *before* he started messing with her, huh?"

"I don't know if he would have *ever* told me on his own; if my homegirl hadn't shown me those pictures, I'd probably still be in the dark now."

Grant sighed. "I guess there's some merit to what they say about social media ruining relationships."

"I guess." Gabrielle sniffed again.

"What can I do to make you feel better?"

"Nothing; I'll be okay," Gabrielle assured him. "Thanks for asking, though. I just feel so stupid right now."

"Stop. You have no reason to feel stupid. *He's* the one who stepped out on you, baby girl. This is *his* screw-up and *his* loss. It's a good thing I'm not there or else I'd *definitely* make him pay for this. Matter of fact, I don't even need to be there to do that...what's the punk's name?"

"Grant!"

"Gabrielle."

"Look, I appreciate you having my back; I really, really do, but he's not worth the resources. Let 'em have each other."

"Are you sure?"

"Yeah, I'm sure."

"You're taking this awfully well."

"I mean, I'm upset. I'm hurt. But if I'm honest about it, I can't be too mad at him."

Grant frowned. "Why do you say that?"

There were a few quiet moments before Gabrielle replied, "He wasn't necessarily...well, he wasn't exactly *single* when we met. I didn't care and went after him anyway, and eventually he left the girl he was with and got with me. So I guess I'm just getting what I deserve."

That took the wind out of Grant a little bit, and he sat back in his chair. "Oh...I didn't know that."

"It's not something I'm necessarily proud of, especially now," Gabrielle said, her voice low. "I tried to justify what I did by saying that I was the better woman for him and all that, but at the end of the day, I was still wrong. When he told me he had a girlfriend, I should have just left him alone. But nooo...I wanted him and decided I deserved to have him. I even snuck into his dorm room and...well, I'm sure you don't want to hear that part. But you can probably guess. And now karma is bitch-slapping me for it."

Grant couldn't make himself say anything. The similarity of Gabrielle's situation to his was a little too close for his comfort. "Damn," was all he managed to eventually croak out.

"Yeah, I know," Gabrielle agreed sadly, misinterpreting his tone. "You don't even have to say you're disappointed in me 'cause I already know. I'm sorry, Grant. That's why I didn't tell Mama everything, 'cause I know she'd still be preaching to me right now. But I guess I deserve it, huh?"

Grant wanted to tell her not to beat herself up too much, to keep her head up, or offer her *some* kind of encouragement, but the words just wouldn't come out.

"Grant?" Gabrielle called out after several quiet moments. "You still there?"

"Uh, yeah, I'm here; sorry," Grant mumbled, silently telling himself to get it together. "Look, baby girl, I'm not gonna come down on you about this. We all make mistakes. I just hope you learned something from it."

"Oh yeah, I most definitely did. How you get 'em is how you lose 'em."

A cold shower of shame washed over Grant at his sister's words. He tried to shake it off as he said, "Look...how 'bout I treat you and a couple of your girls to a weekend away somewhere? Wherever you want to go."

"Really?" Gabrielle squealed excitedly. "Are you serious? Even after what I did? I thought you'd be yelling at me right now."

"It's not my place to judge you, Gabrielle. And you clearly already know you... you messed up. I just want to put a smile on your face."

"Oh my gosh, you are the best big brother anybody could want," Gabrielle gushed, happiness overtaking her earlier gloominess. "I still don't think I deserve it but it *would* make me feel better to get away for a couple of days. Thank you *so* much!"

"My pleasure. Just let me know where and when you want to go."

"I will. And can you not tell Mama about all this? Please?"

"I won't say anything."

"Thanks, Grant. I appreciate you listening."

"Always, baby girl."

They ended the call and Grant ran a hand over his bald head before leaning forward in his chair, tapping his pressed hands against his lips thoughtfully. A cold heaviness was still sitting at the pit of his stomach, and he knew it was conviction hitting him with an iron fist. Grant had never told Gabrielle of how he pursued Van while she was still with Joe; in essence, what Gabrielle had done to get her man sounded almost exactly like what Grant had done to get Van. But would the situations end up the same? For the first time, Grant felt truly guilty for everything he did to get him and Van together.

Getting up and walking into their bedroom, he stood over his beautiful fiancée, watching her as she slept peacefully. His eyes wandered to her left hand splayed out on the pillow next to her. The engagement ring Grant had been so eager to give her sparkled in the dim lighting of the room. He thought back to their earlier conversation about Joe, and then Gabrielle's words:

How you get 'em is how you lose 'em.

What goes around *always* comes back around. Grant knew this; he knew it when he was pursuing Van, but he apparently hadn't cared. But now he did. Now, he was officially worried.

Chapter 15

• • • •

JOE HAD BEEN LOOKING forward to seeing Raven all day, and as soon as he left work, he headed straight to her apartment. They hooked up at least once or twice a week and the more Joe was around Raven, the more he liked her. And not just because of the sex; he enjoyed lying around talking or just chilling with her as much as he did sleeping with her. She made him laugh, she listened to him and actually enjoyed his stories from when he was growing up in the hood; she cooked for him even though he kept telling her she didn't have to, and they could sit for hours binge-watching shows on Netflix. She had a way of making him forget about everything else. He sincerely just enjoyed her company.

Raven was feeling the same way about Joe. It actually surprised her how much she thought about him when he wasn't around, and whenever they made plans to meet up, she made sure she was looking her absolute best for him. One thing she loved, though, was that he was just as attracted to her in shorts and a t-shirt as he was when she was dressed to the nines. He actually told her she didn't need makeup; that she was gorgeous without it. And Raven sensed he was being sincere. It was such a relief to not have to 'put her face on' every time she knew he was coming over as she had with every man before him; she could just let loose and be herself. Really, she discovered a whole other side of herself during her time with Joe. He made her feel relaxed...like she didn't have to be 'on' all the time or put on some kind of performance and could just *be*, and she hadn't realized how much she needed or wanted that before. It was freeing.

She rushed to the door when she heard him knock, the anticipatory grin coming instantly.

"Hey there, Sexy Chocolate," she greeted him, her grin widening upon seeing him.

Joe couldn't resist blushing at the nickname Raven had given him. He tried unsuccessfully to suppress his smile. "Hey, yourself."

"Come on in here." Raven reached out and pulled him into the apartment by the front of his shirt. She started to hug him, but he eased back.

"I need to take a shower first," he explained, rubbing his hands up and down her arms. "I came straight from work and I'm all sweaty and dirty and-"

"I don't care," Raven dismissed, lunging forward and wrapping her arms around his neck. And she really didn't, to her surprise; usually, she would have insisted a man go straight to the shower before touching her and possibly getting dirt on her clothes. But that's what washing machines were for. She just wanted Joe's arms around her.

Burying his face in the crook of her neck, Joe held Raven tightly, noticing how she pressed her body against his. He inhaled her decadent scent that reminded him of some kind of pastry, in no hurry to let her go. Eventually he leaned back and took her face in his hands, bringing her lips to his. They kissed softly but deeply, soft moans and smacks of their lips filling the air around them as time seemed to obligingly stand still. Raven's hands rubbed all over Joe's bald head; she loved doing that and he loved when she did it.

"You wanna take a shower with me?" Joe asked her after they finally came up for air. His voice was raspy with desire.

"*Hell* yeah. Just let me check on dinner real quick and I'll be right in."

"I told you you didn't have to make anything on my account. I still have a peanut butter sandwich from lunch."

"Please. You need a *real* meal after a long day at work on that construction site," Raven insisted, running her hands up and down his chest. "And anyway, I...I like cooking for you."

She almost looked shy when she said this, biting her lip and looking at him from underneath her lashes. Joe swallowed as he looked at her, feeling something come over him. "Well, I definitely appreciate it."

"I know you do. That's another reason why I enjoy doing it for you."

They just stood there smiling at each other for a few moments before simultaneously snapping out of it, as if realizing what they were doing.

"Don't take too long, okay?" Joe requested, tweaking her chin.

Blushing and grinning like a girl with a crush, Raven assured him, "Don't worry, I won't."

Joe went into the bathroom while Raven hurriedly took the steaks out of the oven, covered them, and turned off the pots containing the greens and sweet potatoes that she knew Joe loved. She could hear the shower turn on, and Joe was already under the water when she entered the bathroom. Quickly shimming out of the short romper she was wearing, she eased back the shower curtain and smiled devilishly upon seeing Joe's flawless, muscular naked body in front of her. Her arousal went from simmering to blazing in a matter of seconds.

Joe took her hand and helped her inside, and wasted no time backing her against the wall and kissing her with way more fire and intensity than he had at the door. Raven started to panic when she realized she had forgotten to cover her hair, but as Joe continued to kiss her and then grip her breast in his rough hand, she no longer gave a damn. She cursed loudly as Joe kissed his way down her body, taking his time and savoring everything. When he knelt down and helped himself to her wetness, lifting her leg over his shoulder, Raven honestly thought she was going to pass out. Joe never ceased to set her body on fire, and this time was no different. Before too long he had her simultaneously begging for mercy and begging him not to stop.

Without word or warning, Joe stood and picked Raven up. She wrapped her legs around his waist and her arms around his neck, holding tight to him as he entered her, soliciting a sigh of contentment from both of them. They sexed with an increasing pace and intensity, Raven's back against the cool shower wall, her nails digging into his strong shoulders.

"*Yes*, Joe..." she moaned.

"Damn, Raven, you feel *so* good," Joe whispered, his lips against her neck.

"Don't stop."

"You ain't gotta worry about that, baby; trust me."

They sexed until the water ran cold, and it was only then that they quickly bathed and got out, taking things to Raven's bedroom so they could pick up where they left off. Raven made sure to spend a considerable amount of time pleasing Joe, his hisses and curses and grunts of pleasure only making her want to do more. She wanted to give him at least a modicum of the pleasure he was always giving her.

"Raven!" Joe yelled, gritting his teeth as his body stiffened. He glanced down at her as she eagerly pleasured him, giving him some of the best head he'd had in years, if not ever. Her mouth was working in unison with her hands, sucking and stroking, and he felt like he was about to explode. And in the next few seconds, he did exactly that right down Raven's throat, screaming as he practically ripped the sheets off the bed with one hand and grabbed her hair with the other. The orgasm hit him like two Mack trucks.

Raven smirked as she continued to lick him, then ran her tongue around her lips.

"Delicious."

"Girl, you gon' make me...*damn*," Joe breathed. He almost said *you gon' make me fall in love with you*, but he stopped himself. That powerful orgasm must have been scrambling his brain.

"That's the goal," Raven replied softly, kissing his inner thigh. Joe wondered if she somehow knew what he'd been about to say, but figured that was impossible.

"Damn, what time is it?" Joe asked breathlessly a few moments later. Raven had just collapsed next to him.

"I don't know but it's way darker than it was before," Raven chuckled. "Our dinner is probably good and cold now. I can go heat it up if you're ready to eat."

"I can do that," Joe immediately offered, starting to get up.

"No, you will not," Raven protested, placing a hand on his chest. "Just lay there and relax; I'll be right back."

Joe just smiled at her, nodding his thanks. Raven winked at him as she left the bedroom, not bothering to cover herself. Joe's smile widened as he watched her, admiring the view and appreciating her wanting him to rest. He had been kind of tired when he arrived at Raven's but as usual, she made him forget all about that.

Joe heard his cell phone ring, and he started to ignore it, but figured it might be one of his daughters. He quickly climbed off the bed and retrieved his work pants from the armchair in the corner of Raven's bedroom where he'd tossed them earlier, digging his cell phone out of his pocket. He smiled when he saw it was Canton calling.

"Hey, what's up, man?" he greeted him.

"Hey, Joe," Canton replied. "Are you busy?"

"Nah, you're good. What's going on?"

"Can I talk to you about something? It won't take too long; I know you're probably tired from work."

"Don't worry about that, man," Joe assured him. "You know you can talk to me about whatever. What's on your mind?"

"Okay. Well, I'm still a little mad at Ma," Canton admitted. "I tried to start being nicer to her like you told me to, but I still don't really have all that much to say to her."

"Why do you think that is? You still upset about me and her not being together?"

"A little."

"What else is it?"

"I don't know if I can explain it...things are just *different* now and I can't make myself really like it. *Ma* is different; she said that we moved in with Mr. McCallister to have a better life but she's still all tense and stuff like she was before; *she* doesn't seem any happier. And she doesn't even cook! We have takeout most of the time. She used to actually cook for us but now it's like just because she has more money, she doesn't even bother."

Joe searched for the proper way to respond. "Canton...look. I'm sure your mama has her reasons for that, just like I'm sure there are reasons she still seems stressed. But I'm sure she probably doesn't want you worrying about that; the best thing you can do is be the good, obedient son she always knew you to be. I'm sure if you went back to how you acted before you all moved over there, that would be one less thing for her to stress about."

"I guess."

"Trust me. Always do your best to make things as easier on your mama as you can, and that means watching how you act and staying on top of your schoolwork, and helping out around the house as much as possible, without them having to tell you to. You remember how when I saw something broken or dirty or whatever, I just took care of it without asking if she needed me to do it? I'm gonna need you to do that the best you can."

"Yes, sir."

"And speaking of your schoolwork, are you still back on track with that?"

"Yes, sir," Canton replied, his voice brightening slightly. "I've been getting A's on all my tests, and I do my homework every day. I'm supposed to be getting a progress report in a couple of weeks."

"I want to see that when you get it," Joe informed him. "But I'm proud of you for turning things around, man, for real. I understand you were disappointed about some things but you still have to handle your business. That's what a real man does, and that's what I want you to grow up to be. You understand?"

"Yes, sir; I get it. I'm gonna be a real man just like you are."

That made Joe grin, as well as filled him with a sense of pride. He knew Canton looked up to him as a father figure, but he never really thought he'd want to emulate him, considering how different they were; Joe was a rough and tumble, dirt-under-your-fingernails kind of guy who cared enough about school to try his best but he could never say he loved it. Canton could; a lot of people might have described him as preppy or even a nerd. Joe and Canton didn't even have a lot of similar interests; really, Joe thought Canton would have immediately taken to Grant since the two of them seemed so much more alike. But

Joe found the fact that Canton looked up to him so much extremely, extremely flattering.

"I appreciate that, man, thank you," Joe replied, the smile still on his face. "A real man also respects authority, so make sure that you respect both your mama and Grant. Ask your mama about her day and if there's anything you can do to help her out when she gets home from work...try to get to know Grant. You might find that you actually like the dude more than you think you do."

"Ehh," Canton grunted, and Joe had to suppress a chuckle. "I don't see it happening, but I'll do that if you tell me to."

"It *won't* happen if you keep telling yourself it won't. You've gotta change your mindset, man. Grant isn't a bad guy."

"Nah, he's not," Canton admitted.

"See there? Think positively, man...you've got it pretty good over there. I know you wish things could be like they were, but that's just not how it turned out. Things change and sometimes all you can do is roll with it. But you've got *way* more good stuff in your life than you do bad stuff."

"That's true. Some of my friends don't even have lunch money sometimes; I share mine with them."

"I'm proud of you for that. And I want you to remember your friends' situation the next time you want to complain about something. Be thankful for what you have, and appreciate your mama and Grant wanting to take the best care of you and Cassie. Okay?"

"Yes, sir. I understand that."

"Good."

"I appreciate the advice, Joe, and you talking to me. I actually do feel better."

"Anytime, man. No thanks necessary."

"Are you still going to take me to your construction site?"

"If it's cool with your mama, I absolutely will."

"Awesome!"

Joe smiled, still blown away that Canton even wanted to do that. "You got anything else you want to talk about? Anything else on your mind?"

"No, that was it. I should probably go and finish my homework."

"Yeah, most definitely do that. We'll talk later."

"Yes, sir. Bye, Joe."

"Bye, man. Love you."

"Love you, too."

Joe hung up the phone and smiled as he turned it around in his hands thoughtfully. He really hoped Van let Canton hang out with him because he missed him something terrible; but he was glad that they could at least talk and that Canton still missed him enough to seek out his advice. It was an incomparable feeling knowing he, plain ol' Joe, could have such a positive influence on a young man's life like that. Especially a young man as intelligent and with as much potential and promise as Canton. He felt warm as he sat there already mentally replaying their conversation, still smiling.

Right outside the door, Raven stood with a plate in each hand, sporting a wistful smile of her own. She hadn't intended to eavesdrop on Joe's conversation, but when she came down the hall and heard him talking on the phone, obviously to Canton, she couldn't make herself retreat to the living room. She heard how he checked on how Canton was doing in school, and encouraged him to improve his relationship with Van and Grant, which Raven knew couldn't have been easy for him. The love and concern in Joe's voice for Canton was evident, and it warmed Raven's heart. The more she stood there listening, the more attracted she felt herself becoming to Joe. She already knew he was a good man, but hearing him put his personal feelings aside like that for Canton's sake made her see him in a whole new light. Joe, in his own words, hated Van, but you would have never been able to tell that from his conversation with Canton. Raven bit her lip as a non-sexual attraction towards Joe made her almost as tingly as his tongue had when it was between her legs in the shower. She tried to shake it off, simply because it was unfamiliar, but realized she couldn't.

And if she was honest with herself, she didn't mind that.

• • • •

AS CANTON WAS TALKING to Joe, Cassie was talking to Van about their upcoming birthday.

"I really wanna do it *big*, Mama," Cassie emphasized, spreading her arms wide. "*Way* bigger than last year and the year before that."

Van, really not in the mood to talk about this, sighed as if she was already tired of the conversation. "Why is that necessary, Cassie? You should be satisfied with whatever we do for you."

"But Mama, we're turning *twelve*! That's a big deal!"

"*Every* birthday you get to see is a big deal, Cassie, but that doesn't mean you need a huge blowout party for it. Especially when probably the only reason you want one is so you can show off."

"Show off??' Cassie exclaimed as if she was actually insulted. "Why you say that?"

"It's why *do* you say that, and you know full well what I'm talking about. Every time you get something new, you go running trying to post it on Instagram. That comes off as you flaunting what you have and trying to rub it in folks' face."

"That's not what I be doing!"

"That's not what *I'm* doing," Van corrected. "And yes it is."

"Well, what's wrong with being proud of what I have? I *like* having nice things for a change," Cassie defended.

Van felt that was an insult, whether Cassie had meant it to be one or not. It was no secret that Van hadn't been able to afford many extras before getting with Grant; pretty much anything that wasn't a necessity was out of the question. Canton had accepted that, but Van knew Cassie resented it. She remembered one night overhearing Cassie complain to Canton about how Van never had any money when she asked her for anything, and she made it clear that she didn't want to live like Van when she grew up. That had stung Van then, and it didn't feel much better remembering it now.

"Get this straight, Cassie," Van said, closing the magazine she had been reading and sitting forward in her seat. "We only *have* to get you the necessities; food, clothing, a roof over your head...that kind of stuff. Anything else is a bonus. Now, we've had this talk already. Please don't make the mistake of thinking you're entitled to the cute shoes and the phones and the hair accessories, 'cause I can *definitely* make sure those things stop coming."

Cassie's eyes widened in horror. "Seriously??"

"Yes, seriously."

"Mama!!"

"What?"

"I don't see why you're being so mean about this! All I did was say I wanted a big birthday party!"

"Yeah, you're *always* talking about what you want. But not once do you ever ask what anybody else wants or if you can help them with anything. What does your brother want to do? It's gonna be his birthday, too. Have you even thought about that?"

"I figured we could just have our own different parties like we did last time."

"I bet you did. But it's not always about you, Cassie."

"I haven't even really been asking for stuff recently like I used to," Cassie reminded her. She remembered her talk with Raven and even though there had been a few things she wanted to ask Van or Grant to get for her, Cassie had been trying to heed Raven's advice about appreciating what she already had and not being so greedy. "You haven't noticed that?"

"And did you do that hoping we would grant your wish for a big party now?"

"No!"

"Excuse me?"

"No ma'am! That wasn't why I stopped asking for stuff! You said to be grateful for what I already have and that's what I was doing! I don't get any credit for that?"

"Credit?? Look, Cassie-"

"What's going on?" Grant appeared in the living room, his briefcase in his hand. A slight frown of concern marred his face as he looked back and forth between the dueling mother and daughter.

"Hi, sweetie," Van greeted him, slightly taken aback. "I didn't hear you come in."

"Yeah, I'm not surprised...I could hear you two from the other room." Grant set his briefcase by the couch and went over to give Van a kiss. He was aiming for her lips but she turned her head slightly so his kiss landed on her cheek. His frown deepened but Van just subtly jerked her head towards her daughter. Not wanting to get into it in front of Cassie, Grant again let it go for the time being.

"Hey, Grant!" Cassie greeted excitedly when he walked over to her, seemingly oblivious to the little exchange he and Van just had. Cassie wrapped her arms around Grant's waist and accepted his kiss to the top of her head before looking up at him pleadingly. "I'm glad you're here!"

"Really?" Grant replied with an arched brow. "And why is that?"

"I've been trying to tell Mama that I wanted a big, huge party for my birthday this year," Cassie explained. "I mean,

I'm turning twelve! But Mama is acting like she doesn't want to do it! But *you'll* let me have it, right?"

Grant looked over at Van, who was staring at him with a look that warned him not to override her again. He'd learned his lesson on that, but he honestly wouldn't have minded giving both Cassie and Canton whatever kind of birthday party they wanted, within reason. He would talk to Van privately about why she was apparently so against it, but for now, he knew he had to have her back.

"If your mom says you can't have it, then that's just what it is, Cassie," Grant informed his future stepdaughter, gently squeezing her shoulder.

Cassie, clearly not having expected that response, pouted dramatically. "Really??"

"Yes, really."

"But-"

"Cassie, look here-"

"Go to your room, Cassie," Grant instructed sternly, sensing that Van was about to go off. He shot Van a look before looking down at Cassie and giving her shoulder another squeeze. "Your mom and I will discuss this."

"You gonna get her to change her mind?"

Van was about to lunge off the couch towards her daughter, but Grant quickly stopped her, putting himself between them.

"Go, Cassie," he ordered, his eyes on Van. "Now."

With an exaggerated huff, Cassie stomped off towards the stairs, her arms folded tightly against her budding chest. Van angrily looked after her, then up at Grant, who was still eying her.

He wanted to address the problem she seemed to have with showing him affection in front of the kids.

She mentally noted how he didn't check Cassie for her attitude, like Joe would've done.

Before either of them could say anything to each other, though, Canton wandered in with a thoughtful expression on his face. Van immediately set her magazine aside and turned to her son in concern, deciding she and Grant could discuss Cassie later.

"Hey, guys," Canton greeted them both.

"Hey, baby," Van replied, trying to gage his expression. He didn't seem as apathetic as he usually did.

"How's it going, Canton?" Grant asked him, taking a seat next to Van on the couch. "You all right?"

"Yes, sir," Canton replied politely. He almost looked nervous as he dug the tip of his sneaker into the carpet. "Do y'all have a minute?"

"Of course!" Van responded immediately. She patted the empty spot next to her on the couch. "You wanna sit down?"

"That's okay; I have a lot of homework to do." He pushed his glasses further onto his nose and continued. "I just wanted to come down here and apologize for how I've been acting, and for how I was slacking off at school. That was wrong and I shouldn't have done it. It won't happen again."

Van forgot all about her frustration with Cassie and her eyes started filling with tears at her son's words. He sounded like her sweet little boy that he had always been. She opened her arms to him, and was thrilled when he didn't hesitate to go to her. Holding him to her tightly, she closed her eyes and said a silent prayer of thanks.

"Thank you so much for saying that, baby; it really means a lot to us," she said to her son, still holding him. Leaning back, she held his face in her hands; he was looking more like his father Calvin the older he got. "So you're feeling better about things, then?"

"Yes, ma'am. I just realized I have a lot more than some other kids and I should be thankful. Plus, I don't want to keep slacking off and mess up my chances of getting into my dream college. Do y'all forgive me?"

Grinning as if she had won the lottery, Van couldn't resist pulling her son in for another tight hug. She was so grateful that Canton seemed to be back to his old self and that was one less thing she would have to worry about.

"Of *course* we do!" she assured him, rubbing his back.

"Absolutely," Grant concurred. He reached out to shake Canton's hand when Van finally let him go. Looking at his intelligent future stepson proudly, he added, "That was a very mature thing of you to do, Canton. And we really do appreciate it."

"Thanks, Mr. McCallister."

"You know you can just call me Grant, right?"

"Yes, sir. I will, when I'm comfortable."

"Understood," Grant nodded, not wanting to push him on that. "Well, I'm really glad to hear you're feeling better; I know all of this has been a big transition for you. Just know you can come talk to us whenever you have something on your mind or if you have questions about anything at all; I'm here for you just like your mother is."

"Thank you," Canton replied, even though he knew he still wasn't quite to the point where he felt comfortable confiding in Grant. His now-regular talks with Joe is what got him back on track and what changed his outlook about things. Canton liked Grant okay, but he would never replace Joe. "I'm gonna go finish my homework now, if that's okay."

"Of course."

Canton nodded at both of them politely before turning to leave the room. Van gave him a gleeful pat on the back before he walked off, then turned to Grant, the grin still on her face.

"How great was that??" she gushed, a hand on her chest.

"Yeah, I know," Grant agreed. "Can't say I was expecting that."

"Me, either. I noticed his attitude had been a little better lately but I didn't really expect an apology. He seems to be back to his old self and that is *such* a relief."

"I bet it is," Grant replied, rubbing her leg.

Van looked at him appreciatively. Grant wasn't saying it, but Van suspected that he was the one behind Canton's about-face in attitude. He'd been saying he would talk to the twins about their respective behavior issues, and Van had (reluctantly) agreed, but she didn't know if or when he actually did it. But now, she knew he must have.

Unable to resist, Van grabbed Grant's face and laid a deep kiss on him, her emotions getting the best of her for the moment. She'd gone from incredibly angry and frustrated with Cassie to immensely appreciative and proud of Canton, and she couldn't resist showing Grant her appreciation. He'd been saying for months how he wanted to help more with the twins in other ways besides financial ones, and this was just more proof that she could trust him to do that.

"I love you *so* much," she told him, looking right into his eyes. "Thank you for everything you did."

Grant, not sure what she was referring to but appreciating the sentiment nonetheless, smiled at her. "It's what I'm here for, babe. And I love you, too."

Van hated to bring her good mood down, but she knew she had to go deal with Cassie. Laying one more peck on her fiancé's lips, she ran her hands through her hair and stood up. "Now if we can just get this stubborn daughter of mine on track..."

"We will," Grant assured her, standing himself. "You about to go talk to her now?"

"Yeah. Might as well."

"Want me to come with you?"

"I got it. Plus, you look like you have some work you need to do," Van observed, motioning towards his briefcase.

"It can wait if it needs to."

"No, it's fine. Go on and do your work. But keep an ear out for any screaming," Van half-joked, turning to leave the room.

Grant just chuckled, shaking his head.

On her way up to Cassie's room, Van told herself to stay calm and try to keep something of an open mind. It wasn't that she minded the twins having a big birthday party; their tenth birthday party had been a blowout, with a basketball gym being converted into a playland complete with a bunjee run, laser tag, a dunking booth, obstacle courses, and much, much more, not to mention more food and gifts than the twins could have imagined. That had all been a surprise courtesy of Grant (and Raven), and Van had been over the moon about it, even though part of her was a little bummed that she hadn't been able to do something like that for them herself. The twins had absolutely loved it, and Van had to figure that it wasn't terribly unreasonable for them to want something as big or bigger as they got older. Canton never asked for much, but Cassie had always been over-the-top, and Van certainly knew that. So she told herself to remember that and keep her cool as she opened the door to Cassie's room.

Cassie was in front of the mirror, a dress in one hand and some jeans in the other, alternating holding them in front of her. Her facial expression showed pure concentration, as if she was pondering a major life decision. Van just stood and watched her for a moment; her little girl was growing up right in front of her eyes. Just as much as Cassie was stubborn and loud and flashy, she was also determined and confident and secure in herself, which was more than Van could say about herself when she was Cassie's age. Van had dealt with self-esteem issues for years coming up, but, at least to her knowledge, Cassie never had those issues. She was often *over*-confident, much like her father Calvin had been. Van had always been closer to Canton, personality-wise.

Snapping out of her musings, Van fully entered the room and closed the door behind her. Cassie was so engrossed in what she was doing that she didn't even notice her mother at first. She actually screamed when Van tapped her on the shoulder.

"Oh my *gosh*, Mama!" Cassie exclaimed dramatically. "Why are you sneaking up on me like that??"

"Nobody is sneaking up on you. Though you *do* need to learn to be more aware of your surroundings. What are you doing?"

"Deciding what I'm wearing to school tomorrow."

"Oh. Well, come over here and sit down; we need to talk about that little episode in the living room."

"What episode?" Cassie asked, as if she had already forgotten about the whole birthday conversation.

"The latest episode of the Cassie Chronicles."

Cassie's face lit up, either not realizing or not caring that Van was being facetious. "Oooh! That would be a *good* name for my own show, too! It could be about my life and-"

"Cassie, you know good and well I wouldn't let you have any kind of TV show. That's-"

"It could be an *online* show! All I have to do is-"

"Forget it! And anyway, that's not what this conversation is about. I was referring to that little tantrum you threw in the living room over your birthday party."

"Oh," Cassie sucked her teeth as she plopped down onto her oversized light gray beanbag chair. "What about it?"

Van looked at her incredulously. "What do you mean, *what about it*? You don't have *anything* to say for how you acted?"

"Did Grant get you to let me have the party?"

Van's jaw dropped. "No, he did not."

Sucking her teeth again, Cassie just played with the ends of her long hair.

"Cassie, you *really* need to check yourself. I sincerely cannot believe you're acting like this."

"I don't really see what I'm doing wrong. All I wanted was a big birthday party. You did one for us when we turned ten."

Van remembered that the twins still didn't know that party was thanks to Grant and Raven, not her. "Yes, because you and Canton had never had anything like that before. And it's not that I don't want you to enjoy your birthday. My problem is your attitude about it, baby...you act like all you have to do is snap your fingers and your wish is supposed to be our command. It doesn't work like that."

Cassie looked at her mother. "So what am I supposed to do, then?"

"Some things you have to *earn*, Cassie. Like if you audition for a show or something, you have to do what it takes to prepare for it. If you want that new pink iPhone or whatever else, do some extra stuff around here...Grant and I will pay you for that and you can buy it yourself. And if you want a big party, Cassie, you earn one by being respectful and obedient and grateful for everything that you have. I don't reward foolishness, and that's all I've been getting from you recently. Your attitude needs a *major* adjustment before I spend that kind of money on you for something you don't need."

"Why can't you just use Grant's money, then?"

Van frowned. "Excuse me??"

"Why can't Grant just pay for everything?"

"Girl…" Van took a deep breath, telling herself to keep it together. "You are missing the *entire* point. Where the money comes from is irrelevant. What I'm saying is that with the way you've been acting lately, you don't *deserve* a party. At this rate, you'll be lucky if we take you to Burger King."

This time, Cassie's jaw dropped. Van was amazed that she couldn't seem to even remotely grasp what she was trying to tell her.

"You're a smart girl, Cassie. I *know* you understand what I'm saying."

Looking at her mother as if *she* was the one spouting foolishness, Cassie just shook her head. "Can I ask you something, Mama?"

"Yes."

"What's the point of you even being with Grant if we all can't spend his money? Wasn't that why we moved in here in the first place?"

Fire heated Van's body to the point she felt she would burn a hole in the bed she was sitting on if she didn't get up off of it. She shot up, wringing her hands together to avoid slapping her spoiled daughter across the face.

"How 'bout this," she seethed through gritted teeth, "We don't celebrate your birthday *at all*?"

Cassie gaped at her in horror. "Are you serious?? Is that a joke???"

"I'm dead serious and I'm not joking even a little bit. Your mouth just got any and all birthday plans for you *cancelled*."

"But that's not fair! What about Canton!"

"Oh, *Canton* is still getting a celebration because he actually came and *apologized* to both me and Grant for the way he's been acting, and even before that, he wasn't giving me *half* as much trouble as you do. And his attitude has gotten better recently. If anything, yours has gotten worse." Van turned to leave the room.

"But-"

"Save it," Van cut her off, holding her hand up. "I've been warning you over and over, and apparently you didn't take me seriously. Well, I can show you better than I can tell you. You can act like a little spoiled brat if you want to, Cassie, but I promise you won't be getting *anything* else from me *or* Grant that you don't absolutely need until you straighten up. And that *includes* a birthday party. You only have yourself to blame for it."

She left the room, closing the door on her daughter's horrified face. She didn't feel guilty in the least about her decision; she actually felt at peace with it. Her daughter needed to learn a lesson and apparently it was going to take something drastic to teach it to her.

Grant was on a phone call when Van stormed into his office, but she immediately slowed down when he held up a *give me a minute* finger. She started to leave the room, but he motioned her towards the loveseat in the corner of the room. She took a seat, her mind already replaying her conversation with Cassie. She didn't even realize when Grant sat down next to her.

"I take it the talk with Cassie didn't go well," Grant surmised, looking at her.

"To say the least."

"What happened?"

"Long story short, Cassie isn't getting any kind of birthday celebration this year."

Grant's eyebrows shot up in surprise. "What? Why?"

Van didn't necessarily want to tell Grant what Cassie said, when she questioned the whole point of Van being with him if they couldn't spend his money. "Her attitude just hasn't gotten any better, and I'm tired of it. She apparently thinks she can do or say whatever she wants and still get her way, and I need to show her it's not going down like that."

Grant peered at her before rubbing his hands together thoughtfully. "I see."

Noting his reaction, Van asked, "You disagree with that?"

"Would it matter?"

Van gaped at him. "Of course it would matter!"

"I ask that, Van, because I've gotten the notion that when it comes to the twins, *your* word is always the final one, regardless of what I think."

Gasping, Van exclaimed, "That's not true at all!"

"That's a separate issue for another time, but if you say my opinion will be taken into consideration, I'll give it to you. While I get where you're coming from with the punishment, I don't think cancelling Cassie's birthday festivities completely is the solution."

"So what *is* the solution?"

"Still acknowledge it but make it really, really simple. Get a cake or some cupcakes or something, a couple of her friends, one or two *small* gifts at the most...make her see she doesn't need extravagance to enjoy herself, but we still want to celebrate her being here another year."

Considering his words, Van could admit it wasn't a bad idea. "I get it," she admitted after a few moments, "But she doesn't deserve any gifts."

"I'm not talking about anything big, Van."

"It doesn't matter, Grant. It can be her birthday without her getting gifts."

Grant sighed. While he didn't think Cassie should get away with how she'd been acting (even though it bothered Van more than it did him), he also believed that every child deserved *some* kind of birthday celebration.

"I see we're at yet another impasse," Grant finally said, rubbing his bald head.

"I know you love Cassie and you like to spoil the people you love, Grant, but Cassie needs to learn a lesson. And she's not gonna do that if we just give her a smaller-scale version of what she's asking for."

"You're obviously not giving me any credit," Grant mused, looking at her. "I may not have any kids of my own but I'm not totally clueless when it comes to dealing with them."

"I-I wasn't trying to imply that."

"How about you just trust me on this? Can you please leave everything to me in regards to the twins' birthday? I bet you a diamond necklace that you won't be disappointed."

To her surprise, Van felt the tension immediately start leaving her body. Grant had proven that he could be trusted with many things, so there was no reason to think he couldn't be trusted with this. He knew her stance and how strongly she felt about it, so she would just try to relax and leave it up to him as he asked. And it would be nice to have one less thing to worry about.

"Okay," she conceded, giving him a small smile. "I can do that. But you know I don't need a diamond necklace, satisfied or not. I *will* bet you a two-hour massage, though."

"Oh, I *got* you on that," Grant insisted, pulling her to him. "I might mess it up on purpose just to have an excuse to rub oil all over you."

Van laughed, playfully hitting Grant in the chest. She gazed at him, reaching up to briefly graze his cheek with her fingertips. "I already feel better, baby. Thank you so much."

Grant hugged her to him, resting his cheek on top of her head. "No thanks necessary. I told you, that's what I'm here for."

Sighing in contentment, Van snuggled closer to her handsome fiancé. "Are you going to talk to Cassie like you did Canton, though, before the party?"

"What?"

"Are you going to have a talk with Cassie like you did with Canton?"

Leaning back slightly, Grant looked down at her, confused. "What are you talking about?"

Frowning in confusion herself, Van clarified, "I thought the reason Canton came and apologized to us was because you had a talk with him about how he's been acting."

"I wish I could take credit for that, baby, but no, I didn't."

"Are you sure?"

"I'm positive. He apparently came to that realization on his own."

Van peered at him for another moment or two before resting her head back on his chest, her brow furrowed in thought. Canton realizing he needed to make amends for his behavior on his own was possible, but something told Van that wasn't the case. She had assumed Grant was behind it, but she knew there was really only one person that could make Canton do such an about-face, and that person was Joe. She recalled Canton's recent phone activity, and suspected that was who he had been talking to during those times. Van had suggested a while back that Canton call Joe, and apparently he'd been taking her advice. Canton's behavior had been way better since he and Cassie spent that weekend with Raven while Van and Grant were in Savannah, and now Van wondered if Joe had been at Raven's then, too.

The more Van thought about it, the more she was sure that Joe was behind Canton's attitude adjustment. And despite herself, the more she thought about that, the more she found herself missing him.

Chapter 16

• • • •

JOE WAS ON CLOUD NINE. He was all moved into his new apartment and he couldn't have been happier. It had been years since he had his own place; when he met Van, he was living in his cousin's basement. Before that, he was living with Tanisha. It felt good to be in his own space with his own things; he really felt like things were finally starting to look up for him.

He had gotten a nice two-bedroom apartment close enough to Tanisha's that he could be near his girls, but not so close that he had to worry about Tanisha just popping up on him whenever. Speaking of Tanisha, she was *not* happy about him getting his own apartment; when he told her he signed the lease on one, she threw a major fit. Joe hadn't told her about his plans to get an apartment until it was done, trying to avoid any extra drama. It just made him all the more glad that he had his own place he could retreat to instead of wasting money on hotels when he didn't want to spend the night at Tanisha's.

The smile was still on his face as he wandered through the apartment, even touching things occasionally as if not believing they were there. It might not have seemed like a lot to some, but Joe hadn't grown up with much; his youth was spent either getting into trouble or trying to stay out of it, so he didn't put much effort into getting things, not that his mother could have afforded them, anyway. And most of his adulthood was spent living with other people; nothing was ever in his name. Even though the furniture was minimal and there weren't a lot of extras (Joe was not a decorator, plus he hated clutter), everything in that apartment was his. Nothing was borrowed or handed down, and Joe took a lot of pride in that.

His phone chimed in his pocket and when he dug it out, he smiled when he saw it was a text from Raven. He noticed he did that a lot when he thought about her. She'd been more than helpful when he was trying to get organized for his move, and looked so cute in the scarf and shorts she wore on move-in day, which she insisted on being there for, bringing breakfast and juice because she knew Joe had a tendency to skip that particular meal at times. She even got along well with Duke, who was also helping him. Joe had caught himself staring at Raven a few times as she carried boxes in from the truck or checked things off the list she'd made for him. He found that he actually valued her advice, and deferred to her suggestions as to how to arrange what furniture he did have. When everything was done, they just sat on the floor in the living room, eating pizza and watching a baseball game. It was so simple, but it was one of the best times he'd had in a while. He realized he had a lot of those kinds of times with Raven.

There'd been a point in that evening when Joe found himself just gazing at Raven, and he felt something hit him. It was like his whole body warmed up all on its own, and not from sexual arousal. She was sitting in the middle of the floor, a light blue scarf covering her hair, her face devoid of any makeup, a paper plate piled high with pepperoni and sausage pizza between her long legs that were bouncing to a silent beat as she looked up something on her phone, and Joe had never been more attracted to her. In all the years he'd known her, namely the years he'd been with Van, he liked Raven okay but considered her high-maintenance and even kind of stuck-up at times. But he'd been all wrong. The more he got to know her, the more he realized she was anything *but* those things when she trusted someone enough to let her guard down. And it was very, very endearing.

He even talked to his friend Duke about it, wanting to get another perspective.

"So you're feeling her?" Duke had asked.

"I mean...something like that, I guess..." Joe hedged, feeling inexplicably shy. He rubbed the back of his neck. "I can't lie and say I don't *like* her. A lot."

"You think she likes you, too?"

Joe shrugged. "Seems to."

"Then what's the problem? Go for yours, man."

"I don't know, Duke...not that I care about this part, but Van is already tripping about what she thinks is going on between me and Raven. And I certainly don't need any more drama from Tanisha; she's already pissed that I'm in my own spot and won't be staying with her occasionally like I was. And she and Raven have had a run-in before...I just bet if she were to find out I was messing with her, it would just be a repeat of the bullshit I had to put up with when I was with Van."

"So don't tell her."

"She'll find out eventually. And I'm not trying to hide anything, anyway. If Raven and I take it there, it'll be out in the open."

"I feel you on that."

"Plus, I'm not even sure how I would break all this down to my girls, or even Canton and Cassie, for that matter," Joe continued. "They might not understand how I could be with Van all that time and then end up with her cousin."

"I get it, but I don't think you have to worry about that *too* much," Duke assessed. "I mean, it's not like you cheated on Van with Raven or anything shady like that. Plus, you and Van didn't just break up yesterday; it's been months."

"True."

"I will say that I wouldn't bother saying anything to them unless you and Raven decide to *really* be together, though," Duke continued. "I mean, as long as you're still just gettin' down, keep it to yourself. *But* if y'all decide to actually make that move into a relationship, then just sit 'em down and tell 'em the truth. They might have some questions but I don't think it would be anything they won't understand."

Joe nodded, pondering his friend's words. What he was saying made a lot of sense. Joe just had to figure out what it was he wanted to do. He couldn't lie to himself and say his feelings for Raven weren't deepening. But he had no idea how *she* felt; for all he knew, she was satisfied with the way things were. They'd been sleeping together for months, and had a good time together, but Joe had no idea if Raven liked him for anything more than his sexual abilities. Or if she would want to do anything about it if she did. Joe figured maybe he should just leave well enough alone.

• • • •

HEARING HIS CELL PHONE ring in his hand, Joe snapped out of his reverie and looked down to see who was calling him. He sucked his teeth lightly when he saw it was Tanisha.

"Yeah," he answered, hoping this wasn't about some nonsense.

"Hey, Joe," Tanisha greeted him in a surprisingly-polite manner.

"What's up, Tanisha."

"Whatcha doin'?"

"Nothing much."

"You got everything unpacked and stuff already?"

"Yeah."

"Okay. Well, that's cool, I guess. You, um, you still mad at me?"

"For what?"

"For flippin' out like I did when you told me you were moving."

"I don't trip about that anymore, Tanisha. That's what you always do. What freaks me out is when you're being nice, like you are now. What do you want?"

He heard her suck her teeth. "I just wanted to say I was sorry."

Joe arched a skeptical brow. Tanisha didn't just apologize for no reason. "Thanks. Now again, what do you want?"

"What makes you think I want something?"

"Because I know you."

"Okay, well..." Tanisha hedged, figuring she might as well stop acting like Joe wasn't right. "I want you to come over."

"Why?"

"I just want to see you."

"You saw me yesterday."

"So? That ain't today."

"Is something broke over there or something?"

"No..."

"So..."

"I just want to see you," Tanisha said again, slightly exasperated. "I don't have no reason other than that."

Pursing his lips, Joe checked his watch. "Where are the girls?"

"Mama came and got 'em a little while ago; they're spending the night over there."

"Hmm. Let me check something and call you right back."

Tanisha paused, and Joe waited for some kind of sarcastic comment. But she just mumbled, "Okay, then."

They hung up, and Joe leaned his head against the back of the couch, looking up at the ceiling thoughtfully. He wasn't really in the mood to deal with Tanisha, but she seemed to be in one of her rare not-bitchy moods. He actually didn't mind hanging with her when she was like that. Tanisha could be a lot of fun when she wanted to be, but she let her attitude get in the way more often than not.

Joe picked up his phone and sent a text to Raven:

Hey. U gonna be busy tonight?

About ten minutes passed before he got her response:

Unfortunately. I'm gonna be here late; dinner rush is crazy. I'll hit u up when I get home, though.

Slightly disappointed but understanding, Joe just typed a quick 'that's cool' response before sighing. He knew Raven's job as a chef kept her busy most nights, but he'd really hoped she'd be available to meet up later. Whenever they couldn't hook up physically, they would text or talk on the phone well into the night, and Joe had gotten used to that without even realizing it.

Sighing, he called Tanisha back and told her he would be over there in a little while. For some reason, he didn't really want to be by himself right then.

• • • •

JOE ARRIVED AT TANISHA'S an hour or so later, and Tanisha was grinning from ear to ear when she opened the door.

"Damn, you expecting the Publisher's Clearinghouse people or something? Why are you grinning so hard?" Joe asked her as he stepped inside the apartment.

"I can't just be happy to see you?" Tanisha retorted, closing the door behind him. "And I been entering that Publishers Clearinghouse stuff for years and ain't won nothin'. I think it's fake."

"Yeah, tell that to all the people who won," Joe muttered. He glanced around the apartment and it was surprisingly clean; usually there were clothes or soda cans littered around the living room. Tanisha must have straightened up before he got there. She was even wearing some kind of shorts outfit that looked new, showcasing the tattoos on her breasts and arms. Then he noticed something in the air and frowned slightly as he sniffed, trying to place the scent. "What's that I smell?"

"I'm making some spaghetti," Tanisha informed him proudly. "And burning some incense, too."

Joe looked at her, his eyebrows lifted in surprise. "You're actually cooking something?"

"Yep. I can throw down when I want to."

"Hmm."

Joe appreciated the effort, but he didn't really consider spaghetti *throwing down*, especially since he was pretty sure everything came out of a box or a jar. Tanisha was looking proud like she had actually done something, though, and Joe wasn't about to say anything negative and bring down the rarely-positive vibes. Good thing he liked spaghetti.

"You ready to eat?" Tanisha asked him.

"Um, I guess," Joe replied slowly, still in mild shock that he was even there and that Tanisha was acting like some kind of hood Stepford Wife. "I didn't know I was coming over here for dinner, though."

"You gotta eat, right?" Tanisha shrugged. "I can at least feed you if I'm gon' invite you over here. Come on."

She took his hand and led him to the kitchen, where she fixed them both (plastic) plates full of spaghetti and buttered toast, and they went to eat in the living room. Tanisha was being unusually chatty, telling Joe about how she was thinking about going to Cosmetology school, how she hadn't been watching as much reality television, and how she and the girls had gone to Dunkin' Donuts. She was extremely proud of all of this, especially that last part, and Joe knew she was doing and saying all of this in hopes that he would possibly move back in or even be in a relationship with her again. He chose not to call her on it yet, though, not having the energy to explain that she needed to do all of that for *herself*, not for him. Especially when he knew that it wouldn't make any difference, anyway.

Tanisha polished off her can of orange soda and wiped her mouth with the back of her hand. "You done?" she asked him.

"Yeah."

"It was good, huh?" She eyed his empty plate.

Joe wasn't about to say that there hadn't been anything special about her spaghetti; there was no need to be rude when she was trying to be nice. He couldn't even remember the last time Tanisha made anything for him, so he just chose to be appreciative.

He also didn't want to imagine what Raven would have made for him if he was hanging out with her like he really wanted to be.

"Yeah, it was cool," he casually replied. "I appreciate it."

"I'll take your plate," Tanisha offered, taking it from his lap and standing up. Joe watched her bow legs strut towards the kitchen, then he sighed and shook his head, again wondering what he was doing there.

A few moments later, Tanisha came over and boldly straddled his lap, pushing him against the back of the couch. She wrapped her arms around his neck and smiled at him. Joe got a whiff of peppermint and figured she must have hurriedly rinsed with mouthwash.

Joe eyed her skeptically. "So *this* is what you called me over here for, huh?"

"It's not the only reason. But I'd be lying if I said I didn't want you."

Joe didn't respond.

Tanisha eyed him for several moments before slowly leaning in for a kiss. When she got no refusal, she eagerly pressed her lips against his, jutting her tongue into his mouth. Joe found himself kissing her back, despite the part of him that wondered why he was bothering. Tanisha's arms tightened around his neck and she moaned as she began to grind on his lap. Joe felt his arousal growing, and when Tanisha moved his hands to her backside, he let them stay there. They continued to kiss for a while, longer than Tanisha usually did before trying to move on to the main event, and Joe noticed how tender she was being. Her long blue coffin nails grazed the side of his face as she took her time savoring his thick lips. She even held his face as she looked into his eyes, which was a first. Joe felt himself warming to her as they continued, and eventually both their shirts were off. Joe's hands roamed Tanisha's back and his fingers seemed to unhook her bra all on their own. Their licks and kisses eased downwards, and before too long, their pants and underwear were tossed next to their shirts. Not too long after that, Joe was inside of her. He turned his brain off as he sexed Tanisha on the couch like he had done so many times over the years, giving it to her hard and rough like he knew she liked it,. She loved that hair-pulling, neck-grabbing, ass-slapping kind of sex complete with loads of vulgar sexual trash talk. And that's exactly what Joe gave her.

Tanisha was in heaven, hoping that this whole evening would be enough to get Joe to reconsider their romantic relationship. She knew Joe hated her attitude and her smart mouth, and that he thought she wasn't doing enough with her life or spending enough time with their daughters, so she was trying to fix all of that so he would want her and they could all be a family. Tanisha never had much love or affection growing up; her parents fought all the time, when her dad even bothered to come home. Neither of them paid her much attention, unless it was to yell at her or beat her when she got into trouble. It wasn't until she got with Joe that she *really* felt love and real caring and affection; all the men before him cared about was getting high and having sex. Tanisha loved Joe more than she loved anything or anyone, even if she never could make herself say so. He was the one man, the one *person*, to really show her what true and genuine love felt like. And more often than she would outwardly admit, she always kicked herself for messing that up.

After they finished, Joe just laid there on his back for a little while, his arm over his eyes. Tanisha smiled as she rested her head on his hard chest and slid her arm across his stomach; she couldn't remember the last time she felt so happy. She was oblivious to the torment that Joe was experiencing over what they had just done.

"That was unbelievable," Tanisha murmured after several quiet moments. She ran her nail between his pecs. "Can't believe it actually gets better after all this time."

Joe didn't comment. He just kept his arm over his eyes.

"Can you stay over here tonight?" Tanisha worked up the nerve to ask. She looked up at him. "I don't want you to go."

Joe finally rubbed his eyes with his fingertips before dropping his arm. "I can't stay, Tanisha."

She sat up slightly. "Why? The girls won't be back 'til tomorrow."

"It doesn't have anything to do with that."

"Then why can't you stay?"

Joe didn't want to argue, but he knew if he admitted that he wanted to leave because he was already feeling guilty about sleeping with her, that's exactly what would happen. He wanted to be honest but he didn't want to be cruel about it like he had been in recent months.

Sitting up, he rested his back against the couch and looked at his baby mama, who was looking quite cute and innocent at the moment. Her long black hair was strewn across her chocolate-brown face; she'd always looked younger than she was. Her tattoo-adorned body was still snuggled against his. If only she could be this pleasant all the time. But Joe had known her long enough to know better; her good behavior always ended eventually.

"What was your goal for inviting me over here?" he asked her, even though he pretty much knew the answer. "And be straight up."

Tanisha glanced down at the carpet. "I wanted to get you to agree to move back in here."

"And why is that?"

"Because, I..." Tanisha still wouldn't look at him. "I wanted you to get back with me."

"Just like that?"

"What you mean, just like that? It's not like it's anything new."

"I mean you thought us having sex would change my mind even though it never has any of the other times we got down?"

"But I've been doing better and stuff so I thought..." Tanisha shrugged, looking slightly defeated. "I thought *that* might help change your mind."

"Tanisha...look. I'm glad you're doing better for yourself. And I hope you keep going with that. But I still don't think us getting back together is gonna work."

Sucking her teeth, Tanisha sat up and crossed her arms over her bare chest. "Why wouldn't it?"

"Look, I'm not trying to argue with you so keep the attitude, okay? I just don't have the energy to go there with you again, Tanisha, as far as a relationship. We've tried I don't know how many times over the years and it just doesn't work. So how 'bout we just leave well enough alone and worry about getting along for the sake of our girls?"

Tanisha looked at him with hurt in her eyes, but she quickly looked away. "For the girls, huh? That's it?"

"There's no reason we can't be cool and get along. If you didn't only act right when you want something, we wouldn't have an issue. I get tired of fussing with you."

Tanisha looked away, and Joe could tell she was trying her best to blink back tears. She never did like to cry in front of anybody; he'd only seen her do it once, and that was when he broke up with her the first time. Tanisha didn't like showing that kind of vulnerability. Joe wasn't trying to hurt her feelings, but he wasn't about to let her think something was going to happen with them when it wasn't.

"Fine, whatever," she finally muttered, her face still turned away from him.

Joe just shook his head. At least she wasn't cursing him out. "I'm gonna go...can you hand me my shirt?"

Tanisha looked at his shirt that was right by her leg, then at him. "Can we at least do it again before you go?"

"We probably shouldn't."

Tanisha frowned slightly. "Why not?"

"I just think we need to chill with the sleeping together."

"Even though we *just* got finished fucking not twenty minutes ago?? You didn't seem to think we needed to *chill* then!"

"Well, that was my bad. I guess I shouldn't have done that."

"You *guess*??"

"Hand me my shirt, Tanisha."

"So not only can we not get back together, even though I'm doing all the stuff you said I needed to be doing, we can't even have sex anymore, either? What, you got a girlfriend or somethin'?"

Joe immediately thought of Raven. She wasn't his girlfriend but he still felt like he had wronged her in some way by sleeping with Tanisha. "No, I don't have a girlfriend. But still-"

"I should still be able to do this, then," Tanisha breathed, hopping onto his lap before Joe could stop her. She slid down on his still-erect penis and started grinding frantically on his lap, and Joe hated that it felt as good as it did. If there was one thing he and Tanisha had always been on the same page about, it was definitely sex.

Tanisha grabbed his hands and put one on her breast and the other on her butt, never stopping her efforts. She looked at him, her hair falling across her face, a hint of desperation in her eyes, but she didn't say anything. She just moved and moaned and grunted until the orgasm came, and she screamed expletives so loudly that Joe was sure the neighbors were probably calling the police.

Still breathing heavily, Tanisha reached over and snatched up Joe's shirt. She threw it in his face.

"*Now* you can go," she spat, pushing away from him and stomping down the hall. Her bedroom door slammed, and Joe sighed as a new film of guilt started to creep over him.

· · · ·

"YOU OKAY?" GRANT ASKED Van, looking down at her.

"Mm-hmm. Yeah, I'm okay," Van breathed in response, smiling tightly up at him.

They were in bed making love; at least, that's what they were supposed to be doing. But neither of them were all the way there mentally. Grant's mind was on issues at the office, and Van was stressing about Cassie as well as thinking about Joe and Raven. She knew she was wrong for that, but she couldn't seem to keep her mind off them and what they might be doing. And when she wasn't thinking about them together, she was thinking about just Joe. Ever since she realized he was most likely the one behind Canton's great attitude change, she hadn't been able to get him fully off her mind. And she didn't know what it would take to make that happen.

Grant had hoped that making love to his beautiful fiancée would at least temporarily take his mind off of everything going on at work, but that wasn't happening. Usually, he was pretty good about separating work and home, but there was just so much going on that it was hard to completely switch gears. He had a major deal that was teetering on the edge of falling through at work, as well as one of his longtime executives retiring; Grant wasn't looking forward to the process of replacing him. Shaking his head of those thoughts, he leaned down and kissed Van's lips before burying his face in the crook of her neck and increasing his speed, breathing heavily as he pumped harder into her. Van just wrapped herself tighter around him, but didn't say anything. Neither of them did. They just each worked towards their respective tepid orgasms, their minds never fully getting around to what they were doing.

Afterwards, Grant got up to go to the bathroom and Van turned on her side in bed, biting the nail of her thumb. That had to be the worst time she and Grant had shared sexually, and it worried her. She waited for Grant to come out of the bathroom before sitting up.

"You want some water or anything, babe?" he asked her.

"No, thank you," Van replied. "Grant, come here for a second...we need to talk."

"About what?" Grant asked, crawling back onto the bed.

"About *us*. I'm sure I don't have to tell you that what we just did wasn't...wasn't our best work," Van replied hesitantly, hoping she wasn't insulting him. "I'm worried, sweetie."

"Van, I admit that wasn't the best just now but it was *one* time," Grant protested.

"Grant come on...it wasn't *just* this one time. This was just the worst, but our lovemaking overall is...well, it just isn't on fire like I feel it should be, you know? I mean, don't you agree?"

Grant looked at her thoughtfully, then turned his eyes to the wall in front of him. Eventually, he nodded slowly. "I guess I can't disagree. It *could* be better."

"That's all I'm saying."

"I'm sorry, Van. I hate to think that I don't satisfy you."

"Grant, no," Van immediately protested, scooting closer to him and grabbing his hands. "Please don't take it like that. I still love being with you, but it still seems like we're new to this together when that's not the case. We should be more sexually comfortable with each other than we are. I mean...what do you think the problem is?"

Grant lightly lifted his shoulders. "I don't know," he replied softly.

Van looked at him intently, noting that he still wasn't looking at her. "Do *I* not satisfy *you*?"

"Of course you do." His reply was immediate.

"Well, *something's* wrong. And I don't know about you, but I don't want things to keep going like this. Couples split up all the time over things like sexual incompatibility, or they just cheat on each other. I don't want that to happen to us."

"It won't," Grant assured her, pulling her into his arms. "It won't stay like this, babe. I admit that tonight I was a little preoccupied with work stuff but I'll definitely try to do my part to make things better. And you don't ever have to worry about me stepping out on you; sex is important but it's not the *most* important thing in our relationship. So please get that out of your head, okay?"

Van was still unsure, but she nodded against his chest. "Okay."

"We're gonna be fine, baby," Grant promised, kissing the top of her head.

But as Grant continued to hold her, he had to try to believe his own assurances. Truth be told, he was just as concerned as Van was about their sex life. It didn't take a genius to see it was subpar. He didn't know what the problem was; he was definitely sexually attracted to Van, and he flattered himself to think she felt the same about him. Other women didn't enter his mind when they were together; he only wanted her.

But for some reason, Grant couldn't be totally uninhibited with Van when they were making love. That was never a problem with any other woman, and he didn't know why it was happening now. But he knew he had to figure it out because he certainly wouldn't want to do anything to make Van question her decision to be with him.

Or worse, cause her to start seeing another man behind his back the way she saw him behind Joe's.

. . . .

A COUPLE OF HOURS LATER, Grant was asleep as Van lay awake, looking up at the ceiling thoughtfully. Her sexual issue with Grant had been heavy on her mind ever since they talked about it earlier, and despite his positive assurances that they would be all right, she wasn't feeling quite as optimistic. She didn't know what the problem was so she didn't know how she could fix it, and that scared her. No matter how many times Grant assured her he wouldn't step out on her, she knew that men could only take so much unsatisfying sex before they went looking to be fulfilled elsewhere.

Grant said his mind had been on work that night, and Van felt kind of guilty for not admitting what *her* mind had been on. She knew she had no business thinking about Joe at all, but especially not when she was making love to her fiancé. Her thoughts of her ex weren't even sexual, but it wasn't like she could forget that he was still the best lover she ever had. Just remembering that caused her body to wake up and her legs to rub together all on their own.

Grabbing her phone, she glanced at Grant before turning onto her side, away from him. With her phone underneath the covers, she sent a quick text to Joe before she lost her nerve:

You're on my mind. I hope everything is okay with you.

Still feeling the need to release, Van placed her phone on the nightstand and quietly got out of bed. She tiptoed to the bathroom where she turned on the water, leaned against the sink, and pleasured herself, unable to help thinking about Joe as she did so. Joe had always been able to bring the pleasure, mentally as well as physically.

Van made sure she was completely done before going to get back into bed with Grant. She had already disrespected him enough for one evening.

Chapter 17

· · · ·

VAN COULDN'T HELP BUT notice that Grant had
been spending a lot more time at work than usual. Even
when he had a lot going on and was traveling a lot, he still
tried to be home by a somewhat reasonable hour, even if it
meant he had to continue working in his home office. But
lately, he was staying away from the house and Van couldn't
help but wonder why.

Ever since they talked about their problems in the
bedroom, things became somewhat strained between
them. They hadn't talked about it again or made love since,
and Van tried not to take that as a bad sign. She still felt
a little guilty about masturbating while fantasizing about
Joe, something she indulged in several more times since
that night. When Grant did come home, they slept in the
same bed, but the most they did was cuddle. Van tried to
tell herself that this didn't mean anything; that this was just
a rough patch they were going through, but she couldn't
quite make herself believe it.

As a result of all of this, Van's enthusiasm about
planning their wedding had taken another nosedive. She
just didn't feel like doing it. Her whole mood about the
wedding had shifted, and whenever she was out and was
approached by a reporter or blogger asking about her
relationship with Grant or when the big day was, she was
just reminded of another aspect of life with Grant that
she didn't particularly care for. Getting with Grant caused
a lot more people to wonder about and delve into her,

and Van didn't love that. It only increased the more she accompanied him to benefits or corporate functions he couldn't get out of, with everyone wondering about the woman that had seemingly come out of nowhere and snagged one of the most handsome and notoriously eligible bachelors in town.

Van had of course known that Grant was big-time and being with him would bring a certain amount of attention, but since it didn't happen *every* time she stepped outside, she often forgot about it. More often than not, she could go out and about and remain relatively unbothered. But she groaned when she saw a local entertainment reporter rushing towards her when she was leaving the mall, not terribly eager to gush over her pending nuptials, which she knew they'd ask about.

"Ms. Roseland, how are things going with the wedding planning?" they asked, their recorder aimed and ready.

Van never wanted to be rude, but she really wasn't in the mood for this today. "Just fine, thanks."

"When is the big day?"

"You'll have to wait and see," Van evaded, flashing a forced smile as she continued quickly walking to her car. She and Grant hadn't broadcasted their wedding date as of yet to anyone outside of friends and family.

"Aww, come on," the reporter persisted. "You can give us a *little* hint, right?"

"Wish I could," Van lied, deactivating the lock on her car with her key fob. "But you'll find out when it's time for you to. You have a nice day, okay?"

Van didn't wait for a response before she slid into her car and closed the door on the disappointed reporter. Sighing, she wished she was more enthusiastic about her wedding, but she just wasn't feeling it right now. She and Grant hadn't even discussed it in the past few weeks; he didn't seem any more eager to get down the aisle than she was lately. They both obviously had other things occupying their thoughts, and Van wondered what else was on Grant's mind, because she had a feeling it was more than just work. Was he getting bored with her?

As Van drove, her mind began to drift somewhere it had gone all too often lately, and that was to Joe. She caught herself many times thinking about him, and she hated to admit it, but she even imagined them being married at times. There was no doubt in her mind that Joe would have made a great husband. He had already proven that he would do whatever he needed to do to take care of her and the twins; he was definitely a hard worker, which was one of the things that had always attracted her to him. He wasn't lazy or scared of doing what he needed to do. The twins certainly loved him. Really, the only complaint Van ever had about Joe was regarding his finances, which he had apparently improved upon. She wondered where they would be then if she had let him proceed with his marriage proposal that night, and if she had accepted it. They would probably be living in marital bliss right now, with the simpler life that Van sometimes missed.

And she didn't see sexual issues *ever* being a problem; that had always been top notch. She might not have had all of the extra things that Grant was able to give her, but

Van couldn't imagine that life with Joe would have been anything but a happy one.

But, she had made her decision and chose Grant. And for the first time, she started to think she might've made a mistake by doing so.

Van wished she could talk to someone about all of this. She of course thought of Raven first, even though she knew Raven would probably discourage her from thinking about Joe and basically tell her to sleep in the bed she had made for herself. And despite Van's recent apathy towards it, she remembered that Raven still had yet to start fulfilling her promise to help with the wedding planning. That certainly hadn't helped Van's mood about things any. And she couldn't help but wonder if Raven's foot-dragging about helping with the wedding was due to her relationship with Joe; she and Raven still hadn't really talked ever since Van confronted the two of them at Raven's apartment.

Van picked up the phone to call her mother, but as the phone was ringing she remembered again that her mother still didn't know anything about Grant, or that she had broken up with Joe. When her mother answered the phone, Van kept the conversation to mainly her frustrations with work, giving the impression that that had been the reason for the call, and then she ended the conversation feeling just as alone as she did when it began.

• • • •

VAN HESITATED FOR QUITE a while before finally placing the call she wanted to place. She told herself to think positively as the phone rang.

"Hello?" Raven finally answered.

"Hey," Van greeted softly, hoping she didn't sound as nervous as she felt.

Pause. "Hey."

"How are you?"

"I'm fine."

"Look, I know things are kind of tense between us and I won't even pretend they're not," Van forged ahead, doing away with the forced pleasantries. "The last time we saw each other, things got a little out of hand…"

"That's one way of putting it," Raven muttered.

"And I know I owe you an apology," Van continued. "I was way out of line for how I acted at your apartment that day."

"Yeah, you were."

"I don't want to do anything *else* to push us further apart than we already are," Van admitted, feeling the all-too-familiar tears come to her eyes and swiping at them with her fingertips. She'd been so emotional lately. "Do you think we can get together sometime soon, talk in person? Maybe do lunch or something. I really just want to spend some time with you. I think we need that."

Raven didn't respond for a few moments and Van prepared herself to be denied. But to her surprise, Raven finally responded, "You're right; we do. We can meet up for lunch."

"Really?" Van was shocked.

"Yeah. But it'll have to be sometime this weekend, though, 'cause my schedule is crazy this week at the restaurant."

"Okay, yeah, that's fine; whenever works for you," Van quickly insisted. "How's Sunday?"

"Sunday should work."

When Sunday rolled around, Van was as nervous as she would be for a first date or a job interview; she kept expecting Raven to call and cancel. And when she didn't, Van worried that she would do or say something to make things worse between her and her cousin. She knew she really messed up when she lost her cool after finding Joe at Raven's apartment that day, and she had to rectify that. More than anything, she just wanted to resume mending her and Raven's relationship as much as she could. With everything else going on in her life, she needed that.

She and Raven had agreed to meet at Pappadeaux and Van arrived first. She sat nervously twiddling her thumbs and checking her watch, and felt a cool wave of relief when she saw Raven heading towards her. Smiling, she quickly stood.

"Hey," she greeted her, reaching out for a hug.

Raven obliged her, though it was nothing like their usual hugs. Van told herself not to get discouraged by that. "Sorry I'm a little late; there was an accident on the highway."

"It's fine; I haven't been waiting all that long." Van retook her seat and waved the waitress over. "I didn't know what you wanted to drink so I haven't ordered anything yet."

"That's cool."

After placing their drink orders, they faced each other pensively.

"So...um...before I say anything else, I want to apologize to you to your face about that whole scene at your apartment," Van said. "It was just such a shock to see Joe there and you two looked so cozy and comfortable with each other, and it just rubbed me the wrong way. But I know that's no excuse, especially how I came at you. I sincerely am sorry for that, Raven."

Raven eyed her, gently moving her long bangs out of her eyes. "Yeah, that whole situation was messed up. But I guess I can understand how that would be a shock to you."

"It really was."

"And I suppose we could have handled it better, too," Raven continued. Van noticed how she spoke for both her and Joe and wondered if that was just because Joe wasn't there to speak for himself or if it was because she and Joe were an item. "It was just a jacked-up situation all around."

"Yeah. It was. So do you accept my apology? I really want us to move past this and get back to working on being friends again."

Raven looked at her with pursed lips. "Yeah, I accept your apology."

Van waited for Raven to offer an apology of her own but she never did. "I appreciate that," she said, choosing to let it go. She figured she had been more in the wrong than Raven, anyway. "I'd prefer to just forget about all that, if I can."

"You and me both." Raven's phone chimed and she checked it, smiling almost immediately after reading the text that had come in. Van automatically wondered if it was Joe, but didn't have the nerve to ask.

"So..." Van hedged as Raven typed a response into her phone, "How has everything been going? With work and everything?"

"Oh, girl, work is work," Raven responded, putting her phone on the table. The waitress came with their drinks and they took a minute to place their meal orders before Raven continued. "I made Executive Chef so my schedule is busier and I have a lot more responsibility, but I'm loving it."

"Really? I didn't know you got promoted! Congratulations!" Van exclaimed with a huge grin, reaching over to give her a high five. "When did this happen??"

"A few months ago. With everything we had going on between us I just didn't think to mention it. But yeah, it's pretty exciting. I was a little freaked out at first, though, I admit."

"Why?"

"Because everything is on me; I'm responsible for the menus and the inventory and keeping everything in order, making sure everything runs like it's supposed to...it's a lot. But it's what I've been working towards so I had to check myself and put on my big-girl thongs. It's been going really well."

"Wow, that's awesome, girl," Van marveled. "I am so proud of you."

"Thanks," Raven smiled at her. "So how are things on your end? How are my babies doing?"

"Ugh," Van shook her head, her smile diminishing slightly. "Canton, thankfully, is doing a *lot* better. His attitude has done a complete turnaround and his grades are back up. He actually came and apologized for how he'd been acting."

"That's good!"

"But that Cassie, though," Van continued, shaking her head again as she played with her fork, "She's still testing me."

"What is she doing?"

"She actually had the nerve to ask what the point of me being with Grant was if we couldn't spend all of his money. She stood right in my face and asked me that."

"Van!" Raven exclaimed, her water glass halfway to her lips. "You lyin'!"

"I wish I was. She had been telling me how she wanted to have some big blowout party for her birthday, and I was trying to explain to her how all of that wasn't necessary and she should be grateful for whatever she gets, and it seemed to go right over her head. She apparently figured that since she hadn't been asking for much lately, she would automatically get whatever she wanted for her birthday. And she tried to get Grant to overrule me. I was just so done that I told her she wasn't getting *anything*."

"For real? You're not gonna have a party for the twins at all now?"

"Oh, this has nothing to do with Canton; he hasn't even asked for anything. It's Cassie that was cut off. I'm just sick of her spoiled and ungrateful attitude."

"Wow..." Raven marveled. Apparently Cassie hadn't taken much heed to their conversation they had at Raven's apartment that day. "Well, I can't say I blame you. She *does* need to be taught a lesson, if she's acting like that. Though I hate to think that *nothing* will be done for her on her birthday."

"Well, Grant told me that he didn't think that was the answer and suggested I leave everything regarding the twins' birthday to him, so I'm doing just that," Van responded with a wave of her hand, then looked at Raven as if in panic upon realizing she'd mentioned Grant. She didn't want to ruin the good vibe they were finally having by bringing up what had always been a sore subject.

But Raven was unaffected. Hearing Van talk about Grant didn't bother her like it used to. She knew a big part of the reason for that was due to Joe; he helped her get to the point where she didn't even really think much about Grant or what he and Van did. Like Joe said, what goes around comes around; Van and Grant would pay, in *some* way, for their deception towards the both of them.

As if on cue, her phone chimed with another text from Joe. Another wide smile spread across her face as she read how much he was looking forward to seeing her; the feeling was definitely mutual. They had plans to meet up later that evening and she couldn't deny that she was counting down the hours.

Van eyed Raven the whole time she checked her phone. Again she wanted to ask if the cause for her Kool-Aid grin was Joe, but kept her mouth shut.

"Do you want me to talk to Cassie?" Raven asked as she set her phone back down. "I had a little talk with her when she spent the weekend with me 'cause I could tell she was feeling herself a little too much then. Apparently she needs to be checked again."

"Be my guest. It couldn't hurt. Maybe she'll actually listen to you 'cause she certainly hasn't been hearing me."

"I told her she needs to appreciate what she has and be more grateful; she was over there fussing about some pink iPhone y'all wouldn't let her have."

"Oh yeah, that. Well, really, if it was up to Grant she would have had it the next day. *I'm* the one that said no. The phone she has isn't even a year old."

"Hey, I feel you," Raven agreed. "I don't think kids need all that."

"Well she *hadn't* been asking for as much as she had been so I guess that's due to whatever you said to her," Van admitted as the waitress approached with their food. "But she still doesn't really get it."

"She will. We just have to stay on her."

They continued to talk about various things as they ate their meals. Raven received a couple more texts, which she always stopped to answer while grinning as if she'd just won the lottery. Van would eye her curiously, but never spoke on it. They were having a nice time and she didn't want to ruin it.

But when Raven's phone rang and Van saw a shirtless picture of Joe appear on the screen, she almost dropped her fork in shock. Raven just glanced at her before causally picking up the phone and putting it to her ear.

"Hey," she greeted Joe. She smiled at something he said, and Van arched a curious brow. "No, it's okay...yeah...that's cool. Just let me know when you're on your way...all right..."

Raven paused, then giggled like a giddy schoolgirl. "Me, too....see you then. Okay, bye."

Raven hung up the phone, still smiling. The look on her face was of someone absolutely smitten, and Van wasn't able to make herself resist anymore. She *had* to know.

"Raven," she began, putting her fork down.

Raven looked up at her as if she'd forgotten she was there. "Yeah?"

"Please don't get mad about me asking this but I just have to know. What is up with you and Joe? Are you two together?"

Raven looked at her cousin for several moments, her long fingers playing with her phone. Finally, she replied evenly, "Yes, we are."

Van tried to be cool, but she honestly felt as though someone had just punched her in the chest. Even though she had suspected that, hearing it actually confirmed was still a shock. "Oh."

"Is that a problem?"

Van looked at her. "Would it matter?"

Raven shrugged. "It wouldn't change anything, no."

Van stuffed her now-trembling hands underneath her thighs. Her nerves were racing a mile a minute. "I, umm...I have to admit I don't quite know what to say to that..."

"What is there to say? Joe was single, I was single...we realized we liked each other so we decided to make it happen. Nothing really more to be said."

"I see," Van croaked. She cleared her throat, then tucked her hair behind her ear. She began fiddling with her silverware, then her napkin, then stuffed a forkful of her salmon into her mouth before taking a huge gulp of lemonade. She couldn't help her sudden fidgetiness or bring herself to look at Raven, who was eyeing her with concealed amusement. "So I guess that time you were going on and on about the guy you were seeing being the best lover you ever had...you were talking about Joe?"

"Yeah," Raven smoothly responded. She eyed Van. "You all right?"

"I guess I have to be, huh?" Van replied, forcing herself to look at Raven. It took an even bigger effort to force a smile onto her face. "I can't say I'm not...*surprised*...but I guess if the two of you are happy together..."

"We are."

Van grabbed her glass and drained it, then motioned towards the waitress to bring her more lemonade, almost tempted to make it vodka. "Well...good for y'all."

"I think Joe and I deserve some happiness, right? Just like you and Grant have."

Van couldn't tell if Raven was being snide or not, but her expression seemed pleasant enough. She looked as cool as a cucumber. "Right..."

"Speaking of Grant, how are things going between you two? I haven't forgotten about helping you plan your wedding, either."

"Oh yeah," Van had forgotten all about broaching that subject with her. "Things are fine. We're doing good."

There was no way Van was getting into the issues she was having at home, like her recent apathy towards the wedding planning, Grant seeming to enjoy being away from home more than in it, Van still not telling her parents about Grant, and *certainly* not the sexual issues she and Grant had been having. Raven would probably have a field day gloating about that, if not to her face then definitely behind her back. And Van had no doubt she would tell Joe all about it and they would both be laughing at her, gloating that she was just getting exactly what she deserved.

"I'm glad to hear that," Raven replied sincerely. She picked up her fork and resumed eating as if she didn't have a care in the world. Van had no appetite left, but she forced herself to try to act like her stomach hadn't just been ripped out.

They parted ways a while later, with Raven saying she had some things to do. Van couldn't help wondering if she was going to meet Joe right then, since it was apparent from her brief conversation with him earlier that they had plans at some point later. Raven hugged Van, then slid her shades on and strutted to her car. Van tried to call Grant but it went to voicemail. She walked to her own car slightly dazed, and it was only when she was safely inside of it and sure Raven had already driven off that she put her face in her hands and cried.

· · · ·

GRANT SAW VAN'S CALL come in but ignored it. He wasn't necessarily upset with her, but he didn't want to talk to her right then. Things had been strained between them ever since the night they discussed their lackluster lovemaking. He wasn't a fool; he couldn't deny that they were having issues. That hadn't exactly been a comfortable conversation, and Grant had sensed that Van wasn't being completely honest with him. It was another one of his gut feelings. And given how she had promised to stop keeping things from him, Grant couldn't help but be frustrated. So he started spending more time at the office, even though his mind wasn't really there most of the time.

"Everything okay, boss?" Sheri asked him one day.

"Why do you ask?" Grant responded evasively.

"Just seems like you've been around here a lot more than usual lately, that's all," Sheri replied with a light shrug. "You never used to be here past eight or nine o'clock as much as you are now."

"Oh. Well, I've got a lot going on," Grant muttered, turning his attention to his computer screen. He hoped that answer would be enough to stop all the questions, as he certainly didn't want to get into the specific reasons for his hiding out at work. He was rather close to his assistants, but not so much as to confide in them about issues with his woman.

Sheri thankfully sensed that she should leave it alone and just replied, "Okay then, boss," before going on about her business. As soon as she left the room, Grant leaned back in his chair and wearily rubbed his eyes, feeling more drained than he had in a while.

His mind wandered to his latest conversation with his friend Rick. They both had been pretty busy lately so they hadn't had a chance to meet up in person, but they spoke on the phone while they were each taking a break from burning the midnight oil.

"You sound stressed, man," Rick observed.

Grant hated that he was so transparent but didn't have the energy to deny it. "I guess I am."

"What's on your mind?"

"We don't have to talk about me. We're always talking about my stuff. What's going on with you?"

"Work, wife, a toddler and another baby on the way. Nice try. Now why are you so stressed?"

"Man..." Grant rubbed the top of his head. "Just...home stuff, that's all."

"Things still rocky with the twins?"

"Not really. That's one thing that's actually gotten better, for the most part. But me and Van..."

"What's wrong?"

Grant didn't know how to talk about his sexual issues with Van without telling too much, and without embarrassing himself, to boot. "Overall, things are okay. But they're *just* okay. We're just kind of...going through the motions."

"That happens sometimes, man. You can't be riding high twenty-four-seven."

"Yeah, but something just seems *off*. And neither of us has even mentioned the wedding lately...I don't even know where Van is in regards to planning it. The fact that it really hasn't crossed my mind can't be a good thing."

Rick was quiet.

"I mean, I've had some issues going on here at work and that has taken a lot of my attention, but usually I can put that out of my mind when I get home," Grant continued. "Now I stay at the office longer than I ever have, even when it's not entirely necessary."

"Did you and Van have a fight or something?"

"That's just it; we didn't. I'd feel a little less concerned about things if that was the case. This is just the way things *are* and that worries me, Rick. If they're like this now, how is it gonna be when we get married?"

"I can understand that. Have you talked to Van about it, though? What does she think?"

Grant sighed. "Sadly, no. I haven't talked to her about this."

"Why not?"

"Because we're each too busy pretending that everything is fine to actually acknowledge that it isn't."

Rick paused before speaking again. "And you want to keep pretending so you don't have to face the reality that you have a serious problem in your relationship."

That observation jarred Grant. He knew he and Van had some issues, but he hadn't quite thought of it as a 'serious problem.' But maybe Rick had a point. "I suppose so."

"So what do *you* think the problem is?"

Sighing again, Grant replied, "I don't know."

"Mind if I venture a guess?"

"Go ahead."

"Really, it sounds like karma."

Grant's hand on his head stilled. "Karma?"

"Well..."

"Because of how Van and I got together."

"Look, I know I initially told you to go for Van if you felt that strongly about her, as long as you were all in and would be better for her than what she already had. But maybe I should have also stressed that you two should have been more mindful of how you went about it."

"As in she should have ended things with Joe first before we really started seeing each other?"

"Yes. And you know I would never judge you. But, well, when you start wrong, you usually end wrong. I'm sure I don't have to tell you that our wrongdoings always come back on us at some point. And if you two are going through this before you even walk down the aisle..."

Grant didn't need to hear the end of that sentence. He got the message loud and clear.

If Grant wasn't sure of anything else, he knew he loved Van. And he still wanted her to be his wife. But he couldn't deny that things between them just weren't quite right. A lot of things between them still felt forced instead of natural and effortless. After all this time, they were still like two virgin teenagers in the bedroom. Things might have been better between him and the twins – namely Canton - but he still hadn't really bonded with them like he had hoped to. Van didn't seem to want to show him much affection in front of them, and he wondered if she had been like that with Joe or if it was just him. And there was still the matter of Van not telling her parents about their engagement, which he hadn't forgotten about.

Between all this, his mother's cautions, and his sister's eerily-similar situation in her own relationship, Grant had never been more worried about his and Van's future. And he wasn't quite sure if it was something that could be fixed, or if they were just doomed regardless.

Chapter 18

• • • •

VAN WAS SUPPOSED TO be working, but her concentration was shot. It was almost noon and she hadn't gotten much of anything done. Truth be told, she just didn't want to be there.

As excited as Van had been when she first got the recruiter position and got to move on from being an executive assistant by day and flipping burgers at night, the thrill was gone now. Van liked the job all right, but not as much as she initially expected. Or maybe it was because of everything else that was going on, but when it came to work, she was usually frustrated and apathetic. More and more often lately, Van entertained Grant's suggestion about just quitting, but she didn't want to do that without having some kind of plan for what she would do instead.

"Knock, knock," Mr. Andersen, her direct supervisor, announced himself as he entered her office. Van absolutely hated when he did that.

"Hello, Mr. Andersen," she greeted as politely as she could manage.

"I'm about to head out for lunch but I wanted to let you know about this before I left," Mr. Andersen began, coming over and tapping his blunt fingertips on her desk. Another thing Van hated. "I need you to go to St. Louis next week. Harold won't be able to do it, since he has some personal things he needs to be here to tend to." Harold was the other recruiter who Van often shared work with.

"Honestly, Mr. Andersen, next week really doesn't work for me, either," Van replied.

Mr. Andersen looked at her in surprise; it was the first time she had ever not readily accepted an assignment. "May I ask why?"

"I'd rather not get into the details, with all due respect, but I have some personal things I need to tend to, as well."

"I see," Mr. Andersen frowned slightly, rubbing his chin. His wild, graying black hair stuck out all over his head as it always did and Van wondered if he'd ever heard of hair gel and a comb. "I'm disappointed to hear you say that. But I don't know if I can accept that reasoning as a viable excuse not to do your job."

Van's eyebrows shot up. "I beg your pardon?"

"That's not a good enough reason to not go on this trip, Vanetta," Mr. Andersen emphasized.

Her temper flaring, Van silently told herself to keep it together. She was affronted because she had lost count of how many times she already told this man she preferred to be called 'Van' yet he refused to heed to that, and also that she apparently wasn't getting the same consideration as her co-worker. "So it's fine for Harold not to go for personal reasons, but not for me?"

"I can't discuss Harold's reasons."

"Respectfully, I'm not asking you to. But I *would* like to think that I've established myself enough in the past year as someone who is a team player and always does what is asked of them, if not *more* than what is asked. I have never before said I was unable to go out of town when requested so that *should* indicate that my reasoning is pretty significant. I should be given the same compassion and consideration as Harold."

Mr. Andersen eyed her, then turned towards the door. "I can understand and even agree with some of what you're saying, but the fact remains that *one* of you will need to go on this trip, and I've already excused Harold from it. So if you don't go..."

Van arched a brow. "Yes?"

"Let's just say it might make us question your loyalty to this company and your position here might be in jeopardy."

Van's eyes narrowed as Mr. Andersen left her office without a second glance or giving her a chance to respond. She didn't appreciate her job being threatened like that, and part of her wanted to follow Mr. Andersen and tell him just what he could do with that trip *and* this job. But she stayed in her seat, fuming.

Thankfully, no one really bothered her for the rest of the day, and as soon as it was time to leave, Van sped out of the office, barely speaking to anyone as she did so. She couldn't wait to get out of there; she knew she had a lot of thinking to do about how she was going to handle this whole situation. When she got to her car, she tried to call Grant to get his opinion, but yet again, her call went to voicemail.

It wasn't lost on her that she wasn't as able to reach him during the day as she used to be, and even though she told herself not to, she couldn't help but worry about that. Grant always used to make time for her; even when he couldn't talk, he would shoot her a quick text letting her know he would get back to her as soon as he could. Or even send random messages to her throughout the day, letting her know he was thinking about her. But Van realized he hadn't done that in a little while. They hadn't been communicating much at all recently; he stayed at the office later than usual most nights, and when he did come home, if Van was even still awake, they would have generic conversation before going to bed and doing nothing but sleeping. Something wasn't right, and it scared Van. She knew she'd been a little too consumed with Joe (and now, Joe and Raven together) lately, but she had no idea what Grant's issue was. Had he been more insulted than he let on when she let him know how subpar their sex life was?

Van was just about to pull out of the parking lot when she got a call. She frowned as she looked at the number; she didn't quite recognize it but it seemed strangely familiar. Since she was now debt-free – thanks to Grant – she didn't have to worry about it being a bill collector that she had to dodge. Those days were thankfully behind her.

"Hello?" she finally answered the call.

"Guess who it is."

"Tanisha??" Van couldn't believe her ears. Why in the world was this woman calling her?

"You know you ain't forgot about me," Tanisha replied snidely.

"What the hell do you want?"

"Well damn, you ain't gotta be rude."

"We don't have anything to talk about, Tanisha." One thing Van definitely didn't miss about being with Joe was having to deal with his childish baby mama. She and Tanisha hadn't spoken since Tanisha caught her out to dinner with Grant and the twins and Tanisha threatened to tell Joe.

"Yes, we do. It's about Joe."

That made Van pause. "What *about* Joe?"

"I thought you left him to be with that rich dude, so I don't know why you're coming around trying to break up my groove with him now," Tanisha accused. "We were doing just fine and now he don't want nothing to do with me."

"I don't have anything to do with that, Tanisha. Though I can't say I blame him."

"Yeah, you real funny. But why else would he say he can't have sex with me no more if he's not messing with you? You were the one that took him from me the first time."

Van shook her head. She and Joe met after he had already broken up with Tanisha, so it was funny that Tanisha was still trying to blame Van for the demise of her relationship instead of putting the blame where it belonged, which was on her and her attitude.

But what interested Van more was hearing that Joe was messing around with Tanisha again, or at least, he had been. But he was supposed to be with Raven. Was he seeing both of them at the same time? That didn't sound like Joe, but he clearly wasn't the same man he had been when they were together. He was still angry and bitter and maybe just not interested in being in anything exclusive. But did Raven know that? Van might not have been thrilled about Raven and Joe being together, but that didn't mean she wanted to see her cousin get played.

"If Joe has stopped sleeping with you, it doesn't have anything to do with me," Van replied tiredly. "That's if you're even telling the truth. You're probably lying, trying to mess with me like you usually do."

"I'm *not* lying! Joe came over here and banged my back out just a couple of weeks ago," Tanisha bragged.

Van winced, not enjoying hearing that. "Whatever. Like I said, you're calling the wrong person. I've barely even seen Joe. I'm still very happily engaged to Grant."

"Uh-huh. So what's taking you so long to get married, then?"

"None of your business! Now bye!" Van ended the call, even though Tanisha's question jarred her. Van's chosen far-off wedding date always caused a lot of raised eyebrows, not to mention suspicions. Getting married to Grant hadn't been at the forefront of her mind in weeks. That wasn't good and Van knew it.

Van couldn't get Tanisha's words out of her head as she continued her drive home. There was a big possibility that Tanisha was lying, but if she was telling the truth and *had* actually slept with Joe recently, that meant he was cheating on Raven. Van knew it was none of her business and she had no idea what the dynamics of Raven and Joe's relationship was; maybe they weren't exclusive. Or maybe they became so right after Joe slept with Tanisha. Van had no idea, but she knew she wouldn't be able to just keep this information to herself. Raven had a right to know what she was dealing with, if she didn't already.

But when Van tried to call her, Raven didn't have time.

"Hey, can't talk now; super busy over here," Raven answered the phone breathlessly. Van could hear a bunch of voices and commotion in the background and figured Raven was at work.

"Okay, can you call me back later? It's really important," Van stressed.

"I'll try to, but there's no telling what time I'll get home. I *really* have to go."

"Okay-"

Raven had already hung up. Van could only hope Raven would call her back later, but something told her not to hold her breath about that.

Running a nervous hand through her hair, Van contemplated calling Joe. She started to place the call, then stopped. What would she even say? This whole situation didn't involve her and she was sure Joe would remind her of that, that's *if* he even answered the phone. Never mind that Tanisha had brought her into it by calling her and blabbing about her (supposed) sexual relationship with Joe, and accusing her of being the reason that it ended. Joe wouldn't want to talk to her about this at all.

Van mentally went back and forth about this the rest of the way home. She had to make herself acknowledge the reason she really wanted to confront Joe about all this. Was it just an excuse to talk to him? Did a part of her just want to be nosy and find out if he had in fact slept with Tanisha recently? Or was it just about looking out for her cousin? It could have very well been all of those. But Van had enough sense to know that the jealousy she had no business even having was the main thing fueling her desire for answers.

When she made it home, Van really didn't want to be bothered. She decided to order dinner in, not having the energy or desire to cook anything, and didn't make much conversation with the twins while they ate. Grant, of course, wasn't home. Canton seemed to sense that Van was in a mood and left her alone, but Cassie either didn't get the hint or chose to ignore it.

"Mama, where you going?" Cassie asked when Van started to head upstairs.

Not even having the energy to correct Cassie's grammar this time, Van replied tiredly, "To my room. Why?"

"I wanted to talk to you about something."

"About what?"

"Can you *please* change your mind about cancelling my birthday party?" Cassie pleaded, linking her hands together in front of her chest and bending slightly at the knees. "I won't have an attitude no more if you do."

"Yeah, until there's something else you decide you want, then we'll be going through this all over again."

"Huh?"

"I don't believe you'll change your attitude if we give you what you're asking for," Van clarified. "You might act right for a while but as soon as you see something else you think you should have, you'll be right back to the same mess. And I'm over that."

"Mama-"

"Cassie, do you understand *anything* we've been telling you?" Van interjected, not having the patience for the back-and-forth she and her daughter usually engaged in.

"Raven said she talked to you about this when you went over there. I know *I've* had this discussion with you I don't know how many times. Yet you still don't seem to get it. Or you just don't *want* to, 'cause I know full well you're smart enough to understand it."

Cassie's eyes lowered to the floor.

Van eyed her daughter for a moment, then sighed. "Come in here, Cassie."

They went into the living room, where they both sat on the couch and faced each other. Van tried to gather her thoughts before speaking.

"I really don't know what else I can say to get my point across," Van admitted. "I never thought you'd start acting like this when we moved in here. And to be perfectly honest, I'm very disappointed in you."

Cassie looked at her mother in surprise. She never liked when Van was upset with her, but she especially hated hearing she had disappointed her. "I'm sorry."

"Are you? Cassie, understand something, okay? I did not decide to be with Grant because he has a lot of money. That's no reason to be with anyone. He and I are in love."

"But weren't you in love with Joe?"

Unprepared for that question, Van blinked a few times in surprise. "Yes..." she replied carefully. "But sometimes things just don't work out, and that's what happened with Joe. That's all. It didn't have anything to do with money."

"If it didn't have anything to do with money, how come you said we moved over here so we could live better?"

Van knew she had just put her foot in her mouth, not to mention having just lied to her daughter; money was the main reason she ended things with Joe.

"Okay, let me start over," she began, not wanting to let this conversation continue in the direction it was going in. "Yes, I wanted you and Canton to be in a house where something wasn't always broken, and for you to each have your own room. Plus, this is a nicer area, too. And true enough, Grant is a big part of the reason that I don't have to work two jobs anymore, and also that you and Canton are able to have more of the things you want. I can't deny that. But even more important than that, though, is I'm happier now; I'm not worried about a million things like I always was before. And a big part of the reason I'm so happy, Cassie, is because I can spend more time with you and Canton. I can do more things for you that I wasn't able to do before. As your mother, that's important to me. Do you get that?"

"Yes, ma'am."

"Even if Grant lost all of his money tomorrow, that still wouldn't change how I feel about him," Van continued, wondering if she was telling another lie. "We are not here for Grant's money, regardless of how willing he is to spend it on us. We're a family."

Cassie just looked at her intently.

"Grant loves you, Cassie," Van informed her, placing a hand on her knee. "He loves both you and Canton just like you were his own. And he wants to take care of you; of *all* of us. That's a blessing. How many of your classmates don't have a father in their house, or anyone that is willing to do all the things Grant is willing to do for you?"

Cassie looked thoughtful for a moment. "I know a lot of kids like that."

"And I bet Canton does, too. Even when *I* was growing up, a lot of my friends only had one parent at home, and they struggled like we used to. But we don't have to worry about that anymore. You should be thanking God every day for that. 'Cause I bet any one of those kids would trade places with you in a second, and would be thankful for every little thing."

Cassie looked down at the floor again, an expression of shame starting to take over.

Finally feeling like she was breaking ground, Van forged ahead again. "Think about those people at the food bank where we volunteer. Go in there in the kitchen and look in the cabinets and the refrigerator; it's always full, isn't it? Those people don't have it like that; they might not know *where* their next meal is coming from, or if they'll get to eat anything at all. I want you to think about that. Or when we go to the homeless shelter; those people would love even a portion of what you have, and not so they can post it on Instagram, either. It's because they know what it's like to go without. We go help out there because we choose to; *they* go because they don't have any other choice."

Van knew she was laying it on a little thick, but she felt it was necessary to really get through to Cassie. And it seemed like it might be working; Cassie's eyes actually looked a little moist. Van figured she should go ahead and go for the jugular.

"So...I was going to wait until later on to tell you this but I might as well go ahead and do it now. Due to the way you've been behaving lately, I've decided to send you to stay with Ms. Tanisha. You remember her?"

Cassie frowned a little before her eyes widened in recognition. "You mean Jillian and Tara's mama??"

"Yes."

"Why??"

"Because like I said, you need to be taught a lesson, and apparently us just talking to you isn't cutting it. Jillian and Tara are gonna come stay here, in your room."

Cassie's mouth fell open in horror. "Are you serious??"

"I'm very serious. I know *they'll* be grateful for everything that's in there, because you're taking nothing but clothes with you. No cell phone, no laptop, no games..."

"*What?!?*"

"Since Jillian and Tara have never even lived in a house and have always shared a small room, they'll be in heaven over here; your bedroom is probably as big as their living room. And they won't waste food or walk around here with an attitude or always have their hands out. They'll be grateful for everything because they're so used to having to go without. And you'll get to see what it's like for them, because they're worse off than we were before we moved over here."

Van felt a little bad for lying to Cassie like that. She had made no such arrangements for Cassie to switch places with Joe's daughters. She made all that up in the spur of the moment to get her point across. Dramatics was what her daughter responded to best. It was taking every ounce of restraint not to laugh, too, because Cassie looked absolutely horrified.

"What about Canton, though?" Cassie exclaimed.

"What about him? He gets to stay here."

"B-but we're supposed to stay together!"

"Why, because you're twins? You didn't care about that when you were talking about celebrating your birthdays separately, did you?"

Cassie's mouth fell open, but she knew she had no response for that.

"You and Canton hardly hang out with each other anymore, anyway, so it shouldn't be a big deal," Van said, doing her absolute best not to crack a smile. "And I bet he'll appreciate having Jillian and Tara here; they're actually *nice* to him."

"I'm nice to him, too!" Cassie insisted.

"No you're not, Cassie; you're only nice to people when you want something from them," Van replied coolly, standing up. "Now go ahead and pack your things...and remember, clothes only. I *will* be checking your bags before we go to make sure you're not trying to sneak anything extra over there."

"Mama! Are you really serious??"

"And you can only take two suitcases," Van continued, ignoring her. "Actually, make that one. That will still probably be more than what Jillian and Tara have, or at least almost. You know they have to share stuff."

"But Ms. Tanisha is mean! Why would you let me go over there with her and she's mean??"

"Maybe that's what you need. We're certainly not mean to you here and you don't appreciate that."

"How long am I gonna have to stay there??"

"Until I feel like letting you come back."

"But I don't want to go!!"

"Oh well. I didn't ask you what you wanted, did I? You didn't care what *I* wanted when I repeatedly asked you to straighten up your attitude. So you brought this on yourself. Now go get your stuff together; we're gonna be leaving in a little while."

Van walked out of the room, leaving her flabbergasted daughter behind. It wasn't until Van got upstairs that she actually put a hand over her mouth and giggled out loud. She knew she probably should feel bad for freaking Cassie out like that but she didn't. Clearly something different was necessary to wake her daughter up and get her to really see what she was trying to teach her; as she thought, Cassie responded better to drama. Van just wondered how far she was going to take this little bluff she started.

Going on about her business, Van took a shower and picked out her outfit for work the next day, then watched half an episode of *Family Feud*. She almost forgot to go check on Cassie, and when she got to her room, she was more than a little surprised to find Cassie sitting on her bed, tears running down her face, her pink suitcase on the floor next to her. Her cell phone was on her nightstand, and her laptop and headphones were on her desk. It looked like Cassie had conceded to going to Tanisha's, which Van hadn't expected at all. Cassie looked like she was lost in her thoughts and Van wondered if she had even heard her come in.

"Cassie?"

Looking up at her mother, Cassie sniffed, then looked back down at her hands. "I called my friend Bianca to let her know I wouldn't be able to call her for a while," she began softly. Her voice sounded different than usual. "But she wasn't answering the phone. I called a bunch of times and she still didn't answer, and I thought she might still be mad at me."

"Why would she be mad at you?" Van asked gently.

"'Cause I, um, I didn't let her borrow one of my dresses," Cassie admitted guiltily. "And I wouldn't let her use my phone one time when she asked for it."

Van just shook her head but didn't comment. Sadly, Van couldn't say she was entirely surprised. Sharing had never been Cassie's strong suit, especially after they moved in with Grant; Cassie reveled in having things her friends didn't have and could be selfish with them. Whatever dress it was Bianca had asked for, Cassie had so many clothes, she probably wouldn't have even missed it.

"Then I called my other friend Tiffany to see what was up with Bianca," Cassie continued. "I know they hang out sometimes, too, so I figured she would know. Tiffany told me that Bianca's family's house burned down two nights ago."

"Oh no..." Van breathed, placing a hand to her chest. She went and sat next to Cassie on the bed, wrapping an arm around her. "That's terrible; I feel so bad for them. You had no idea about that?"

More tears streamed down Cassie's face. "No, ma'am. I-I hadn't called her 'cause I didn't want her to ask me for anything else. But I feel bad about that now; Tiffany said Bianca's family lost everything." Cassie put her hands over her face and cried, hard.

Van hugged Cassie to her, tears coming to her own eyes. She hated to hear about what happened to Bianca's family; it was always devastating to her when she learned about a family losing everything like that. But she also hated to see her daughter so distraught; Cassie was clearly taking this hard, especially knowing how selfish she had been towards her friend. Van could just imagine the guilt that Cassie was feeling right then.

Van couldn't even remember the last time she saw Cassie break down like this. She just let her daughter cry as long as she needed to, knowing there was nothing she could say to ease the pain Cassie was feeling in that moment.

After a while, Cassie sat up and wiped her sad eyes before looking up at her mother.

"Okay, I'm ready to go now," she said softly.

Van felt awful. She knew she needed to come clean about this whole house-swap ruse.

Cassie stood. "On the way to Ms. Tanisha's, do you mind if we stop by the hotel that Bianca and her family is staying in? I wanted to give her these clothes." She pointed to another bag by her bed that Van hadn't noticed. It was chock full of clothes and shoes, and Van was willing to bet that the dress that Bianca had wanted to borrow was in there, too. Cassie just looked down at the floor, as ashamed as Van had ever seen her.

And the small part of her that had briefly questioned if this was all an act to get out of going to Tanisha's was silenced; Cassie was good, but she wasn't *that* good. Van could see the conviction in her child and knew she finally learned her lesson, even though it had taken something this terrible to teach it to her.

"You know what?" Van said, standing herself. "Don't worry about going to Ms. Tanisha's. I'm cancelling that."

Cassie looked at her, sniffling. "Why?"

"Because I think you finally get it," Van replied, smoothing some hair away from her daughter's face. "There's a reason you feel so guilty, and I know you won't forget why that is. I just hate that it took something like this happening to your friend for you to learn this lesson."

"Yes, ma'am."

Van took Cassie's pretty face into her hands, wiping her tears with her thumbs. "I hate that you're feeling so bad right now. But I really hope you remember this the next time you're even tempted to complain or catch an attitude about *anything*. Just think about Bianca and her family and what they're going through."

"Oh, I will. Tiffany said Bianca said they don't know when they're gonna be able to get another house. They're all in a hotel. Bianca has three brothers, too."

"Oh my goodness," Van shook her head. Her heart hurt for that family, and she had to remind herself to be grateful, also. That could have just as easily been them. "Well, look; here's what we're gonna do. We can absolutely take these clothes to your friend, and I'm also going to talk to Grant and see how else we can help them. I hate the thought of all of them being crammed into a hotel room."

"Me, too." Cassie glanced around her bedroom, and Van guessed that she was imagining losing it and everything inside it. "Especially since one of her brothers is just a baby."

"Oh no! Yeah, we're *definitely* gonna try to help them, in any way we can. I'm just glad they all made it out okay."

"I am, too." Cassie looked up at Van, her red eyes still shining with convicted tears. "I really don't have to go to Ms. Tanisha's? I know I deserve it."

Van smiled tightly at her daughter before leaning down and placing a kiss to her forehead. "Really, no you don't have to go."

"Okay. Thanks, Mama. Can we go see Bianca now?"

"Absolutely. We'll get Canton in here to help with these bags." Van started to turn to leave the room when Cassie gently grabbed her wrist, stopping her. Van looked at her, eyebrows raised.

"I really am sorry for how I've been acting, Mama," Cassie said sincerely. "Do you forgive me?"

Van felt like she had her sweet little girl back. She cupped Cassie's chin lovingly before pulling her into another hug, holding her tightly. She noticed how Cassie clung to her and realized how much what happened to her friend had really gotten to her.

"Of course I forgive you, baby," Van informed her, kissing the top of her head and rubbing her back lovingly. "Let's just get better from here."

• • • •

A FEW HOURS LATER, Van fell across her bed, exhausted. She and the twins had gone to see Bianca and her family; when Canton found out where they were going, he wanted to give them some of his things, too. Van spent some time with Bianca's parents, hugging and encouraging them, and offered to help them get out of that cramped hotel room and into somewhere more comfortable for their family. She was thankful that they accepted her assistance, and she wasted no time calling Sheri, Grant's assistant, to help her find somewhere to move them to. She tried to call Grant but he was unavailable as usual, but she couldn't worry about that right then.

Van had ordered dinner for everyone and they all sat and talked and got to know each other a little better. Bianca's mother, Renee, looked so drained and defeated, and Van's heart ached for her. But even with everything they'd gone through, the entire time Van and the twins were there, she didn't hear any of them complain once. She really hoped Cassie noticed that, too. It was just another reminder that in the grand scheme of things, Van's problems might have been significant enough to her, but they weren't *nearly* as bad as they could've been.

She made sure to leave her contact information with Renee and her husband Caliph, and insisted that they call her if they needed anything. It warmed Van's heart when she heard Cassie apologize to Bianca for being so selfish, and tell her that she would share anything she had with her from then on. The two girls hugged, and Van had to blink back tears.

When they got back to the house, Canton went to his room and Van and Cassie sat in the living room and talked. Van let Cassie know how proud of her she was for wanting to help her friend like she had, and informed her that they could talk about resuming the birthday plans. Van still didn't know what Grant was planning for that, but Cassie didn't need to know that her birthday plans had never *fully* been cancelled like she thought.

Cassie did have one request for her birthday that Van wasn't expecting:

"Whatever we end up doing, can we invite Joe?"

Van's eyebrows shot up in surprise. "Really? You want to invite Joe?"

"Yes, ma'am. I miss him."

"Oh..."

"Do you think he'll come?"

"I don't know, baby. We can ask."

"I hope he does come. Jillian and Tara, too."

"Yeah, that would be nice. Well, look, go on up and get your shower so you can go to bed; it's been a long day."

"Yes, ma'am."

Now, Van rolled over and grabbed her phone off the nightstand. She sent Joe a text, citing Cassie's request for him to come to her birthday party, and left it at that. She laid the phone next to her by the bed, hoping he would respond.

• • • •

JOE SAW VAN'S TEXT, just like he'd seen all the other ones she'd sent him lately. He got one from her at least once a day, and he never acknowledged any of them. And he never knew what they were going to be about from one time to the next:

Hey...just wanted to check on you. Hope everything is ok.

How is the new job going? I know you're awesome at it.

I've been thinking about Jillian and Tara recently. Is Tara still afraid of the dark?

Do you remember that time we played hooky from work and spent the whole day together doing nothing? I miss days like that. Just a random thought.

It would be cool if we could hang out. I miss our friendship.

I know I probably shouldn't ask this but...do you miss me at all? I'm just curious.

Joe always just shook his head whenever one of her messages came in; she was really trying to get back into his good graces. He didn't know what was up with her. She chose to leave him and be with another man, so he didn't understand why she couldn't just leave him alone. He figured there must have been some kind of trouble in paradise, since she had so much time to worry about him.

He couldn't deny, though, that it was nice to hear that Cassie wanted him to come to her birthday party. He had no problem going for her; he just wished he didn't have to see Van or Grant. But he knew he couldn't turn Cassie down; if she wanted him there, he'd put his feelings towards her mother and future stepfather aside and be there for her.

And truth be told, he realized he wasn't as upset at Van and Grant as he used to be; he was just indifferent. The talk he had with Van had actually served some purpose, as far as cementing that it really was over between them. Part of the reason he avoided having such a sit-down with her for so long was because he didn't want to risk all of his old feelings for her rushing back; Joe had truly never loved a woman like he loved Van, and it had taken him a long time to finally start to get over her. He thought that maybe being alone with her might derail that progress, but thankfully, that's not what happened. He'd been angry and annoyed with her when they met up, but he didn't miss her even a little bit.

And he couldn't deny that Raven probably had a lot to do with that.

They'd been spending a lot of time together, as much as their schedules would allow, and Joe was a little surprised that they were still going like they were. He figured that their little rebound fling would have fizzled out by then; that the feelings they'd been experiencing for each other were just fueled by a mutual distaste for Van and Grant and wanting to get back at them, while also helping each other relieve their sexual frustrations. But that hadn't been the case, at least on his part. He genuinely liked Raven, a lot. She was on his mind more than he expected, and he actually liked that. Thinking about Raven almost always made him feel better, and if he was honest with himself, he knew he stopped seeing her as just a fling a while ago.

He went to her place after work one evening, and as soon as he saw her, he pulled her into a long, tight hug. Then he kissed her for what stretched into several minutes, holding her close to him, and she returned his kiss with just as much intensity as he was giving her.

"Would it freak you out if I told you I missed you?" he asked her when they finally parted.

Raven's grin came instantly. "Not at all. 'Cause I missed you, too."

Now Joe was smiling. He pulled her in for another kiss, and they slowly began taking each other's clothes off. Once they were in their underwear, Joe picked her up and carried her to her bedroom, where they proceeded to have slow, intense sex on top of her duvet. There was a lot of face caressing, eye gazing, and lingering kisses; more than usual. This time seemed different from all the rest; like it actually meant something. And they both felt it.

Afterwards, they laid side-by-side on their stomachs, each hugging a pillow, and talked about their respective days. When Joe mentioned how Cassie had apparently requested his presence at her birthday party, Raven's eyebrows shot up in mild surprise.

"Really? I figured Canton would definitely want you there, but I'm a little surprised to hear that from Cassie," she commented.

"You and me both, really," Joe admitted. "She seemed happy to see me when we were all here that time but I figured she'd be too over the moon with all the stuff she has now to be thinking about me like that. But I'm not mad about it that I was wrong. It made me feel good that she wants me there."

"So are you gonna go?"

"Yeah," Joe replied, blowing air through his thick lips. "I don't want to disappoint Cassie and Canton if I don't have to."

"I know they'll be glad about that. Especially if you bring Jillian and Tara."

"Yeah. You're going, right?"

"Of course, whenever they figure out what they're gonna do."

"What do you think about us going together?"

Blushing like a schoolgirl who had just been asked to the prom, Raven smiled. "I think I like that idea."

"It's a date, then." Joe winked at her, causing Raven to blush harder. "But maybe you can help me out with something, though…"

"What's that?"

"Why do you think Van has been texting me so much lately?" Joe asked, resting his head in his pillow. "She's been hitting me up damn near every day, talking about how she misses me and our friendship and a bunch of other random stuff. I don't know what's up with her. Y'all have talked, right?"

"Yeah, but not so much about that," Raven replied, playing with the edge of the pillowcase. "I had no idea she was reaching out to you so much. Do you respond to any of the messages?"

"Nah. I don't have anything to say to her."

"Hmm."

"Do you think something happened between her and her man?"

Raven looked at him thoughtfully before turning her eyes back to the pillowcase. "Actually, Joe, I wouldn't be surprised if she wanted you back."

Joe's eyebrows shot up in surprise. "Word?"

"Yes. I mean, why else would she keep trying to contact you after all this time?"

Joe shrugged. "I figured she was maybe still feeling guilty. I told her I hadn't forgiven her and she said she hated that. It seems she's just gonna keep trying until I do."

"Would you take her back, if you could?"

Raven's question was soft, almost timid, as if she was afraid of the answer. She couldn't even look at him as she asked it. Joe turned to look at her, not responding until she eased her eyes to him.

"No," he stated decisively, looking right into her eyes.

"Really?" Raven wondered if her relief was obvious.

"Yes, really," Joe confirmed. "My attention is somewhere else now."

A slow smile spread across Raven's face. Joe gently grabbed her chin and brought her lips to his. He kissed her intently, letting her know that she was the one he wanted. Raven slid her arms around his neck, surprised at how emotional she felt right then and the eagerness with which she returned his kiss; the thought of Joe going back to Van actually made her feel a little sick. She didn't want to see them together; she didn't want to see Joe with anybody but her.

They clung to each other, each wanting to get as close to the other as they could. Raven held Joe's face in her hands, feeling something for him that she knew she'd never felt for any other man, and it didn't freak her out. She had told Van that she and Joe were a couple just to mess with her, but Raven realized she had actually begun to think of Joe as hers.

And the feeling was definitely mutual. Joe had been wondering for a while what Raven would think about the possibility of them actually being together for real, but hadn't quite had the nerve to ask. But as they joined their bodies again, clinging together more intensely than ever, they both knew they were falling for each other.

Chapter 19

• • • •

GRANT KNEW HE COULDN'T keep hiding out at work. He and Van had been doing this evasive dance for too long now, with him taking his time coming home and Van not even bothering to ask him about it, not to mention him letting most of her calls during the day go to voicemail and opting to respond to her later via text. The most they communicated recently was about how to help Cassie's friend's family after their house burned down. As soon as he found out about that, he had the family moved to one of his rental properties and paid their expenses for the next year so they could just focus on getting back on their feet. It wasn't lost on him that Van hadn't even commented on the fact that he was away from the house so much, or that he wasn't taking her calls like he used to. He didn't know if that meant that she was incredibly understanding of his schedule, preoccupied with other things, or that she just didn't care.

So after another long day at the office, he headed home, determined to finally talk to Van about things. It was rather late so the house was quiet when he got there; the twins were both sound asleep. He could hear the television in his and Van's bedroom, and hoped that she was still up and hadn't dozed off watching a movie, as she often did.

Thankfully, she was still awake. "Hey, babe," he greeted her upon entering the room.

"Hi," she replied simply, glancing at him before turning her eyes back to the television.

Grant set his briefcase down and stuck his hands in his pockets. "Van, we need to talk."

She looked at him and pursed her lips before clicking off the television with the remote. "I suppose we do."

Going to join her on the bed, Grant almost didn't know how to start things off. "You doing okay?"

Van shrugged a shoulder. "I guess. You?"

"Not really. I don't like how things have been between us lately."

Van sighed. "I don't, either."

"It feels like we're pulling away from each other."

"Yeah. It does. And that scares me."

"Me too, babe. And I know I haven't been helping things by being so scarce around here lately; and I can't even totally blame it on work. My mind has been all over the place these past few weeks, Van. Ever since we had that talk about our sex life, things have just been different."

Van lowered her eyes. "I figured you were probably upset about that. I'm so sorry if I embarrassed you."

"That's not it. I can't say I enjoyed hearing that, but if I'm honest about it, you weren't wrong. And anyway, I'd been having concerns even *before* we had that conversation."

Van looked at him in surprise. "Really?"

"Yeah. I never mentioned this to you, but a while back, I talked to my mother and she was asking if I was totally sure about me and you getting married. I assured her that I was, and she just stressed that marriage was serious and we had, as far as she was concerned, gotten together and escalated kind of fast."

"I can understand that."

"Then she told me my sister was having issues with her boyfriend, so I called to check on her. Turns out he had dumped her for someone else. I wanted to make him pay for that, but she claimed she was just getting what she deserved."

Van looked at him curiously. "What do you mean?"

"Apparently, he was with someone else when they met and she pursued him anyway. Didn't stop until she had him. It sounded amazingly similar to our situation, and I can't lie and say that didn't worry me. It's not like I didn't know I was wrong for going after you while you were with Joe. But at the time, I felt I deserved you more than he did and that's all I cared about. I tried to justify it with the reasoning that you and Joe weren't married. I really felt like we were made for each other. And I still do, but now it's like I'm finally remembering that karma always makes its way back around. And with the way things have been going between us..."

"You think we're just getting what we deserve?" Van finished his thought.

Grant looked at her. "Don't you?"

"Maybe," Van mused. "I hadn't quite thought of it like that but it *does* make a lot of sense. We knowingly hurt two people we claimed to care about; of course that's going to come back on us at some point. And you're right; we *didn't* think about that when we were sneaking around behind Joe and Raven's backs. We were pretty selfish, I hate to admit."

"Yeah. We absolutely were. And now I have to wonder if we're doomed because of it."

"Grant, don't say that..."

"I'm trying to be realistic here, Van. Things haven't gone smoothly between us for a while now, if ever. If it hasn't been issues with the twins, it's been various things between us. It's just always *something*. And I know that's life, in general, but it shouldn't really be like that in a relationship; not to this degree."

Van looked at him, then slumped a little in realization. "I guess you're right."

"We're supposed to be getting married and I can't even remember the last time we've talked about the wedding," Grant continued. "It's been too easy for us to get distracted by other things."

Van knew she couldn't deny that. "You're right," she agreed again. "And since we're talking, Grant, I might as well admit this, too...Raven confirmed that she and Joe are a couple and I've been more upset about that than I probably should be. I don't even know how to describe how I feel about it, but it's been on my mind a lot. I know you probably don't want to hear that..."

"Not really but it's understandable, to a degree. Are you jealous?"

"No, not *jealous*..."

"You just don't want them to be together?"

"No, I don't," Van admitted. "It just seems like they did it to spite me or something. I know it's really none of my business either way, and it's hypocritical of me, but I just don't like it. It bugs me. But the fact that I'm worried so much about that instead of focusing on what should be the happiest time of our lives has to mean something."

Grant just looked at her for several moments before releasing a long breath and rubbing his bald head. He wasn't surprised to hear that Van was so upset about Raven and Joe being together; she'd been upset when she just *suspected* they were, even though she tried to deny it. Grant could understand it to a degree but it just further cemented his concerns about their relationship.

"Van," he began, taking her hands in his. "Do you still want to be with me?"

"Yes," Van insisted automatically. And in that moment she did, despite her recent doubts.

"Then that just means we need to work that much harder to make this work," Grant emphasized, gripping her hands tighter. "The deck is clearly stacked against us but I believe if we both *really* want this - and I know *I* do - then we can make it happen together. I don't want to lose you, Van, I really don't."

Van blinked back tears. "I don't want to lose you, either. You're absolutely right; we need to re-focus."

"Right. And if we're having issues or doubts, we need to agree to talk to each other about it *then*, and not let it linger on like everything is okay," Grant stressed. "Communication is going to be all that much more important now, baby. We *have* to be honest with each other; we just have to."

Knowing she still hadn't been completely honest with him about a couple of things, Van swallowed nervously. "You're right," she softly agreed.

"I love you."

"I love you, too."

"Come here."

Van quickly went to him, closing her eyes as his arms wrapped around her. She rested her head on his shoulder, hoping that they could actually do what they said and get things back on track.

Especially since Joe was now officially with Raven.

• • • •

A COUPLE OF DAYS LATER, Grant decided to finally spend some extended alone time with the twins. He cleared his schedule, sent Van to the spa, and he and the twins went to Dave & Busters, which was the only place they could agree on. A few people recognized him and one was bold enough to ask for a picture, but otherwise they were able to enjoy their time undisturbed. They spent a couple of hours playing games, with Canton going off on his own while Cassie pulled Grant to seemingly every game in the building. Grant kept an eye on Canton the whole time, wondering why he automatically veered off on his own. He had learned over time that Canton was something of a loner, but he couldn't help but wonder if he would have done the same thing it was Joe there with them instead of him.

After a while, they took a break to get something to eat. As usual, Cassie dominated most of the conversation, talking a mile a minute. Canton wasn't saying much, but that was usual for him, also. Grant noticed that he either debated or fussed with Cassie endlessly, or he didn't say anything at all. At least he wasn't looking completely disinterested; Grant could tell he was listening. He just didn't seem to have much to say. Several times, Grant tried to engage him in the conversation and Canton would give a thoughtful but succinct response, then go back to his quesadillas.

"How's your friend Bianca doing, Cassie?" Grant asked.

"Oh, she's doing good!" Cassie replied enthusiastically. "She said they love the house you gave 'em; it's better than the one that burned down. And her dad has already started going back to work."

"I'm glad to hear that," Grant smiled. "What about her brothers? They're good, too?"

"Yes, sir. She said one of 'em has nightmares sometimes but other than that, they're okay."

"Oh, no. I can only imagine how traumatic that must have been for them. But I'm glad they all made it out okay and no one was hurt. Be sure to keep me posted on how they're doing."

"I will."

"Canton, are you still looking at Harvard as your school of choice or have you changed your mind?"

Canton finished chewing before responding. "I haven't changed my mind. Still Harvard."

"Do you have any other contingencies?"

"What's 'contingencies'?" Cassie interjected.

"Like a backup plan," Grant clarified.

"Oh."

"I'm certainly not saying you shouldn't try to go to Harvard if that's what you really want, but it's always good to have other options, also," Grant continued to Canton. "I know I had a top five list."

"I have a couple of other ones I like, if Harvard doesn't accept me," Canton informed him. "Especially since they don't give merit scholarships like other schools. I didn't want Ma to have to pay for anything."

"You don't *need* a scholarship now, though," Cassie chimed in, chomping on a French fry. "Right, Grant?"

Grant noticed how Canton cut his eyes at his oblivious sister, frowning slightly. Clearly she'd hit a nerve.

Trying to keep the pleasant-enough vibes going, Grant hurriedly asked Canton, "What is it you want to do after you graduate?"

"I'm going to be a lawyer. I just haven't decided what kind yet."

"That's awesome, man. I actually considered going into law, myself, when I was in undergrad. But I always knew entrepreneurship was going to be my thing. I've always had a better head for business."

"I plan on owning my own business, too. Franchises, though."

"Oh okay, so you want to own your own Smoothie Kings or McDonald's?"

"Not *those*, but yes, sir."

"And then I can come and eat whenever I want for free, right?" Cassie asked her brother, sticking two fries in ketchup before jamming them into her mouth.

"Uhh, *no*," Canton replied, looking at her as if she was crazy. "I'm not gonna make any money giving stuff away all the time."

"I'm your *sister*, though!"

"So what?"

"Canton!"

"I'll probably give you a discount or something," Canton conceded seriously, and Grant had to stifle a laugh at the look on Cassie's face.

"A *discount*?? That's all?? Grant, can you tell him he can do better than just giving me a discount if he *owns* the business??" Cassie exclaimed.

Grant actually had to pretend to wipe his mouth with his napkin and cough a couple of times to quell his laughter. These two were hilarious to him.

Finally he replied, "Well, Cassie, you have to understand that it's a business and not just expect to be given whatever you want just because you're family." He looked over at Canton. "But at the same time, if the business is being run correctly, it will still be profitable if you feed your sister for free, as long as it's not excessive."

Canton looked at him then at Cassie for a beat before shaking his head. "*She* would be excessive."

"I would not!" Cassie loudly protested.

They continued to go back and forth, and Grant just sat back and listened, amused and intrigued. He was glad that Canton was engaging more, but he noticed it was only talk of school and future career plans that got him to open up. This was the most Canton had said all day.

When they went home a couple of hours later, Grant sent Cassie on into the house and asked Canton to hang back in the car.

"Am I in trouble?" Canton asked.

"No, you're not in trouble," Grant assured him. "But I *do* want to talk to you."

"About what?"

"Well, I can't help but notice that you still don't seem all that comfortable around me," Grant observed. "It's like I'm your teacher or something instead of your future stepfather. After all this time, I thought you would have loosened up around me by now."

Canton pushed his glasses up onto his nose. "Oh."

"What's going on, Canton? Do you not like me or something? You can be honest."

"It's not that I don't like you," Canton clarified. "You're cool. You're just not Joe."

Grant nodded, having kind of expected that. "So you miss Joe, huh?"

"Yes, sir. Is that bad?"

"No, of course not," Grant quickly replied. "Joe has been all you've known as a father; of course you're going to miss him. I don't take offense to that at all. But I *do* want you to know, though, that I'm here for you, too...you can depend on me just like you depended on Joe."

Canton just looked down at his shoes.

"I want you to understand that I'm not trying to replace Joe or make you forget him," Grant continued. "I love your mother and your sister, and you, too. Y'all are just like my own children. And I understand if it'll take you some time, but I just hope you're at least *open* to the two of us building a better relationship."

Glancing at him, Canton nodded. "Yes, sir. I'm open to it."

"I'm glad to hear that." A thought came to Grant and he hesitated only slightly before requesting, "So tell me about Joe."

Canton looked at him curiously.

"I realize that I really don't know that much about him and he was such a big part of you all's lives for so long," Grant continued, realizing it must have been strange to hear him ask about his fiancée's ex.

Perking up slightly, Canton pushed up his glasses again and said, "Joe's great. He works really hard, and can fix just about anything. And he's a lot of fun, too...we used to wrestle and stuff."

"Oh yeah?" Grant smiled.

"Ma used to always freak out when he would throw me up in the air, but I thought it was fun," Canton continued, smiling at the memory. "I was never all that good at sports or anything but he always said there was nothing wrong with that; that there were other things I could be good at besides sports. He made me feel better about myself when the kids would tease me about being a nerd or whatever."

"That's awesome," Grant said sincerely.

"Ma said I used to always follow him around. He taught me a bunch of stuff, like how to fix things around the house, how to cook, how to do my own laundry...he said a man needs to know all of that," Canton said. "He didn't have a lot of money, but he took the best care of all of us that he could, including his other two daughters, Jillian and Tara."

"That's very admirable," Grant acknowledged. "He sounds like a really good man."

"He's the kind of man I want to be," Canton declared. "I'm glad I can at least still call him whenever I want to. He's the one that told me I needed to apologize to you and Ma for how I'd been acting, and get my act together in school."

"Really?" That was news to Grant; he thought Canton had come to that realization on his own.

"Yes, sir. He told me that I was stressing Ma out with the stuff I was doing, and I needed to respect you and give you a chance."

Grant hadn't been expecting that. He could only imagine how much pride had to be swallowed for Joe to say something like that to Canton, and he couldn't deny that his respect for Joe went up significantly.

If he was honest, he had yet to hear one negative thing about Joe from *anyone*. Grant didn't count his financial situation because that was something that could be improved with enough effort, and from what he'd heard, Joe was anything but lazy and tried his best. And Van had told him that Joe had gotten the promotion he'd been working towards when they were together, as well as getting his degree.

Grant started to feel even guiltier for stabbing a good brother like that in the back like he had.

"It means a lot that you respected him enough to do what he said," Grant told Canton, suppressing the momentary feeling. "I hope you realize how fortunate you are to still have him in your life like he is; the fact that he still wants to be there for you despite no longer being with your mother says a lot about how much he must love you. And by all means, I *want* you to continue your relationship with Joe. But I want you and I to have one, also, man...I'm a pretty cool guy, too, I think."

Canton chucked, causing Grant to smile. "You are."

"I'm glad you think so."

"But if I'm honest, there's something else."

Grant sat forward slightly. "What's that?"

"I guess...part of me doesn't wanna get too attached to you in case you end up gone, too, like Joe," Canton admitted, turning his eyes to the window. "Missing him has been bad enough. It would be hard to deal with that again."

Grant felt his chest constrict at Canton's words. He hadn't expected to hear that from him but now his standoffishness made even more sense; Canton didn't want to develop a bond with Grant only for him to disappear from his life like his father and Joe did. And he realized he never *really* grasped just how deeply losing Joe from his daily life affected Canton.

"I can understand that," Grant replied, his voice thick with an almost overwhelming level of emotion. "And I know you might not want to hear any grand promises right now but I can assure you of one thing. And I need you to look at me when I tell you this."

Canton wordlessly turned back to Grant.

"If I can help it, I'm not going *anywhere*," Grant assured him, looking right into his eyes. "I'm sure you know there aren't any guarantees in life and sometimes things are beyond our control, but I *promise* you, Canton, I will be here for you and your sister as long as it's within my power to be. I hope you believe that."

Canton's expression didn't change and Grant sensed that he probably wasn't convinced, but still he said, "All right."

"You'll see. I'm trying my best to be a good dad to you and your sister, too, even though I know you still don't really think of me that way," Grant continued. "We're going to be a family, man. I can't wait to marry your mom."

Canton's eyebrows shot up. "I almost forgot about that."

"Forgot about what?"

"That you and Ma were getting married. I hardly ever hear either of you say anything about it."

Reeling, Grant sat back in his seat, trying to resist the thoughtful frown that was aching to bend his brows. It hadn't even occurred to him what the twins might be thinking about his and Van's pre-marital foot-dragging.

He and Canton only sat out in the car for another couple of minutes before going in the house. Canton's words were on Grant's mind as he went up to his and Van's bedroom, where she was curled up on the chaise lounge with her phone in her hand. She was so engrossed in the message she was typing that she didn't seem to hear him enter the room.

"Hey babe," he greeted her.

She looked up, slightly startled. "Hey," she smiled guiltily, as if she'd been caught. Grant told himself not to be paranoid. "I was wondering when you were gonna come in. Cassie told me you and Canton were still in the car."

"Yeah, we were; just having a discussion." He went over and gave her a peck on the lips.

"Everything okay?"

"Yeah, we're good," Grant assured dismissively, his face a picture of concentration. "I think we need to make a change, though."

Van looked up at him, surprised. "What kind of change?"

"I think we should move up the wedding."

"Wh-what? Why?"

"I just don't see what we're waiting for. Even if you want a big wedding, we can hire somebody to make that happen as fast as we need."

Van looked visibly nervous, and Grant noticed.

"It's not about the wedding, Grant...I *do* want a nice one but it doesn't have to be huge. You know I'm not into extravagance just for extravagance sake. More important than that, I think we need to be more focused on working on our issues, don't you?"

"Who says that has to stop if we get married?"

"Well...it doesn't, but I would just feel better if we worked through all this stuff *first*," Van replied, turning her eyes back to her phone. "I mean, wouldn't that make more sense? To not have all this ugliness hanging over our heads when we walk down the aisle?"

Grant just looked at her. She was fidgeting, and avoiding his eyes. Van was not a very good liar, nor did she have a great poker face. Something was up; there was a reason that Van didn't want to move up their wedding date, and Grant knew in his gut that there was more to it than just her wanting to work out their issues beforehand.

"So you want to just leave things as they are?" Grant clarified, looking at her intently. "You really think it'll take that long for us to work through things?"

"The date isn't *that* far away, Grant," Van tried to chuckle casually.

"Damn near fifteen months."

"That's not long when it comes to planning a wedding."

"But I've told you multiple times that you don't have to do that by yourself. I know several excellent wedding planners, Van."

"But I've always wanted to plan my *own* wedding," Van declared. "And besides, you know Raven is helping me."

"So what have you all done so far?" Grant inquired, folding his arms. "Might as well keep me abreast of everything, right?"

"Oh..." Van looked away again. "Well, I admit we haven't gotten *that* far yet, with everything that's going on..."

Grant just continued to look at her.

"I promise, there's nothing more to it than what I'm telling you," Van assured him, standing and going to him. She wrapped her arms around his waist. "I'm just as anxious to marry you as you are to marry me."

"Really? 'Cause if it was up to me, we'd be married *now*."

Van pursed her lips. "You know what I mean, though. We agreed to slow down and just continue to get to know each other, and not rush anything. Not to mention everything that we've been going through recently. You can't say things between us are exactly ideal right now. I don't want to start our marriage off like that."

"I'm not talking about moving it to tomorrow, Van. I was thinking four, *maybe* six months from now. Not fifteen."

Van blushed as she smiled up at him. "We'll see how things go over the next few weeks. Is that okay?"

Grant's eyes continued to bore into her. There was something she wasn't telling him; he could feel it. "Van, I thought we agreed to be honest with each other."

Her eyebrows flew up at the reminder. "We did."

"So why do I get the feeling that there's something you're not telling me? Like there's another more pertinent reason you'd rather not move up the wedding?"

Her mouth fell open. "I don't know what you're talking about, Grant."

"Van, please don't insult my intelligence. I don't appreciate being lied to right to my face."

Van looked up at him, then sighed. "I just don't think we should speed things along," she admitted softly, her eyes downcast. "Please don't take that the wrong way; I'm still going to be your wife. For now, I would just rather leave things as they are. I'm simply not ready, Grant. I don't know how else to explain it."

"You're not ready. What happened to 'I'm just as anxious to marry you as you are to marry me'? Isn't that what you *just* said a minute ago?"

Her face reddened, caught. "I..."

"Which one is it, Van?"

"Oh my god..." Van briefly covered her face with her hands. "I *want* to be ready, baby. But..."

Grant nodded, taking a step back. She eyed him pleadingly as her arms fell to her sides.

"All right, then." Grant gave her one last knowing look before leaving the room, ignoring her when she called after him.

Chapter 20

• • • •

JOE WAS OVER THE CONSTANT texts from Van.
She had just sent him another one, trying to reminisce
again. First thing the next morning, he got his number
changed; he didn't want to just block her. He was sure to
text Canton his new number and specified that he was not
to share it to anyone.

It was amazing how things had changed. Just a couple
of years before, Joe was head over heels in love with Van
and figuring out how to go about making her his wife.
Now, he wanted nothing to do with her. If he was honest
with himself, he was a little surprised at how strongly he
felt about that. He always thought that if he and Van ever
split up, for whatever reason, that he would always take
any chance to get back with her that he could, because he
just couldn't imagine being without her. But that wasn't the
case. Maybe it would have been different if things hadn't
gone down the way they had, with her cheating on him and
then announcing she was leaving him for another man just
as he was about to propose to her, but Joe had felt nothing
but anger towards Van since that night. There was a very
brief period when he felt like he wanted her back, but it
was fleeting; all he had to do was think about the things
she told him the night of his ruined proposal and his anger
was automatically reignited.

But that anger wasn't there anymore. It had been
replaced by his rapidly-growing feelings for Raven. What
he told her about his attention being somewhere other

than Van was the truth; it was all on Raven, and had been for a while. She seemed happy to hear that when he said it. And he was starting to think that maybe a relationship between them might actually work.

Joe was going to be spending the weekend with his girls, and played with the idea of inviting Raven to join them for dinner one night. After going back and forth about it for a good five minutes, he went ahead and made the call, figuring the worst she could say was no.

"Of course!" Raven replied enthusiastically when he extended the invitation. "I'd love to come hang with y'all!"

"Really?" Joe was a little surprised; part of him had expected her to have (or find) a reason why she couldn't.

"Absolutely. I'm actually a little flattered that you even want me there. I know how you are about your time with your girls."

"Well yeah, but you're..." He hesitated, not wanting to freak her out.

Raven paused. "I'm what?"

Joe hesitated again before forging ahead, "You're important to me so I want them to spend some time with you, too."

He could hear Raven gasp, and he hoped he hadn't just sent her running for the hills. But to his relief and delight she responded, "I am *so* glad to hear you say that, Joe."

"Word?"

"Word."

"Well, then..." Joe actually felt nervous now, and was glad that Raven couldn't see him fidgeting. "I'm glad you're glad."

Raven chuckled, suddenly pretty nervous herself. "Yeah, um...this is actually a perfect weekend for this 'cause they're closing the restaurant for renovations and stuff, so I'll have some extra time. What day do you want me to come over?"

"Friday or Saturday night; whichever works for you. I'll be taking them back to Tanisha's Sunday afternoon."

"We can do Saturday night then; that'll give me a little more time to tie up the loose ends and stuff before the restaurant closes. Can I bring anything?"

"Nah, woman, I invited you...I'll provide the food. And I remember you're allergic to peanuts."

"Oh," Raven was pleasantly surprised, touched, and impressed. She'd told him about her peanut allergy during one of their lazy days together; she hadn't expected him to remember. She barely remembered telling him. "I appreciate you remembering that. But there must be *something* I can bring."

"Just yourself," Joe insisted. "I mean, I'm no chef or anything like you are so don't expect anything fancy. I can make a decent meat loaf, though."

He could hear the smile in Raven's voice when she replied, "I'm sure it's delicious. But I refuse to come over there empty-handed so at least let me bring some dessert. What do the girls like?"

"Hell, they're easy to please. My girls are both adorable *and* greedy as hell, especially when it comes to sweets. I swear they can both eat like some linebackers when they want to."

Raven laughed loudly, and Joe automatically smiled. He could just imagine how he must have looked right then because his cheeks were actually starting to hurt, he was grinning so hard. Raven had a knack for putting a smile on his face and making everything just seem...better.

When she calmed down, she cleared her throat and said something that caused his smile to get even wider:

"I can't wait to see you, Joe."

His voice dripping with sincerity, Joe replied, "Believe me, I can't wait to see you, either."

When Saturday night rolled around, Joe felt the nervous, anxious anticipation he felt recently when he knew he was going to be seeing Raven. He actually contemplated what to wear, as if they weren't just going to be spending the evening in his apartment. After telling himself to stop tripping, he put on a black v-neck t-shirt and some jeans, and made sure he had on deodorant and that his face and teeth were clean. He didn't really wear cologne but Raven had long since commented that she loved the smell of the soap he used, and he'd taken an extra-long shower about a half hour before she was to arrive.

Jillian and Tara were watching a movie in the living room when there was a knock on the door. Joe was in the kitchen and quickly went to answer it, trying to keep his smile in check.

"Is that Ms. Raven, Daddy?" Jillian asked, turning around. Joe had already told them she would be coming over.

"Should be, yeah."

"I like her," Tara commented.

Yeah, I like her, too, Joe thought to himself as he quickly checked the peephole before opening the door. Raven stood in front of him with two handfuls of grocery bags and a sheepish smile on her face.

"Don't fuss at me, Sexy Chocolate," she greeted him, stepping inside the apartment. "I know I had insisted on just bringing dessert, but I remember you saying one time how much you and the girls liked mac and cheese, and then I remembered you never tasted *mine*..."

Joe just shook his head as he closed the door behind her and took the bags from her hands. He couldn't resist smiling, and had to resist the urge to take a quick kiss like he wanted to. It was only because his daughters were nearby that he didn't.

"And the next thing I knew, I was getting the ingredients for that, along with some other stuff," Raven continued. "I was at the farmers market, and I'm like a kid in a candy store when I'm there."

"Candy?" Jillian and Tara chorused, whirling around excitedly.

Joe and Raven laughed. "I don't have any candy but I *do* have something sweet for y'all later on," Raven assured them, going over to give them each kisses on the forehead, which they happily received. "How are my little sugar babies doing?"

"Fine," the girls chorused.

"We're watching *Frozen*," Tara informed her.

"For the millionth time," Joe muttered jokingly as he took the bags into the kitchen.

"You wanna watch it with us, Ms. Raven?" Jillian asked. "We can start it over."

"Oh, most definitely! Y'all go ahead and finish and then we'll all watch it together from the beginning after we eat, if it's okay with your dad. I'm gonna help him in the kitchen...we're gonna be good and full when we watch it!"

"Are you really making mac and cheese? Is it out of the box, like our mama makes it?"

Raven did her best not to laugh out loud. "Yes, I most certainly am making mac and cheese and nope, it's definitely not out of the box. Hopefully you'll like it. I put a whole bunch of gooey, yummy cheese in mine, and bacon."

"Ohh, that sounds *good*!" Tara exclaimed. "Can you hurry up and make it??"

Laughing, Raven blew them a kiss before turning towards the kitchen. "Coming right up. Y'all just stay right there and enjoy your movie...whoever stays put the longest gets the most dessert!"

Joe was in the kitchen taking the groceries out of the bags. "You're just hardheaded, ain't you?"

"Feel free to spank me," Raven flirted, lowering her voice so the girls couldn't hear.

"Girl, you better watch yourself," Joe playfully warned. "Don't make me bend you over this counter."

"How wide do you want my legs?"

Instantly as hard as steel, Joe reached out and yanked Raven to him, eliciting a delighted shriek from her. Not even trying to resist, he planted a deep kiss on her, letting his hands roam into her hair then down to her backside, squeezing it as he pulled her closer against his erection. He usually wouldn't engage in such a thing with his daughters right in the next room, but he couldn't help himself. He hadn't seen Raven in days and couldn't keep his hands off her any longer.

They kissed hungrily for several minutes before Joe reluctantly pulled back. "We better stop," he whispered, his chest heaving slightly. "'Cause I'm not gonna be able to keep controlling myself too much longer and I don't want to risk the girls coming in here and catching us."

"Why do you think I bribed them with sweets to stay put?" Raven whispered in response, sliding her hands up his chest and around his neck. Her body had started burning for him as soon as she saw him in that tight black shirt; Joe was just too fine for words, to her. "I *had* to get my hands on you."

Joe bit his lip as Raven's hand slid down to his crotch. She sucked on his neck as she quickly unbuttoned his jeans, then proceeded to give him the best hand job of his life. Usually, that wasn't enough to make him explode but Raven obviously had the secret; in just a couple of minutes he was literally weak in the knees and using every ounce of restraint he had not to yell out loud. He clutched Raven to him as she continued licking and sucking his neck, occasionally running her tongue up and around his ear, her hand working him into a frenzy. And of course when Raven felt he was getting close, she dropped to her knees and finished him off with her mouth, swallowing every drop of his release.

"Wouldn't want you to mess up your clothes, right?" she smirked at him, slowly licking her lips as she stood. "We have to get this dinner going."

Joe just shot her a look as he tried to get his bearings; she had moved over to the sink and was washing her hands, actually whistling. Once Joe got the feeling in his legs back, he fixed his pants before going over and standing behind her, leaning close to her ear.

"You know I'm gonna get you back for that, right?" he warned in a low voice.

"Promises, promises," Raven winked. She squealed when Joe swatted her behind.

"So what is all this you brought that I told you not to bring?" Joe asked, looking at all the groceries.

"Just stuff for my mac and cheese, and I was gonna roast some vegetables and make some homemade biscuits. What were you planning to serve with the meat loaf?"

"To be honest, I was just gonna pop open a can of corn or something."

Raven shook her head, chuckling. "No offense to the corn, but I think we can do a little better than that, if it's okay with you."

"It wouldn't have been *plain* corn. I would've put a bunch of seasoning in it."

Raven threw back her head and laughed, and Joe couldn't resist laughing with her. He had been running late and hadn't even started on his meat loaf, and had forgotten all about sides. All he had were canned goods. He hated grocery shopping and tried to get the simplest things that he could while still being at least somewhat healthy. The most he would ever do as far as produce was grab a bag of apples or oranges.

Joe and Raven proceeded to cook dinner together, occasionally going to check on the girls and also helping themselves to several kissing breaks. Joe could cook all right though it was never something he particularly enjoyed doing, but he loved every second in the kitchen with Raven. She would playfully bump him with her hip while they were side by side at the counter, tell him about things going on at work and was genuinely interested to hear about his job, give him tips on how to make his cooking easier and better without making him feel stupid for not knowing as much as she did. When everything was in the oven, they fooled around in the kitchen some more before going to join the girls in the living room. Joe noticed how easily Raven got along with Jillian and Tara, and how quickly they took to her. For a while, none of them were even paying him any attention; they were engrossed in a Chris Brown vs. Trey Songz debate, and something about lip gloss. Joe just checked on the food every now and then and watched a basketball game on TV, smiling to himself.

When it was finally time to eat, they all sat at Joe's small table with full plates of food. The girls raved about Raven's mac and cheese, and begged her to come over and make it again the next time they were there. Joe couldn't deny it was probably the best he'd ever had, too. Raven even agreed to help teach the girls how to cook, at their request.

Then Jillian asked something that neither Joe nor Raven had been expecting:

"Daddy, is Raven your girlfriend?"

Blinking a couple of times in surprise, Joe put his fork down and looked at his daughter, then at Raven. Normally he would have gotten onto Jillian for getting into grown folks' business, but he found that he actually wanted to answer this particular question.

"Yeah," Joe replied, his eyes still on Raven. "She is."

Raven's breath quickened slightly, and a smile curled the corners of her mouth. A warm gush flowed through her, hearing Joe claim her like that. She hadn't expected that, but inside, she was thrilled at his response.

"Good," Jillian declared, clearly pleased herself.

"And I hope y'all stay together longer than you and Ms. Van did," Tara added.

That startled both Joe and Raven for a few moments, but Raven recovered quicker than Joe did. "Don't you worry your pretty self about that, but between you and me," she leaned in dramatically and Tara quickly and eagerly leaned in, too, prepared to hear the secret of a lifetime, "I don't plan on going anywhere any time soon."

It was Joe's turn to smile.

After they finished dinner, they watched *Frozen* as promised while they devoured Raven's dessert, which was a layered treat of thick chocolate chip cookie and fudge brownie – both from scratch - with Oreos in between. And she brought salted caramel swirl gelato to go with it. Joe had to stop the girls from getting more than two servings apiece. He knew if he left it up to them, they'd eat the whole pan.

"You trying to have them bouncing off the walls or somethin'?" he asked Raven while the girls were getting ready for bed.

"Hey, a little decadence is good every now and then," Raven defended, winking at him. "And you know it was good, too. You sure tore up yours."

"Oh, it was damn good," Joe confirmed. "I can't be eating like that too much, though; gotta keep it tight." He lifted up his shirt, revealing his six-pack.

Raven wanted to dive on him. Biting her lip, she eyed him lustfully. "Unless you want me to maul you like an alley cat, I suggest you put your shirt down."

Joe smirked, then moved like he was going to take the shirt completely off. Raven started towards him, then they heard the girls call out that they were ready for bed.

"I'll be back," Joe tweaked her chin as he passed her. Raven just turned and looked after him thoughtfully as he went to kiss his daughters goodnight. She lowered herself onto his bed, rubbing her hands on her thighs as she waited for him to come back. She knew it was time for them to have a talk.

When he re-entered the room several minutes later, he noticed the look on her face.

"What's wrong?" he asked, closing the door behind him.

"Can you come sit down?" Raven requested, patting the spot next to her. She was still biting her lip, only now it was out of nervousness.

Joe obliged, his concerned eyes on her. "You okay?"

Raven didn't respond for several moments; she just continued to get her thoughts together as she looked at the blank television in front of her. Finally, she turned towards him, looking right into his eyes. "What are we doing, Joe?"

Joe returned her gaze, knowing full well what she was talking about. "Are you mad at me about what I told the girls at dinner? I know we've never discussed all that..."

"Well, let's discuss it now," Raven suggested eagerly. "We've been doing what we do for a while now, and it's been awesome, but I'm starting to feel differently about things...I need to know what page you're on. I know which one *I'm* on..."

"I know which one I'm on, too," Joe assured her. "And I want what I told the girls to be true."

Raven felt her heart speed up. "You do?"

"Yeah. I want us to do this, for real. I want to be your man, Raven. I have for a while."

Raven had to get her bearings for a moment; she thought Joe might've just told the girls they were together to appease them, but that he wasn't quite ready to go there with her yet. She'd been imagining herself as Joe's woman for weeks now, and to hear him say he wanted the same thing sent her over the moon.

"Well we *are* on the same page, then," she replied, her smile spreading into a full-fledged grin. "'Cause that's most definitely what I want, too."

Joe couldn't remember the last time he'd been so relieved. He had no idea how Raven was going to react to that; when she said she wanted to talk, he thought she was going to put an end to things...maybe say that things were getting too heavy and she wasn't ready for it. He knew he was stepping out on a limb claiming her as his girlfriend to his daughters, but there was really no other answer he wanted to give. And hearing that Raven wanted him the same way he wanted her made him feel like he hit the lottery.

"Are you sure?" he still felt compelled to ask. "I come with a lot, Raven. I have two daughters with a very difficult woman. Being with me means having to deal with Tanisha, and I can tell you right now, she's not gonna like hearing about us being together."

"I'm absolutely sure," Raven assured him. "I can handle Tanisha. And I already adore your daughters. You're not gonna scare me away that easily, Joe Miller...it's gonna take a lot more than a couple of kids and a bitchy baby mama to get rid of me."

Grabbing her face, Joe kissed her deeply, a sudden overwhelming swell of emotion hitting him. He hadn't felt like this since he fell for Van, and he welcomed the feeling. He wrapped his arms around Raven tightly, pulling her onto his lap. He couldn't get close enough to her. She straddled his lap as they shared the most heartfelt and emotional kiss yet.

Raven didn't think she'd ever been so happy. She never would have imagined it, but Joe was the man she felt she'd been waiting for all of her life. The realization both scared and thrilled her at the same time. She finally found a good one.

Their kiss continued as they fell onto their sides on the bed, not letting each other go even for a second.

"I thought we both said we didn't want a relationship," Raven reminded him in a whisper against his lips between kisses. She dared to look into his eyes, part of her not even wanting to remind him of that. But she felt she should offer one last out, if he wanted to take it. "Remember, when we started all this..."

"Things change," Joe retorted emphatically. "I *didn't* want one then. But I absolutely want one now...but only if it's with you."

Happy tears pricked Raven's eyes. That was all she needed to hear. "Well, it's settled, then," she said, her voice breaking as she grinned at her new man. She didn't even try to stop the happy tears from streaming down her face. "I'm all yours."

"Music to my ears." Joe smiled before lowering his head and claiming her lips again.

They laid on top of Joe's bed, fully clothed, holding each other for the rest of the night. Raven snuggled close to Joe, her head on his chest, feeling the most content she had ever felt. Joe held her to him, his thumb softly stroking her shoulder, his eyes looking blankly out of the window in front of him into the Atlanta night. Raven was officially his woman, and he couldn't have been happier.

But now, he wondered if he should tell her about his last tryst with Tanisha. He didn't know how she would take hearing that he slept with Tanisha during the time he was sleeping with her. He hadn't technically done anything wrong, but she still might take offense to that. Joe didn't know if Raven had been seeing anyone else while they'd been messing around, because he hadn't asked; part of him felt it wasn't any of his business but the bigger part of him simply didn't want to know. He hadn't wanted to think about her with another man, even before he started really wanting her for himself.

Joe started to wake Raven up and tell her what happened with Tanisha, just for the sake of having everything out on the table. After what went down with Van, he wasn't trying to have any secrets - or anything that could even be misconstrued as a secret - messing things up with Raven before they really got going.

But he didn't want to taint the vibe of what had turned out to be an awesome evening, so he hesitantly decided to wait, promising himself he'd tell her soon.

Chapter 21

. . . .

IT WAS THE DAY OF CASSIE and Canton's birthday dinner, and despite the occasion, there was a lot of dissension and tension in the McCallister/Roseland house. Grant was on edge about issues at work; they had identified who was stealing money and him and his attorneys were pressing every charge they could against them. Grant didn't appreciate being taken advantage of, and he was going to make sure that this individual paid for doing just that. Aside from that, it irked him that as good as he tried to be to his employees, there was someone greedy and stupid enough to steal from him and think they could get away with it.

Van was trying to figure out how she was going to tell Grant that she had quit her job the previous day. Things had come to a head with her and her supervisor, Mr. Andersen, and when he threatened her job again, Van lost it. She told him exactly where to go, what to pack, and how to get there, and stormed out of the office. She felt exhilarated, like a weight had been lifted off of her shoulders, but it wasn't long at all before another one replaced it.

Even though Grant had been the one to suggest she quit in the first place, Van hadn't discussed this with him; she had always insisted that she wouldn't quit without a plan, and she had no plan. As miserable as she had been at work recently, she hadn't taken the time to really figure out what it was she wanted to do instead, and she couldn't deny that was because she knew she had Grant as a safety net. It wasn't like before when everything was on her; she would never have been able to just up and quit her job just because her boss pissed her off before she got with Grant. But she hadn't hesitated to do just that today; she was just fed up. Grant would probably understand that, but how would she explain it to her children, especially Cassie? What kind of example was she setting for them?

Van tried her best to block those thoughts out and just concentrate on celebrating her babies turning twelve, but between her inner turmoil, Grant's obvious attitude that he kept trying to deny, and the twins arguing like it was going out of style, Van was already ready for the day to be over.

And on top of everything else, Van was wondering if Joe was going to show up, and if he would be with Raven if he did. Van had discovered that Joe had changed his number, and she couldn't help being insulted by that. Had he done that because he was tired of her contacting him? It wasn't like he ever responded to her. Surely he wouldn't go that far just because of her...would he?

Van kept eyeing the clock, counting down until the birthday dinner was to start and hoping to high heaven that Joe actually showed up. They had some things to talk about, though she knew actually getting him to talk to her wouldn't be an easy task at all.

Grant had arranged a catered dinner for the twins at the house, and told them they could each invite a couple of friends. When he'd told Van what he was planning to do, she was all for the idea; it was nice but small, just like she wanted. Canton had no problem with it, but she could tell Cassie was slightly disappointed at the thought of her birthday just consisting of a dinner at home, even though she tried to hide her disappointment. Van had noticed a significant change in her attitude ever since the whole situation with her friend Bianca, but Cassie still had her moments every now and then, which Van expected. She *was* still just a child, after all.

Van was trying to get ready, since guests were going to be arriving at the house soon. The caterers were already there setting up. She wasn't willing to acknowledge even to herself that the extra care she was putting into her appearance wasn't solely for the benefit of the man it *should've* been for. Part of her couldn't help wanting Joe to still be attracted to her, even if he didn't acknowledge or act on it. Why that mattered was still something she wasn't willing to face.

But as she was doing her hair, the sounds of Canton and Cassie arguing, again, caused her hands to fall onto the vanity with a thump and a long, already-exhausted sigh to flow from her lips.

"Cassie, get out of my room!" Canton demanded.

"Not until you give me my phone charger back!" Cassie snapped.

"I don't have your stupid charger; I have one of my own. Now will you get out of here and leave me alone?!"

"No! I know you have it 'cause I can't find it in my room!"

"Maybe if you *cleaned* your room..."

"My room *is* clean!"

"You should be able to find stuff in there, then. I know where all *my* stuff is. So if you can't find your charger, that's not my problem."

"I'm tellin'!"

"Go ahead!"

"*Mama!!*"

Van heaved another sigh before standing up and stalking to Canton's room to put out this latest fire. She had hoped that as the twins got older all this senseless arguing would dwindle down, but no such luck yet.

"What is the problem now?" Van asked upon entering Canton's room, even though she had heard their entire conversation.

"Canton has my phone charger and won't give it back!" Cassie accused, pointing at her brother.

"I *don't* have her charger!" Canton insisted.

"Aren't y'all getting a little too old for this? How do you know he has it, Cassie?" Van asked.

"Because I can't find it!"

"That's it? So because you can't find it, you automatically blame somebody else?"

"Where else could it be?" Cassie didn't understand why they couldn't see her point. "I need it back 'cause my phone is about to die!"

"Cassie, we really don't have time for this," Van informed her, trying to ignore her growing headache. "Where did you last have it?"

"I don't remember."

"Where all did you look?"

"In the living room and in my room, a little bit."

Van knew that meant Cassie had hardly looked at all; if it wasn't in plain sight, she just claimed she couldn't find it and went on her accusation tirade. "You need to look more than just *a little bit* before you go accusing people. Go look in the den; you were in there yesterday with your phone."

The look of realization on Cassie's face indicated that she hadn't even thought of that, and Van turned out to be right; her charger was right in the den where Cassie had been the night before. Van got on to her for starting some nonsense, made her apologize to Canton, then went back to her room to finish getting ready. She tried to take a deep breath and pray that the rest of the day went more smoothly than it began.

But that prayer was out the window when she got a call from her mother. Telling herself to chill out, she picked up her cell phone; of course her mother was going to call on the twins' birthday. No need to get nervous.

"Hey, Mama," she greeted, raking her nails through her freshly-trimmed bangs as she looked in the mirror.

"Hey, sweetheart," Florence greeted. There was a lot of commotion in the background. "What are you doing right now?"

"Trying to get myself together; it's been kind of a full morning. Where are you? There sure is a lot of noise, wherever it is."

"Well, I have some good news that hopefully will make you feel better. We're at the airport."

Van felt her stomach drop. "*What* airport?"

"The one in Atlanta; Hartsfield, I think it's called. Our flight just arrived a little while ago."

Almost dropping the phone, Van had to fight to not sound as panicked as she was feeling. She honestly felt like she was going to faint. What in the world were her parents doing in Atlanta?? They hadn't said anything to her about coming today; this was the *last* thing Van needed!

"Ummm...I didn't know-" Van cleared her throat, which was suddenly as dry as the desert, "I didn't know you all were coming. You should've told me..."

"Then it wouldn't have been a surprise, would it?" Florence chuckled. Van could hear her father, Mitchell, laughing in the background. "Can you come pick us up?"

Why, God?? "Of course, sure," Van croaked, then cleared her throat again. "Just, um...just let me get myself together and I'll be on my way. What airline did you come in on?"

"Southwest. Are you okay? You sound strange."

"No, I'm fine," Van quickly insisted. "Just a lot going on at once, that's all."

"I'm sorry to just spring this on you, baby, but we really wanted to be here for our grandbabies' twelfth birthday," Florence explained. "Your father wanted to give you a heads-up but I thought it would be a nice surprise."

"No, it is; it's a *great* surprise," Van lied, placing a hand on her forehead. Her head was pounding. Any other time, she would have been thrilled to get a surprise visit from her parents. But this was the absolute last thing she needed today; she still hadn't told them about Grant, and now she had no choice but to do just that.

Assuring her parents that she would be on her way shortly, Van took a few moments to gather herself. Why was this happening?? How was she going to swing this? This day was turning out to be a disaster, and the main event hadn't even happened yet. Van really wished she could just go somewhere and hide, but she knew she was about to finally face the music.

Grant was in his office, perched on the edge of his desk, arms crossed, his phone at his ear. There was a frown on his face and Van couldn't tell if it was from concentration or anger; he'd been on edge all day himself, and they hadn't said very much to each other outside of plans concerning the dinner and the twins, or other generic things. Van wanted to just leave for the airport without telling him, but she knew that would just cause more issues.

After noticing her, Grant put whoever he was talking to on hold and looked at her. "What's up?"

"I'm sorry to interrupt, but I just wanted to let you know I have to run to the airport to get my parents; they just called to let me know they were in town."

Grant's eyebrows shot up, intrigued. "Oh really?"

"Yeah, it was a total surprise. I had no idea they were coming."

"I'm looking forward to finally getting to meet them. It's about time I get to know my future in-laws."

"Right; and they'll sure love to finally get to know you, too," Van replied with a forced smile.

Grant just eyed her for a moment before asking, "Would you like me to send Tommy to get them so you can continue with whatever you were doing when they called?"

"No, no; that's not necessary," Van quickly insisted. She knew she needed the time in the car to finally come clean and prepare her parents before they got to the house. "I can get them myself."

"All right, well, be careful. I'll keep an eye on everything here. Love you."

"Love you, too. I'll try to hurry."

"All right."

Van could feel her anxiety rising as soon as she walked away from Grant's office, and it shot through the roof as she drove to the airport. Over and over, she thought about how she was going to work this situation, and she knew the only thing she could do was tell the truth. There was just no way she could put it off any longer. She just knew her mother was going to fuss at her until the cows came home, and there was no telling *what* her father would say.

So once Van arrived at the airport, she hugged and kissed her parents, grabbed their bags, and hustled them back to the car. She gripped the steering wheel and took a deep breath, knowing she only had the length of the drive home to get this out.

"Mama, Daddy, I have something really important I need to tell you and I *have* to tell you now."

"What is it?" Florence asked, concerned, from her spot in the front seat. Van's father Mitchell was in the back. "And is this some new route to your house? I thought it was in the other direction."

"Um, yes, that's part of what I need to tell you. There's no other way to say this than to just come out with it...Joe and I broke up. A while ago."

"What?" Florence gasped.

"Why??" Mitchell chimed in. He and Joe had always gotten along great and were like best buddies from the beginning.

"Y'all, I really don't have time to get into every detail but I made the decision to be with someone else."

"Why are you just now telling us? How long ago was this??" Florence demanded, a frown marring her face.

Van knew they were going to flip out. "A little over a year ago-"

"Excuse me?!" Mitchell exploded, making Van jump. Her father didn't typically say too much but he made up for it when he got angry.

"Over a year?? How many times have we talked in all that time? And how many times have I specifically asked you about Joe and you never said anything about *any* of this!" Florence exclaimed, angry herself. "So you were just *lying* to me?!"

"Yes, and I'm sorry but you might as well know that when I left Joe, the twins and I moved into this other man's house, and...we've been engaged for several months now."

"Have you lost your damn mind??" Mitchell yelled.

"So, let me get this straight," Florence turned towards her daughter. "You're with Joe for years then all of a sudden leave him for another man, move your children into his house, get *engaged* to this man, and don't say anything about it to us? If we hadn't just shown up here like we had, you wouldn't even be telling us now, would you?"

Van was crying now. "I'm sorry!"

"There is no excuse for this!" Mitchell fussed at her. "What, are you pregnant, too?"

"No!"

"What??"

"No, sir," Van quickly corrected, shrinking in her seat a little. "I'm *not* pregnant."

"Why did you feel you couldn't tell us all this?" Florence asked, shaking her head. Van didn't even want to look at her because she could feel the disappointment radiating like the heat from the vents. "The fact that you felt you needed to lie to us is what upsets me the most."

"What did Joe do?" Mitchell demanded. "Why did you decide to leave him after over five years together? What, he wouldn't marry you or something?"

Van's eyes squeezed shut momentarily. "No, that's not it at all. Joe didn't do anything wrong. He was...he was actually about to propose to me when I ended things. I just didn't think it was working anymore, that's all."

"That's all," Florence repeated, glaring at Van intensely. Van knew she knew there was more to it than what she was saying.

"And who is this man you're engaged to?" Mitchell demanded to know.

"His name is Grant McCallister."

"Umph. Sounds like you left Joe for some rich guy."

Van gasped. "Daddy!"

"I've heard that name before..." Florence mused.

"I know who he is," Mitchell grumbled. "What, a regular hard-working man wasn't good enough for you anymore?"

"It wasn't like that!" Van protested tearfully. She wiped her eyes with the back of her hand. The tone in her father's voice was like a slap across the face. "I have all the respect in the world for Joe!"

"What did you leave him for, then? You said yourself he didn't do anything wrong."

Van knew she couldn't get into all that by the time they arrived at the house, which would be in the next fifteen minutes or so. It was one time that the notoriously bad Atlanta traffic wasn't terrible. Figures. "I promise I will tell y'all all the details later, but for the time being, can you *please* not let on that you're just finding out about all this?"

Florence glared at her. "And why do we need to do that?"

Van wanted to just vanish into thin air. She kept her eyes straight ahead when she mumbled, "Because Grant doesn't know that I hadn't told y'all about him yet."

"Hmph," Mitchell scoffed, shaking his head.

Florence just glared at Van, then turned her eyes towards the passenger side window. Her thin salt-and-pepper hair was pulled into its usual tight bun and her hands clutched her purse beneath her large breasts as she sat stiffly in her seat. No one said anything else the rest of the drive.

When they got to Van and Grant's, everyone went into the house as if that whole talk in the car hadn't happened. Van took a couple of minutes to gather herself and make sure her eyes weren't red or glassy from the crying, then plastered a smile on her face and led her parents into the house. The guests hadn't started to arrive yet but the caterers were just about done setting up. The twins were dressed and in the living room when they walked in. Cassie was on her phone and Canton was reading a book.

"Guys, look who's here," Van called out.

The twins looked up and gasped.

"There go my babies!" Florence grinned, opening her arms to them.

They both ran and practically jumped on Van's parents in one collective group hug. Van smiled at the sight and kept an eye out for Grant, who she knew would be making his appearance any second.

"I didn't know you were coming," Canton commented to his grandparents.

"It was a surprise. We didn't want to just call you and send you something this year," Mitchell replied.

"Did you *bring* us anything?" Cassie asked.

"Cassie!" Canton admonished.

"What? I was just asking."

"You're not supposed to ask that!"

"How come I'm not? It's our birthday!"

"Y'all hush; you know we have gifts for both of you," Florence admonished with a smile.

The four of them were still talking when Grant came into the room. Van noticed him first, and her chest immediately started pounding. She prayed her parents heeded her request to not let on that they had just found out about him a mere ten minutes before.

"How's everybody doing?" Grant announced his presence.

Van's parents looked up at Grant. Their expressions remained even as Grant approached them with a smile on his face.

"I'm Grant," he introduced himself, going to shake Mitchell's hand first. Van bit her lip nervously. "I'm so glad to finally meet you all."

"It's great to meet you, too, Grant," Mitchell replied, shaking Grant's hand firmly. He looked him right in his eyes. "I'm looking forward to spending some one-on-one time with you; getting to know you better."

"Me too, sir." Grant turned to Florence with his hand extended. "Mrs. Roseland, it's my honor."

Florence glanced at him, at his hand, then back up at his face. Van just knew she was going to say something snide but to her relief, Florence surprised her.

"Come on over here, Grant," she said with a smile, nudging his hand away and opening her arms wide for a hug. Grant grinned, seemingly slightly relieved himself, and leaned down to oblige her. Florence hugged him tightly, just like she used to do to Joe, and Van said a silent prayer of thanks.

A little later, guests started arriving. Grant hadn't invited all that many people; it was mainly just a few other family members along with Canton and Cassie's friends, and their parents. Van hadn't heard from Raven recently but the last they had talked, she was coming. Van was just glad that she hadn't refused like she had the previous year on the twins' birthday because she didn't want to be in Grant's house.

Once the twins' friends got there, they all went to the den for a while. Van didn't really want to get things going until Raven arrived, even though everything was ready to go. She knew this day was supposed to be about the twins, but it was more important to her than she realized that Raven be there for the entire dinner.

"Baby, I think we need to go ahead and get started," Grant said, coming over to her and checking his watch. "Everything is ready and waiting."

"Let's just wait a few more minutes," Van pleaded. "The kids aren't in any hurry, anyway."

"Maybe not, but their parents will be," Grant reminded her. "Have you called Raven?"

"I did but it went to voicemail. She texted me, though, and said she was on her way."

"Well then she can just join us when she gets here. It's not a movie, it's a dinner; she won't be missing anything if she starts after everybody else. We have plenty of food."

"Grant, please?" Van looked at him with puppy dog eyes.

Grant sighed, knowing he couldn't deny her when she looked at him like that. "Fine. But just a few more minutes, Van. We can't keep everybody waiting just because Raven can never be on time."

"Thank you," Van smiled at him, not even bothering to defend Raven's tendency to be tardy.

About ten minutes later, Raven finally showed up. It was Grant who let her in, and he was more than a little surprised to see her arrive with Joe and his daughters.

"Hey, come on in," he smoothly greeted, stepping aside. "Welcome. It's good to see you all."

"Thanks," Joe replied simply, not looking at him as he stepped into the house.

"Hi, Grant," Raven greeted politely, giving him a small smile. Her animosity towards him had pretty much evaporated; she was too happy about her new official relationship with Joe. But she knew Joe wasn't quite there yet, as far as being cool with Grant. "You remember Joe's daughters, Jillian and Tara?"

"I sure do. How are you beautiful young ladies doing?" Grant smiled at the girls, who giggled in response. Joe tried not to frown when he noticed they were actually blushing.

"Fine," Jillian and Tara chorused.

Just then, Van came into the foyer and stopped in her tracks when she saw Joe there with Raven, unable to stop the slight frown that appeared when she saw their linked hands. She tried to gather herself quickly, but Grant saw it and he was sure everyone else did, too. He eyed her as she seemingly forced herself to continue towards them.

"Hey; I didn't hear y'all come in," she said, forcing a smile. Her smile turned into a grin when she looked at Jillian and Tara. "Wow, y'all have gotten so big! Come here and give me a hug, babies!"

Jillian and Tara went into her open arms looking glad to see her, but they weren't as excited as Van or even Joe had expected. Their requests to see Van had dwindled since Raven had been coming around.

With her arms still around the girls, Van turned her eyes to her other guests. "Raven, I'm so glad to see you;

we've been waiting on you to get here. Hey, Joe; I'm glad you could make it."

"Yeah, Canton and Cassie invited me so I wanted to be here for them," Joe replied, only glancing at her. The implication that he wasn't there because of her was clear.

"Sorry we're late; I didn't know we were holding things up," Raven commented. "It's just been one of those kinds of mornings."

"It's fine. You're here now," Van assured her.

"I can take your coats," Grant offered.

Joe immediately moved to help Raven out of her black trench coat, and she smiled back at him appreciatively. Van swallowed hard, unable to stop watching them.

Just then, Joe got a call on his cell phone and stepped outside to take it while Grant showed the girls where all the other kids were. Van went over and linked her arm through Raven's, noting the obvious glow her cousin had.

"So everything's good, huh?" she asked, her voice low.

Raven grinned. "Everything's *great*."

Van itched to ask her to elaborate and bombard her with questions, but she knew that would have to wait. "Well, I'm glad you decided to come; it means a lot. Just a heads-up, though, we had a little surprise this morning. My-"

"Is that my Raven?" Florence exclaimed, rushing into the foyer with her arms already outstretched and a huge grin on her face.

"Oh my gosh!" Raven gasped, clearly shocked. She glanced at Van and tried to recover quickly. "Auntie!"

"You come on over here and give me a hug, girl!" Florence ordered, still grinning.

Raven quickly went over and gave her a huge hug, genuinely happy to see her aunt but clearly thrown for a loop. "It's so good to see you! I didn't know you were gonna be here; is Uncle Mitchell here, too?"

"Yeah, he's in there. We decided to come down and surprise everybody."

"Well, you sure did *that*! I haven't seen you in so long...and you're gonna have to let me know what face cream or magic potion you're using up there in Ohio 'cause your skin is on *point*, Auntie."

"Girl, that's nothing but black soap and cocoa butter, and drinking a whole lotta water," Florence informed her, even though she was clearly pleased with the compliment. "You're just as beautiful as always."

"Thank you, Auntie!" Raven beamed.

Florence eyed her. "You're *radiant*, actually," she observed, her eyes traveling up and down Raven's body. "You aren't pregnant, are you?"

"Pregnant? No!" Raven insisted, actually blushing. Van eyed her, now curious about the possibility herself. Even when Raven was high on Grant, she wasn't looking like she did now.

"You sure?" Florence pressed.

"I'm *absolutely* sure. There aren't any buns in this oven. Ooh, speaking of buns, I've gotta tell you about my promotion at the restaurant!"

"You got a promotion?! Congratulations!" Florence hugged her niece again. "I knew when you were always hovering in my kitchen that you were gonna be a big-time chef one day."

"I'm not quite big-time yet, but I'm working on it," Raven grinned.

"So is that why you're walking around here like a night light? I used to love my teaching job, but it never had me looking like *this*."

Raven actually looked bashful, an uncommon thing for her. "I don't know what you mean, Auntie."

"Girl, please, the only thing that can have a woman glowing like you are is-"

Just then, Joe stepped back into the house, still looking down at his phone. The three ladies turned to him.

"Joe??" Florence exclaimed.

Joe looked up and almost dropped his phone when he saw Florence. His eyes shifted to each of the women before he managed a slightly uneasy smile. "Wow...Mama Florence! Hey!"

Florence's eyes were full of questions as she glanced at Van, then Raven, before rushing over to give Joe a big hug. She leaned back and took his face in her hands, smiling at him adoringly. "I am so glad to see you, baby! I've missed you!"

"I missed you, too. I didn't know you were going to be here," he commented, giving Van a quick but clearly accusatory glance. Van mouthed *I didn't know she was coming*, but Joe had already turned his eyes away from her.

"Yeah, we're shocking everybody today," Florence chuckled. She turned to face the women and seeing the slightly uneasy expressions on Van and Raven's faces, she frowned curiously. Glancing between the three of them, she asked Joe, "You're just getting here?"

Joe looked slightly uncomfortable; he didn't know how much Van had told her about their breakup or the state of their non-existent relationship now. "No, ma'am; I got here a few minutes ago."

"Oh." Florence glanced at the ladies again. "You came by yourself?"

"No, ma'am...I came with Raven."

"With Raven?" The surprise was clear in Florence's voice. "You two are friends? That's really nice."

Raven cleared her throat. "Actually, Auntie-"

"Everybody ready to eat?" Grant asked with a clap of his hands, entering the foyer. Everyone looked at him with varying expressions, and Grant could tell he had walked in on something. "Everything okay?"

"Yes, everything's great," Van insisted, glad that Grant had interrupted Raven about to tell Florence about her and Joe's relationship. She quickly stepped over to him and wrapped an arm around his waist, placing her other hand on his chest. She smiled up at him then at everyone else, trying to ease some of the obvious tension. "We're ready; I know *my* stomach's growling."

"Yeah, it smells great in here," Raven commented, seemingly a little relieved herself, even though she had been about to tell her aunt the true nature of her and Joe's relationship. It certainly wasn't anything she was trying to hide, but she didn't want to cause any more tension than was already there. Today was supposed to be about Canton and Cassie.

"Well, let's go, then," Grant suggested, his eyes sweeping across all of them before turning to head to the dining room, his arm around Van. Everyone followed suit, with Florence casting one more thoughtful glance towards Joe and Raven, who drifted close together as they walked but not touching.

Chapter 22

• • • •

THE ADULTS CONGREGATED in the dining room while the kids stayed at the table in the kitchen. Mitchell was surprised to see Joe, and Florence quickly went over and whispered something into his ear. Mitchell frowned at her in confusion, and Florence just shook her head slightly. Van would have given anything to know what her mother said to her father and what was behind those exchanged looks. She had a feeling Florence suspected there was more to Raven and Joe than just friendship.

After Mitchell prayed over the food, everyone sat down to eat. The food was delicious and the vibe was pleasant enough, but still a little strained. Joe and Raven were sitting next to each other and Van tried not to watch them too much, but she couldn't seem to keep her eyes from straying in their direction. Then she would look at Grant and see his eyes already on her, watching her watch them, and she would blush and look down at her plate. She was glad that she had already expressed to Grant her disapproval of Raven being with Joe, so at least he would know why she was so fixated on them, but she could tell that he wasn't thrilled to see her paying them more attention than anything else. She told herself to get it together, because she certainly didn't want any more issues with Grant than she already had.

"Excuse me, y'all, I've gotta use the little girl's room," Raven announced a while later, dabbing her lips with her napkin. She turned her eyes to Grant. "I forgot where it is, though..."

"I'll show you," Van quickly volunteered before Grant could respond, standing from her chair.

"Cool." Raven squeezed Joe's arm before standing up.

"Yeah, enjoy your girl talk," Joe commented, winking at Raven. "We all know that's why y'all women always go to the bathroom in pairs."

Everyone at the table chuckled, including Van. Joe was absolutely right; that's exactly why she was accompanying Raven to the restroom. She had to tell Raven something and she couldn't make herself wait anymore.

"Yeah, we're gonna go talk about all y'all handsome men," Raven teased, playfully nudging Joe's shoulder. More laughs. The smile was still on Raven's face as she followed Van out of the room.

"Why are we going up here?" Raven asked when she saw Van heading towards the stairs. "I know there's a bathroom downstairs somewhere. Is it broken?"

"No, it's fine; I just wanted to talk to you in private and didn't want to risk getting interrupted," Van explained, opening the door to her and Grant's bedroom.

Raven paused at the door. "You seriously expect me to come in here?"

Van stopped and looked back at her, realizing her lapse in judgment. "I guess not...I wasn't thinking. We can use the one in the hallway, if that makes you feel better."

"Yeah, let's do that," Raven agreed, already turning away. She wasn't angry, but she still had no desire to go into Van and Grant's room.

Van led Raven to the bathroom down the hall and waited for her to handle her business. As soon as Raven stepped back out, Van grabbed her arm. "We need to talk."

"About what?"

"I didn't know you were coming with Joe," Van hissed.

"Why wouldn't I? I told you we were together."

"So you're an actual couple?" Van clarified. "Like, *exclusive*-exclusive?"

Raven looked at her strangely. "Yeah..."

Van pursed her lips.

"Why didn't you tell me Auntie and Uncle Mitchell were gonna be here?" Raven retorted. "A little heads-up about that would've been nice."

"I had no idea they were coming until they called me from the airport telling me they were here."

"Wow," Raven marveled. "What's up with them, though? They've been looking kind of strange all through dinner."

Van ran a hand through her hair and glanced down the hall to make sure no one was coming. "That's probably because of the bomb I dropped on them in the car on the way to the house."

"What bomb?"

"That Joe and I broke up. And that I'm with Grant. And that Grant and I are engaged."

Raven gasped. "Shut *up*! Van, you're *just* now telling them about all that??"

"I didn't know how to bring it up..." Van defended weakly.

"In over a year?"

"Look, that's not really what's important right now," Van hastily dismissed. "They don't know about you and Joe, either."

"I gathered that. I was about to let Auntie know when Grant walked in earlier. What, am I supposed to be keeping that a secret, too?"

Van would have liked that, but she knew Raven probably wouldn't go for it. "I wouldn't ask you to do that."

Raven eyed her. "But you wish I would, right?"

"It *would* make things a little less complicated," Van admitted.

"I'm sure it would, but I'm not trying to be keeping any secrets," Raven informed her. "I don't have anything to hide, Van. Joe and I aren't doing anything wrong."

"Maybe *you're* not," Van muttered before she could stop herself.

"What's that supposed to mean?"

Van hesitated, still unsure if she should say what she had brought Raven upstairs to say. She didn't want Raven to be hurt, be she also didn't want her to be made a fool of, either. And if she was honest, a tiny part of her just wanted to throw some kind of shade over all of their glowing happiness.

"Okay, look, please know that I do not enjoy telling you this..."

"Telling me what?"

"Did you know Joe was sleeping with Tanisha?"

Raven just looked at her, then frowned. "Wow, Van."

"What?"

"You're gonna try that, huh?"

"I'm not *trying* anything. It's the truth."

"And how do you know that?"

"Tanisha told me. She thought he and I were back together and told me he had just recently been over there with her."

Raven eyed her. "And when was this?"

"A few weeks ago."

Raven breathed a little easier; it sounded like this had happened before she and Joe made things official, if it was even true. And if that was the case, she couldn't get mad, even though she wasn't thrilled about the thought of Joe sleeping with both her and Tanisha at the same time. She knew she'd be asking him about it later and was already telling herself not to have an attitude when she did.

"Well, thanks for the information but we're good," Raven informed her cousin, lifting her chin confidently. "Whatever it is you're trying to do isn't gonna work."

Van frowned, as if insulted. "What are you talking about??"

"Don't play. I know you aren't happy about me and Joe being together. You can't hide it."

"Okay, I'm not, but I would never try to deliberately cause trouble between you two," Van informed her. "I was really just trying to look out for you, Raven. I didn't want you to be in the dark about anything."

"And I appreciate that," Raven replied sincerely. "Believe me, my eyes are wide open."

"Okay, then. That's good to know."

They went back downstairs and were surprised to see both Joe and Grant getting drilled with questions from

Van's parents. It didn't seem malicious, but it was clearly making the men slightly uncomfortable.

"So you don't have any kids of your own, Grant?" Mitchell asked, looking at him intently.

"No, sir; though I do love Cassie and Canton as if they were my own," Grant replied.

"Hmm," Mitchell nodded. "And how have y'all been getting along?"

"Everything is good." Grant glanced at Van as she retook her seat. "It was an adjustment at first but we worked through it."

"What about Jillian and Tara? How did they adjust to all of the...changes?" Florence asked Joe.

Van saw Joe's jaw clench. "They're good, Mama Florence. Raven has helped a lot with that."

Raven grinned as Van felt her own jaw clench. She didn't like the idea of Raven essentially replacing her in Jillian and Tara's eyes, though she knew she couldn't expect any differently. Breaking up with Joe meant breaking up with his daughters, too, even though she still loved them as much as she always did. It wasn't lost on her that they weren't as excited to see her as they used to be; Van had been a little hurt by that. Yet another casualty of her decision.

"So you two are a couple, then?" Mitchell clarified, slightly waving his fork at Joe and Raven.

"Yes, sir," Joe replied without hesitation. Raven lightly grabbed his arm, leaning into him, and he smiled at her.

"I see," Florence mused, eyeing them with a light smile. Van couldn't tell if she was sincerely pleased or just trying to look polite.

Van's parents continued to alternate questions at Joe and Grant before Van decided to say something; she didn't think this was the time or place for this line of questioning, especially since there were other people at the table who were essentially being ignored.

"So Daddy, how's that car of yours running?" she asked, referring to the old Mustang that Mitchell had been restoring for years.

"Oh, it's coming along just fine," Mitchell replied, always glad to talk about his project. "I found some nice parts for it that I can't wait to use."

"So you're a car man, sir?" Grant asked, also seemingly grateful for the change in subject.

"Big time; love 'em," Mitchell nodded, putting the last of his steak into his mouth.

"I love cars, myself," Grant informed him. "What kind is it that you're working on?"

"It's a '67 Mustang," Mitchell replied proudly. "My baby."

"Sweet...you've been working on it a while?"

"To put it mildly," Florence joked, winking at her husband.

The other people at the table started to chime in on the conversation, and Raven's mind wandered back to what Van told her upstairs about Joe and Tanisha. She didn't want to believe it, but she also didn't think Van would flat-out lie about something like that. She had planned to ask Joe about it later when they were alone, but the more she thought about it, the more she knew she wasn't going to be able to wait. She lightly tugged on his arm, getting him to lean closer to her.

"What's up?" he asked where only she could hear.

"So...you and Tanisha?" Raven whispered, trying to keep her voice even.

Joe blinked, clearly caught off guard. "There *is* no me and Tanisha. What are you talking about?"

"So you haven't slept with her recently?"

Sweeping his eyes around the table to be sure no one was listening, Joe answered honestly in a lowered voice, "It was weeks ago, the last time me and her hooked up. Definitely not since you and I decided to really make it happen."

Raven eyed him. "Really?"

"Yes, really, Raven. I'm not a cheater; never have been and never will be, especially not after *that*," he emphasized, lightly jerking his head towards Van and Grant. Raven's face softened in understanding. "I had every intention of telling you about it myself sooner and I apologize for that but I swear, since then I've only seen Tanisha when I'm over there to get my daughters, that's all. I told her I'm not messing with her like that no more."

Raven continued to eye him, then her lips slowly stretched into a smile. She was usually very suspicious of men, but she believed Joe was telling the truth. And she knew how he felt about cheating after what Van had done.

"Okay," Raven acquiesced. Her hand squeezed his arm as she gave him a quick peck on the cheek. "Thank you for letting me know what the deal is."

"Always, baby."

Raven grinned like a schoolgirl, as she often did when around Joe, and leaned in to press her lips to his, temporarily forgetting they were at a table full of people.

"Y'all cut all that out," Florence teased from across the table. "Save that for the bedroom."

Raven gasped, clearly blushing. Even Joe chuckled. "Auntie!"

"What? Girl, don't try to act like you two ain't doing nothin'. I told you I recognize that glow."

Grant couldn't help but join in the laughter that was spreading around the table, and Van wanted to get up and run into another room.

"I'm gonna go check on the kids," she announced, standing. Her feet couldn't carry her out fast enough.

Grant looked after her, but kept his seat. She might've tried to hide the fact that she didn't enjoy Joe and Raven's PDA but it was as clear as day.

Another thing that was clear to him was that Van's parents had just recently found out about him. If he wasn't sure about it before, he was sure about it now. The looks on their faces when they first saw him were polite, but blank and void of recognition. And all the questions they were drilling him with indicated that, also; facts like whether or not he had children was something Van would have told them by now if she'd told them about him. He knew Van hadn't told her parents about their engagement, but now he was suspecting she hadn't told them about him, period. And that thought didn't sit well with him. At all.

Van reentered the room, a look of resolve on her face. She avoided everyone's eyes as she retook her seat. "Grant, honey, when are we doing the slide show?"

"Slide show?" Raven asked.

"Yeah, I put together something for the twins; kinda like a montage," Grant explained.

"That sounds interesting."

"Van, I've been meaning to ask you how things were going at that job of yours," Mitchell commented. "When's the next time you have to go out of town?"

Van wished she hadn't come back in the room. She wished this whole day could just be over. "Well, about that...I don't really work there anymore."

Grant's eyebrows shot up in surprise. This was news to him.

"Why not? What happened?" Florence asked.

Van hesitated slightly. "I quit."

"You quit?"

"You quit your *job*??" Cassie exclaimed, having just come into the room.

Van wanted to curse out loud. She turned to her daughter. "What are you doing in here, Cassie?"

"I was going to ask when we could cut the cake. But you really quit your *job*?"

"Get on back in that room and stay out of grown folks' business!" Florence reprimanded before Van had a chance to. Van looked at her mother gratefully. "We'll get to the cake when we get to it."

Knowing better than to say anything other than a meek "Yes, ma'am," Cassie turned and quickly exited the dining room.

There was an awkward silence at the table. Grant was silently tapping his thumb against the arm of his chair, eyeing his empty plate, his lips twisted thoughtfully. Van's parents were looking at Van, seemingly waiting for an explanation as to why she was now unemployed. The other guests were looking like they'd rather be anywhere else, and Joe and Raven were watching everything with intrigued amusement.

"All right, well," Grant finally spoke, "If everyone is done eating, we can go on into the media room. We can do the cake and presents after that."

Van dared to look at her fiancé and tried to read the expression on his face, but she couldn't quite place it. She knew she was going to have to do some explaining later, and wondered at what point she became someone who hid things from her loved ones. That never used to be her, but she was now keeping things from her parents and not sharing things with the man she had agreed to spend the rest of her life with, not to mention the sneaking around she did behind Joe's back and how she kept her growing feelings for Grant from Raven. What had happened to her?

They went and got the kids, who were all as happy and oblivious to all the tension among the adults as could be, and everyone congregated in the media room. It was a home theater, with two tiered rows of leather recliners, two loveseats on the opposite ends of the lower level, and a couple of large beanbags in the middle. The seating, carpet, and baseboards were a light tan and the walls were a smoky gray; Van hadn't been in the room in a while but had always loved it.

The room wasn't ridiculously huge but it was big enough to hold everybody comfortably, and Joe and Raven wasted no time claiming one of the loveseats. Van wanted her and Grant to curl up on the other one, but he took a seat in one of the recliners on the upper tier. She sat in the one next to him, noting how he rarely looked at her.

Once everyone was seated, Grant stood and went to the side of the room, facing everyone.

"I want to thank everyone for being here today to help us celebrate Canton and Cassie," he said, smiling at the twins. They beamed back at him. "I hope you enjoyed your meal and if you want any more, please help yourselves; consider yourselves at home here."

"Daddy, does that mean we can take home the rest of that chicken?" Tara asked Joe, turning to him from her beanbag.

Everyone laughed, including Joe.

"Maybe not all of it but some, if it's all right with the hosts," Joe replied, still not wanting to say Grant's name.

"She can take as much as she likes," Grant confirmed with a smile and a wink at Tara, who grinned in response.

"Now, I know I haven't been in the twins' lives terribly long, but I wanted to do something to show them show special they are to me, and to their mother, of course," Grant continued, glancing at Van with a smile. She returned his smile, even though it only further confused her...was he upset with her or not? "We hope everybody enjoys it. It's only about twenty minutes long so we'll be getting to that cake before you know it."

Amid all the chuckles, Grant dimmed the lights and started the film. Van's jaw dropped as she watched the professionally-done tribute showing countless pictures from when the twins were babies until now, some of which Van had never even seen. There were captions under each one, and a soft musical accompaniment. Towards the end, Grant appeared on the screen and he gave a from-the-heart speech to the twins about how much he loved them already that had just about everybody dabbing the corners of their eyes. Van's hand was on her chest; she was absolutely blown away. When in the world had he done all of this? *How* had he done all of this, without her knowing?

The twins apparently loved it, because when it was over they both got up and hugged Grant, which sent the brimming tears rolling down Van's cheeks. Everyone commented on how beautiful and touching the film was, and Van noticed that Cassie held on to Grant a little longer than expected. Canton had already gone back to sit on the floor near Joe's feet as he had been before.

Next, it was time for cake, and Grant asked Van to help him bring everything into the TV room so everyone wouldn't have to move again, and could enjoy watching a movie as they ate. When they were in the kitchen, Van tried to use that opportunity to talk to Grant.

"You got something on your mind, sweetie?"

"There's always something on my mind. The plates and forks are over there; the caterers left the serving cart so we can use that to take everything in," Grant replied, not looking at her.

"That's not really what I meant..."

"There's strawberry cake, red velvet, and yellow cake with chocolate frosting," Grant continued, as if he hadn't heard her. "I think I requested a pound cake, too..."

"Grant, I know you're probably upset with me," Van surmised, her eyes fixed on him. He still wouldn't look at her. "Can we talk about this, please?"

"There's ice cream in the freezer, if anybody wants any."

"Grant!"

He finally sighed and turned his eyes to her.

"Why are you ignoring me?"

"Because, Van," Grant slowly responded, as if trying to patiently gather the right words, "A house full of people is hardly the place to discuss the fact that your parents didn't know I existed until today."

Van's mouth fell open. How in the world did he know that? She thought he was upset with her about all the attention she had been paying to Joe and Raven, and not telling him she quit her job. She had no idea he had figured out that she hadn't told her parents about him.

"Wh-what?"

"Tell me I'm wrong."

Swallowing hard, Van took a step towards him. "Grant, I..."

"Don't risk digging your hole any deeper, Van," Grant ordered crisply, giving her a no-nonsense glare. "If after all this time of us being together *and* engaged you still haven't told your parents about me even though you talk to them damn near once a week, then you just didn't *want* to tell them. And now is not the time to discuss why that is. So let's save this particular discussion for later...think of it as more time to get your excuse together."

She just stood there with her jaw on the floor as Grant steered the cart with the cakes out of the kitchen. She knew she was in trouble, and she knew there was no excuse she could give to justify not telling her parents about him before then. Her hands were already shaking thinking about their eventual conversation, and what might come of it. The thought of Grant calling off the engagement and even ending their relationship caused a burn in her stomach that she didn't like.

She knew she had to hold it together until the end of the party, though, especially with Joe and Raven there. Petty or not, she didn't want them to know that there was trouble between her and Grant while they were apparently swimming in bliss. Joe would probably be thrilled that she was so miserable after what she did to him.

She grabbed the tray with the napkins, plates, and utensils and quickly followed Grant to the theater. Everyone pigged out on the cakes, and then the twins opened all of their presents, which Grant had apparently informed the guests shouldn't be worth over twenty-five dollars, the only exception being Van's parents, since they weren't expected and weren't aware of that stipulation. To look at Grant, you would never think he was absolutely livid with his fiancée, and Van was doing her absolute best to keep her game face on. She wanted all of these guests to leave, but at the same time, she was afraid of them doing so because that meant she would have to face Grant alone. The twins had been invited to a sleepover at one of their guests' house and Van had given them permission to go, so it would just be her, Grant, and her parents, since Grant had already insisted they could stay with them instead of at a hotel.

Finally, everyone started to gather their kids and head home, thanking Van and Grant for the invitation. Van busied herself preparing to-go plates for anyone who wanted them, purposely avoiding Grant. He seemed to be avoiding her, as well, getting everyone's coats and seeing all the guests outside. When she was finally alone the kitchen, Van stood at the counter, gripping the edge, and released a shaky breath. As far as the twins were concerned, the day had been a success; they got to celebrate their birthday, they got some presents, but nothing was over-the-top, just like Grant had planned it. Van had to acknowledge that he had done a great job planning the party, and it made her realize how fortunate she was to have him in her and the twins' lives.

So why did it seem like she was hellbent on messing that up?

Feeling another headache coming on, Van headed to the guest bathroom to get some Tylenol. Just as she reached for the door, it swung open. She felt her heart thump when she realized she was face to face with Joe.

"Oh!" she gasped, glancing down the hall before turning her eyes back to him. "I, um, I didn't know anyone was in here."

Joe glared at her before turning out the bathroom light. "Yeah, well. I'm done. Excuse me."

"Joe, wait," Van protested when he attempted to step around her. She placed a hand on his arm, then quickly retracted it when he glared at her. Her voice was hushed when she asked, "Can we please talk for a minute?"

"What do we have to talk about, Van?"

Now that he asked, Van realized she didn't know *what* exactly they had to talk about. Her earlier thoughts of asking him why he changed his phone number and even possibly confronting him about Tanisha vanished into thin air now that she was in front of him. She just didn't want him to automatically rush away from her like he seemed to want to do. "Are you still upset with me?"

Joe looked at her, and Van was slightly encouraged to see less of the venom in his eyes than when they last saw each other. After a couple of moments, he shook his head. "I can't say you're my favorite person or anything, but I'm not trying to keep wasting energy hating you."

Relieved, Van smiled, "I'm so glad-"

"But that doesn't mean I'm trying to be friends, either."

Van's shoulders slumped. "Joe-"

"I've gotta go, Van," Joe cut her off, moving to step around her again. "Raven and the girls are waiting in the car."

"Joe, please," Van pleaded, placing a hand on his chest. This time, she didn't retract it when he looked down at her hand. With another glance down the hall to make sure no one was coming, she forged ahead. "I-I miss you."

Joe's eyebrows shot up in surprise before he just shook his head and chuckled wryly. "Yeah, I bet you do."

"No, really," Van insisted, taking a tiny step closer to him. Her fingers shifted against his hard chest. Daring to look up into his eyes, she licked her lips. "I *really* miss you, Joe."

Joe peered at her, not missing the inflection in her voice. There was something in her eyes that told him she wasn't just talking in general terms. His eyes roamed the face he used to be so enamored with, those beautiful brown eyes and strawberry-shaped lips. She had let her hair grow longer but she still had those brow-skimming bangs, and he remembered how he used to always think they were so sexy on her. Van was still a beautiful woman, he could acknowledge that...but when he looked at her, he didn't feel anything. Maybe pity, since she apparently wasn't able to let go of the past even though she'd been the one to end things between them. But Joe had Raven now; Van wasn't even on his radar anymore.

Closing his hand around hers, he brought it to his lips and lightly pressed her fingers to them. Van's eyes looked hopeful, and she released a hitched breath before a small smile played at the corners of her mouth. She took another step closer to him, feeling her body heat up from being so close to Joe again. It wasn't something she planned or was able to help. And as wrong as it was, every part of her wanted Joe's lips to be on her lips instead of her fingers.

Before she could stop herself, she pushed him back into the bathroom, quickly closing the door behind her and locking it. She cornered Joe against the wall, getting closer than she knew she had any business being to him. They eyed each other in the dim light provided by the lighted plug-in near the sink. Joe didn't bother asking what she was doing because he already knew. Her eyes were saying she wanted him. But instead of turning him on or tempting him, it just showed him what kind of woman she was; she had already cheated on him with Grant, and now she was engaged to Grant and pushing up on him with Grant right outside. Even if Raven weren't in the picture, Joe wouldn't have gone for that.

"Please, Joe," Van pleaded in a whisper, her eyes on his lips. "I need this."

Her fingers trailed down his chest to his belt, where she grabbed hold with both hands; the awareness of what she was doing was being overtaken by her overwhelming arousal. She had visions of Joe finally grabbing her and blessing her with one of his panty-drenching kisses before whipping her around and bending her over the counter, sexing her until she couldn't walk straight. The fantasy made her chest heave with anticipation and pent-up desire; just thinking about Joe's kisses and what his lips and hands used to do to her had her body aching. She pressed her breasts against his body, hoping he could feel her excruciatingly beaded nipples through their clothing, and her leg rubbed against his. She itched to rip off the snug Henley he was wearing and tear off her own dress so they could be skin-to-skin again, and if Joe gave her even the slightest go-ahead, she would have.

In that moment, she didn't care about Grant or their engagement. She wanted Joe that much.

"You have *no* idea how much I think about you; *yearn* for you," she breathed, pressing her body closer. Her rational mind and good sense were forcibly muted as she let the unbridled lust that she hadn't felt since their relationship ended overtake her. "I've never admitted this out loud but I'll say it; I never should have left you, Joe. My heart misses you. My body misses you. I *know* you haven't forgotten how good we were together, baby. I need you. *Please* fuck me. Kiss me, touch me, *something*, just once..."

She was subtly grinding against him, mildly surprised that she didn't feel him hardening even a little between them but undeterred. She yanked down the top of her dress and bra, baring her breasts to him. She moaned as she slowly squeezed and caressed them in the way that used to drive him crazy, but Joe didn't move; his eyes stayed on her face. Even when her hand drifted between her legs under her dress, he didn't flinch or respond. She'd fully expected him to be ravaging her by now but it was like she had no effect on him whatsoever. If anything, he looked like he pitied her.

Even more blindly determined instead of finally accepting the obvious reality, Van lunged for Joe again, needing to feel him. He grabbed her hands, stopping her just as she was about to grab his crotch. Holding them firmly between them, he looked right into her pleading eyes.

"You made your choice," he stated, his face close to hers. "And you're embarrassing yourself."

With that, he dropped her hands, stepped around her, and exited the bathroom.

Chapter 23

• • • •

GRANT NEEDED TO GET out of the house.

It had taken everything in him to hold it together until the birthday party was over. He was usually very good under pressure, but now he felt that pressure was getting ready to explode. Acting like he wasn't upset with Van when he was absolutely furious with her had been a gargantuan task, and he just had to get away from her before he totally lost it.

He went back into the house after seeing the last guest off, and Joe was in the foyer, adjusting the collar of his jacket. He paused when he looked up and saw Grant, then just lightly shook his head and started to step around him.

"Get home safe, man," Grant felt compelled to say. He knew he wasn't one of Joe's favorite people but there was a part of him that wished they could be on better terms.

"Yeah. Thanks," Joe muttered, continuing to the door. He didn't even look at Grant as he stepped outside, closing the door behind him.

Grant sighed. He knew he deserved Joe's anger, regardless of how long it had been since everything happened.

Van emerged from the hallway, wiping her eyes with a tissue. She looked startled when she saw Grant.

"Oh!" she gasped. Her eyes were slightly red, as if she had been crying. Her dress was slightly rumpled, namely around the collar. She looked nervous, guilty. Scared, even. To Grant, she looked like someone who knew they had been caught in something and was about to get their ass handed to them.

Grant just stuck his hands in his pockets, his eyes shooting daggers at her. She looked away guiltily. Feeling his blood start to boil again, Grant gritted his teeth and turned his eyes away, as well.

"I'm leaving," he informed her, his voice low. He made a move to walk past her.

Panicked, Van grabbed his arm with both hands. "What?? What do you mean, you're leaving?"

"I have to get away from you right now," Grant informed her. "I don't need to talk to you when I'm this pissed off."

Van looked slightly relieved, but still worried. She tightened her hold on his arm. "I-when are you coming back?"

"When I can stand to look at you again," Grant seethed, his eyes still focused on the wall to his left. "Now please let go of my arm."

Fresh tears filled Van's eyes as she reluctantly released her hold.

"Van!" Florence called from the direction of the living room.

Quickly wiping her eyes, Van took a tiny step back. "I'm coming, Mama!"

Unable to make himself say another word, Grant stepped around her and headed towards the stairs.

Van took a few moments to gather herself, stepping to the oval mirror hanging in the foyer to check her face. She knew her parents would be able to tell she had been crying, and she didn't have the energy to try to hide it. After Joe had rebuffed her in the bathroom, she leaned against the wall and cried tears if embarrassment and shame. Embarrassment over Joe shutting down her impulsive seduction, and shame for trying to seduce him in the first place. She didn't know what had come over her; she never thought she was the kind of woman to come on to another man while her fiancé was in the same house. But at the time, all Van could think about was how much she missed Joe, and how he used to make her feel. She'd been completely outside of herself, not even considering the consequences of her actions.

She actually told Joe she shouldn't have left him. And meant it. It was like a weight lifted as soon as the words left her mouth. She bared herself to him, physically and emotionally, and he'd had no reaction whatsoever. He was truly over her.

And when she finally emerged from the bathroom and saw Grant, part of her wondered if he somehow knew what she had done. Guilt clouded her body with every passing second; she was completely in the wrong, and if Grant found out about that, she figured they would be as good as done. But he appeared to not know anything about it, which only provided her marginal relief since he still had plenty other things to be mad at her about.

Combing her fingers through her hair and taking a deep breath, she headed to the living room to face the music with her parents. She could just imagine the barrage of questions they were about to throw at her. Her nerves were already going into overdrive. She was just thankful the twins weren't there to possibly hear her get reprimanded like a child.

When she got to the living room, her parents were side-by-side on the couch, talking amongst themselves. When they looked up at her, their expressions were even; they didn't look particularly upset, but they didn't exactly look pleasant, either.

"Come sit down, baby," Florence instructed.

Van did as she was told and waited for the assault. But to her surprise, that's not what she got.

"Where's Grant?" Mitchell asked. His short graying afro had receded more since Van last saw him.

"Oh, he...he had to go to the office for a little while," Van replied, trying to keep her voice even. She could only hope that Grant would just be gone a little while. It was the first time he'd been this upset with her so she really had no idea *what* he would do.

"Oh okay. Well, look, I know you think we're gonna fuss at you," Florence began, "But we're not. You're a grown woman who can live her life as she pleases. But what we *would* like, though, is for you to talk to us, finally. Your father and I are so lost as to what's really going on."

"I know," Van said softly, looking at her hands. "I'm sorry."

"Can you tell us what really happened? What made you leave Joe and get engaged to another man so quickly?"

Sighing, Van sat up straighter in her seat. She felt a little better knowing she wasn't about to get dragged through the mud, but she still wasn't particularly enthusiastic about having this conversation. But she knew her parents were just concerned about her and not asking out of nosiness.

"I left Joe because, basically, I was just tired of things being the way they were," Van stated. "We were always struggling when it came to money, and I was stressed from having to work two jobs and still not really making a dent in our debt. Not to mention always having to turn the twins down when they would ask for things. It just got to be too much."

"That doesn't sound like Joe," Mitchell said, frowning slightly. "I never knew him to be lazy."

"Joe *isn't* lazy," Van quickly corrected him. "He isn't lazy at all. Joe was working twelve-hour days most of the time, or longer. Then he would always come home and help out around the house however he could. This isn't on him, at least not totally."

"Not totally?"

"The mother of his children never forgave him for leaving her and she was always demanding more child support or finding some other way to milk his pockets, and he usually gave in to her to keep the peace around his daughters," Van explained. "And while I understood that, it often meant he didn't have much left to contribute to *our* household, 'cause it's not like he didn't have his own bills to pay. And eventually I just got tired of it."

"So you left him just because of that? He didn't cheat on you or anything?"

Van's eyes squeezed shut momentarily. "No, he didn't. Joe was always good to me."

"Did you talk to him about the situation at all? Let him know you were reaching the end of your rope?" Florence asked. "I just can't imagine he wouldn't have made some kind of change if he knew you were thinking about leaving."

Shame burned Van's skin. "I-I *did* let him know I was getting tired of the way things were. But to be honest, no, I didn't let him know I was thinking about leaving."

"So you just up and left him one day and then got with Grant after that?"

"That's not how it went," Van softly admitted. She couldn't even look at them. "Raven and I met Grant randomly one night and Raven made it clear she wanted him, and they started dating. But it turned out Grant was only seeing her to get closer to me. I didn't learn this until later, even though Grant always found excuses to call or try to see me, so I suppose I should have known or at least suspected. And my feelings for him started to grow, and I was getting more and more frustrated with how things were at home, and...things just progressed from there."

"Oh," Florence sat back in realization.

"So *you* cheated on *Joe*," Mitchell clarified.

Van told herself not to cry. "Yes. Even though I didn't think that's what I was doing at the time, I guess I did. Grant and I never...we kissed but we never slept together until *after*..."

"Sex isn't the only way you cheat, baby," Florence informed her daughter. "If you were doing or feeling anything with Grant that you should have only been doing or feeling with Joe, then that's more than enough right there."

Van nodded. "I understand that. And I know Joe didn't deserve it; I'm still ashamed of myself for how I treated him. And don't even get me started on how all this has damaged my relationship with Raven."

"So..." Florence began, "Let me see if I've got this. Raven was seeing Grant though he actually wanted you. You were with Joe. I'm guessing Grant pursued you anyway. You started seeing Grant behind Joe's back. You left Joe for Grant...and now Joe is with Raven."

"Pretty much."

"I didn't even know they were friends."

Van tucked some hair behind her ear. "Apparently, Raven had been helping Joe plan my proposal. He was gone from the house more than he was in it, and it turned out he was working a lot of overtime to pay for my engagement ring and the honeymoon, and going to school to complete his degree, which explained why he never had any money when I asked him for it. He wanted to surprise me with everything, but the night he was going to propose is when I ended things and told him me and the twins were moving in with Grant. Raven happened to come in the room then and heard everything. I guess she and Joe consoled each other."

Mitchell rubbed a hand down his face and Florence exhaled a long breath.

"I know you're disappointed in me..." Van hedged, eying them.

"Yes, we are," Florence admitted with no hesitation. "I just...I didn't think you were this kind of person. Cheating on a good man just because things weren't perfect. Betraying your own family for a man. We're absolutely disappointed, Vanetta."

Van couldn't stop the tears from falling this time. This was what she had been trying to avoid and why she kept putting off telling her parents the truth about her and Grant. She didn't want her parents to think of her in such a way, but she knew she deserved it. There wasn't anything she could say in defense of herself.

"I'm so sorry," was all she managed. She'd lost track of how many times she'd said that throughout the day.

"It's not *us* you need to apologize to," Mitchell replied. Van could only imagine what was running through his mind, given how close he and Joe were. She knew he probably wasn't happy finding out Joe wasn't going to be his son-in-law like he hoped.

"I've apologized to Joe. Repeatedly and profusely," Van insisted. "He doesn't seem to hate me anymore but he's so indifferent towards me now. Really, I can't believe he hasn't forgiven me, given all the time that has passed. I just can't stand the thought of him wanting nothing to do with me but every time I try to reach out to him, he shuts me down. And to be honest...I miss him."

Florence looked at her. "What do you mean, you miss him? You want him back?"

"Well, even if I did, he's made it more than clear that it wouldn't happen," Van wryly replied, thinking of their meeting at Waffle House and their encounter in the bathroom earlier. "I'll admit that I...if I could do everything over again, I'd make different decisions. I truly love Grant but I can't help still wanting Joe in my life. I miss our relationship, our friendship. But...I screwed all that up. And now I have to see him with Raven..."

Van looked down at her hands, which were clasped between her knees. Florence could see the torment running rampant through her daughter, and how hard it had been to admit all of this to them. She was disappointed in Van's actions, but she knew it wasn't necessary to come down too hard on her about it. As she'd said, Van was a grown woman. And it was clear she felt bad enough already.

"So how did this engagement come about?" Mitchell inquired with a tired sigh.

Van lifted a weary shoulder. "Grant asked me to marry him a few months after the twins and I moved in here. And I said yes."

"You don't seem too happy about it," Florence observed. She eyed the large engagement ring on Van's finger. "Matter of fact, usually whenever I talked to you over the past few months, it was evident you were going through something. I could tell. I knew there was something going on with you but you always insisted everything was fine."

"Why didn't you feel you could tell us about any of this?" Mitchell asked her.

"I-I was afraid of what you might think of me," Van admitted.

"You sure that's the only reason?" Florence pressed, looking at her daughter pointedly.

Van blinked in surprise. "What do you mean? Of course that's the reason."

"It might be *a* reason but I don't think it's the only reason, or even the main reason. But I'll leave that for you to think about," Florence said. "Van, just know that you don't have to keep things like this from us, baby. We might be upset or disappointed but at the end of the day, we will always be here for you. We raised you to be strong, and that includes living with the decisions you make and dealing with whatever comes from them."

Van nodded again. "You're right, Mama."

"And if I can offer you a little piece of advice," Mitchell chimed in.

"Sure, Daddy."

"Leave Joe alone."

Van resisted the automatic frown that wanted to come to her face. That wasn't what she expected him to say. "Uhh, sir?"

"Leave him alone. Let him move on, and you need to move on, too. Concentrate on the man you agreed to marry."

Van knew what he was saying was right, but she just didn't want to accept it. "But Daddy-"

"But nothing. You can't expect that man to want to be friends with you after what you did," Mitchell interrupted with a slight edge in his voice.

"Mitchell..." Florence warned.

"Look here, you gave her the nice response, now I'm about to give her *my* response," Mitchell told his wife. Looking back at his tearful daughter, he continued, "You made your bed, now lay in it. You got what you wanted; somebody that's got money, which you apparently need even more now since you done went and quit your job."

Van gasped. "Daddy!"

"Don't 'Daddy' me. I never thought you were one of those kinds of women that would leave a perfectly good, hardworking man that treated you like gold just because he wasn't rich enough. You think your mother and I didn't struggle when we were younger? You think it was always *easy* for us? Hell no, it wasn't. But we stuck it out, *together*. This generation don't know nothin' about that; y'all just look for the quick and easy way out."

"Th-that's not what I was doing!" Van cried. She couldn't believe her father was saying these things to her.

"The hell it ain't. Joe wasn't the reason for all the debt you had; you had most of that when you met him. *You're* the one that got knocked up in college and had to drop out, then you and Calvin stupidly bought a ton of stuff on credit with no way to pay it off, and I'm sure there's more we don't know about. But Joe was willing to do whatever for you *and* your twins, loving them like they were his own kids, and it wasn't good enough. And I could even respect *that* more if you had been woman enough to tell him that to his face *before* you started messing around with another man. But that's not what you did. And *we've* offered to help you out more than a few times, and you never wanted to accept *our* help. You just kept lying to us, saying everything was fine when it obviously wasn't, and then Mr. Deep Pockets comes along and you're more than willing to take *his* money. I bet he paid off all your debt, didn't he? Since you gave him what he was chasing after."

"Mitchell!" Florence admonished.

Van was now crying uncontrollably, covering her face with her hands. She couldn't make herself respond if she wanted to.

"Yeah, that's what I thought," Mitchell shook his head, taking her lack of denial as confirmation. "I am a simple man who works hard and takes care of his family, and Joe is, too. And I don't take too kindly to folks who don't respect that. So yes, I *am* pissed off and I ain't gon' try to hide it. I expected better from you, Vanetta. And I'm just ashamed that my daughter is both a cheater and a liar."

With that, he stood and stalked out of the room. Florence immediately went over to Van, who was doubled-over and crying her eyes out. She wrapped her arms around her daughter and pulled her close.

"Oh my god!" Van wailed against her mother's chest.

"He's just upset, baby," Florence assured her, rocking her and smoothing her hair.

"How could he say those things to me??"

"Your daddy is old school; he believes in people making their own way. And there were plenty of times after talking to you that we'd tell each other that you were just too proud to admit you needed help. And I can't say I'm not a little hurt, myself, that you would accept the help of some man before us, your own family."

"Mama, I didn't mean to-"

"I know, baby," Florence reassured her. "I'm sure you were doing what you thought was best at the time."

Van sniffed, then sat up slightly. "I am so sorry, Mama. I know I could have handled all of this better. When I think of everything I did…"

"You can't dwell on that, Van. What's done is done. Your daddy was right about one thing, though; you *do* need to move on and let Joe move on in peace, too. He'll decide to forgive you in his own time but if he doesn't, that's for him to live with. But you don't need to be worrying about Joe while you're walking around here wearing Grant's engagement ring."

Sniffling again, Van nodded. "You're right."

"And since you have so much time to think about Joe, I take it things aren't going so well with Grant?"

"Things aren't great. Especially now."

"What does that mean?"

"He could tell you and Daddy just found out about him today," Van admitted. "He knew I hadn't told you about our engagement, but he didn't know I hadn't told you about him *at all*. That's the real reason he left the house; he's pissed at me. I can't say I've been very honest with him these past few months, either, despite how many times he's asked for me to be. And it finally seems like he's fed up."

"And he should be," Florence agreed. "But without knowing much about him, I can tell he's a good man at heart; I'm sure he'll be more open to talking to you when he comes back. And whatever comes from that, you'll just have to deal with it."

That's what Van feared; what was going to come from her eventual conversation with Grant. "I know."

"In the meantime, baby, you need to examine yourself. Marriage is too serious to go into it lightly, and if you don't sincerely want to be Grant's wife and spend the rest of your life with him, you need to let him know that. I'm not trying to be cruel when I say this, but don't do him like you did Joe. Be honest. *Finally*."

The words hurt, but Van knew they were true. Honesty hadn't exactly been her strong suit lately.

After talking to her mother for another few minutes, Van headed upstairs to her bedroom and closed the door. She trudged over and fell across her bed, drained and with a pounding headache. She moved her wrist in front of her face to see her watch, and wondered how much longer it would be before Grant came back. She still had no idea what she would even say to him when he did.

It had been some day; her parents showing up unexpectedly, Joe and Raven arriving together and confirming their relationship to everyone, her parents meeting Grant for the first time, her losing her mind and coming on to Joe and him shutting her down, Grant walking out on her, and her father blasting her and making her feel like the slut of the century. And to think when Van woke up that morning, all she wanted to do was celebrate her twins' twelfth birthday.

Van hadn't liked seeing Joe and Raven together. At all. She couldn't deny how genuinely happy they looked, and despite how much Van knew she needed to, she still didn't want to accept it. She didn't even know what it would take to get her to that point; she realized how it made her look that she was still so consumed with them. But whatever it was going to take, she knew she would have to force herself get over it. Joe was with Raven; any interest or love he had for Van was gone. The kiss he applied to her fingertips had apparently been a final good-bye. That realization brought tears to Van's eyes that she had to make herself blink back.

Van really did love Grant. And when she thought about her life without him in it, it made her heart hurt. Van didn't know what it said about her that she still considered Joe the love of her life, even after everything that had happened. Her words to him in the bathroom might've been fueled by lust but that didn't mean they weren't true; she could no longer deny that she regretted her decision to leave Joe. That was why she dragged her feet about marrying Grant, why she couldn't be totally uninhibited with him, why she didn't think of him as a father figure to her twins the way she did Joe, why she just hadn't been as happy as she should've been. Her mother's words about her reasoning as to why she kept their relationship to herself made all the sense in the world now; Van didn't tell her parents about Grant because, deep down, she knew he wasn't the man her heart wanted, despite how much she genuinely loved him. And telling her parents would have been like cementing the decision she foolishly made.

She'd been justifying her decision to be with Grant for months, trying her best to make herself believe it, but if Joe had obliged her in the bathroom and said he'd take her back, she'd have gone in a heartbeat. It was a hard reality to admit, but at least she was finally being honest with herself.

But Joe and her parents were right; she made her choice. It was a realization she had come to many times but eventually, she always ended up concentrating on Joe more than Grant. Despite her admitted epiphany, Van's feelings for Grant were sincere and she believed she could be happy with him if she let herself. Why couldn't she just be grateful for what she had the way she was always preaching to Cassie?

Reaching for her phone, Van tried to call Grant, but of course it went to voicemail. Biting her lip, she tried to call Joe, just with the intent of apologizing for her actions earlier, but was reminded that he changed his number when the one she dialed was no longer in service. She had seen him talking on his phone earlier and hated that she hadn't thought to ask him for his new number, not that he would've given it to her. Van sensed that he changed his number in the first place because of her, and she had to make herself blink back the tears again.

Feeling guilty for caring so much, Van knew she needed to check herself yet again before she ended up without Joe *or* Grant.

That is, if Grant didn't decide she was more trouble than she was worth and leave her first.

• • • •

GRANT DID GO TO THE office for a while, but he ended up at Coco's with Rick. He was thankful that his friend was willing to meet him on such short notice, because Grant was feeling like he didn't know which way was up.

"She's not over him," Grant insisted, downing the last of his beer and motioning to the bartender for another. "I know in my gut that Van is not over Joe."

He had told Rick all about the party and other events of the day, including coming to the realization that Van's parents had only heard of him minutes before they met, and Rick just listened in stunned silence. Grant couldn't remember the last time he had been so hurt and angry, but mostly hurt.

"I just...I don't know what to think about all of this, man," Grant admitted, his voice anguished. He clunked his bottle down on the counter and hung his head, absentmindedly rubbing it with his hand. "My mind has been all over the place ever since I left the house. I just...umph." He sighed, as if too exhausted to talk anymore.

Rick clamped a hand on his friend's shoulder in comfort. He'd never seen Grant so distraught.

"I hate seeing you like this, Grant."

"I don't want to think I've made a mistake choosing Van but..." Grant sighed again. "It's starting to look like maybe I did."

"Maybe it wasn't so much a mistake choosing Van, but a mistake not giving her time to close that door with Joe before opening one with you," Rick suggested. "From what you've told me, Grant, Van seems like a great woman who loves hard. And she loved Joe. That doesn't mean she doesn't love you but she didn't give herself time to let herself heal from that long-term relationship before you two started yours. You came into all this fresh; she didn't."

Grant had never thought of it that way. "I can see your point on that. So you think she's just conflicted?"

"Perhaps but also, maybe she just feels plain guilty," Rick clarified. "You told me Joe said that he hated her and still hadn't forgiven her for what she did, and how much that bothered her. Maybe she wouldn't be so consumed with Joe if that wasn't the case."

Grant nodded, pondering his friend's words. "And what about her being so against Joe being with her cousin, Raven?"

"Well, I can't imagine too many women that would be cool with that, in *any* situation. Even if Van and Joe had ended on good terms, Raven is still her cousin and Joe is still her ex. That can't be comfortable."

"Hmm. So you don't think she's jealous at all?"

"It's definitely possible. But only she would be able to confirm that."

Grant grunted. "She'd probably just deny it like she's been doing."

Picking up his beer, he downed most of it in one long gulp. He lifted his hand to motion for another from the bartender but Rick stopped him, waving the bartender off.

"This isn't the way to deal with it, man," he assured him. "Go home and talk to your woman. With a *clear* head."

"Rick, honestly, I don't even know what I would say to Van right now."

"Well, let me ask you this: do you want to end things with Van?"

"No," Grant quickly replied. "I don't *want* to..."

"So this is something you two can work out, then. 'Cause I doubt she really wants to leave you, either."

"Rick, Van hasn't been honest with me about so many things, and I probably don't know the half of it. More than that, I don't know how to deal with the woman I'm supposed to be marrying being so consumed with another man, regardless of the reason," Grant admitted, a frown marring his handsome face. "Could *you* deal with that?"

"No. I couldn't."

"Exactly." Grant exhaled a long breath, then his frown cleared and a look of worry replaced it. "But...Melissa wasn't with another man when you pursued her. Van was. And maybe all of this is just me being punished for that."

Rick just nodded as he twiddled his thumbs, silently agreeing with his friend's assessment.

"And if that's the case," Grant continued with a sigh. "I'll just have to learn to live with it."

• • • •

BY THE TIME GRANT MADE it back home an hour or so later, Van was sprawled across the bed, still fully clothed, fast asleep. Her phone was lying by her hand. He saw when she tried to call earlier, but he hadn't been ready to talk to her yet. And really, he still didn't know exactly what he was going to say whenever they *did* talk about all this. Part of him was glad that she was asleep and he would get a reprieve, even if it was a temporary one.

Not wanting to wake Van, Grant went back downstairs and into the kitchen, where his stomach growled on cue.

He opened the refrigerator and was contemplating what he wanted to eat when he heard a noise behind him.

"Mr. Roseland," he said in surprise when he saw Van's father standing there. "You, um...you finding everything okay?"

"Yeah, I'm finding things just fine, thanks," Mitchell replied, his hands stuffed into the pockets of his bathrobe. "You raid the fridge at night, too, huh?"

"Sometimes, yes," Grant replied, feeling more nervous than he was used to. It had been years since he had to deal with a woman's father, and never in a situation such as the one they were in. Van had told him some things about Mitchell, but not all that much. And Grant hated that he just didn't know how to read the man yet.

"Let's talk a lil' bit," Mitchell said, jerking his head towards the kitchen table.

Knowing this wasn't a suggestion, Grant joined him at the table, subtly wiping his damp palms on his pants.

"I've heard of you, Grant, but I don't know much about you," Mitchell began. "And here you are about to be my son-in-law."

Grant cleared his throat. "Yes, sir...I know these aren't exactly ideal circumstances."

"Not at all. From what I hear, you went after my daughter while she was still with Joe. Is that right?"

Resisting the urge to hang his head, Grant replied, "Yes, sir."

"Is that something you usually do? Go after another man's woman?"

Not used to being reprimanded like this, especially by another man, Grant felt his face burn in shame. His own father was pretty much non-existent in his life and always had been, leaving all the parenting of Grant and his sister Gabrielle to their mother. Being a father had never fit into his carefree, playboy lifestyle.

Summoning the steel spine he had to use at work, Grant sat up a little straighter in his chair. "No, sir, it's not. And you may or may not choose to believe this, but I have been feeling very conflicted and very guilty about that, especially recently."

Mitchell's bushy eyebrows rose slightly. "Why recently?"

"Mr. Roseland," Grant began, trying to gather his words, "From the first time I laid eyes on your daughter, I was hooked. And not just by her beauty; she had this...this spirit, this glow, this aura about her that just drew me in. I have never, ever been as captivated by another woman as I was by Van. And when I found out she was in a relationship, true enough, I should have just left her alone and concentrated on Raven, who was actually single and very interested in me. And I sincerely tried to do that, more than once. But I just could not make myself stop thinking about Van; it always went back to her."

Mitchell just looked at him, listening.

"I did a few things I'm not proud of, including how I used Raven and stabbed a good brother like Joe in the back," Grant continued. "Neither of them deserved that. At the time, all I cared about was getting Van with me...I had never met a woman so beautiful and humble and appreciative, not to mention hard-working. When I learned everything she had on her plate, it just made me want to do whatever I could for her."

"So she never asked you for anything?"

"Absolutely not. Whatever I did for her, I did because I wanted to do. And when I saw how much she always sincerely appreciated it, it just made me want to do more. Even now, she still gets on to me about spoiling her and the twins so much; if it were up to me, Van would have a lot more than she does. But she insists she doesn't need it."

Rubbing his chin, Mitchell looked down at the table, his expression thoughtful.

"How are things between you and Van now?" he finally asked.

"They could be a lot better," Grant replied truthfully. "Things haven't felt right between us for months. It's become too easy for both of us to lose focus...we haven't even discussed the wedding in a while. There's no doubt in my mind that I want Van to be my wife, sir. But I'm well aware that she's not over Joe, and that's a hard pill to swallow. But knowing my past actions and just how everything played out, part of me feels like I simply have to be understanding and patient about that. As I'm learning, karma always comes back.

"You're right about that," Mitchell agreed. He leaned his elbows on the table and looked at Grant earnestly. "Look...I always liked Joe and was looking forward to him putting a ring on my daughter's finger. He reminds me a lot of myself. You and I don't seem to have much in common, but I can tell you're a good man. And that you love my daughter."

"Very much so."

"I came down on Van pretty hard earlier," Mitchell informed him. "And I was gonna come down on you, too. But at least you're owning up to your part in all this. So now, you need to figure out what you're gonna do about this whole situation; are you gonna step up and make the most out of the cards you swiped, or are you gonna fold?"

Grant looked at him.

"And keep in mind, it's not just Van affected in all this," Mitchell continued. "Those twins are in this, too. I'm sure you took that into account when you decided to go after Van."

"I did. Though I can be honest and say that neither I nor Van considered them enough when we started all this, and it affected them both. I regret that. It's a mistake I won't make again because I would never want to do anything else to hurt Canton and Cassie. I really do love them as if they were my own children, like I told you at dinner. Folding isn't in my blood, sir, but it's also about what Van wants."

"True."

They continued to talk for a while longer, with Grant confiding in Mitchell about several things about his relationship with Van and Mitchell giving him much-needed fatherly advice. Mitchell warmed to Grant over time and realized he wasn't the spoiled, entitled rich guy that he had initially thought him to be. He still didn't approve of Grant and Van's actions, but he appreciated that Grant at least showed remorse. And he could tell that Grant sincerely loved Van and just wanted to provide the best life he could for her. Grant might not have been blue-collar like him and Joe were, but he still worked hard to get to where he was. His companies and his success wasn't inherited or gifted, they were earned. Mitchell could do nothing but respect that.

After they indulged in some pound cake and ice cream, Mitchell went back to the guest bedroom and Grant peeked in on Van. She was still in a deep sleep across their bed, and he couldn't resist going over and gently brushing her bangs to the side, placing a soft kiss on her forehead. She stirred slightly, but didn't wake up.

Knowing he had way too much on his mind to get any sleep right then, Grant went to his office. Plopping into his leather chair, he leaned his head back, his eyes closed.

Then as if something occurred to him, he sat up and pulled up the security cameras on his computers. He scanned back to the time of the party, not even sure what he was really looking for but somehow knowing he would find *something* to help with his dilemma. His eyes perused the screen, watching the dinner with the adults in the dining room, the kids in the kitchen...he saw when Van and Raven had left the table and gone upstairs instead of to the closer guest bathroom, which Grant found curious. They didn't look like they were arguing or anything, and Grant was tempted to turn up the sound to hear what they talked about, but decided against it. Whatever they discussed was between them.

But when he got to the end of the evening when everything was filing out, Grant sat forward in his chair. While he'd been outside seeing everyone off, Van apparently had an encounter with Joe. He watched as Van headed to the downstairs bathroom, and looked surprised when Joe came out. Joe tried to walk away but Van stopped him, and they exchanged some words before Joe took Van's hand that had been on his chest and kissed it. Rewinding it a little bit, Grant turned on the audio and braced himself for anything:

"Oh! I, um, I didn't know anyone was in here."

"Yeah, well. I'm done. Excuse me."

"Joe, wait. Can we please talk for a minute?"

"What do we have to talk about, Van?"

"Are you still upset with me?"

"I can't say you're my favorite person or anything, but I'm not trying to keep wasting energy hating you."

"I'm so glad-"

"But that doesn't mean I'm trying to be friends, either."

"Joe-"

"I've gotta go, Van. Raven and the girls are waiting in the car."

"Joe, please...I-I miss you."

"Yeah, I bet you do."

*"No, really...I **really** miss you, Joe."*

Then Van pushed Joe into the bathroom and closed the door.

Grant felt his anger surge. He had been right outside, and Van was pushing up on Joe. He paused the film and turned away from the computer, telling himself to calm down. His first instinct was to go right then and confront Van about this, but he decided against it. Nothing good could come from him saying anything to her right then, especially with her parents in the house.

Making himself turn back to the screen, he resumed the tape. Not even three full minutes passed after Van pushed Joe into the bathroom before he stormed back out, heading straight for the front door where Grant had seen him when he re-entered the house. Van came out of the bathroom herself shortly after, wiping her eyes with a tissue and obviously crying. That explained the guilty expression she was wearing when Grant saw her.

He stopped the tape. There was no way he could let this go; any thoughts he had of reconciling with Van were now no longer on his mind. It was one thing for Van to miss Joe and feel guilty for how she treated him; Grant could understand that. But Van making a move on her ex in Grant's house was an entirely different issue. He felt disrespected, and that was something he couldn't deal with. Even though there were no cameras in the bathrooms and he had no idea what really happened when Van pushed Joe in there, the fact that she did that at all was enough. And he didn't miss the inclination in her voice or the look in her eyes when she said, "No, really...I *really* miss you, Joe."

Grant made a decision. Van was about to have a lot more time to yearn for her ex-boyfriend.

Chapter 24

· · · ·

"WHO IS THAT BANGING on the door??"

Raven came out of the bathroom, frowning. She was at Joe's apartment and someone was pounding on the door like they were trying to break it down.

"I don't know, but they're about to wish they didn't," Joe stated emphatically, emerging from the bedroom. He stormed past Raven and looked out the peephole, his hand on the doorknob.

"Aww hell," he muttered with a sigh.

"Who is that?" Raven asked, coming up behind him.

"It's Tanisha."

"What the hell? I didn't know she was coming over here."

"Yeah, you and me, both," Joe replied, finally opening the door. Tanisha stood there, her fist poised to bang on the door again, a deep scowl on her face that only got deeper when she saw Raven standing there.

"What you want, Tanisha?" Joe demanded.

Sucking her teeth, Tanisha stormed into the apartment without invitation. She purposely bumped Raven's shoulder, and Joe had to grab Raven's arm to keep her from snatching Tanisha by her long ponytail.

"Tanisha, look here-"

"So you weren't even gon' tell me, huh?" Tanisha cut her off, facing the two of them with her arms folded. She glared at Joe accusingly.

"Tell you what?" Joe asked, closing the door.

"Don't play dumb, Joe. You weren't gon' tell me about *her*," Tanisha spat, pointing an acrylic nail at Raven.

"*Her* has a name," Raven interjected.

"Yeah, whatever," Tanisha waved her off. To Joe she said, "How come I gotta find out from our kids that you in a relationship now? Is that why you said we can't have sex no more?"

"That's the main reason," Joe replied, his hand still gripping Raven's arm. "And for the record, I don't have to tell you anything about who I'm dating."

"How you figure that??"

"How do you figure I *do*? You and I were not together, Tanisha, and hadn't been for a while. I can do what I want."

"Oh, so you can get with this heffah-"

"Come over here and say that!" Raven warned, starting towards Tanisha but Joe restrained her. "You've got *one* more time to call me out my name, Tanisha, for real."

"And what you gon' do??"

"Let me go, Joe, so I can show her better than I can tell her!" Raven ordered, trying to pull her arm free of his grasp.

"Nah, bump that. Y'all need to chill out," Joe demanded, moving to stand between them. He let go of Raven but kept her at arm's length. "This is ridiculous. Tanisha, I don't know what it's gonna take for you to get this. Your attitude is what gets you in trouble with me every time. You're always flying off the damn handle for no reason. You need some anger management or some counseling or something, because you're never gonna get anywhere with me or anybody else acting like you do."

Tanisha just glared at Joe, then looked away in a huff. Joe and Raven eyed her, waiting on the inevitable comeback. It looked like Joe's words might have struck a chord with her, but Joe knew better than to expect her to admit it out loud.

"I just don't get why you'd get with your ex's cousin but you won't just be patient with me," Tanisha finally griped, her face still turned away. "I told you I was tryin' to do better."

"And I told *you* that while that's good, you need to be doing that for *you*, not for me," Joe replied. "It'll be good for our girls to get to spend quality time with you and to see you actually trying to do something with your life. But the reason shouldn't be because of a man. Damn, don't you wanna be a better woman for *yourself*?"

Tanisha looked at him, then her eyes slid to Raven.

"She ain't even all that," she muttered stubbornly.

Raven chuckled, then before Joe could stop her, shot over and got right in Tanisha's face, glaring down at her.

"Let me let you know something," she said, her voice strong but even, "I ain't Van. You're not gon' just talk to me any kind of way, disrespect me because you feel like it, or think you're gonna be messing with my man just because you're too stubborn to realize it's your own fault that he's not with you. If you *really* love Joe, let him be happy. I'm not just gonna sit and take your bullshit like Van did; I *will* come back at you. So how 'bout you get the damn chip off your shoulder, grow up, and let's all get along the best we can for the sake of your daughters. 'Cause whether you like it or not, I'm not going *anywhere*."

Tanisha opened her mouth to respond and Raven cut her off, "Oh, and the next time you feel like messing with Joe or calling yourself harassing me or anything like that, I'd advise you to rein that in. 'Cause I *will* toss your little ass like a Caesar salad. 'Kay?"

Joe remained quiet, but he loved how Raven was putting Tanisha in her place. That was something Van never really did; like Raven said, Van had always just taken Tanisha's nonsense, choosing to ignore her. But Raven was setting the tone up front and Joe loved that. And he appreciated how she had his back.

Tanisha was glaring at Raven, and Joe readied himself to break them up in case Tanisha lost her mind and decided to try to jump on his woman. But to his and Raven's surprise, Tanisha's face actually broke out into a huge grin.

"I can't front; I *like* you!" she exclaimed to Raven. "You just might be all right!"

Clearly not expecting that, Raven looked at her skeptically. "What?"

"You ain't all stuck-up like that Van was; I like that. If Joe gotta be with anybody other than me, I'm glad it's with somebody that can hold him down like that. You got a little *hood* in you. And here I thought you was just some bougie lil' princess or somethin'."

"Oh," Raven was clearly surprised, but she was glad that Tanisha was standing down some. She glanced over at Joe, who looked cautiously pleased himself. "You for real?"

"Yeah, Tanisha, don't be saying this today then trying to raise hell tomorrow," Joe warned.

"I ain't gon' do that," Tanisha assured them. "As corny as this shit is to say, I *do* want you to be happy, Joe. Yeah I wish it was with me, but like I said, you got you a ride-or-die right here. She won't do you like Van did you. I can respect that."

"You're right about that," Raven confirmed with a wink. "And as long as you stay in your lane, Tanisha, we won't have any problems."

"Yeah, well," Tanisha shrugged. "I ain't sayin' we gon' be best friends or anything like that..."

"And neither am I..."

"But I'll chill out. At least, I'll try to."

Joe wasn't quite sure he should take her at her word, but he *could* say Tanisha had never conceded like this before. He knew he had to keep an eye on her but he could also tell she swallowed a lot of pride in saying what she said.

"Well, I sure hope you mean what you say," Joe told her. "We'll get along a lot better if you do."

"We're getting along better, anyway, since you're not the mean and hateful bastard you were acting like a few months ago," Tanisha retorted with a smirk. "But I guess that's thanks to Ms. Long Legs over here. I didn't even think you were into chicks that were taller than you."

"She's not taller than me."

"I bet if she puts on some heels, she is."

"Well, whatever. I don't care about that."

"Yeah, I bet. So what y'all doin' tonight?"

Not expecting the question, Joe and Raven glanced at each other. "Why?"

"Since we're all cool and everything now, I figured we could have some fun together or somethin'."

Joe arched a skeptical brow. "What kind of fun? Raven and I don't smoke."

"I ain't talking 'bout getting high. I'm talking about getting *down*."

"What?!" Joe exclaimed as Raven burst out laughing.

"Come on, now, don't act like you ain't never done that."

"Are you seriously asking us to do a threesome??"

"What's wrong with that?"

"What's wrong with -bye, Tanisha," Joe dismissed, trying his best to resist the strong urge to laugh. Raven was actually leaning against the wall, still laughing hysterically.

"What you mean, *bye*? I'm asking nicely, ain't I?" Tanisha asked as Joe gently pushed her towards the door.

"It don't matter how you ask; that ain't happening."

"I know y'all be doing some freaky stuff; I'm down with whatever," Tanisha insisted as Joe nudged her out the door. "Hell, I'll even-"

"Bye, Tanisha!" Joe called out, closing the door in her face. Making sure it was locked, he finally released the laugh he'd been holding in.

"What the hell?!" Raven exclaimed through her laughter, trying to catch her breath.

"You see the affect you have on people?" Joe teased, going over and grabbing her by the waist. "Not only did you get her to chill out with the attitude but you got her wanting to sleep with you, too."

"That certainly wasn't the goal, believe me," Raven insisted, wiping the tears from her eyes before sliding her arms around Joe's neck. She smiled at him as her eyes roamed his face. "I'm down for some freaky stuff but I'm not trying to go there with your baby mama. And I'm not sharing my man, either."

"I like that," Joe said, his smile widening. His hold around her waist tightened as he backed her against the wall. "And I like how you had my back with her, too."

"Absolutely. That's how it goes, right? You have my back and I have yours?"

"Most definitely." Joe leaned in and kissed her, the urge overtaking him. Any residual amusement from the episode with Tanisha was quickly replaced by a quickly-escalating passion that had each of them holding tighter to the other as the kiss progressed. Joe's hands slid down Raven's hips and upper thighs before drifting back up to her face, taking it in both of his hands and breaking the kiss to look right into her eyes, not speaking until she was looking back into his.

"I love you, Raven," he said, his voice low but strong.

Momentarily stunned, Raven broke out into a grin. "Really?"

"Really."

"Joe, I love you, too."

It was Joe's turn to grin, and he knew he was blushing but he didn't care. "Word?"

"Word."

Joe leaned in to kiss her again, this kiss being deeper and more fervent. His body pressed hers into the wall, unable to get close enough. He never in a million years would have imagined that he would end up here; he always thought Van was his future, but now, she was the furthest thing from his mind. He was actually grateful for Van doing what she did because it led him to who he felt he was really supposed to be with. His life was going better than it ever had, and Raven was a huge part of that. When they started messing around months ago, if someone had told him that they would actually fall for each other, he would have laughed in their face. Raven wasn't his type, or so he thought. But she turned out to be his best friend, his lover, and his woman. And he was getting to where he just couldn't imagine his life without her.

Raven's heart was bursting all over the place. She'd been carrying around that declaration for weeks; she'd never really been in love before, but she knew with everything in her that she loved Joe. He wasn't the kind of man she ever imagined she would end up with; when she planned her future before, it was always with a baller or businessman of some kind. She had really thought Grant was perfect for her, with his model looks and bottomless bank account, but it took being with a man like Joe to make her realize that someone looking like Boris Kodjoe or having money didn't make them ideal. Joe treated her better than all her past men combined, and that made him irresistible as well as irreplaceable to her. Raven finally felt like she had everything she ever wanted.

• • • •

MEANWHILE, GRANT WAS finally ready to talk to Van.

He had taken his time and thought long and hard about what he wanted to say and what he wanted to do. His anger over seeing Van make a move on Joe in the house they shared together had dissipated into a mild burn, and whenever he felt himself wavering about his decision, all he had to do was think of that and he was right back on track again. He was very interested to get Van's side and see if she was going to try to defend her actions. Her parents had gone back to Ohio and the twins were at school, so they would have no distractions.

"Let's talk, Van," he ordered after he found her in the media room curled up on one of the loveseats, a blanket over her legs. She was watching *Brown Sugar*, one of her favorite movies.

She glanced at him warily before grabbing the remote and turning off the movie. Grant could see the nervousness in her eyes as he moved to sit next to her.

"Okay," she softly replied.

Grant didn't want to waste any time with preamble. "I'm sure I don't have to tell you that we have a little problem here. Well, really, a big problem."

Van looked down at her lap.

"You're not over Joe, Van," Grant stated. When she opened her mouth to protest, he held up a hand. "Let's not keep pretending here, okay? You've been acting like you're not over that man and I've been acting like I didn't know you were lying. Notice I didn't *ask* you if you were over him; I'm *saying* you're not 'cause I know. So just go ahead and admit it so we can move on from there."

Sighing, Van figured she might as well be honest. She was already in enough trouble with Grant and the truth was the only way to get herself out. "Okay; no, I'm not fully over Joe. I tried to tell myself I was but I realized a while ago that I'm not, and I have to admit that."

Grant started to ask if her realization came when she was all up in Joe's face telling him how much she missed him, but he stopped himself.

"Van, I have been over and over all of this in my mind," he said, "And I've come to the realization that something between us has to change. I can be patient; I think I've proven that. I can be understanding; I've proven that, also. But all of that goes out the window when I'm being lied to or when information is withheld from me."

Van's eyes widened. "Grant-"

"There's nothing you can say," Grant cut her off. "I'd prefer it if you didn't disrespect me any more than you've been doing."

"Grant, please, I know I don't have much of a defense-"

"You have *no* defense," Grant interjected again. "And I'm not going to say it's all on you; my letting things get to this point without doing anything about it is just as bad. I didn't want to believe that I wasn't enough for you. But I'm willing to take my share of the blame because I set all of this in motion when I began pursuing you while you were still with Joe. You went right from him and came to me with no time to heal in between, so knowing that, I can't totally fault you for your residual feelings for Joe."

Looking slightly relieved but still fearful as to how all of this was going to end up, Van tentatively reached for Grant's hand. "Sweetie...you've been so good to me. I really don't deserve it. And true enough, I *didn't* heal from how things ended with Joe...I'm seeing now that maybe I should have. But Grant, I hope you don't think for one second that I don't love you. I truly *do* love you."

"I believe you love me, Van," Grant conceded, his voice low. "But obviously, that isn't enough. I mean, look at how things have been between us."

"But we can work them out, right? I want us to work them out."

"Do you?" Grant eyed her intently.

"Of course! How could you doubt that?"

"You *really* don't want to ask me that right now, Van."

Van frowned. "What do you mean? Why do you say that?"

Not having the patience to drag it out anymore, Grant's voice turned harsh when he snapped, "Because I saw you make a move on Joe."

All of the color drained from Van's face. "Wh-what?"

"There are cameras all over this house, Van. Did you forget that?"

Van *had* forgotten all about the security cameras. That had been the furthest thing from her mind when she was all up in Joe's face. The fact that Grant saw that made her feel a burning mixture of shame, regret, and embarrassment. She didn't even want to look at him. "Oh..."

"Yeah, *oh*," Grant scoffed. "I heard you tell him you *really miss him* right before you pushed him into the bathroom to do God knows what. Do you have any idea how it felt for me to see that?"

Tears brimmed Van's eyes. "I'm so sorry..."

"What happened inside the bathroom? Did you kiss? Touch each other? I know you weren't in there that long but something happened, I imagine. Just tell me what it was and don't try to leave anything out."

If Van could have vanished into thin air right then, she would have. "We didn't do anything."

"So why did you push him into the bathroom? What was your purpose for that?"

Momentarily covering her face with her hands, Van admitted, "Okay, I-I wanted something to happen. I'm so ashamed to admit that to your face, but I did. I propositioned him and...told him I still had feelings for him. But he refused me. Said that I made my choice and then he walked out."

Grant's respect for Joe went up yet another few notches. It seemed like he really was over Van. "Were you disappointed by that?"

"I was embarrassed. As *soon* as he walked out, I felt...I just knew I had made a mistake. It was a stupid, disrespectful thing to do and I know that, Grant. And I know that doesn't make it any better and you have every right to be mad at me..."

"I'm furious, I'm disappointed, and really, I'm just tired, Van," Grant confirmed. "I'm tired of all of this."

Van looked at him with fear in her eyes. "What does that mean?"

"It means we need some time away from each other."

"Time away?? Grant-"

"This isn't a suggestion; it's happening," Grant stated emphatically. "You need to figure out if I'm really the man you want to commit yourself to or if I'm just who you're stuck with because you mistakenly left the man you really wanted. And I need to decide if I want to be patient with a woman who isn't all in like I am."

"I don't want to lose you, Grant," Van insisted, moving closer to him on the couch. She desperately placed her hands on his thigh, looking at him with tears running down her face. "I am so sorry if I made it seem like I don't really want to be with you, but I do!"

"Let's not kid ourselves, Van," Grant said, a sadness starting to creep over him. The idea of leaving Van made his chest hurt, but he knew it had to be done. "You couldn't keep your eyes off Joe and Raven when they were here; the jealousy was written all over your face. You didn't even tell your parents about me; a woman happy to be engaged doesn't keep a secret like that. You won't show me affection in front of the twins. It took forever for you to choose a wedding date, then you choose one way off into the future swearing – and lying – that it doesn't mean anything, and then you didn't even seem interested in planning the wedding. You quit your job and didn't say anything to me about it. It's too easy for you to keep things from me, and I've asked you repeatedly to be honest. And I just refuse to go another day like this."

Knowing she couldn't refute anything he said, Van hung her head.

"I'll go stay in one of my other properties for a little while," Grant continued, trying to keep his own emotions in check. "I need to get my head together."

"How long is a little while?" Van asked softly, her eyes on her trembling hands.

"A few days. However long I feel is necessary," Grant replied, looking at the floor by his feet. "Just tell the twins I'm away on business; they don't need to know our drama."

Unable to speak, Van just nodded.

"When I get back, we can make a final decision about us and this relationship," Grant continued. "I'm going to be thinking long and hard about what it is I really want and what I'm willing to do to get and/or keep it. I suggest you do the same."

With that, he stood and walked out of the room, not looking at her. He heard her break down in sobs behind him, but he made himself keep walking, despite the tears that started to sting his own eyes. All of this was killing him, but he knew it was necessary. He just hoped that he would be able to live with whatever decision was made.

Chapter 25

• • • •

VAN FELT LIKE THE STUPIDEST woman alive.

Here she was about to lose yet another good man who loved her more than anything simply because she didn't know how to be grateful for what she had. She already left Joe, which was a decision she finally acknowledged that she regretted. But Joe was with Raven now, and had made it perfectly clear that he didn't even want to be friends with Van, let alone anything else. And now, because she couldn't accept the decision she had decided to make, she might very well lose Grant, too.

Ever since Grant told her he was leaving the house for a while, Van hadn't been able to keep her emotions in check. Whenever the twins were around her, it was a gargantuan task to act like everything was fine, especially when one of them asked about Grant. He hadn't even been gone a day and Van already missed him as if it had been a year. She wanted to be encouraged that he didn't just end things as soon as he saw that footage of her making a move on Joe; it still horrified her that he had even seen that at all. She could just imagine how it must have felt for him. And sadly, she knew that was something she probably never would have told him about if he hadn't found out on his own, despite her promise to always be honest with him. But it's not like she'd been keeping that promise before that happened, either.

After the twins were in bed, Van went to her bedroom, but one look at Grant's side of the bed had her quickly walking right back out. She went back down to the den, perusing the books on the large built-in bookshelf even though she knew she didn't have the concentration to read anything right then. Plopping onto the corner of the couch, she used the remote to turn on the television then dropped it to the floor, already not interested in whatever was showing on the screen. She grabbed her favorite blanket and covered her legs, curling up into a ball as she mindlessly looked at the wall ahead of her. The tears were already starting to make their reappearance. The thought of losing Grant was threatening to push her into a heart-crushing depression that she was trying her best to fight. She knew that wasn't going to get her anywhere; she needed to do like Grant said and figure out what she really wanted.

"What am I doing??" she muttered to herself. "How have I made such a mess of everything?"

Van knew that whether she and Grant ended up staying together or not, she needed to find a way to get over Joe. He had moved on, and she needed to do the same. She was so sure when she made the decision to leave him for Grant that she was doing the right thing, and for the right reasons, but the fact that she hadn't been able to get him out of her head or her heart made her realize she should have done what her father said and just stuck it out. But that was all moot now; Joe was with Raven, and they were very happy together. Van just wished that she and Joe could be friends, but she knew she had to give him the space to forgive her on his own, if he ever did. And if he didn't, she would have to find a way to be okay with that.

When she thought about the love she had for Joe and the love she had for Grant, Van knew it wasn't the same. With Joe, it was so unadulterated and raw and all-consuming; with Grant, it was...safe and comfortable and routine. It didn't compare. But Van had been happy; Grant was nothing but a blessing to her. And if he walked away from her after everything...it would be the third man she loved and lost. She wasn't sure how she'd recover from that, especially since two out of the three would be her fault.

But she couldn't deny Grant had made several very good points. She hadn't even realized that she didn't show him affection in front of the twins. She certainly used to kiss Joe in front of them. All of the things Grant pointed out just further confirmed that she wasn't as all in with Grant as she tried to tell herself she was.

Van knew it would make her look incredibly shallow and superficial if she left Grant. She had left Joe because he didn't have enough money, then Grant helped her become debt-free and if she left him now, it would come across like she had been just using him for his money. Nothing could have been further from the truth. Her feelings for Grant were genuine. Yes, he fixed her financial troubles, but she liked to think that that wasn't the main reason she was with him.

But if she was honest with herself, she knew that if Grant had been just another regular guy who loved her but didn't have the financial means she needed, she probably wouldn't have left Joe for him. She probably wouldn't have entertained him at all.

Coming to that realization made Van sit up in her seat. She had never before thought of herself as a gold digger; she always prided herself on being independent. But she wasn't. Grant had come in and taken care of everything for her, and now she had gone and quit her job, so she couldn't even say she was still doing something for herself. She would have had to just suck up her work frustrations if she was still with Joe; she'd had to do it many times over the years. But now, knowing that Grant would take care of her, she just walked out of work because her boss ticked her off. No wonder her father called her out like he did.

Van looked down at her engagement ring, biting her lip thoughtfully. Did she really want to be Mrs. Grant McCallister? Was she ready for that? She knew that was something she should have been sure of before ever accepting Grant's proposal. There were so many things she should have done differently. Grant deserved a woman who would love him wholeheartedly, and Van knew she wanted to be that woman. She'd made a lot of mistakes, and she didn't want to lose Grant on top of everything else. And the twins had already been through enough changes...she would hate to put them through any more.

She so wished she could call Grant and ask him what he was thinking; she wanted him to come home so they could talk about things face to face. But she understood that he had to handle all of this his way. A man could only take so much, and she had put him through a lot in their relationship. As angry as he was and the way he spoke to her before he left, Van wondered if she shouldn't just go ahead and prepare herself for the possibility that she and the twins might need to start looking for another place to live.

• • • •

THE NEXT DAY, VAN WOKE up renewed, telling herself that she was going to think positively. While the twins were at school, she called her mother and told her what was going on, and appreciated it when Florence gave her encouragement instead of an 'I told you so.' Van still hadn't spoken to her father since he went off on her and basically accused her of being a lazy, cheating liar, and Van couldn't deny that she was still hurt by that. She hated that her father thought of her in such a way but it wasn't like she could say much to refute his accusations. His words may have been harsh but they weren't entirely untrue, and as hard as it may have been for her to do, Van had to admit that.

Another thing she did was think about what she was going to do about her jobless status. If Grant decided he wanted to end things between them, she would certainly have to have a way to support her children and herself. And if she and Grant ended up staying together, she didn't want to be a housewife; it would drive her crazy staying home all day every day. She liked to work; she just needed to figure out what she could do that she actually enjoyed, which was a luxury she never had before. Getting the bills paid had always been the most important thing. She wanted to love what she did every day, like Grant and Raven and even Joe did. And she wanted her twins to finally see her enjoying her job instead of just tolerating it.

Speaking of the twins, she knew it was past time for her to have a talk with them. There had been so much going on and Van was ashamed to admit that they had become something of an afterthought. She had been letting all of her issues take precedence and even their birthday party ended up being more about her drama than about them. That was definitely something she needed to fix.

"How was school, guys?" she asked them as they filed into the living room.

"It was good," Canton reported simply.

"Ugh," was Cassie's dramatic response, dumping her colorful bookbag onto the nearest chair and plopping onto the couch. "My homeroom teacher punished the *whole* class just because two people were talking. We had chicken sandwiches for lunch and they're usually good but today they were *so* nasty...it was like they had been sitting out all day or something. And then Ms. Murray is making us write some long paper about some war and is only giving us a week to do it! *And* I chipped my nail polish, *see*?"

"Oh my gosh, how will you ever make it after a day like that??" Van gasped facetiously, plastering her hands to her chest and looking at her daughter in mock horror. Canton snickered.

"I know!" Cassie exclaimed, not getting the joke. "And the girl I was sitting next to on the bus kept popping her gum in my ear. And I know she was reading my texts I was sending on the sly, too."

Shaking her head, Van closed her laptop that was next to her on the couch and moved it to the coffee table. "Why don't you and Canton sit together on the bus?"

"Because Canton was sitting next to *Shantell*," Cassie teased, looking at her brother with a smirk.

"Why don't you be quiet, Cassie?" Canton hissed.

"Shantell? Who's Shantell?" Van asked, turning to look at Canton.

"Canton's girlfriend," Cassie replied immediately.

"What??"

"She is *not* my girlfriend!" Canton quickly insisted, blushing.

"Yes, she is! They're always sitting together on the bus and walking together in between classes," Cassie informed Van, glad to spill the beans on her brother. "I even saw them holding hands one day."

"No we didn't!"

"Okay, I made that part up, but the other stuff was true!"

Van listened to them go back and forth for a minute or two before finally stepping in; Canton was getting agitated and Cassie was having too good a time teasing him. Van had to admit it was cute how much Canton was blushing, though.

"All right, that's enough," she announced over the sound of Cassie making kissing noises and Canton telling her to shut up. "Cassie, stop teasing your brother. And Canton, I look forward to hearing more about this Shantell. You're too young to have a girlfriend, though."

"She's *not* my girlfriend!" Canton exclaimed, exasperated.

"Uh-huh," Cassie muttered.

"Anyway, y'all, there's something I want to talk to you about," Van hedged, tucking some hair behind her ear. "It's about...well, everything that's been going on around here lately."

"What do you mean?" Canton asked, glad for the change in subject.

"Well, I already told you that Grant is gone," Van said, fighting to keep her face and voice even. "He'll be away for a few days or so; I'm not sure exactly how long."

"He's gone on business?"

"Yes." Van hated lying to her kids but Grant was right when he said they didn't need to know their drama.

"I hope he can tell me about it when he gets back. And plus I wanted to ask him something about starting my own business...he said he was doing stuff when he was around my age."

Van smiled. "So you're really warming up to Grant, huh? I'm glad to see that."

"He's cool," Canton shrugged. "Plus he knows a lot about what I want to do when I grow up. And he doesn't mind answering all of my questions."

"I'm glad to hear that, baby."

"Speaking of questions, I have one," Cassie piped up.

"What?"

"I know you're probably just gonna tell me its grown folks' business, but how come Joe came with Raven to our birthday party?"

That caught Van off guard; this wasn't something she was prepared to talk about. "Oh, umm...well Joe is Raven's boyfriend now."

"But he was your boyfriend first. I didn't know cousins were supposed to do that."

Yeah, I didn't either. "Well, baby, they were both grown and single...they can do whatever they want. And if they make each other happy, those kinds of rules shouldn't matter. Life is too short to not be with who you really want to be with."

Cassie eyed her, pondering her words. "And you don't care?"

Again, Van had to fight to keep a straight face. "If they're happy, I'm happy for them. Plus, I have a wonderful man, myself, you know."

"Right. You still don't have a job?"

"No, not right now," Van replied evenly.

"Why did you quit?" Canton asked.

"I...had a difference of opinion with my boss. And I just didn't enjoy the work; I hated having to go out of town and leave you guys," Van said, putting an arm around each of them. "But please believe, I'm going to find something else soon."

"Why?" Cassie asked incredulously.

"Why what?"

"Why do you want to find another job? Did Grant say you had to?"

Telling herself not to get upset, Van replied, "No...I *want* to get one, Cassie. I can't just sit around the house all day; I like to work. I just would finally like to do something I enjoy."

"Good for you, Ma," Canton commended. "Maybe you won't be so stressed all the time once you get a job you like."

Van wanted to say that her job hadn't been the main cause of her stress, but she wasn't about to tell them everything that was. "I sure hope so, sweetie. That's the goal."

"Hmph," Cassie scoffed. "I know *I* wouldn't worry about trying to work if I had a rich husband."

Van frowned. "Cassie, let me tell you something...you do know what being *independent* means, right?"

"Yes ma'am. There's a couple of songs about it and they're my jam. *'All the women, independent, throw your hands'* - "

"Okay, I got it," Van interrupted her before she continued with the rest of the song. "Well if you actually listened to the words of those songs, you would know that women shouldn't depend on men like that. They should be able to take care of themselves and handle their own business."

"But I thought a husband was supposed to take care of his wife," Cassie protested.

"Yes, he is. But a woman should always be able to take care of *herself*. You never know what's going to happen. If your man leaves you, he can take all of his money with him and you'd be left with nothing. Then what?"

"Do you think Grant would leave *you*?"

Van knew she needed to change the subject before she lost it. But she still made herself answer, "I sure hope not. But in any case, I need to always be sure I can take care of you two, and myself. And there's nothing like making your own money and paying your own bills. It's a very satisfying feeling."

"So Grant doesn't pay any of your bills?"

"Cassie!" Canton admonished.

"What? I was just asking."

"That's not any of our business."

"How come it's not? She *said*-"

"Look y'all, just know that I'm trying to figure out what my next move is going to be, as far as my job situation," Van interjected before they got into a full-fledged argument. "We're going to be just fine. But I *do* need to ask y'all something, though."

They both looked at her expectantly.

"How do you *really* feel about Grant? And be honest."

"I like him a lot," Cassie immediately informed. "He's really nice and he does things for us and, you know, he's cute."

Van chuckled, then looked over at her son. "And what about you?"

Canton shrugged. "He's cool. I like him more than I used to."

Van wanted to ask if he liked him as much as he liked Joe, but she stopped herself. Plus, she was pretty sure the answer would be no. "Do you love him?"

"I guess; I don't know. Never really thought about it."

"*I* love him," Cassie chimed in. "But I still love Joe, too. Is that okay to love them both?"

"Sure it is. There's nothing wrong with that at all." Van rubbed her daughter's shoulder with a smile.

"Do *you* still love Joe?"

Vans smiled and tweaked her daughter's chin. "I'm gonna always love Joe. But I'm with Grant and Joe is with Raven; we're all happy where we are."

Van could only hope that was a true statement as far as she and Grant were concerned and that she hadn't just lied to her children again.

· · · ·

A COUPLE OF DAYS LATER, Van was starting to feel a little stir crazy. She missed Grant something terrible, and several times tried to think of some excuse to call him just to hear his voice. But she knew she needed to respect his request for space, and take advantage of this time apart, herself. She had mentally worn herself out analyzing this whole situation with Grant, and just needed a reprieve. And she had done all the laundry and cleaned out the kitchen cabinets and whatever else she could find to do around the house...she just wasn't used to being home all day. She had already read until her eyes crossed and shopping when she didn't really need anything didn't appeal to her.

The twins were at school, so Van's mind wandered to Raven. She grabbed her phone, wondering if her cousin would be available to hang out. They hadn't spoken much since the twin's birthday party. Part of her wondered if Joe had told her about Van's proposition in the bathroom, but she figured she would have heard from Raven by now if he had.

"Hey, girl," Raven answered cheerfully.

"Hey," Van replied, slightly taken aback by Raven's tone. She hadn't been that happy to hear from Van in forever. "You okay? Am I catching you in the middle of anything?"

"Nope, not really. I'm going over some stuff for work but that's about it. What's going on?"

"Oh...I'm just here at the house and feel like I'm about to lose my mind; I need to get out for a while. Can you meet me for lunch or something?"

"Right now?"

"Whenever is good for you. It's not like I have anything to do and the twins won't be home for a few hours."

"Oh yeah, I forgot you left your job. What's going on with that? What are you gonna do?"

"Ugh, girl, I'm still figuring all that out. But I need to come up with something 'cause if I didn't know it before, I know now that sitting around the house all day is *not* for me."

"I feel you."

"Can you come out right now?"

"If you give me about an hour, I can. I can't go too far, though, so you'll need to come this way. I don't have to be at the restaurant until later but I never know when somebody is gonna call me with some kind of crisis."

"Not a problem. How about that Applebee's down the street from your complex?"

"I'm not a fan but I'll deal with it. I'll see you over there in about an hour."

"Sounds great." Van hung up the phone feeling relieved and encouraged. Part of her expected Raven to have some excuse as to why she couldn't meet her. Raven had actually sounded happy to hear from her, and not like Van was interrupting something or bothering her as had been the case the past few months. She must have still been on cloud nine from her relationship with Joe.

So after Van took a shower and changed clothes, she headed over to meet Raven. As usual, Raven was a little late.

"I'm sorry; I lost track of time," Raven explained as she sat down across from Van. "I'm working on some new things for the menu and I almost forgot I had agreed to come over here."

"It's fine. I'm just glad you were able to come out at all. How are things going at work? Still loving the new job?"

"Oh yeah, I love it. It can be a lot, though. Oh, can I get a *big* ol' margarita, please?" Raven asked their server who had just appeared at their table. "And some fries."

"And I'll just have some salsa verde nachos and a Mud Slide, please," Van told the server, handing him her menu.

"Drinking in the middle of the day, huh?" Raven teased with a smile. "I know why *I'm* doing it, but why are you?"

"Ugh," Van shook her head. "Don't ask."

"I just did. What's going on?"

Van hesitated. "I know you don't want to hear about all of this, Raven."

"It must have something to do with Joe."

"Honestly yeah, it does. And I don't want to ruin the vibe or anything so I'll just keep it to myself."

"Does it have anything to do with you trying to sex Joe in the bathroom after the twins' birthday party?"

Heat rushed to Van's face like a roaring wave. So Joe *had* told her about that. Van suddenly felt very embarrassed. But Raven didn't look the least bit upset.

"I'm sorry about that," Van muttered softly, looking down at the table. "I know there's no excuse."

"Nah, there's not. And I was pissed when Joe first told me about it. But I'm okay now."

Van looked up at her, surprised. "Really? When did he tell you?"

"He told me about it later on that night. Joe and I made a promise to not keep secrets from each other; trust and fidelity are big deals to the both of us, especially after everything that's happened. He wasn't going to keep something like that from me."

"So...not that I want you to be, but how come you're not more upset?"

"Oh I wanted to beat your ass at first, trust. And I was putting on my shoes and pulling my hair back to go right back to your house and do exactly that. But Joe reassured me and calmed me down, and made it clear nothing was ever going to happen between you two. Then the more I thought about it, I actually felt sorry for you."

Van reared back in her seat. "Sorry for me?"

"Because I know you. And despite all the crap you've done, I know you're not really a bad person. There has to be something going on with you to make you do the things you've been doing. And it's not like I've never done shady stuff before."

"Well yeah, but..."

"To be honest, I expected you to make a move on Joe at some point," Raven revealed. "You were just too consumed with him, and any idiot could see you aren't really over the man. I just can't understand why you're not happy, girl...didn't you get what you wanted?"

"I obviously didn't know *what* I really wanted," Van admitted.

Raven peered at her. "The grass isn't always greener, huh?"

Van looked at her cousin. She could tell Raven wasn't trying to be snide; she was just stating a fact. The grass certainly *wasn't* as green as Van had thought it would be when she decided to leave Joe.

"No, it's not."

"Look, I know I never wanted to hear anything about you and Grant before, but I'm past all that now. I'm not angry about what you two did anymore so I can talk to you about this stuff. Be real with me...what's *really* going on?"

Just then, the server brought their drinks and Van wasted no time taking a large chug of her Mud Slide. She couldn't deny that it was a relief that Raven seemed like her old self towards her again, and that she was finally willing to listen. Licking her lips, Van forged ahead.

"When I made the decision to leave Joe for Grant, I sincerely thought I was doing the right thing," Van began. "But I totally underestimated the hold Joe had on my heart, and how much he really meant to me. And while I *do* love Grant, I can't deny there's a huge part of me that wishes I had just stayed and stuck things out with Joe. I still love him. The kind of relationship he and I had...you just don't meet men like him every day."

"You sure don't."

"Grant has been nothing but good to me," Van continued. "And I've tried and tried to just be grateful for what we have and concentrate on him and the wonderful life he's provided for me and the twins. But my mind kept going back to Joe, for some reason. And then when I found out you two were together, I felt...I don't know...angry, betrayed..."

"Jealous," Raven offered.

"Yes, that, too. I'm not gonna deny it. I didn't like the idea of you two together, and to be honest, it's still gonna take some more getting used to. But that's *my* issue, and I know that."

Raven looked at her thoughtfully. "What did you really expect to happen when you pushed Joe into the bathroom that night?"

"I honestly thought he would at least kiss me, though I won't deny I wanted much more than that," Van admitted. "I thought that if I could just get him alone, in close quarters, and look into his eyes, something would spark in him and reignite all those feelings he had for me, even if just temporarily. That he would remember how close we used to be and want me as much as I wanted him in that moment. But when he looked at me with such indifference and turned me down flat, I knew it was *really* over. That he wasn't just being difficult to make me sweat or playing hard to get...he was just *over* me."

"So if he *had* given in and sexed you or even kissed you...then what? Did you even think about the consequences of that? How it would affect me or Grant if we found out?"

"Honestly no, I didn't. In that moment, Raven, I wanted Joe – wanted Joe *back* – more than I've ever wanted anything and it blocked out all rational thinking. It was like all the months of begging for his forgiveness and pent-up emotion about our breakup just exploded."

"Wow."

"Which is another reason why it's a good thing Joe turned me down. As embarrassing as it was, it was the wake-up call I needed. Like Joe said, I made my choice. And it's not fair for me to only think of myself and my own feelings and not consider other people any more than I've been doing. I've really had to check myself."

"Well, at least you finally realize all this. Does Grant know about that whole episode?"

"Yeah, he knows. He saw it."

Raven's eyebrows shot up. "What do you mean, he saw it? I thought he was outside when this was happening."

"Yeah, he was. But he saw it on the security camera footage later."

"Oohhh, damn..." Raven sat back in her seat, a look of shock on her face. "Did he go off? I bet he went off. When I had busted up in his office and accused him of being gay, he threatened to buy my restaurant and fire me and everyone I ever smiled at."

"He didn't confront me about it immediately; I'm sure I would have gotten it good if he had. But it was far from pleasant when we *did* talk. He let me know that he was tired of how things are and we needed some time apart to both figure out what we really want."

"Seriously?"

"Yes."

"How long has he been gone?"

"A few days. The twins think he's away on business."

"And how are you feeling?"

"Not great. I've been doing a lot of thinking about all of this; analyzing, re-analyzing, evaluating…"

"But does it really have to be that difficult? Van, do you love Grant and want to spend the rest of your life with him or not?"

"Is it that *simple*?"

"Why can't it be? Van, you know you have a tendency to over-think and blow things up in your head, making things way more dramatic and difficult than they need to be."

Van couldn't deny that.

"The only thing you need to *evaluate* is if you really want Grant to be your man or not," Raven advised, leaning forward. She looked at her cousin sympathetically; she honestly felt for her. "And if you do, would he just be a fallback since you can't have Joe or would you sincerely give your all to the relationship? Don't waste the man's time any more than you already have."

"I don't want to do that," Van replied immediately. "Grant means so much to me. Thinking about a life without him brings tears to my eyes. I can't even *tell* you how much I've missed him these last couple of days. As I've said, I love him."

"Loving him and wanting to be his wife and spend your life with him are two different things, Van. Are you ready to commit to him like he's committed to you?"

Van hesitated briefly and Raven arched a brow. "I can be all in with Grant. I don't want to lose him."

"Because you've already lost Joe and don't wanna end up with nothing?"

Feeling her face flame, Van averted her eyes.

"Van, I'm not trying to make you feel worse," Raven assured. "I'm just making sure you're being honest with yourself. And if you're willing to be honest with Grant, finally, about all of this you're feeling. Y'all can't be truly happy together if you can't even keep it real with him."

Van chewed her lip as she considered her cousin's words. She could only imagine Grant's reaction if she admitted that she felt she made a mistake in choosing him; the fact that she was willing to be all in now might not be much of a comfort, knowing that.

Still, she sat up straighter, looking right into Raven's challenging eyes. "If I didn't know before how detrimental secrets and dishonesty can be, I surely know now. I realize I need to earn Grant's trust back, and I can't do that by telling half-truths. Hopefully the love Grant and I share is strong enough to get us through."

"Well, I hope it is," Raven said with a smile. "I do want you to be happy."

"Me too. I sincerely want to make this work with Grant."

"Well, Van, baby, that's a start. Just concentrate on building your relationship fresh from here. Take getting married off the table for the time being; I think it's clear y'all aren't ready for that. You two need to just be easy and enjoy each other, and let things happen as they happen."

Van knew she was right. Her relationship with Grant had been clouded in drama since it started. No wonder they were such a mess.

"I would love to do that," Van sighed wistfully, realizing just how much she did. "But if Grant decides he's fed up, that's it. And I can't even say I'd blame him if he did."

"He's not gonna do that," Raven declared. "Grant loves you too much."

"I wish I was as confident about that as you are. I've given that man a *lot* of headaches. He might decide I'm just not worth it."

"Hmph. I won't front like that's impossible. But let's not act like Grant is blameless in all this, himself. *Both* of you contributed to this mess your relationship is in. And if he could sit and watch you push up on another man in his house and not put you out right then, then he just needs to clear his head. He doesn't *really* wanna leave you."

"I hope you're right." Van looked at Raven and couldn't help but smile.

"What?" Raven asked, smiling herself.

"I've missed this," Van replied, motioning her hand back and forth between them. "Us talking like this, sharing advice. I'm so glad it feels like we're starting to be friends again."

"Yeah, I've missed it, too," Raven admitted. "It took me a while to get past everything that happened but I'm good now. The past is the past. I'm in a great place in my life and just want to spend my energy enjoying it, not holding grudges. And it's not like you haven't apologized a hundred times."

"At least," Van chuckled.

"So we're good. I just want you to get to where you're truly happy, yourself."

Van's smile faded slightly. The server came with their food and she waited until he was gone before speaking. "I'll admit it might take me a minute to really settle in with the idea of you and Joe. He and I were together for so long, and you're my cousin as well as my best friend…it's just a little strange for me. But I'm sincerely and honestly trying. And I mean it when I say that I'm happy for you; you still have that glow Mama was talking about when she was down here."

Blushing, Raven hunched her shoulders, an automatic grin adorning her face. "Hey, I can't deny it. I'm in love with a great man who's everything I didn't even know I wanted; I'm enjoying the hell out of it. But I'm sure it won't be too long before you have that glow again, yourself."

"That would be great; I miss that," Van smiled. "Now, on to the really important thing in the moment: are you gonna share some of your fries?"

Raven laughed. "Girl, as good as I'm feeling, I might just give you half of 'em." She grinned at her cousin, truly feeling the happiest she had ever felt. "But you can't have any of my margarita, though."

Chapter 26

• • • •

AFTER ANOTHER COUPLE of days, Grant came back home.

He hadn't let Van know he was coming; he just showed up. Van was in the living room at the small desk in the corner, her laptop in front of her. She was concentrating so hard on whatever she was looking at that she didn't even hear him come in at first. When she looked up and saw him, she jumped and almost knocked her computer off the desk.

"Oh my gosh!" she exclaimed, catching her laptop before it slid to the floor. "Grant! I didn't hear you come in!"

"I'm sorry for scaring you," Grant replied evenly, unable to deny to himself that he was happy to see her. He couldn't help missing her terribly during his time away and had the physical urge to grab her and hold her until his arms went numb. But he just set his leather bag by the couch and slid his hands in his pockets, eying her.

Van was so relieved to see Grant. Him standing right in front her only cemented her decisions over the past few days; she would do whatever it took to make it work with him. She could only hope he wanted the same and would be willing to give her more grace and patience so she could do that.

Resisting the urge to go to him like she wanted to, she just closed her laptop and nervously slid her hands under her thighs. She couldn't quite read his expression;

he didn't look that happy to see her, but he didn't look as upset as he was when he left. There was no way she could guess what was on his mind by the way he was looking at her, and the realization sent her nerves into overdrive. But, remembering Raven's advice, she told herself to think positively. It wasn't over until it was over.

They continued to stare at each other until Van just couldn't take it anymore. She stood and quickly went over to him, wrapping her arms around his waist and burying her face in his chest. Her body immediately filled with a mix of emotions that had her squeezing Grant tighter. Her heart surged when she felt his arms hug her back almost equally as tight.

After several long moments, Van eased back and slid her hands up his chest, lightly grabbing the back of his neck. She looked up into his dark eyes, almost overwhelmed by how glad she was to see him. "I am *so* glad you're back. I-I missed you."

Grant's hands tightened on her waist. He fought to keep his voice even when he replied, "I missed you too, Van."

Van wanted to kiss him more than anything, but she knew she needed to clear the air first. Grabbing his hand, she led him to the couch and sat down, gently pulling him down with her. She scooted closer to him so their knees were touching.

"I don't know what you've decided, but I have to let you know this, regardless," she began, keeping her hold on his hand. "I am so sorry for everything I've put you through, Grant. I know it's been one thing after another and just about any other man would have left a long time ago. But you've been so good and so patient and I simply just haven't appreciated it like I should have. And I would love the chance to make it up to you."

Grant just looked at her, his expression still unreadable.

"If how I've been feeling while you've been gone these past few days is any indication of what it would be like with you out of my life, then I don't want any part of it," Van continued. "I want us to make this work. And let me go ahead and address this, about my feelings for Joe and all that...as hard as this is to admit to your face, I *did* feel like I wanted Joe back that night I propositioned him. I finally realized that the way I'd been acting was because..." She ran her hands down her face, anguished. "Oh god, how can I say this..."

"Just say it."

"I questioned my decision to leave Joe," Van blurted, making herself look at him. "This is freaking me out, telling you this, because I can only imagine how it'll make you feel, but you deserve my honesty, finally. I finally admitted that truth about why I was so consumed with him; I felt I'd made a mistake in leaving him. But I'm getting over that. And not just because he's with Raven; it's just time. He's moved on, and I finally realized I need to really move on, too. I can't keep hanging on to the past if I want a future with you, and that's what I want, Grant."

Grant's expression barely changed. "Really?"

"Absolutely! And I'm not going to act like it will be the easiest thing to see him and Raven together, at least for a while, but I've even told Raven that I'm just happy for them because they're happy together. And I meant that...he's the kind of man she needs."

"That's big of you."

"Grant, in all the thinking and pondering I've done these past few days, I realized that despite whatever uncertainties I may have had, you had to have been pretty special for me to walk away from Joe. And it wasn't just because of how much you've helped me and my kids. It's because you're *you*. You mean the world to me, Grant. Please..." Van brought his hand to her chest. "Please don't give up on me."

Grant looked away, pondering her words. He wasn't entirely surprised to hear just how deep her residual feelings for Joe went, or even that she had doubted her decision to leave him. While he was away, he analyzed their situation left right and sideways, and once he had some separation, the reason for how she'd been acting should've been as clear as day. And when he finally swallowed his pride and confided in his mother, including admitting his dishonorable actions in pursuing Van, she not only checked him for his actions, she checked him for his anger. While he had plenty to be upset with Van for, he also had to turn the mirror on himself for his part in everything.

He didn't want to leave Van. She had upset him, disappointed him, even embarrassed him, but he knew her well enough to know that it wasn't because she was a malicious person; she was just caught up in a whirlwind of changes and emotions that she didn't know how to handle. And as much as Grant had wanted to make himself stay angry and tell her that maybe this just wasn't going to work out, there was something specific holding him back from that.

He'd been waiting to hear the part about her and Joe; that was the tipping point of everything. If she had told him that she was still consumed with her feelings for him and was still upset about him being with Raven, then any kind of relationship between them would've been a wrap. Grant simply wasn't willing to put up with that anymore.

"I'm not going to leave, Van," he finally informed, running his free hand up and down his thigh. "Or ask you to leave, either."

Van grinned, hope surging through her. "You're not?"

"No. Look...I need to admit some things, too. If I'm honest, my proposing to you was an act of jealousy. I knew you weren't over Joe, and I foolishly thought that us getting engaged would get your mind and heart on me. But my rational mind knew you weren't really ready...I just wanted to believe you when you said you were, so I stuck my head in the sand to the reality right in front of me."

"So you didn't really want to marry me?"

"I had every intention of proposing, but not that soon. It was out of desperation more than of being ready. So I acknowledge that we both played a part in how everything turned out."

"But I played a way *bigger* part," Van insisted, scooting closer. "I wasn't fair to you, Grant. I agreed to live and spend my life with you knowing my heart and mind was still partially with another man. I'm so sorry for that; for everything."

"I believe you..." Grant squeezed her hand. "But since we're disclosing everything, I'll admit that I feel some kind of way about you basically admitting you made a mistake in choosing me."

"Grant, I-"

"And if I'm honest, that's not something I can let go of or brush under the rug just because I love you so much. Because the fact of the matter is, if Joe would have taken you back, you would have gone. Am I wrong?"

Van started to protest, but the hard look in his eyes squelched her words. "I can't say that you are."

"That's what I thought. And maybe you *do* want to work things out with me now, and you might feel you're being sincere. But I'm basically just a consolation prize. In any other situation, I'd be ending this, knowing that. Because I have no desire to go through life worrying about if your mind is really on me like it's supposed to be. I just can't share your heart with another man anymore."

"You're not," Van immediately insisted, shaking her head emphatically. She clutched his hand on her chest with both of hers. "I promise, baby, I'm all in with you, and I'm willing to do whatever's necessary to prove that. I love you, Grant, and I want this. And I just can't apologize enough for everything."

Grant eyed her. Everything in him wanted to just accept her apology, wipe the slate clean, and go on with their relationship. But hearing her admit that she wished she hadn't left her ex for him was a blow he couldn't shake off, regardless of what she might be feeling towards him now.

"So this is what it is," he finally said, clearing his throat. He eased his hand from her grip. "I own my part in everything, but I'm still hurt – and yes, angry – about all of this. But I believe I'll get past that in due time. As I've said, I'm not leaving you. But that move you made on Joe was the final straw for me. So, know that things aren't going to be like they were before."

Van frowned in confusion. "What do you mean?"

"We're still together and everything. But my enthusiasm about it is practically in the gutter."

"Oh...so why are you-"

"For the twins."

Van's mouth clamped shut momentarily, not having expected that. "You're staying with me because of my kids?"

"Yes. Canton and Cassie have been through enough, losing their father, then losing Joe. I'm not going to be another man that disappears from their lives, especially when they've both finally recovered from the craziness we forced on them. I love them enough to stay with you despite my unhappiness with how things are between us."

Unable to believe her ears, Van blinked rapidly before rubbing her fingertips across her eyes. Was this really happening?

"Understand, Van, that I *do* still love you," Grant continued. "And I certainly won't mistreat you in any way. I want us to get along and, hell, maybe at some point I'll be able to move past this state I'm in now and go all in with you again. Maybe not. But for right now, this is what I feel is best for everyone."

"So we'd just be playing the role of a happy couple for the twins' benefit? When they're not around, you'll have nothing to say to me? Will we sleep in separate beds? Or the same bed but you'll never touch me? I just...I don't know how to take this, Grant. I don't want to live like that."

"Well, if you want to yank the twins from yet another happy home because things aren't ideal for you, feel free," Grant clipped, folding his arms. "But know that *you'll* be doing that to them, not me."

That erased any further complaints or protests. Van just looked down at the engagement ring she had been mindlessly twisting around her finger, wanting to cry but figuring there was no point. Grant wouldn't be moved by her tears. She'd brought this on herself.

"So this is going to just go on indefinitely? You'll just tolerate me until...what, the twins go off to college? Then you'll leave me for good?"

"Possibly. But how about we cross that bridge when we get to it. I'm not thinking that far ahead right now."

"I see," she finally whispered. "I guess I should give this back to you, then..."

"Keep it on," Grant ordered before she could remove her engagement ring. "You and I both know the twins will notice if you take it off, and Cassie will ask a million questions. Like I said, they don't need to know this new dynamic between us. As far as they're concerned, we're fine."

"But we're basically lying to them, Grant. Acting one way when we're around them and another when we're not is deceit."

"You mean like living in my house and wearing my engagement ring when you're wishing you could be with your ex?"

Van gasped. "Grant!"

"Don't act like that's not the truth, Van. You deceived me for basically our whole relationship."

"I didn't-"

"And it won't be totally an act," Grant interrupted, not interested in hearing more of her excuses. "Like I said, my feelings for you are still there, because I can't make them leave. My heart still wants you, wants us...and sitting here next to you confirms that my physical attraction to you is still intact, whether I want it to be or not. But after months and months of ignoring my gut feelings and letting my heart foolishly take the lead and override my common sense when it comes to you and us, my head is overruling everything right now and for the time being, I need to let it." His stern expression eased some and he sighed, running his hands down his face. "This has all been a lot, Van. I'm trying to keep it together here. I need you to give me this."

Van knew there was no way she could protest anymore. Most men would have been out the door already after everything she did, without giving second thought to what it would do to her kids. Van might have been hurt that he was staying more for Canton and Cassie than for her, but at least he was staying.

"All right, Grant," she finally acquiesced, her voice barely above a whisper. "If this is what you need from me, so be it. I owe you at least that much. I'll...learn to live with it. I suppose I should thank you for caring about my babies enough to stay for them."

Grant released a breath at her agreeance, closing his eyes momentarily before running his hands down his face and dropping his head. Several long moments passed before he looked up at her, his eyes glassy.

"Know that you're not the only one that's disappointed," he muttered. He released a sardonic chuckle, looking away with a slight shake of his head. "I resent you *so* much for doing this to us. Hell, I resent myself. I really just can't believe this is my life right now."

With that, he stood and walked out of the room.

• • • •

VAN AND GRANT ADJUSTED to their new dynamic the best they could. They put on their happy faces for the twins, acting like the so-in-love engaged couple that Van couldn't help but still wish they were. And thankfully, the twins had no idea that anything had changed between them. When they were alone, Grant had few words for her, though that was improving slightly with time. At first, they were just coexisting, giving each other wide berths and only making obligatory conversation. They did sleep in the same bed, only because Grant didn't want to risk the twins noticing either of them sleeping in a different one, but there was practically no touching. Van ached for Grant to put his arms around her, kiss her, show *some* proof of the attraction he claimed to still have for her. But he just stayed to his side of the bed and she stayed to hers.

After a few months, things got a little warmer between the two of them. Van vented to Grant about the frustrations regarding figuring out what her next career step would be, and Grant would share happenings from his business trips or even something funny that happened at the office, usually something to do with his sibling main assistants, Sheri and Lee. It was like music to Van's ears, hearing Grant laugh again.

And when the yearning for his touch got to be too overwhelming and she'd grab his hand or rest her head on his shoulder and he didn't pull away, it gave her hope that they would get to the point where they could give their relationship another try. She wanted that, but she knew she had to let Grant get there on his own, if he ever did.

Joe still entered Van's mind occasionally, but she was grateful that it didn't come with the anguish and yearning that used to come with thoughts of him. She left him alone, only discussing him whenever Raven mentioned something about their relationship. Van was determined not to fail again at moving on.

By the time he came by one day to pick up Canton, Van felt thankfully at ease.

"Hey, Joe," she greeted pleasantly when she answered the door.

"Hey, wassup." Joe nodded at her as he somewhat hesitantly stepped into the house.

"Canton should be down in a minute. He's so excited about going to your construction site. This is all he's been talking about all week."

"Yeah, he's called me every day to make sure it was still happening," Joe revealed, chuckling. "I'm still surprised he wants to go so bad."

"Canton loves to learn, almost regardless of what it's about. He loves seeing how things are made. I wouldn't be surprised if he ends up owning a construction company or gets involved in real estate or something when he grows up. Everything is a learning experience for him."

"I can definitely respect that." Joe stuffed his hands into his pockets.

"I'll go get Canton for you," Van offered, turning to walk away.

"Hey Van, hold up."

Mildly surprised, she turned back and looked at him.

"I, um, I just wanted to thank you for letting Canton come with me today, that's all. That's cool of you. I can admit that I've been looking forward to this as much as he has."

Van smiled. "Of course. You two are still close and I'd never stand in the way of that. I appreciate you taking him. I hope y'all have a good time."

"No doubt. I won't keep him too long...I'm just gonna take him around, introduce him to some of the guys, show him what I do and how things go. Then we might grab a bite to eat or something."

"That sounds good; I know he's in good hands so no rush. Just have Canton shoot me a text when you're on your way back."

Joe was a little thrown by Van's attitude. She was being as pleasant and cool as he had always known her to be before things exploded between them, but there was none of the lingering looks or subtle flirtations or even desperation that she'd been exhibiting whenever he had seen her post-breakup. She looked at peace...there was almost a glow to her. He guessed she was really happy with Grant.

"That's cool," he agreed, giving her a small smile.

"I'll go get Canton," Van said again, the smile still on her own lips as she turned and walked out, releasing a somewhat shaky breath when she was out of his sight. She had been a little nervous before Joe got to the house, wondering what affect seeing him was going to have on her, if any. But when she opened the door and faced him, she realized she felt okay. It was nice to see him and she could admit he looked good, but that was truly as far as it went. Continuing to pine for Joe was a dead end and she knew it; her concentration was on earning back Grant's trust and rebuilding their relationship.

Part of her considered apologizing to Joe for the scene in the bathroom the night of the twins' birthday party, but she decided to leave well enough alone. No need in dredging up old stuff, especially since he didn't seem to be holding a grudge about it, so she preferred to just forget it ever happened.

• • • •

VAN HAD BEEN HARD AT work researching and gathering information for the foundation she decided to start. She had always imagined working with young women in some way, and one night it just came to her to start her own thing. She wasn't sure of the exact details of everything yet but she would figure all of that out. For now she was researching how to get everything going and how to go about securing funding. Grant had graciously given her his full support, but she had declined his offer to give her the money to get everything off the ground. She appreciated the offer, but she wanted to do this on her own.

She knew she had a lot to be grateful for. But Van still kicked herself for messing things up with Grant the way she had, and she doubted she'd ever stop as long as they were living as polite acquaintances.

Though they did finally share some physical intimacy beyond Van's tentative touches. One night in bed, she looked over at him with his back turned to her, feeling the neglected tingles she'd been trying to ignore for months take over her body yet again. She slid over to his side of the bed and hesitated slightly before placing a hand on his torso, noting immediately how warm his skin felt through his t-shirt.

"Grant." She eased her body closer. "You awake?"

He didn't move for a moment and Van started to retract her hand when he grumbled, "What is it?"

"I need a favor."

"It's after midnight, Van."

"I know." She swallowed, actually nervous. "But this is important. Can you please turn around?"

She heard him sigh before he finally did as she asked, his eyes boring into her in the darkened room. "What?"

Before she lost her nerve, she slid her hand between them and grabbed his manhood, feeling emboldened when she felt it harden in her hand. "I need this. It's been so long, Grant."

He sucked in a breath when she began slowly stroking him. "Van..."

"I'll beg if I need to."

"Van." His hand grabbed hers, and her body sagged with disappointment. "I purposely haven't touched you because I didn't want you to feel I was only using you to selfishly satisfy my primal urges. That's not what I'm about."

"I know, Grant. And I appreciate it. But I'm telling you, I need this and from the feel of it," she squeezed him, "So you do."

He groaned. The grip on her hand loosened as he let her continue to slowly stroke him. He couldn't deny it felt good.

"I don't want to complicate things," he managed to say, a hint of anguish now scraping his voice. "We've been getting along well enough and as good as this feels-"

"I'm not overthinking it." She placed his hand on her slightly-heaving breasts before eagerly going behind the waistband of his silk pajama bottoms, needing to feel his skin. His hand on her stayed still while hers resumed stroking him, loving how he hardened in her hand even more. "It can be just sex; I won't read any more into it than that. I'm *suggesting* we use each other; we can't very well go on indefinitely without affection. I know *I* can't." Her movements stilled and she sat up slightly, something occurring to her. "Or *have* you been going without?"

"I'm not seeing anyone else, Van, if that's what you're asking."

She breathed a sigh of relief. The possibility of Grant with another woman was something that hadn't occurred to Van until that moment, and the thought almost brought a level of panic. But she knew it wasn't the time to freak out about that.

"Let's at least give each other this, then," she pleaded. "We don't have to talk about it. We don't have to analyze it. It doesn't have to mean anything beyond this moment. I'm just..."

When her voice trailed off and she stayed quiet for a moment, Grant urged, "You just what?"

"I'm tired of forcing all this restraint. It's torture lying next to a gorgeous man every night and having to get myself off when I ache for you to do it for me. I've agreed to your stipulations, Grant. Please give me this."

He didn't respond right away and she steeled herself for him to shut her down and roll back over. But then she felt his thumb slide over her hardened nipple, and she gasped then moaned a little too loudly, but she couldn't help it.

"As long as you understand this doesn't change anything between us..."

"I do," she immediately panted, nodding vigorously. "I promise. I *swear*."

"If we're gonna do this, I insist on wearing protection."

Van's head reared. "Why? We haven't been using-"

"I'm not risking getting you pregnant," he said bluntly. "That is as off the table as us getting married. So I hope that wasn't your aim for this proposition."

Van was hurt and a little insulted, but she forced herself to calm down. She hated the reminder that Grant no longer wanted to marry her or share a child together. She'd been hoping that would change over time but he hadn't budged even a little bit, and it saddened Van. Especially when she remembered how excited he used to be about making her his wife.

But as she had to do almost daily since this new dynamic between them started, she reminded herself that they were mostly in this place because of her. She had ruined everything.

"I understand," she finally muttered, swallowing her disappointment. "Whatever you say."

"Let's go, then."

That night, Grant sexed her like a man possessed, and Van loved every delicious second of it despite the fact that there was no tenderness, no words of endearment, no longing looks. It was sex and sex only, as promised, though Grant did grant her some intense kisses as they went at it. And there was plenty of sexual urging and dirty talk from the both of them, each releasing months of built-up frustration.

They finally shared the raw, uninhibited sex that they didn't seem to be capable of when they were together before. Van couldn't help but marvel at the irony.

From that point on, they had an unsaid understanding; when either of them felt that certain physical urge, they just ventured to the other's side of the bed and placed a hand on their hip. That was their signal. If they were in the mood, they'd turn around. If not, that would be it, no questions asked.

It wasn't ideal by any means. But Van was basically taking what she could get at this point.

And she continued to hold out hope that over time, if she continued to respect Grant's boundaries, they'd slowly begin to disappear and the two of them could ease back to how they used to be. She had to believe that was possible so she wouldn't keep crying herself to sleep on nights Grant stayed on his side of the bed.

• • • •

ONE DAY AS SHE WAS working on her computer, Van sat back and rubbed her eyes, feeling the effects of several hours of work on her foundation to-do list. Needing a reprieve, she pulled up her Facebook account, which she didn't check as much as she used to. She scrolled through the posts mindlessly until she got to a post from Raven. When she saw what it was, she bolted up in her chair.

"They're engaged???" she exclaimed, her eyes bugging at the screen. Leaning forward, she peered at the post again and saw it was from a couple of weeks earlier. Raven hadn't told her anything about this, and they had spoken several times since then. Van wondered why Raven hadn't mentioned getting engaged; she thought their friendship was back on track, as far as confiding in each other and sharing important news. How could Raven not tell her that Joe had proposed?

Grabbing her phone, she quickly dialed Raven's number, continuing to scroll down her timeline. There was another picture of Raven happily flashing her engagement ring, and Van couldn't help but wonder if that was the same ring Joe was going to propose to her with the night she left him.

"Hello?" Raven answered, practically singing.

"Hey girl," Van greeted. "What's going on?"

"Oh, not too much. Just trying out some new recipes. What's up?"

"You tell me."

"Huh?"

"Raven, how come you didn't tell me you and Joe got engaged? Why did I have to find something like that out on Facebook, of all places?"

"Oh yeah," Raven replied guiltily. "I'm sorry about that. I wanted to tell you the day after he popped the question, but I just...I guess I didn't know how you would take it."

"What? Girl, I'm fine! I meant it when I said that I was happy for you two. I'm actually a little hurt that you kept this from me, Raven."

"I wasn't trying to keep it from you to hurt your feelings, Van. Like I said, I wasn't sure how you would react. I know things have been good between all of us lately and I just wanted to keep that going. It's one thing for Joe and I to be dating but us getting married is a whole 'nother ball game."

"Yes, it is. And I'll say it again, if you're happy - and I can tell you are - then I'm happy for you."

"Well, that's good to know," Raven said, sounding a little relieved. "I'm really glad to hear you say that 'cause you know you're gonna have to help me with all this."

"Of course!"

"What about you and Grant? Have you started back talking about getting married yet? I saw you were still wearing his ring the other day."

Van had told Raven that Grant decided not to leave, and had admitted that things weren't the same between them, but couldn't bring herself to admit that he was mainly staying for Canton and Cassie's benefit more than out of any love for her. Her pride didn't want Raven – and possibly Joe – to know the mess that her life with Grant had become, especially when they were so happy together. Everything she and Grant did when they were being sneaky and deceitful and dishonest when they got together had come back on them tenfold, not to mention Van's actions during their relationship. And as much as Van wanted to be straightforward with her cousin, it was simply too embarrassing.

"Yeah, I still wear it," Van managed to reply evenly. "We, um, agreed I should. Since we'll be staying together and all."

"That's awesome, Van, for real. I am so glad y'all decided to work things out."

"I'm just grateful he's still here." Van was glad that this was a phone conversation. She didn't know if she'd ever fully get used to how things were now between her and Grant; it still wasn't the easiest to talk about. Her parents knew the real deal, only because she didn't want to imagine the consequences with them if they caught her in any more lies or withheld truths. "But enough about me; we need to start planning this wedding. Have y'all set a date yet?"

"Um, soon...*real* soon."

"Oh really? What's the hurry? You got a bun in the oven or something?"

Raven paused. Van was too busy giggling to notice that she hadn't responded.

When Raven was still quiet after several moments, Van stopped laughing. "Raven?"

"Yeah."

"How come you didn't say anything?"

Raven paused again and Van felt her stomach start to churn a little bit. "Raven..."

"Van..."

"Are you *pregnant*??"

There was only slight hesitation before Raven responded with unbridled joy in her voice, "Yes. Three weeks."

"Oh!" Van gasped, surprised. She felt like the wind had been knocked out of her. Raven was going to have Joe's baby...hearing that made Van feel some kind of way. She couldn't really explain the feeling, but it was definitely there.

"You okay?" Raven asked cautiously.

"What? Oh...yeah, girl! Congratulations!" Van made herself say. She wanted to mean what she was saying, and she knew she would after she had a chance to process everything. It was just a shock to her in the moment.

"So...you're really not upset?" Raven verified.

"Of course not!"

"*Really?*"

"No, Raven, I'm not upset. This is wonderful news. And I know the twins will be thrilled to get a new baby cousin."

"I can't wait; the thought of being a mother kind of freaks me out but I know I'm gonna love it."

"You sure will. There's nothing like it. And you have a great man right there next to you; you see how good of a father Joe already is to Jillian and Tara, and how he was with Canton and Cassie."

"You're right about that; that's one of the reasons I fell for him, among other things," Raven gushed. Van was glad they were on the phone and not in person because her smiles were getting tighter and tighter by the second.

"Well...that's great," was all she could say.

"Van, girl, I am so glad to hear you say you're cool with all this," Raven admitted. "Because, well, I wasn't totally honest with you about something just now."

Van frowned. "What do you mean? You're not really pregnant?"

"Oh, no, I'm most definitely pregnant. But Joe and I aren't engaged....we're married."

Van literally dropped the phone. Scrambling to pick it up, she realized her hands were shaking. Did Raven just say what she thought she said?

"Van! Van, you there?" Raven was calling out.

"Yeah, I'm here; sorry," Van fumbled. She wiped at the tear that she didn't even know had formed in her eye.

"What did you just say, though? You and Joe are married already?"

"Yep. We eloped two days after he proposed. We just...didn't want to wait."

"Wow..." Van marveled. Tears were now flowing down her face, and she just let them fall. She didn't even know why she was crying. "Raven...wow."

"I am Mrs. Joe Miller," Raven boasted. "I'm telling you, girl, I honestly could not be happier than I am right now."

"Raven, that's...that's awesome," Van forced herself to say. "We'll have to go out and celebrate or something soon."

"Absolutely! I'm so glad you're gonna be right there with me through all this."

"Of course I will," Van replied sincerely. She squeezed her eyes shut. "Whatever you need, you know all you have to do is ask. And since you're already married, I guess I can just focus on planning your baby shower, huh?"

"Yep!"

They talked for a few more minutes before Raven had to go. Van hung up the phone and started to put her head in her hands and let the tears flow some more, but she shook her head vehemently and wiped her eyes.

"Stop it!" she admonished herself. "There is nothing for me to be crying about!"

She said the words, but the tears didn't stop. Telling herself she would only allow this final pity party to last just a minute or two, she put her head down on the desk in front of her and cried.

Thank you so much for reading *Trade Rumors*! When I finished *Take One For the Team*, that was supposed to be it; I didn't plan on a sequel. But one day the opening scene of Joe showing up at Raven's door came to me and I wrote it just to get it out of my head. Then more of the story began to form, and I found myself wanting to stick it to Van for what she did. LOL

I so appreciate your support; please consider leaving a review on Amazon and/or Goodreads, or wherever you purchased this. Reviews are vital. Social media shoutouts are also appreciated. ☺

I'm on Twitter/X at @ItsJessicaTerry, and Instagram, TikTok, and Facebook under @AuthorJessicaTerry. You can also sign up for my sporadic emails at www.jessicaterry.com[1].

---

1. http://www.jessicaterry.com

Also by Jessica Terry

Some Like 'em Thick
It's All Right...Now
Not By a Long Shot
Get Right
Decisions and Consequences
Take One For the Team
When You Share Too Much
Backtalk
Emasculated
Restless
The Beginning of Again
Always and Nevers
She is Me
Split By the Bell
The Karma Call
Forehead Kiss
All Because of Ava
Love Intolerant
Mr. Time Waster
The Stubborn Kind
From Meltdown to Mistletoe
Mrs. Soul Crusher
I Want Us
The Introvert Series
An Introvert's Christmas
Wooing the Introvert
The Introvert Roast

I, Take Thee Introvert
The Introvert Series Compilation (paperback only)

Discussion Questions

1. Do you feel Raven and Joe were wrong for hooking up?
2. Van was conflicted throughout the book. Do you believe she sincerely loved Grant?
3. How much fault do you place on Grant for everything that happened?
4. Van had a problem with Joe and Raven being together. Was she a hypocrite or do you think her anger was valid?
5. Was Van a golddigger?
6. Did you feel Van's father Mitchell was too hard on her when he found out how and why she dumped Joe?
7. If you read *Take One For the Team*, you know how much Joe loved Van. Do you feel he was going overboard in *Trade Rumors* with how angry he was at her or was it understandable?
8. What do you think of Grant's decision regarding his and Van's relationship after he saw what Van tried with Joe?
9. What affect do you think it would have had on Canton and Cassie if Grant had decided to leave?
10. Were you rooting for Joe and Raven? What about Van and Grant? Did you think Joe might eventually want Van back? Would you have wanted to see them back together?
11. Why do you think Van was crying in the final

scene?

12. Did Van get what she deserved?

Did you love *Trade Rumors*? Then you should read *I Want Us*[1] by Jessica Terry!

Jazlyn Mackie and Rome Ellis were platonic best buddies...until they're snowed in together during a blizzard and end up keeping each other warm *all* night. After that, they're feeling anything but platonic about each other.

All would be beautiful except for the fact that they were both in relationships, however imperfect, and only one of them is feeling the guilt over what they did. Then Rome's jilted girlfriend Nell hits Jazlyn with a strange

1. https://books2read.com/u/mq9k7Q

2. https://books2read.com/u/mq9k7Q

request: 'give' Rome back to her for one month so she can prove her love for him.

Who will Rome choose after the month is up? Will he decide his evolved feelings for Jazlyn are just a fluke and go back to Nell, or will he stay with the woman who took over his heart after one amazing night?

Read more at https://www.jessicaterry.com/.

About the Author

Jessica Terry caught the writing bug at a young age and loves little more than holing up at home in Douglasville, GA, cranking out contemporary novels. And eating. www.jessicaterry.com

Read more at https://www.jessicaterry.com/.

www.ingramcontent.com/pod-product-compliance
Lightning Source LLC
Chambersburg PA
CBHW021839010726
47493CB00005B/1472

9 7 9 8 9 9 0 1 7 6 9 2 8